Acclaim for Tom Bradby's

THE WHITE RUSSIAN

"Brilliant. . . . St. Petersburg . . . illuminates *The White Russian*. . . . Ruzsky is a character to remember. . . . A complex mystery."
— *The Columbus Dispatch*

"*The White Russian* [has] a poignancy and urgency that go perfectly with its portrait of a nation on the edge of the abyss."
— *The Flint Journal*

"Exceptionally rich. . . . *The White Russian* is a masterful creation of suspense set in deadly times." — *The Manhattan Mercury* (Kansas)

Acclaim for THE MASTER OF RAIN

"In this ambitious, atmospheric crime novel . . . a city on the brink is re-created with impressive diligence. The physical details are strong and the politics appropriately ominous." — *The New York Times*

"Bradby has done for Shanghai what Raymond Chandler did for Los Angeles." — *Time*

"A crackling murder mystery. This is an immensely atmospheric, gripping detective story with just the right mixture of exoticism, violence, and romance." — *The Times* (London)

Tom Bradby

THE WHITE RUSSIAN

Tom Bradby is the United Kingdom editor for the British television network ITN. He has spent the last nine years covering British and American politics as well as conflicts in China, Ireland, Kosovo, and Indonesia. Bradby now lives in London with his wife and three children.

Also by Tom Bradby

The Master of Rain

THE WHITE RUSSIAN

THE WHITE RUSSIAN

A NOVEL

Tom Bradby

ANCHOR BOOKS
A Division of Random House, Inc.
New York

FIRST ANCHOR BOOKS EDITION, JUNE 2004

The Library of Congress has cataloged the Doubleday edition as follows:
Bradby, Tom.
The White Russian : a novel / Tom Bradby.—1st ed.
1. Police—Russia (Federation)—Saint Petersburg—Fiction.
2. Russia—History—Nicholas II, 1894–1917—Fiction.
3. Saint Petersburg (Russia)—Fiction.
PR6102.R33 W48 2003
823'.912—dc21
2002041474

Anchor ISBN: 1-4000-3200-8

Book design by Elizabeth Rendfleisch

www.anchorbooks.com

Printed in the United States of America
10 9 8 7 6 5 4 3 2

For Claudia, Jack, Louisa, and Sam.
And Mum and Dad.

ACKNOWLEDGMENTS

Thanks to Constantine Beloroutchev, for conducting key research in St. Petersburg, Moscow, and Yalta, for showing me around and advising me on all matters pertaining to the history of the period, Russian culture and language (all mistakes are mine not his); to my mother, Sally Bradby, for assistance with historical research in the UK; to my editorial team, Bill Scott-Kerr and Jason Kaufman, for their support, endless encouragement, and clever insights; to Mark Lucas, for being the greatest agent known to man; and to my inspirational wife, Claudia, for more reasons than there would be space to list.

THE WHITE RUSSIAN

St. Petersburg (Petrograd), January 1, 1917

Vengeance is mine, and I will repay.

ST. PETERSBURG 1917

OKHRANA
HEADQUARTERS

ALEXANDROVSKY PROSPEKT

Malaya Neva

MALY PROSPEKT

SANDRO'S
APARTMENT

THE STRELKA

Vasilevsky Island

*Bodies found
on the ice*

WINTER PALACE

LINE FOURTEEN

Bolshaya Neva

The Alexander Garden

ST. ISAACS

IMPERIAL YACHT CLUB/
ASTORIA HOTEL

OFITSERSKAYA ULITSA

MARINSKY
THEATRE

CITY POLICE
HEADQUARTERS

SADOVAYA ULITSA

MARIA'S
APARTMENT

© 2003 Jeffrey L. Ward

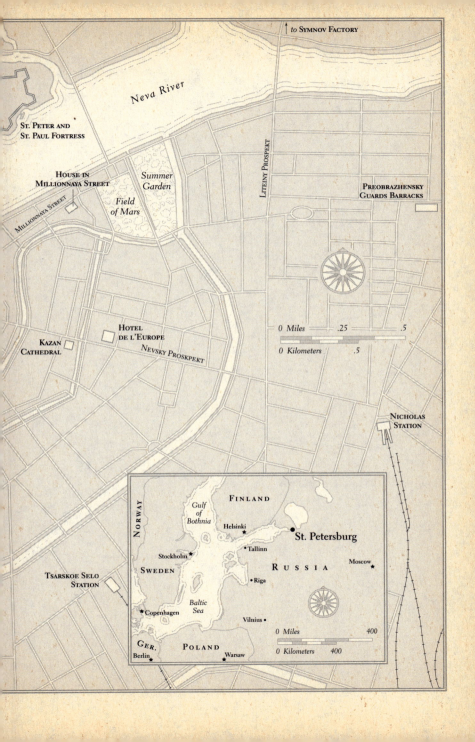

to SYMNOV FACTORY

Neva River

ST. PETER AND
ST. PAUL FORTRESS

HOUSE IN
MILLIONNAYA STREET

Summer
Garden

Field
of Mars

MILLIONNAYA STREET

LITEINY PROSPEKT

PREOBRAZHENSKY
GUARDS BARRACKS

HOTEL
DE L'EUROPE

KAZAN
CATHEDRAL

NEVSKY PROSKPEKT

0 Miles   .25   .5

0 Kilometers   .5

NICHOLAS
STATION

TSARSKOE SELO
STATION

NORWAY

FINLAND

Gulf
of
Bothnia

Helsinki

St. Petersburg

SWEDEN

Stockholm

Tallinn

RUSSIA

Moscow

Baltic
Sea

Riga

Copenhagen

Vilnius

GER.

POLAND

Berlin

Warsaw

0 Miles   400

0 Kilometers   400

The arctic wind sliced through Ruzsky's thin woolen overcoat. His boots were damp and his toes numb with cold, but he was oblivious to everything except the frozen expanse before him.

All he could see was ice.

Ruzsky's heart was beating fast. He tried to place a foot on the ice, before shifting his weight back to the step. He looked down at his boots, but his vision was blurred. He fought to control his breathing. "Christ," he whispered. His first day back from exile and it would have to begin like this.

The constables were ahead of him, in the center of the frozen river Neva, illuminated by a ring of torches. The snowfall had tapered off through the night and the sky was now clear. The narrow spire of the Peter and Paul Cathedral on the far side of the river was bathed in moonlight.

There was a sudden flurry of movement, and a burly figure broke away from the group, the flame of his torch dancing as he walked. Ruzsky watched his partner stride toward him.

"You're waiting for an escort?" Pavel halted, one hand thrust deep into his pocket. Small crystals were lodged in his beard and along his drooping mustache.

"No."

"It's the ice?" They'd had to deal with a body on the ice once before, years ago, on a small lake outside the city.

Ruzsky cleared his throat. "No," he lied.

"It's January. The river's been frozen for months. If anyone was going to fall through, it would have been me," Pavel said, gesturing to his own girth.

Ruzsky stared at him. Pavel had a round face that exuded warmth even when he was frowning. He was right, of course.

"Oh, shit," Ruzsky muttered. He closed his eyes and stepped forward, trying to ignore the jolt of fear as his foot crunched down on the frozen surface.

"The city's bravest investigator, afraid of the ice," Pavel said. "Who would believe it?"

Ruzsky opened his eyes. They were walking forward briskly and he was starting to breathe more easily.

"I didn't mean that," Pavel said.

"I know."

"I don't blame you, my old friend. You've barely been back twelve hours and look what it has delivered up to us." Pavel nodded in the direction of the Winter Palace. "And here, of all places."

They walked with their heads bowed against the damp, bitter wind that whistled in from the Gulf of Finland. It was several degrees colder out here on the river.

Ruzsky thrust his hands deep into his pockets. Only his head, beneath one of his father's old sheepskin hats, was warm.

Next to the bodies, the constables stood, smoking. They were dressed in long greatcoats and black sheepskin hats, the uniform of St. Petersburg's city police.

The woman was closest to Palace Embankment and lay on her back, long dark hair spread out around her head like a fan. "Torch." Ruzsky held up his hand.

One of the men marched forward. He couldn't have been older than seventeen or eighteen, with a pronounced nose, narrow eyes, and a nervous expression. He was lucky not to be fighting at the front, Ruzsky thought, as he took the torch and bent over the body of the woman. He got to his knees.

The victim was—or had been—pretty, though with poor skin. He removed one of his gloves and put his hand against her cheek. Her skin was frozen solid. Her face was almost peaceful as she stared up at the night sky. The fatal wound was to her chest, probably to her heart; he could see that she had lost a good deal of blood. He tried to ascertain exactly where she'd been stabbed, but her clothes were rigid and he decided to leave any further investigation to Sarlov.

Ruzsky's hand was already numb, so he put it back into his glove and thrust it into his pocket. He straightened again, looking at the gap between the two bodies. The area around them had been well trodden by the constables, so he could make no attempt to determine a pattern of events from the footprints. "Don't they teach them anything these days?" Ruzsky grumbled, gesturing with the torch at the trampled snow.

"It's good to have you back." Pavel offered him a flask.

Ruzsky shook his head. He walked around to the other body, the spitting of the flame and the crackle of his boots in the snow the only sounds above the whistle of the wind.

The man lay facedown, surrounded by a sea of crimson. He had bled like a fountain.

"Turn him over," Ruzsky said. Two of the constables moved forward and heaved the body onto its back.

Ruzsky breathed out.

"Holy Mother of God," Pavel said.

There were stab wounds to the man's chest and neck and face, one through his nose, and another peeling back his cheek.

"Who were they?" Ruzsky asked.

"I don't know."

"Have you checked their pockets?"

"Of course. Nothing, except this." Pavel handed over a roll of banknotes—small denomination Russian rubles.

"That's it? No identity papers?"

"Nothing."

"Cards? Letters?"

"There's nothing."

"Have you looked properly?"

"Of course I have."

Ruzsky bent down and pulled back the man's overcoat. He thrust a gloved hand into the inside pocket. It was empty. He straightened again and shoved the roll of rubles into his own coat. "The girl?"

"Same."

"Any sign of a knife?"

"No."

"How far have you looked?"

"We were waiting," Pavel said slowly, "for you."

The constables started to move about again. "Stay where you are," Ruzsky instructed them. He walked back to the girl. As he looked down at her, he felt suddenly sober. She was young, probably no more than twenty; well dressed, too. They both were. It was difficult to be sure, but he didn't think she had been stabbed more than once. He looked across at the other body. They were about seven yards apart.

"You've checked *all* of their pockets?"

"Twice."

"We'll have a look when we get them inside," Ruzsky said, mostly to himself. He didn't want to take his gloves off again out here.

Ruzsky looked up toward the Admiralty spire above Palace Embankment, and the golden dome of St. Isaac's Cathedral in the distance. They were in full view of the austere blue and white facade of the Tsar's Winter Palace, but at a distance of fifty yards or more. Pavel followed his gaze.

"Perhaps a servant saw something," Ruzsky said.

"Not if they were killed in the middle of the night."

"We should make it our first port of call."

"Of course. We'll get the Emperor out of bed."

Ruzsky didn't smile. They both knew the Tsar hadn't spent a night in the Winter Palace for years—not since the start of the war, at any rate.

Ruzsky raised the torch higher, then began walking again. "Tell them not to move, Pavel."

He walked slowly and carefully until he found the footsteps he was looking for, implanted in the thin layer of snow that covered the ice. He examined them for a moment, before returning to the bodies to check the size and shape of the victims' shoes.

Once he got away from the melee around the murder scene, Ruzsky found the trail easily enough. The couple had been walking close together, perhaps arm in arm. He followed their footprints for about twenty yards, then stopped, turned, and looked back at the scene of the crime. Pavel and the constables were watching him.

Ruzsky swung around ninety degrees, held the wooden oil flame torch in front of him, and began to walk in a wide circle around the bodies. He expected to encounter another set of footprints—or several—left by the killer, but there was nothing here except virgin snow.

Ruzsky returned to the orginal path and got down on his knees again. He looked carefully at the tracks, moving the torch closer to the ground, so that it hissed next to his ear.

He raised his hand. Pavel was marching out to meet him.

"You search like a hunter," Pavel said.

"I used to hunt wolves with my grandfather."

Ruzsky struggled to throw off the remains of his hangover.

"It's New Year," Pavel went on, "the couple are lovers out for a romantic stroll."

"Perhaps."

"Just the two of them, alone. They leave Palace Embankment, walking close together, arm in arm. They turn toward the Strelka, then gaze up at the stars above. The city has never looked more beautiful. Some bootlegged vodka perhaps, all troubles forgotten."

Ruzsky was now completely absorbed in his task, the fragility of the ice only a dim anxiety at the back of his mind, the biting cold a dull ache in his hands and feet and upon his cheeks.

He began to trace the victims' path backward once more, ignoring Pavel, who followed him in silence. It was not until they had almost reached the embankment that Ruzsky found what he was looking for.

The killer had followed the tracks of the dead man, both before and after he'd struck. Only at the very last moment, barely three yards from the embankment, had he lost patience and stepped outside them.

Ruzsky reached into his pocket, took out a cigarette case, and offered it to his colleague. He felt more confident within reach of the steps.

They lit up—no easy task with gloved hands numb with cold—and turned their backs against the wind. The smoke was pleasantly warm, but Ruzsky could still feel his temperature dropping. Perhaps he was just sobering up.

"They must have been lovers," Pavel said. "Their footsteps are close."

"Why doesn't the girl run?" Ruzsky asked.

"What do you mean?"

"How many times has the man been stabbed? Ten? Twenty? In his chest, his heart, his nose, his cheek. Does the girl just stand there watching?"

"Perhaps she knows her attacker."

"Mmm." Ruzsky stared out across the river.

"It was planned. She knew of it."

"Possibly." Ruzsky turned to his colleague. "But why did she have no idea that she was also to be a victim?"

Pavel shook his head. He flicked his cigarette high into the air and they heard it fizzle as it hit the ice.

Ruzsky gazed at a cloud passing across the face of the moon. A photographer walked over from the St. Peter and St. Paul Fortress. They watched as he prepared his camera and lined up the first shot. He bent down, his head beneath a cloth, and they saw a light flash. The noise—a dull thump—reached them a split second later.

"Were there any witnesses?" Ruzsky asked.

"Do you see any?"

"We should begin at the palace."

Pavel's expression told him he did not wish to go anywhere near the palace. "So I'm taking orders again?"

Ruzsky looked up sharply, then shook his head, embarrassed. "Of course not. I'm sorry."

Pavel smiled. "Better things return to the way they were. Welcome back, Chief Investigator."

Ruzsky met his affectionate gaze and tried to smile, but his frozen face wouldn't obey.

He reached into the pocket of his greatcoat for a notepad and pencil, then handed Pavel the torch and crouched down in the snow. He shakily traced the outline of one of the footprints the killer had left in front of the steps, then stared at it for a few moments. He stood and put his own boot alongside it. "About my size. A little bigger."

"Why didn't he go over to the Strelka?"

"Who?"

"The killer." Pavel gestured at the Winter Palace. "There are guards here, the road is busy. Much less chance of being seen if he'd gone on to Vasilevsky Island."

Ruzsky did not answer. He was staring at the group out on the ice, deep in thought.

"Oh, by the way," Pavel added. "New Year, New Happiness."

It was the traditional greeting for the first day of the year. "Yes," Ruzsky answered. "Quite."

2

They climbed onto the embankment and approached the riverside entrance of the Tsar's Winter Palace.

Ruzsky stepped forward to knock on the giant green door. There was no answer, so he tried to look through the misted glass of the window to his right. He climbed up on a stone ledge to give himself a better view.

"Be careful or they'll shoot you," Pavel said.

A light was dimly visible in the hallway. There was little obvious security, but then it was well known that the Tsar and his family preferred their country palace outside the city at Tsarskoe Selo.

Ruzsky stepped forward and knocked once again. He glanced up at the light suspended on a long iron chain above him. As it swung slowly in the icy wind, its metal links creaked.

"This cannot be right," Pavel said.

"If anyone saw it, it will have been the guard here."

Pavel hesitated. "Let's go around to the office of the palace police at the front."

"Then we'll never find out who was on duty back here."

They waited, listening to the wind. Pavel forced his hat down upon his head. "Maybe it's colder than Tobolsk."

Ruzsky saw the guilt behind Pavel's uncertain smile. "It's the damp here," Ruzsky said. "You know how it is. In Siberia, it's a dry cold." Ruzsky wanted to assuage his friend's guilt, but did not know what else he could say. Pavel had been responsible for his exile, but Ruzsky did not hold it against him. In fact, far from it. The thought still filled Ruzsky with bitterness, as though it had happened yesterday.

Three years before, in the darkened, piss-strewn stairwell of a tenement building in Sennaya Ploschad, Ruzsky and Pavel had arrested a small-time landlord who'd assaulted and strangled the ten-year-old daughter of one of his poorer tenants. The man had not imagined the terrified mother would dare complain, but his insouciance as they led him down to the cells in the city police headquarters ought to have set their alarm bells ringing. Throughout that night, both Ruzsky and Pavel had struggled to retain their tempers as the fat, sweaty toad had drummed his pudgy fingers upon the table and answered their questions with a contemptuous insolence.

Pavel had a distinct intolerance for these crimes, and while Ruzsky was upstairs dealing with the paperwork, Pavel had decided to put the man into a cell with a group of armed robbers. He'd informed the men of the nature of their new companion's crime.

Ruzsky had no moral objection to this solution, but it had resulted in the world falling in upon their heads. The man turned out to have been the foreman of an arms factory over in Vyborg and, more damaging, an agent of the Okhrana—the Tsar's vicious secret police. Within a few hours of his lifeless body being dragged from the cell, the city police headquarters had been swarming with hard-faced Okhrana men in long black overcoats.

Pavel tried to take responsibility, but Ruzsky had overruled him. It had been his own idea, he told the secret police chief, Igor Vasilyev, and his thugs.

Ruzsky's punishment had been effective banishment to Siberia as the chief investigator of the Tobolsk Police Department.

Ruzsky tried to return his friend's smile. They both knew that Pavel's punishment would have been much worse. Ruzsky might have been the black sheep of his distinguished, aristocratic family, but the Ruzsky name itself and the fact that his father was a government minister still carried weight. It had limited the scale of punishment—back then, at least.

Ruzsky finally heard a bolt being pulled back and the palace door swung open. Three men in the distinctive uniforms of the Yellow Cuirassiers emerged from the darkness. The elder of the men—a sergeant—had white hair and a mustache like Pavel's. His two young companions were nervous and held their rifles firmly in both hands. In the grand hallway behind them, Ruzsky could just make out the tip of a chandelier.

"City police," Ruzsky said. He wasn't in the mood to offer felicitations for the dawning of a new year.

"You should have come to the other side."

"There have been two murders, out here, on the ice."

The sergeant walked forward, followed by his companions. They stood in a small group looking out toward the torches in the middle of the frozen river. "Yesterday it was a drunk," he said, pointing at the deserted road in front of him. "Froze to death just here."

"I fear this is a little different. The victims were stabbed—"

"A week ago, someone was stabbed out in front of the Admiralty."

"A domestic dispute," Pavel corrected him. "Two brothers. Both still alive."

"Have you been on duty all night?" Ruzsky asked.

"Of course."

"You're on detachment?"

The Yellow Cuirassiers—officially His Majesty's Life Guard Cuirassier Regiment—were based out at Tsarskoe Selo, in the small town that surrounded the royal palaces there. It was about an hour's train ride from the capital.

The sergeant did not answer.

"There are other guards?" Ruzsky went on.

The man shrugged. "On Palace Square. They don't move unless we call for them."

Ruzsky looked down the embankment toward the Hermitage. "There is no one out here?"

"A sentry either end until midnight. After that, it is not necessary. The shutters on the ground and first floors are closed. We would hear any commotion." He was defensive.

"There are no patrols?"

His cheeks flushed slightly. Ruzsky didn't wish to press the point; it had been New Year's Eve, after all. "What time did you and your men come on duty?"

"If you wish to ask questions, you will have to apply to the head of the guard detachment or the office of the palace police."

"Come on," Pavel said softly, before Ruzsky could get annoyed. "A couple of lovers have been sliced up out there. We just want to check to make sure no one saw anything, then be on our way."

The man's face softened. He breathed out. "Cigarette?" Pavel asked, taking out a tiny tin case from the pocket of his coat and offering it around the group.

The men hesitated—smoking on duty was strictly forbidden—before each taking one in turn. They lit up and smoked in silence, suddenly conspiratorial.

The sergeant looked out at the constables still guarding the bodies on the ice. It was marginally less cold here, in the shelter of the giant porch.

"We came on duty at midnight. I did my last rounds about an hour later. I walked along the embankment to check for drunks. Then I locked the door."

"You stand here, inside the hallway?"

"We check the rooms periodically, but, as I said, all the shutters are locked, except those by the door."

"You didn't see or hear anything?"

The sergeant shook his head and so did his young companions. Ruzsky could see they were telling the truth. He suspected they'd probably been playing cards as the New Year dawned.

That, and the fact they had accepted a cigarette while on duty, was, he thought, a sign of the times. He wondered if the men had seen action at the front. The sergeant, certainly. The others looked too young.

"When you came out at one o'clock, you didn't see anyone at all?"

"There was a group farther down, by the Admiralty. I think they'd just crossed the river, but they were going home. It was quiet after that. If we'd heard anyone else, we'd have moved them on. We don't allow people to linger."

"Could anyone have seen something from one of the upstairs windows? A servant?"

He shook his head. "These are all state rooms at the front. There are family bedrooms on the top floor, but none are occupied." The sergeant gestured toward the group on the ice again. "It's quite far out."

"But extremely visible on a clear night."

"Yes." He shook his head and looked genuinely apologetic. "You can talk to the head of the household later on. He could tell you whether there might have been anyone in the front rooms, but I'm afraid I cannot help you."

The sergeant turned and retreated, taking the younger men with him. The door shut with a loud bang and the silence descended once more, save for the iron chain above them creaking in the icy wind. An ambulance had parked on the Strelka and two men were carrying a stretcher out to retrieve the bodies.

"It's a strange place for a murder," Pavel said. "At this time."

Ruzsky didn't answer. He glanced over his shoulder. They were only a few minutes from his parents' home here, and he thought of his son Michael sleeping, curled up with his teddy bear pressed to his nose.

"We'd better start looking for the knife," he said.

Ruzsky returned to the edge of the ice. As he reached the bottom of the steps, he heard the sound of a car door being shut and turned to see two men in fedoras getting out of a large black automobile farther down the embankment.

The men leaned over the wall and surveyed the scene on the ice.

"The Okhrana?" Ruzsky asked quietly.

It was only half a question. They both knew perfectly well that these were Vasilyev's men. The change in Pavel's demeanor was palpable.

"What are they doing here?" Ruzsky asked.

Pavel did not answer. He was staring at them, trying to conceal his unease.

The two secret policemen sauntered back to their automobile and got in. The car swung around and returned the way it had come.

Ruzsky and Pavel watched as it disappeared down the embankment before turning left over the bridge in the direction of the St. Peter and St. Paul Fortress.

3

Ruzsky didn't want to go back onto the ice, so he got Pavel to instruct the constables and then stood on the embankment and watched as they searched across the river. It was a huge area and they moved quickly, reminding him of a pack of hunting dogs eager to pick up a trail. Maybe they just wanted to get home.

The wind had dropped a little, but it was still bitterly cold. The dim light gave the appearance of fog and Ruzsky could now only just make out the spire of the cathedral on the other side of the river. It wasn't going to make their search any easier.

It was still early, but they were not alone on the ice; two constables from the marine police had begun working the section of the river around the Strelka. As Ruzsky watched, one leaned forward and probed gently with his foot, before reaching back, taking a pole with a red flag from his colleague, and sticking it into the ice.

The pair appeared oblivious to the fact that a murder investigation was going on around them. They were looking for hazards, patches of black water, where a thin covering of ice concealed a pocket of five or six feet of water and a thicker layer of ice underneath.

Pavel was marching back toward him. Ruzsky wondered why none of the constables had bothered to go and tell the marine policemen to be on the lookout for a murder weapon.

"Not helping with the search, Deputy Chief Investigator?" Ruzsky asked Pavel as he climbed the steps toward him.

"They'll never find anything." Pavel glanced at him. "You look terrible, by the way."

Ruzsky did not respond. Pavel had picked him up from the station upon his return from Siberia the previous night, and they had demolished a bottle of bootlegged vodka in the dingy room Pavel had rented for him.

They stood together in silence, their breath billowing out into the morning air. Pavel coughed.

The bodies had already been removed by the ambulance, but watching the constables scanning the ice, Ruzsky had a clear vision of the dead girl's face. He could picture her laughing, her head resting on her companion's shoulder as they stared up at the stars and the cold beauty of the city around them. The dawn of another year. Had they been wondering what it would bring? How could you not?

Ruzsky heard the sound of movement and turned to see a servant brushing snow from the porch of the Winter Palace behind them. The man was a tall Tartar in the distinctive cinnamon-colored coat of rough cloth and cap trimmed in silver braid worn by these most menial of palace staff. He, too, stopped what he was doing to watch the dark figures moving about on the ice.

"You must be excited about seeing your boy," Pavel said.

Ruzsky frowned. His wife, Irina, had left him in Tobolsk six months earlier and returned to the capital, taking their son with her. Pavel knew the bare facts, but, so far, Ruzsky had managed to avoid all but the most cursory discussion of the subject. "She won't allow me to see him," he responded.

"She won't allow it?"

Ruzsky could see that Pavel also blamed himself for the state of his marriage, but the surprise was not that Irina had left him, but that she had ever agreed to go to Siberia with him in the first place, as was the fact that she had stuck it out for two and a half years. It had been a last attempt to make the marriage work, and for a few months it had even looked as if it might succeed.

"Irina has gone to stay with my father," Ruzsky explained. "She's sheltering behind them."

With a talent for deliberate provocation that he now recognized as one of her most striking attributes, Irina had, upon her return to Petersburg—or Petrograd, as it had been renamed at the start of the war—gone straight to live with his father rather than her own parents. The old man doted on his grandson and would deny him nothing.

Pavel shook his head. "He's your son, Sandro. Just demand it."

Pavel seemed about to go on, so Ruzsky forestalled him, wishing to change the subject. "When you think about it—"

"I'm not paid to think anymore," Pavel responded.

Ruzsky gave him a stern look and continued. "I can't understand those last three paces. The killer doesn't come back and make any attempt to conceal them, and they're clearly visible to even the most ignorant detective."

"It shows you what people expect."

Ruzsky stared at the steps in front of him. He wondered what the man had done to encourage such brutality in his assailant. "Who found the bodies?" he asked.

"An old woman walking home."

"Did you speak to her?"

"Of course. She didn't see anything."

"What time did the constables call you out?" Ruzsky asked.

"I don't know how you stand it, Sandro," Pavel went on. "I wouldn't manage a month without seeing my boy. Why did she leave?"

Ruzsky watched one of the constables talking to a marine policeman, thinking of how his wife had detested their stifling provincial life in Tobolsk, from the exaggerated respect afforded the governor, a petty tyrant from Petersburg, to the crumbling homes and small-town mind-set of the local gentry. He didn't blame her. Not for that.

"A disintegrating marriage is not an attractive thing," he said, quietly, reflecting upon the arguments that had raged in that tiny house at the end of a dusty street.

Ruzsky took a pace forward. He surveyed the river once more. "Is there anywhere else from where someone might have witnessed the murder?" he asked. But the wide expanse of ice answered the question for him.

The constables were working their way back toward the embankment.

"Well, we survived another night without a revolution," Ruzsky said, turning toward his deputy. It was a teasing reference to Pavel's vodka-induced doom and gloom the night before.

"I told you what is said in the khvost."

The khvost was a phenomenon talked about even in faraway Tobolsk, but you had to see the lines of people snaking around windy street corners to believe them. The poor had to queue for anything and everything these days: food, oil for their lamps, clothes. They joined lines even when no one seemed aware of what lay at the front; it was bound to be something in short supply.

"What you don't understand," Pavel went on, "because you have not been here, is that people don't read newspapers anymore. No one believes what little slips past the censors and so they treat what is said in the khvost as news, not rumor. They believe it."

"Maybe the war will be over soon."

"Maybe I'll become the tsar." Pavel leaned forward earnestly. "The word in the khvost—and it has been so for months—is *treason.*"

"That's not exactly new."

"One of our neighbors was in a line last night for bread. She told Tonya it was a four-hour wait. One woman said she'd heard from a cousin in the Life Guards that the imperial family had already left for England. Another said China had invaded. The day before, the khvost talk was that the Empress had agreed to be paid by the Germans to starve the peasants to death. Last week, it was said she had promised to sell the western half of Russia to Berlin. And the things that have been said about the Empress and Rasputin . . ."

"Perhaps things will improve now that the priest's no longer with us," Ruzsky said. They'd talked about Rasputin's murder last night. The case had been taken over by the Okhrana, as had all recent cases that were deemed to have political significance.

"No. And it was too late, anyway. Do you know where the biggest khvost is? There's a new railway ticket bureau since you left, in Michael Street. Now that so few trains run, the line there is five-deep. Thousands are leaving—to the Crimea or the Caucasus, or Haparanda."

Haparanda was just over the border, in Sweden. "And here's another thing," Pavel went on, getting into his stride, "who would defend them? Tell me that. If it blows, who would fight to save the Romanovs?"

They'd had this discussion last night too. "The same people who always have."

Pavel shook his head violently. "The blue bloods are not here. They're at the front. Dead. You have seen it yourself; the capital is full of reservists, the wounded, deserters."

"There's one lot who would defend him," Ruzsky said, pointing at a group of dark figures who had left the Strelka and were walking toward the Winter Palace. They were dressed in black and the man at the center carried a picture of the Tsar mounted on a wooden pole. They were singing the national anthem, "Bozhe, Tzaria Khrani"—"God Save the Tsar"—in loud, tuneless voices.

"Another night of Jew bashing," Ruzsky muttered as he and Pavel watched their approach. The Black Bands were gangs of street thugs funded by the secret police to attack opponents of the Tsar. Mostly, they spent their time organizing pogroms against the Jews.

The men mounted the steps, still singing. The figure carrying the portrait was a young man with a fleshy face flushed red from alcohol and exertion, and a thin, pencil mustache. In his left hand, Ruzsky could see a knuckle duster. He stopped. "New Year, New Happiness," he said.

Neither Ruzsky nor Pavel answered.

"God save the Tsar!"

This was what all of these gangs did, demanding a show of loyalty as an excuse to beat anyone who wouldn't offer it. "Fuck off," Ruzsky said.

The man took a pace forward, his face livid.

"We're police officers," Pavel added. "There's been a murder. Move on, please."

Pavel's tone had been more conciliatory, but the leader of the group brushed him aside. "If you're police officers, you should want to show your loyalty to the Tsar."

"Go away, before I arrest you," Ruzsky went on.

"You? Arrest us?" The man did not move, and, for a moment, he looked as if he would strike them. Ruzsky felt the weight of the Sauvage revolver in his pocket. As it had been often before his exile, the temptation to bring these kind of scum down to size was overwhelming.

There was a shout from the river. Close to the embankment—about fifty feet away—one of the constables was holding something above his head.

Ruzsky and Pavel pushed past the thugs and strode out onto the ice.

Behind them, the men of the Black Bands began to sing "God Save the Tsar" again.

"I've found it, sir!" the constable shouted as they approached him. He offered Ruzsky the knife.

"Christ," Pavel whispered.

It was an old, crude black dagger. Ruzsky held it up so that he could see the twisted iron handle more clearly. There was some inscription by the base of the blade, partly obscured by dried blood. It looked like Sanskrit, or Arabic. He turned it over in his hand and then passed it to Pavel.

Ruzsky faced the embankment. The gang of thugs had disappeared from view, the sound of their singing now just a faint echo across the river. "Why would he do that?" Ruzsky asked.

"Do what?"

"He follows them so carefully out here, then throws away the murder weapon."

"He must have been wearing gloves. There won't be any fingerprints."

"It's still careless. Why throw it away?"

"Panic."

"He wasn't panicking when he retraced his steps, going backward."

Pavel returned the knife to the constable. "Take it straight to the office and give it to Veresov. If he's not in his room, telephone him at home and say the chief investigator would like his help and he is to come in immediately."

The constable ran off in the direction of the palace. They watched him go. "In its way, it's all a bit theatrical, isn't it?" Pavel said, gesturing toward the patch of blood in the center of the ice. "Following in the footsteps and so on."

"If you call being stabbed a dozen times theatrical." Ruzsky turned to his partner. "It's certainly not straightforward, I'll grant you that."

4

Pavel was hungry, so Ruzsky agreed to go briefly to a café for breakfast. The route to their favorite haunt took them around the front of the Winter Palace, past the Hermitage, and into Millionnaya Street, where the wind funneled down from Palace Square had swept deep drifts up against the walls of the houses. Outside the barracks of the first battalion of the Preobrazhensky Guards—his father's regiment—a sentry stamped his feet hard.

As they walked down Millionnaya Street, they heard a muffled shout and turned to see a detachment of the Imperial Guard Cavalry entering the street behind them, the horses' hooves clattering on the treacherous cobblestones, their breath hanging on the cold morning air.

Ruzsky and Pavel waited as they passed. The men were from the elite Chevalier Guard Regiment, mounted on their distinctive chestnut mares. They were in full parade uniform, the soldiers' white and red jackets visible beneath long blue overcoats, their swords clanking beside them, their scabbards bright. The officer wore a cape over his blue and red jacket, fastened at the throat with a gold buckle. All of the men had upon their heads the curved brass helmet of the guard, with the large imperial eagle at its peak.

There were no shouts or barked commands; they were trying to avoid waking the aristocratic residents of one of the city's wealthiest districts. As they reached a stretch of the street that was covered in snow, their progress was suddenly silent.

Halfway down, Ruzsky stopped outside a house with a delicately sculpted, soft yellow facade. The shutters were closed. This had always been his family's home in the city. He'd been born here. So had both of his brothers. Pavel stood behind him and Ruzsky found it hard to move on. In the cold dawn light, a sense of overpowering loneliness settled upon him.

He thought of Michael in his room in the attic and wondered which of his own toys were still on the shelves above the small bed.

Pavel waited patiently. He knew the truth—or some of it—and did not wish to intrude. "They'll still be asleep," he said quietly.

Ruzsky tore himself away and forced himself to keep walking. As they emerged from the far end of the street onto the Field of Mars, past the Pavlovsky Guards barracks, he felt like a champagne cork escaping from the neck of a bottle. Just to be in the street was to feel the pressure of his own history.

The Field of Mars was a sandy expanse designed for military training now shrouded in a thick layer of snow. The detachment of cavalry cantered around it, turning and wheeling as it exercised as a unit, still quiet but for the snorts of the horses, the clank of metal, and the occasional barked command.

Pavel and Ruzsky walked around the square, past the giant yellow-stone palaces that faced onto it. All the windows were dark, but outside one a private sled driver stood next to his horse, banging his hands together. Just in front, beneath a gas lamp, another servant waited for a small, dirty-white Pekinese to do its business. Neither man acknowledged them as they passed.

Walking on toward the Summer Gardens, Ruzsky felt his heart lurch as he saw a tall man striding in their direction, trailing behind a big brown hunting dog. The man's purposeful gait and the type of hound—big dogs were unusual in Petersburg houses—made him think for a few seconds that it must be his father Nicholas. As they came closer, the realization that it wasn't brought both relief and disappointment.

The café was on a ground floor of a large tenement block the other side of the Moyka Canal. Pavel ate bread. Ruzsky sobered himself up fully with Turkish coffee and cigarettes. Their drinking had gone on into the early hours and the alcohol was still circulating in his bloodstream. His feet were sore and damp and he only gradually regained feeling in his toes.

The café was run by a short, swarthy Ukrainian from the Crimea and was full even at this time in the morning, the air thick with steam, body heat, and cigarette smoke. A small group of the abjectly poor milled around outside the door, glancing in at the warmth and the food, their faces gradually obscured by the mist gathering on the thick glass windows.

The black Romanov eagle was etched in the center of the panes either side of the door, and there was a line drawing of the royal palace at Livadia on the wall above Pavel's head. The owner's father had been a member of the imperial household at the Tsar's summer home in the Crimea and the son remained fanatically loyal not only to the Tsar and his family, but to the principles of autocracy. But his food was good and, more importantly, cheap.

Sitting here this morning, Ruzsky felt as though he had never been away. Had he been inclined by nature to self-pity, the scene would almost have been poignant, since the last time he had sat here, before his fall from grace three years ago, he had felt happier than at any point since the early days of his childhood.

It had mostly been because of her. Instinctively, Ruzsky touched the letter in his jacket pocket. Like Michael, Maria would still be sleeping.

"It hasn't changed," Pavel said, smiling, as Ruzsky looked around him.

"Clientele still as shabby as ever."

"It's no place for a prince," Pavel went on, stretching. "Dear me, no."

Ruzsky smiled too. It had been a long-standing joke between them. The Ruzskys drew a continuous line of service and loyalty to Tsar and Empire stretching back more than a hundred and fifty years to the reign of Peter the Great. The eldest son always served in the Empire's most prestigious infantry regiment, the Preobrazhensky Guards. Ruzsky's decision to shun the Guards and, as a result of a childhood passion for Sherlock Holmes, enter the service of the St. Petersburg Police Department—as lowly an occupation for a man of high birth as it was possible to imagine—had provoked a final severance of any form of connection with his father.

Ruzsky looked at Pavel. With his drooping mustache and lugubrious expression, he seemed to have aged dramatically these past three years.

Ruzsky made a sudden decision and stood. "I'll see you back in the office."

"Where are you going?"

"I won't be long. Make sure Sarlov is in," he said, referring to the medical examiner.

In the street outside, Ruzsky walked at first, but then gathered speed, so that by the time he reached Millionnaya Ulitsa, he was running.

His father's home was one of the most beautiful on the street. It was four stories high, not including the attic or the basement. To the left of the steps leading up to the doorway was the yard in which all of the family's transportation was kept. Ruzsky watched a servant oiling the runners of one of his father's upended sleds, with its distinctive green and gold livery.

He climbed the steps and knocked. The door was opened, but not by Ivan, the family's old butler.

Ruzsky stared at the young man before him. He was tall and thin, handsome but for his pimples, with wavy dark hair curling over his collar. He wore the red and gold uniform of his father's house.

"Can I help you, sir?"

It took Ruzsky a few moments to get over the shock of not being recognized in his own home. "Where's Ivan?"

"Ivan is not here. And you are?"

"I'm the son of the house," Ruzsky said as he walked forward into the hallway. He stopped, realized his manner had been churlish, and offered his hand. "I apologize, I'm Sandro."

"Master Sandro, sir, yes." The young man's handshake was firm. "I'm Peter. I believe your father is out."

"I'm here to see my son."

"Yes, sir. Would you like me to find the boy?"

Ruzsky forced himself to smile. "I will be all right, thank you."

"Of course. New Year, New Happiness."

"And the same to you."

The young man shut the door and withdrew discreetly, down the wooden stairs toward the kitchen in the basement.

Ruzsky stood for a moment in the semidarkness of the hallway. He realized he had been holding his breath.

He shoved his hands into the pockets of his coat and slowly exhaled. Ahead of him was a fir tree, decorated for Christmas. He took a pace closer and touched one of the round pink and white gingerbreads his mother had always instructed the servants to bake. The decorations were the ones she had bought at Peto's all those years ago: tiny sedan chairs, violins, bears, monkeys, and thin candles in tin candlesticks. Ruzsky imagined Michael helping his grandfather and the servants decorate the tree. He thought of the excitement that would have lit up his son's face.

He'd heard that Christmas trees had been banned as too Germanic, but the rule clearly did not apply to such high servants of the Tsar.

The hall was wide, leading onto the formal rooms to his right and left. His father's study and the winter room were at the back, before the stairs leading down to the kitchen. The hall was dominated on one side by a giant gilt-edged mirror above an ornate chestnut dresser, and on the other by a dark tapestry hanging from a long metal pole. There was an iron coat stand in the corner. Beside it, on top of a wooden pillar, was a bust of Ruzsky's grandfather. In the style of Roman emperors, his brother Dmitri had always said, and with similar pretensions to grandeur.

Next to it was a portrait of their mother, with a cold smile playing at the corner of her lips. Ruzsky stared at it for a moment.

The memory it triggered was of the scene in this hallway on the day Ruzsky had begun as a cadet at the Corps des Pages—the last time he had seen her. Standing by the door in the uniform of the school, next to his father, he had raised his hand to her to say goodbye and she had failed to lift her own in response.

He had hesitated, waiting for something more, his face reddening as he realized that nothing would be forthcoming.

The door to the drawing room was open and Ruzsky walked through it, conscious of the noise of his footsteps on the wooden floor. This room, too, was in semidarkness. His father forbade the servants from lighting a fire until after four in the afternoon, even in the depths of winter.

It had been redecorated since Ruzsky's last visit, with a rich red wallpaper that matched the Persian rugs. On the wall closest to him a curved saber hung below a painting of a mountain from the northern part of the Hindu Kush. Next to the saber was a tall wooden table upon which stood an elaborate, bejeweled box, and on the wall above that, portraits of his two brothers.

His mother had wanted a society artist, but his father had chosen someone cheaper and less fashionable. Ruzsky could no longer even remember the man's name, although he had forced them all to sit for long enough.

Ruzsky pulled back the curtain, to allow in a little more natural light. The man had caught none of Dmitri's charm, but the portrait of Ilya—Ilusha as he had been known to them all—had greater warmth, capturing perfectly his impish grin.

Ruzsky wondered what his father had done with his own portrait. Even though it had been many years since it had hung alongside the others, its absence still caused him pain. It was as if he did not exist.

He let the curtain fall, haunted by the resemblance between Ilya and Michael. Or was it just that his own son had almost reached the age at which Ilusha had been taken from them?

Ruzsky turned around and walked swiftly from the room and through the hallway. He glanced out of the rear window and caught sight of his son in the garden.

Michael was on his own. He had built a wall of snow and behind it assembled a small mound of snowballs.

Ruzsky watched as his son came back behind the wall, picked up the first missile, and hurled it toward its target. He missed, so repeated the exercise with the second and then with all the others, ducking down between each throw, as if dodging gunfire.

When he had finished, Michael mounted an imaginary horse and rode out beyond his rampart.

He dismounted and began to run through the small garden, with his arms outstretched. He was a plane, or perhaps a bird. He was alone in his world.

Michael's isolation reminded Ruzsky of his own in the years after Ilusha's death.

He rested his forehead against the window and the glass slowly misted up with the warmth of his breath. How the months had dragged since he'd last set eyes upon his son.

"Perhaps you should leave him."

Ruzsky spun around. His father stood quite still in the hallway, apparently unchanged by these past three years. He was an older and more distinguished version of his eldest son. He was no taller than Ruzsky and not much broader, but he carried about him the gravity of his wealth and position.

His mustache was completely white now and drooped neatly around the edges of his mouth. His hair was longer than usual, but also a distinctive silver-white. Neatly brushed across his forehead, it was wavy and thick. If only you were as handsome as your father, Irina had once said to him with a sigh.

Today, Russia's assistant minister of finance wore a morning suit, his gold pocket-watch chain looped across the front of a dark waistcoat, highly polished boots catching what little light filtered through the window.

"I'm sorry?" Ruzsky asked. He felt his face flushing.

"He's your son. It's your choice."

"What is?"

"Whether to see him."

Ruzsky faced the window again. Michael had discarded his hat and was standing in the middle of the garden staring at the gray sky. "Why is that a choice?" he asked.

Irina emerged from the kitchen below and hurried toward their son. She tried to shoo him back inside, but he was reluctant to come. She picked up Michael's hat and forced it onto his head.

Irina was not an unattractive woman. Her dark hair had been recently cut and styled to frame her narrow face. She glanced up briefly, but did not appear to see him.

"Perhaps you should give him more time."

"Time for what?"

"To settle in."

Ruzsky had forgotten how much authority his father carried in his voice. "To settle in where?" he asked.

"You know perfectly well what I mean."

Ruzsky watched as Michael finally allowed himself to be led by his mother back into the house. He heard the door being shut below and could dimly make out the sound of their voices in the kitchen.

"Fatherhood carries responsibilities."

Ruzsky turned and, as he did so, caught sight of a wooden train in the corner of the doorway to his father's study, by the base of a large palm tree. "What do you mean by that?"

"Sometimes you have to act in the best interests of the child, and not of your own."

"And what are the best interests of my child?"

The elder Ruzsky gazed solemnly at his son. His face was deeply lined, his forehead creased by a severe frown. "If she finds you here, there will be a confrontation."

Ruzsky stared at the train. It was part of a set his father had commissioned for him on his seventh birthday from St. Petersburg's leading toymaker. Once, they had enjoyed playing with it together in the attic room at the top of the house.

Ruzsky forced himself to meet his father's glare. "He would be better off without me. Is that what you think?"

There was no reply and Ruzsky felt the weight of the past upon him. He was no longer the chief investigator of the Petrograd Police Department, but a frightened eleven-year-old boy in the study at Petrovo.

Ruzsky lowered his eyes and kept them fixed on the train as he fought to contain his emotions. He breathed in deeply. "Can a man never escape his past mistakes?" he asked.

The elder Ruzsky did not flinch, his eyes fixed upon his son. "It is the boy's welfare that concerns me now."

He turned around and walked slowly toward the study door. At its entrance, he bent down to pick up the wooden train engine and then, without a further glance, shut the door behind him, leaving Ruzsky alone in the corridor.

The house was silent.

Ruzsky heard a banging sound below, like a wooden bowl being hammered on a table. One of his father's Great Danes gave a single bark and then was quiet.

Ruzsky waited. Ever since Ilusha's death, his life had been about that closed door. He wanted to move beyond it, but felt paralyzed once again.

He could hear the sound of the Tompion clock on the mantelpiece in the drawing room.

He recalled the dark winter afternoons of his childhood, marked out by the steady, rhythmic ticking of that clock. It was the sound of the inflexible regimentation of his father's world.

Ruzsky closed his eyes and let himself return to that day at Petrovo. He could almost feel the icy water's embrace as his mind drifted toward a place that he knew deep in his heart would end the pain and guilt forever.

His father had instructed him to make sure that Ilusha did not play on the ice now that spring was upon them. And even if he had not been there at the moment his little brother had made those fateful steps, even if he could have claimed that it was not his fault and that he had heard the cry and run to the lake and dived in and done his best to save him, there was no one who blamed Ruzsky more than he blamed himself.

He should have gone with Ilusha.

It was snowing heavily when Ruzsky emerged, but he didn't take this or his surroundings in, until he had reached the corner of the Nevsky Prospekt. He stood on the street corner opposite the Alexander Garden, now, in winter, just dark, skeletal trees reaching for the sky, and tilted his face upward.

He tasted the flakes as they fell.

A detachment of soldiers in long greatcoats marched past him, then wheeled right onto the Nevsky. Ruzsky recognized them as members of the Semenovsky Regiment, though they hardly did justice to its reputation. They looked scruffy and marched without any of the precision that would have accompanied them before the war, when no regiment had moved anywhere in Petersburg unless immaculately turned out and in perfect order.

Ruzsky thought for a moment of the painted soldiers he had kept neatly in boxes in his attic room in the house in Millionnaya Street. He wondered if they were still there, and if Michael played with them, also. The contrast with the St. Petersburg of his childhood was pervasive. It was the first day of the New Year, but he was certain there would be no reception in the great halls of the Winter Palace.

Aside from the soldiers, the capital's main thoroughfare was almost deserted. Two private sleds waited outside the Wolf and Beranger Café and, beyond them, a motor car was clanking noisily in his direction.

Ruzsky pulled out his pocket watch. It was not yet ten o'clock in the morning; the city was only slowly coming to life.

He continued noticing that this section of the city had borne few physical changes. The huge windows of Alexandre's were packed with scarves of woven Persian silk, jade, ivory, leather goods of all descriptions, and jewels beyond the imagination of most passersby. Druce's, the famed *magasin anglais*, still had Harris Tweed and English soaps in its smaller windows, and Cabassue's had fine French silk ties and linen along with fashionable botinky, the low-cut velvet boots with rubber soles so favored by the rich. All the stores had signs declaring "English spoken" or "Ici on parle français," though, of course, they had all lost the once common "Man spricht Deutsch."

Ruzsky stopped dead. He had reached Wolff's, the capital's largest bookstore and his favorite as a child. The latest casualty lists from the front were posted in the window. The names stretched for column after column.

He read through them all.

Ruzsky turned around, deep in thought. Beyond the shop, tucked into the corner of the wall, was a bearded Circassian in traditional sheepskin coat, his wares—mostly silver bangles and brooches—spread out on a colored rug.

The man was clutching the cape around him, head bent. These traders were a commonplace sight in summer on the Nevsky, but Ruzsky had never before seen one here in winter.

The city police department was housed in a grand, classical building situated on Ofitserskaya Ulitsa—Officers Street—not far from the Mariinskiy Theatre. Pavel was waiting for him by the gate and the pair strolled in through the side arch of the courtyard, past a group of horses being exercised in a tight circle. Behind them, men from the transport department had already hauled out sleds and carriages from the garage, ready to be hitched up.

Ruzsky led the way into the lobby. It was warmer in here, but gloomy and run-down, blue and gold paint peeling from its walls.

Directly ahead of them was the duty desk, then the incident room and the narrow stone steps leading down to the cells. To the right, behind a closed door, was the senior officers' mess. Ruzsky stepped into the constables' mess opposite, where small groups of men gossiped, sipping tea or perhaps vodka from steel cups. Few lamps were lit in the vaultlike room, and the warm air was thick with the smell of tobacco smoke, wet leather, and wool. The three constables who'd been out on the ice earlier sat on a bench in the corner, smoking. One had his boots off and was rubbing the circulation back into his toes.

The men got immediately to their feet. "I should have introduced myself out on the ice," Ruzsky said. "Investigator Ruzsky."

They thrust out their hands and announced their names in turn, with an eagerness borne of the fact that service here earned an exemption from the front.

"You searched well," Ruzsky said.

They did not reply. They were just boys, and looking into their faces made him feel old. He hesitated, wishing he had something more to say, then turned and walked back into the hallway. He didn't recognize the constable at the duty desk either, and Pavel didn't bother to introduce him as he pulled across the report book. "Anyone missing last night or this morning?" he asked. A glass-fronted cabinet behind the desk was filled with rifles and revolvers.

"No, sir." The man had a wide, flat face. He wasn't from Petersburg. Probably one of his parents was from the Far Eastern provinces.

"They must have some form of identification on them," Ruzsky said.

"They haven't," Pavel responded. "I've just been down to check. We have two nameless victims."

Ruzsky watched his partner flick back through the pages. "Would you get us the missing persons book?" Pavel asked.

The desk clerk went into the room behind, running his hand along the rows of files.

Pavel slammed the incident book shut. Ruzsky leaned back against the desk, examining the posters on the wall. He moved closer. Alongside the grainy police photographs of wanted men, there was a caricature of Rasputin dancing alongside the Tsar and a half-naked Empress. Next to the Tsar sat his English cousin George. The caption read, "Little Father plays with Georgie, little Mother lies with Grigory."

Alongside the poster was a row of photographs of Rasputin's body. The first was a close-up of his face, which looked as if it had been rubbed in soot. There appeared to be a bullet hole in the center of his forehead. The other two showed the priest's frozen corpse, with its legs and hands bound, arms raised above his head.

"I thought you told me we never got called to the scene," Ruzsky said.

"The photographer arrived first. By the time I got there, Anton had handed jurisdiction to the Okhrana."

Ruzsky frowned at his friend, who seemed nervous or embarrassed, his eyes evasive. Last night, he'd told Ruzsky that the constables had called the Okhrana direct—indeed they'd had a mild altercation over it. The Tsar's secret police normally dealt only with sedition and terrorism and the ruthless suppression of opposition to the Tsar. This was the first time they had ever taken direct control of a murder case.

"You think Anton should have fought for the investigation?"

"No."

"But you still had a look?"

Pavel didn't answer and Ruzsky turned back to the photographs. "This was taken by Great Petrovsky Bridge."

"Yes."

"So it's true he was still alive when they threw him into the river. His arms are like that because he was trying to escape when his body froze?" Rumors had even reached Tobolsk about the manner of Rasputin's death—that he had been almost impossible to kill, and had still been breathing after being shot, bound, and thrown into the ice.

"I don't know," Pavel said.

"And you weren't curious?"

Pavel stared at the photographs, without responding.

"We should have insisted on making it our investigation," Ruzsky said easily.

"There was no investigation. The dogs on the streets knew who had done it. If the relatives of the Tsar want to murder his wife's lover, then who are we to get involved?"

"You don't really believe that they were lovers?"

Pavel shrugged. "People do. I got called out to an incident—about a year after you left. It was at one of the new gypsy restaurants. He was drunk."

"Rasputin?"

"Yes. Somebody telephoned to complain and I happened to be working late. When I arrived he was dancing in the middle of the restaurant, boasting of how he could make the Empress dance like this . . ." Pavel shoved his hips forward. "Then he dropped his trousers and started waving his penis at the spectators."

"I don't believe it."

"On my son's life."

Ruzsky shook his head. He had met the peasant priest only once, just before the war, after the imperial favorite had appeared at the police department late at night, drunk, claiming incomprehensible threats on his life.

The constable shuffled back with the book and pushed it across the desk. There had been no entries for more than a week. "I suppose it is too early for anyone to have missed them," Ruzsky said.

He turned around and led Pavel past the entrance to the armory and up to the first floor. The door to Anton's office at the top of the stairs was shut, the corridor dark. To their right were the administrative offices—finance, the records library, constables and senior officers' administration—but Ruzsky flicked on the light and turned left to the Criminal Investigation Division.

Their office was small—far too cramped for the number of people who worked here—a series of wooden cubicles arranged around a group of desks in the center reserved for the secretaries and the junior constables on attachment. Vladimir's cubicle had the words *Investigator, Street Crime* inscribed in the door. Next came Sarlov, under the heading *Pathology*, then Maretsky under *Modus Operandi*, and finally the corner office that Ruzsky and Pavel had shared for many years with the words *Chief Investigator/Deputy Chief Investigator, Murder* inscribed heavily in black. Ruzsky pushed open the door of his cubicle, flicked on the wall light, took off his coat, and threw it onto the stand in the corner. He removed his gloves and bashed the last of the snow from his boots before sitting down at his desk.

"See, I tidied up," Pavel said.

Ruzsky was gratified that no one had occupied his desk, but it was obvious that Pavel had simply spread the mess during his absence and swept it up and dumped it back on his own desk prior to his return. "You're a pig," Ruzsky responded.

Pavel took a piece of chalk and wrote the date at the top of the blackboard on the wall beside him. Underneath, in capitals, he scrawled NEVA BODIES. He turned around. "A great start."

He moved to the city map next to it, took a black pin from its edge, and placed it in the center of the river Neva. "Black for murder, red for muggings, green for random street violence, orange for anti-Jewish violence. Vladimir puts his up. It's a kind of competition. We get five points per pin to Vladimir's one. We ran out of pins so many times last year, I got bored of it, but today we can begin again . . ."

"Did you call Sarlov?"

"Yes."

"He said he was on his way?"

Pavel raised an eyebrow. "This is Sarlov we're talking about. He didn't say anything."

Pavel straightened, turned, and walked out of the office. A few moments later, Ruzsky heard the door to the toilets at the end of the corridor bang shut. He reached into his pocket, pulled out the roll of banknotes taken from the dead man's jacket, and put it in one of his drawers.

He sat down. In the center of the desk was a piece of wood with a carved inscription carrying the words of the oath all soldiers and officers of the Imperial Army swore to the Tsar. *I promise and do hereby swear*, it read, *before Almighty God, before his Holy Gospels, to serve His Imperial Majesty, the supreme Autocrat, truly and faithfully, to obey him in all things, and to defend his dynasty, without sparing my body, until the last drop of my blood.*

It had been given to Ruzsky by his brother as a joke. In the light of the carnage at the front, it no longer appeared funny.

Ruzsky pulled over his "in" tray and took out the only item that had been placed within it. It was a clipping from the newspaper *Novoe Vremia.*

He glanced over it. The article had been written by the liberal Maklakov and it compared Russia to an automobile being driven at breakneck speed toward a precipice by a mad chauffeur whose passengers were too scared to attempt to seize control of the steering wheel.

Ruzsky opened the central drawer of his desk and was surprised to find that his old notebook was still there. He opened it and flicked through the notes of his last case, that of the ill-fated girl from Sennaya Ploschad. He turned over a fresh page and wrote *Neva Murders.*

One of the office telephones rang and Ruzsky got up to answer it.

"Ruzsky."

There was a confused pause, then the caller spoke.

"Ruzsky? Is it really you? It's Veresov."

Ruzsky was heartened by the pleasure he detected in Veresov's voice. He was a small, studious man who occupied the tiny fingerprint bureau, located, much to his chagrin, in the basement, between the canteen and the cells.

"You're back," Veresov said.

"Don't sound so surprised."

Veresov was silent. "Not the best of times to return to," he said.

There was a moment's silence. "I have the dagger," Veresov continued. "Is it criminal suspects only?"

"What do you mean?"

"We don't have automatic access to the Okhrana's files of political suspects anymore. If I have to apply to work through their records as well, it's going to take twice as long."

"I thought we shared files?"

"New regulations."

"Well," Ruzsky said. "It doesn't look like a political case. Start with your own files."

"Petrograd or Empire-wide?"

"Start with St. Petersburg, then Moscow, then work through the other cities."

Ruzsky put the mouthpiece back on its hook and it rang again immediately.

"It's Sarlov. You can come down now."

Sarlov's laboratory was next to Veresov's fingerprint bureau in the basement and it was equally damp and even more tiny. Sarlov always complained about this, but Ruzsky thought the pathologist enjoyed the fact that it forced detectives to stand too close to the bodies.

There was a bright lamp in the ceiling and the two victims lay side by side on a steel table beneath it. The table had been designed for one, and the man's body looked as if it was about to tumble onto the floor.

Sarlov had a mask across his face and wore a white apron spattered with blood. He had a small saw in his right hand. "Ruzsky," he said, surprise in his voice. "I didn't know you were back. To what do we owe the pleasure?"

"Did you see Rasputin's body?" Ruzsky asked, ignoring his question.

"No."

"Is it true he was still alive when they put him in the river?"

"I don't know."

"Don't you doctors talk?"

"Sometimes." He leaned over the man's body and raised the saw.

"Please, Sarlov," Pavel said. "Not now."

"You can see for yourself. There's not much to tell you. I'll give you a full report upstairs when I'm finished." Sarlov leaned back and pulled down his mask. "The man was in his early forties, died around three A.M. Between three and four. Severe loss of blood from the stab wounds. Seventeen in all. Look at him."

Ruzsky realized he had been consciously not looking at either of the victims, but he forced himself to do so now. The man was bulkier than he'd imagined, a thick pelt of hair running from his chest to his waist. His body had been punctured repeatedly, but his face looked less distorted now that the wounds had been cleaned. He'd not been a handsome man, Ruzsky thought; his cheeks were too fleshy and nose too broad. The girl, by contrast, was prettier than she'd appeared. She had a neat face, with a petite nose and long eyelashes. She'd been stabbed only once, precisely, in the center of her chest. She was naked and Ruzsky instinctively wanted to reach forward and cover her up.

"So?" Pavel asked.

"They were followed from behind," Ruzsky said. "And yet stabbed from the front."

"I can certainly tell you they were stabbed from the front," Sarlov responded.

"The man has no marks on his arms, so the first blow must have been sudden and unexpected. He was caught unawares."

"Very good, Ruzsky. I'm pleased to see provincial life has not dulled your powers of observation." Sarlov's eyes twinkled with laughter. He liked to hide his affection beneath a manner that was alternately curmudgeonly and playful.

"Who was killed first?" Ruzsky asked, failing to return the smile. He knew the game. He was supposed to be the butt of their humor—now more than ever.

Sarlov shook his head. "I don't know. Common sense dictates it must have been the man."

"One of them was expecting this to happen," Ruzsky went on, "because neither ran. Perhaps the girl was killed first, but the man was expecting it, so he stood and watched. Then the murderer turned unexpectedly on him."

"And stabbed him seventeen times?" Pavel asked.

"Have you found anything on them, Sarlov?"

"No. Their pockets have been cleared out."

"But nobody took the money."

Sarlov shrugged.

"Have you found any clues at all?"

The doctor shook his head. "The man has had some dental work. It's gold foil treatment, very elaborately performed. That is not to say it couldn't have been done by a dentist here, just that it is more likely to have been done somewhere else. Europe, or maybe America. Somewhere like New York."

"A foreigner, then?"

"His shirts have no markings, and the labels from his jacket and overcoat have been removed. His underpants were Russian, his boots made to measure, probably somewhere in the Empire, I couldn't tell you where."

"The man was the real target," Ruzsky said.

"Perhaps."

"Why else would he have been stabbed seventeen times?"

"He was certainly no Rasputin. I should think he was dead after the first blow."

"Anything else?"

"No. Oh, yes. I almost missed this. Look here, on his shoulder."

Ruzsky and Pavel examined the man's skin. He had a small, branded black star there.

"What does that mean?" Pavel asked.

"I have no idea," Sarlov said.

"Have you seen anything like it before?"

"No."

Ruzsky noticed the pile of clothes on the far end of the shelf. The man's clothes were stiff with dried blood. His overcoat was thick and, Ruzsky thought, expensive. There was nothing in the inside pocket and the outline where the label had been was clearly visible. He pulled the pocket out, but there was nothing there, except a little dirt.

The jacket was made of thick, dark wool, probably of cheap Russian manufacture, since the stitching appeared primitive. He turned all the pockets inside out, but again found nothing. He examined the boots for a moment. They were old and worn down and if the maker's name had ever been visible in the sole, it had long since faded.

Ruzsky pushed the pile to one side and turned to the girl's clothes. He was struck immediately by their quality. The seams were immaculately stitched. He started with her corset, but then picked up the dress and saw the tiny label sewn into the hem.

"Pavel," he said. "Tell one of the constables to go down to the Nevsky and bring Madame Renaud here, whatever her objections."

"Why?"

"Because my wife's expensive taste in dresses has finally served a purpose."

Ruzsky made his way upstairs to the first floor. He saw that Anton's office door was ajar. Anton had always come to work on Saturday mornings. It was a ritual. He was bent over a drawer, searching for something. The desk itself was covered, as always, in loose papers. On the wall, below a white clock, was a picture of Napoleon's retreat from Moscow. The bookcase was full of leather-bound volumes, some Anton's own work.

Anton straightened. He had his glasses in his hand and spun them slowly.

"You're in early," Ruzsky said.

Anton looked at him for a moment more and then came toward him. "My boy," he said, gripping his shoulders and looking into his eyes. "How wonderful to have you back. Come, let's celebrate."

Anton reached down to the bottom drawer of his desk and pulled out a bottle of vodka. As he filled two glasses, a large mop of dark hair hung over his forehead, the gray now visible at his temples. His face exuded the warmth of a loving father, his manner the absentmindedness and eccentricity of the college professor he had once been.

Anton pushed one glass across the desk and raised the other. He looked carefully at his protégé. "Fantastic to have you back."

They drank. Ruzsky almost choked. "Christ."

"I know, it is dreadful."

"It's worse than dreadful."

"The city is an island, cut off from decent vodka."

"I should have brought you some from Tobolsk."

Anton raised his eyebrows. "Better keep your voice down. It's still illegal, you know."

Ruzsky smiled. "I'm sure prohibition has been observed to the letter, especially inside this building."

Anton took another slug. "It's been an excellent idea which, as the chief of the city police, I have, of course, fully supported. It has made a huge contribution to improving the general level of sobriety." Anton refilled his glass.

Ruzsky took a pace closer to look at the photograph on Anton's desk. It was of the five of them—Ruzsky, Pavel, Anton, Vladimir, and Maretsky. "Good God," Anton said. "A proper reunion is in order. Where is Pavel?" He picked up the telephone earpiece. "Professor Maretsky," he told the operator, then: "Maretsky. Anton. Come around, will you, I've got a surprise. And bring Vladimir." Anton listened. "What about Sarlov?" He shook his head. "All right, just get over here."

Anton put down the receiver and refilled both glasses.

"Pavel will be back in a minute." Ruzsky threw the vodka to the back of his throat, shook his head once, and put the glass down. He picked up the photograph and looked at the faces that stared back at him, one a much younger version of his own.

"You were a baby then," Anton said.

"So were you."

Ruzsky stared at the photograph. The words *Criminal Investigation Division, St. Petersburg City Police Department* and the year—1900— had been written by hand across the bottom of it. Ruzsky took out his cigarette case and pushed it toward Anton, who removed one and shunted it back.

"Have you seen her?" Anton asked. Ruzsky saw the warmth and affection that shone in his friend's eyes.

"Irina? No."

"I wasn't talking of Irina." Anton was smiling. "I saw you together, don't forget. That night at the Mariinskiy."

Ruzsky did not answer. He wondered how his feelings could have been so transparent.

"One of the dancers told me she kept a photograph of you on her dressing table after you went."

Ruzsky felt his face flush with embarrassment and pleasure as he thought of Maria.

Anton stretched his legs. "So?"

Ruzsky shrugged. "It's complicated."

"I know that you will say that I should not, but I cannot help feeling in some way responsible for this mess."

Ruzsky sucked heavily on his cigarette. Irina had been one of Anton's students.

"Pavel has been filling me with the usual gloom," Ruzsky said, anxious to change the subject.

Anton leaned forward again. "This time he's right. I never imagined that the Tsar's absence would be a handicap, but since he ran off to the front to try and win the war single-handedly, it has gotten worse. It is like being on a ship headed for an iceberg with a madman at the controls."

"I got the article."

"Yes, but the worst of it is that the woman is at the steering wheel. That's what's frightening."

"Do you still attend the weekly meetings at the Interior Ministry?"

"Yes."

"What do the Okhrana say?"

"We don't need them to tell us what is going on. Stand in a line for bread. You'll get the idea."

Anton came around the desk and leaned against it. "I took a look at the bodies," he said.

"And?"

"People are desperate, but this kind of savagery . . . Have you identified the victims?"

"No. Their bodies have been systematically stripped."

Anton looked up. His eyes were washed out and bloodshot. There was deep concern there. "It troubles me. At this time, right out there on the ice, in front of the palace, in the very heart of the city."

Ruzsky wondered what lay beneath Anton's concern. "I don't think the location was chosen for its symbolic value, if that is what you mean."

Anton toyed with his eyeglasses.

"I don't understand what you're driving at," Ruzsky said.

"These are complicated times, Sandro."

"What has that to do with us?"

Anton sighed. "It's a time for caution. The Progressives and even some members of the government have been writing to senior generals at head-quarters to demand the Empress be arrested on her next visit to the front line, and sent to the Crimea. I've heard that some of your contemporaries at the yacht club discuss in hushed tones whether it would be justifiable to assassinate the Tsar."

"And what has that to do with us?"

"Nothing, I just want you to be aware."

"Of what?"

"No one operates in a vacuum, that's all."

Ruzsky did not see what Anton was driving at. "And our friend Vasil-yev?"

"The chief of the Okhrana sits in his office playing the loyal police chief. The plotters' letters are opened, their contents divulged to the Empress. She in turn writes to her husband and demands another round of ministers be sacked and sent into exile. We call it ministerial leapfrog. At a meeting yesterday, the latest bulletin to be sent up to Tsarskoe Selo was pushed around the table. It contained extracts from a letter written by the Grand Duchess Maria Pavlovna to a leading member of the Duma, de-manding that the Empress be . . . annihilated."

Ruzsky did not answer. Maria Pavlovna was one of the most senior members of the Romanov family and what Anton was telling him was not khvost gossip. "Pavel tells me Vasilyev tolerates no opposition," he said, memories of his confrontation with the city's secret police chief three years ago still fresh.

"You have to question the currency of a regime that relies for its sur-vival on such a man."

"You exaggerate."

"No."

"And he is rewarded for his loyalty?"

"Yes, but you're missing the point. Vasilyev is not stupid. Think about it for a minute. Some of these strikes . . . what lies behind them? Are the Okhrana up to their old tricks? We know they have provocateurs in these factories and strike committees. Is Vasilyev deliberately stirring up trouble so that whichever group of revolutionaries he favors can seize power under the guise of saving the Empire?"

"The incorruptible Vasilyev? Devoted servant to the Tsar?"

Pavel appeared in the doorway. "What's this, a wedding reception?"

Maretsky was half a step behind him. "Professor," Ruzsky said, unable to conceal his pleasure. Maretsky stepped forward and offered himself for a bear hug, and Ruzsky ducked into it as he would have done to his son. Maretsky gripped him tight, then took a pace back, unsteady and misty-eyed for a moment, before he sat down next to Anton. His legs didn't quite reach the floor and he looked like a child in an adult's chair. His face was round, a few wispy strands of gray hair protruding from the top of his shirt belying an otherwise almost feminine appearance. He wore a gray jacket and shorter boots than was the fashion.

"You look thinner," Maretsky told him. "Don't they have food out there?"

"Which is more than can be said for you, Maretsky," Pavel said.

"How was Tobolsk?"

"Cold and boring."

"Is it true they eat each other when they get hungry?"

"More or less."

Anton clinked his glass against the metal vodka bottle and then poured out a measure for each of them. He pushed the glasses across the table and they all raised them together. "Older, wiser," he said, looking at them meaningfully. "But still here."

They drained their glasses.

An awkward silence followed. Their attempt to pretend that nothing had changed only served to reinforce the fact that something had. Maretsky—even Anton, or was he imagining that?—seemed almost wary of him.

"How is Irina?" Maretsky asked.

"She's fine, thank you. Or so I believe."

Maretsky frowned. "She survived Tobolsk?"

"Just about."

"I'm surprised she went. My wife wouldn't have."

"It's surprising," Ruzsky said, "what guilt can make you do."

They were silent once more.

Ruzsky heard Madame Renaud's haughty voice at the other end of the corridor.

6

Madame Renaud burst into the room, an anxious constable alongside her. "Bonjour, madame."

"You are Irina Ruzskya's husband." It was an accusation. She surveyed the room, glancing coldly at each of his colleagues.

"I am."

"You should be ashamed of yourself."

Ruzsky stood, then leaned back on the balls of his feet trying to imagine the stories Irina must have invented about him. They stared at each other like predators. "We have the body of a woman downstairs, wearing one of your dresses."

"I have a business to run, don't you know that? You drag me in here like some common criminal, and in these times. Don't you have anything better to do?" She glared at the others.

Ruzsky kept his tone level. "As the constable will have told you, madame, we are the Criminal Investigation Division and we are investigating a murder. I'm sure the Okhrana does have better things to do with its time, if that is what you mean."

"How can you be sure it is one of my dresses?"

"A man whose wife is bankrupting him recognizes the cause."

"Only cheap husbands complain," she said icily.

Madame Renaud exuded a haughty arrogance. She had a long, bony nose, narrow eyes, and white skin heavily powdered in a vain attempt to conceal her age. Her fingers were thin and, like her neck, bedecked in jewels that sparkled even in this dull light. Her expression reflected disgust and astonishment that the scion of a great family could work in such surroundings.

"These are my colleagues, Anton Antipovich . . ."

"I did not come to attend a social occasion."

"You make no concession to the times," Ruzsky said, pointing at her diamond necklace. "For that I admire you."

"I am not normally dragged through the streets."

"Your sled was not ready. I apologize. But this is a murder case, the victim one of your clients. I thought you would wish to help us."

She relaxed a little, breathing out. Ruzsky realized his irritation and hostility had more to do with Irina. He imagined the two of them together, clucking and cooing over a dress that would cost ten times more than most people earned in a year. Since their marriage, Irina had received an allowance direct from his father, as well as a smaller stipend from her own parents. Behind the desk, Anton was staring at his empty glass.

"I'd be grateful if you would accompany us to the basement," Ruzsky said.

A hint of a smile played at the corner of her lips. "You make the invitation sound so attractive, Prince Ruzsky."

He could tell both Pavel and Maretsky were watching him. "We're not in the habit of such formality here, Madame Renaud."

"Are you ashamed of your fine ancestry?"

Ruzsky saw Pavel roll his eyes theatrically.

Without replying, Ruzsky led them along the corridor and down the stairs. Madame Renaud kept both hands in a fur muffler and her back rigidly straight.

As they came down the last flight of stairs, Ruzsky could hear Sarlov working with the saw and he hurried along the dark corridor. "For God's sake," he said, and Sarlov looked up, startled. "I thought I asked you not to do that."

"I have a medical practice to run, Ruzsky. I can't wait on your pleasure all day. As even you must be able to see, the bodies are rock hard and will take a considerable time to properly thaw."

Sarlov's coat and mask and face were splattered with tiny flecks of frozen blood and flesh. There was an incision across the woman's chest, a small pool of thawing blood on the metal table beneath him, a thin stream dripping onto the floor.

Ruzsky heard a sharp intake of breath from Madame Renaud behind him and he rushed forward to pull a sheet over the body. He turned to face her. "My apologies, Madame Renaud. I was not aware this process had begun."

He expected her to turn away, but found instead that she was struggling to compose herself. Pavel stood alongside her. Maretsky and Anton had remained upstairs.

"Come forward, if you would."

She put a black gloved hand to her mouth, then took out a white lace handkerchief from her bag and placed it over her nose. She stepped forward and looked calmly at the girl's face, before shaking her head confidently. "I don't recognize her."

"Are you sure?"

"Of course I'm sure."

Ruzsky walked over to the pile of clothes in the corner and picked up the dead girl's dress. He carried it to Madame Renaud, pulling the hem through his hands until he found the label. She took the dress from him and half turned, holding it up toward the light. She returned it to him and removed a pair of eyeglasses from her bag, before examining it once again. "Yes," she said, simply. She let the hem of the dress drop, holding it up by its shoulders. "I see you are as capable as your wife claims."

Ruzsky felt momentarily confused.

"Sherlock Holmes, she calls you. Isn't that so?"

Ruzsky realized she was taunting him.

"This is one of your dresses," he said.

"It is much too big for the dead girl. A terrible fit." She turned to him with a caustic smile. "Surely you can see that."

"Who did you make it for?" Ruzsky didn't expect an answer.

"Vyrubova," she said.

"*Anna* Vyrubova?"

"Yes." She was enjoying her power now. Ruzsky saw the color drain from Pavel's face again.

"You are referring to the intimate friend of the Empress, Anna Vyrubova?"

"The same. It's an old dress—two or three years. She must have given it to the dead girl."

Ruzsky hesitated. "You haven't seen this woman before?"

"No."

"Definitely not?"

She tilted her head to one side, but it was a gesture of amusement, not irritation. "No." She was watching him. "Your wife came in this morning."

He didn't answer.

"She wishes to have a dress for the Vorontsov ball."

"Of course."

"She said you would not be accompanying her."

Ruzsky stared at the floor.

"She says you were once handsome, but she does you a disservice."

Ruzsky looked up. He could hardly credit the fact that this harsh-faced woman was attempting to flirt with him in front of two half-dismembered corpses. "Thank you for coming in, Madame Renaud."

Pavel was silent as they walked upstairs to the office.

The dagger had been placed on the corner of Ruzsky's desk, with a tag attached stamped *Petrograd City Police, Criminal Investigation Division*. Alongside it was a set of crime scene photographs, which they examined in silence.

Ruzsky opened the drawer, took out the notebook, and slipped it into the inside pocket of his jacket. He replaced it with the piece of paper on which he had drawn the outline of the footprint traced from the snow.

"What do you want to do?" Pavel asked.

"Go down to the embankment and start checking all residential buildings in the neighborhood. Go to the Winter Palace and try and get hold of the head of the household. See if there is any chance anyone did see anything. And if you have time, try the embassies. British, French, American. Ask if they've received any reports of a missing national. We'll see if Sarlov was right about the man being a foreigner. I'm going to go out to Tsarskoe Selo."

"You don't want me to come with you?" Pavel didn't sound enthusiastic.

"We'll make more progress if we split up."

"Who are you going to see?"

"Count Frederics. One of the other senior household staff. Vyrubova herself."

"Why don't you telephone?"

Ruzsky frowned at Pavel's caution. "If I call, they will decline."

"They will decline to see you anyway."

Ruzsky looked up and saw Maretsky going into his cubicle. He picked up the dagger and walked around to join him. Pavel followed.

Maretsky was scanning a document, his glasses pushed to the top of his head. He looked up at them, chewing his lip, as if concentrating on something else, his round, piggy eyes staring into thin air.

Ruzsky held up the knife.

"It's a dagger," Maretsky said.

"Correct." Ruzsky handed it to him.

"It has blood on it."

"That's not uncommon in murder cases."

Maretsky pulled his glasses down and glanced at Ruzsky. He held it up to the light.

"There's some writing on the blade," Ruzsky said.

"I can see."

Ruzsky waited as Maretsky turned the knife over in his hand. The professor handed it back without comment.

"And?" Ruzsky asked.

"And what?" Maretsky glanced at Pavel. For some reason, Ruzsky thought, the professor never felt as comfortable when Pavel was around.

"Have you ever seen this kind of knife before?"

"You're the chief investigator, Chief Investigator."

Ruzsky shook his head. Ever since the professor had joined the department, they'd had a strong protective bond. Maretsky had once been a highly regarded academic at St. Petersburg University—a professor of philosophy—but an incident with a young male student had destroyed his career. Anton had offered him a home here, and for some reason Maretsky thought Ruzsky was the only other member of the department who did not judge him. Over the years it had paid dividends more often than Ruzsky could remember.

"The Black Bands?" Ruzsky asked. "Political organizations? Revolutionaries? Does this kind of knife, or the inscription, have any connection with any of them?"

"I've not seen anything like it."

"What is the script?"

Maretsky shrugged.

"Can you find out?"

The professor sighed, which Ruzsky took as a sign of acceptance. He examined the knife once more. "It's an unusual weapon." Ruzsky looked up. "Do you still do liaison work?"

Maretsky had been made responsible a long time ago for liaison with the Okhrana, but since Vasilyev's appointment, relations between the two organizations had grown so hostile that there was virtually no communication at any level.

"I never wanted to." There was a note of bitterness in Maretsky's voice.

Ruzsky looked at the professor. Perhaps it was his imagination, but all of his colleagues seemed more evasive these days. Was it his fate that had frightened them? Or something else? "Have you heard any whispers about this case?" Ruzsky asked. "Has anyone called you?"

"No."

Ruzsky nodded at Pavel, who returned a minute later with the photographs. Ruzsky spread them out on the desk and waited as Maretsky examined them. The professor shook his head. "No," he said.

"You don't recognize either of them?"

"No."

Maretsky was saved from further questioning by the appearance of one of the constables, his face puce with exertion and alarm. "Sir. You had better come."

7

Sarlov's voice was audible from the top of the stairs.

Three men in long dark overcoats waited outside the laboratory. Sarlov and Anton stood between them. "This is outrageous," Sarlov said, his face red with anger.

Ruzsky pushed past them. Ivan Prokopiev was standing in the center of the room, smoking a cigarette. He was a tall man, bigger even than Pavel, with a bulbous, ruddy nose and closely cropped hair. He wore only a shirt which, despite the cold, was open to the middle of his chest, dark trousers and high leather boots. The head of the Okhrana's Internal Division still held himself with the swagger of the Cossack officer he had once been.

He was watching two of his officers wrap the bodies in a single canvas sheet.

"What are you doing?" Ruzsky asked.

"Prince Ruzsky. What a pleasant surprise. Welcome home."

There was a moment's silence as they stared at each other. Prokopiev made no attempt to offer an explanation.

Ruzsky took a step closer. "You've no authority to do this."

"Sandro," Anton said, taking hold of his arm.

Prokopiev's expression was dismissive.

"Let's see your authorization."

"Sandro," Anton said again. His and Pavel's faces were white with shock. Only Sarlov echoed Ruzsky's anger.

Prokopiev finished his cigarette and stamped it out under his boot. From the inside pocket of his jacket, he took a piece of paper and handed it to Anton, who looked at it before giving it to Ruzsky. It contained a single sentence instructing the Okhrana to remove the bodies for *urgent po-*

litical investigation. It was signed by Major General Prince Alexander Nikolaevich Obolensky, the city mayor and titular head of all of Petrograd's police departments.

"Did Obolensky even see this?" Ruzsky asked. "Or did you just sign it yourselves?" In theory, Obolensky was the most senior police official in the city, but they both knew he'd never dare stand in the Okhrana's way. Prokopiev might easily have forged his signature to save time.

Prokopiev lit another cigarette, then pointed at the pile of clothes on the side. "Where are the contents of their pockets?"

"Are you assuming control of the investigation?" Ruzsky pressed.

"I don't believe any mention is made of it."

"Then why do you wish to remove the bodies?"

"You have emptied their pockets?" Prokopiev countered.

Ruzsky shook his head. "They had been stripped of all personal items by the time we arrived." He omitted to mention the discovery of the roll of banknotes.

Prokopiev nodded, his face expressionless. Ruzsky thought it was the answer he had expected, or wanted.

Anton stepped aside and forced Ruzsky to do the same, as Prokopiev's men took hold of the canvas sheet and began to carry the corpses out of the room and down the corridor. Prokopiev clicked his heels. "We shall return them when we are done. Good day, gentlemen."

Ruzsky followed them, shaking off Anton's restraining hand. Pavel stared at the floor as he passed.

Upstairs, Ruzsky's constables stood and watched as the corpses were carried out into the courtyard and thrown into the back of a large truck. The Okhrana men climbed up beside them. Prokopiev made his way around to the cab.

"Urgent political investigation," Ruzsky said. "What does that mean?"

Prokopiev turned back.

"Who were they?" Ruzsky asked.

"I have no idea."

"Then why do you want them?"

"They were murdered in front of the Winter Palace. That will do as a reason for now."

"So, in your estimation, it was a political murder?"

"I didn't say that, did I?" He raised his finger. "You mustn't misquote me, old man." He took a pace back. "I'm glad you're home. See how our city has changed?"

Ruzsky did not respond.

"You haven't, perhaps, but you will. You'll telephone me if you ever need anything, won't you?"

Ruzsky still held his tongue.

"So much crime, such difficult times. We need to help each other, isn't that so? How is your son, by the way?"

Ruzsky went cold. "He's fine, thank you."

"Michael, isn't it?"

"Michael, yes."

"A good name. Perhaps if I ever have a son, I'll call him Michael." Prokopiev looked at him with his piercing blue eyes. "Good day, Prince Ruzsky." He climbed up into the truck. "And, once again, welcome home."

The engine started up and diesel fumes billowed across the courtyard.

Ruzsky watched until it had disappeared from view. He turned to find Anton standing on the step behind him. "So, we let them get away with it?" he asked quietly.

Anton stared up at the sky. "Sometimes you're not very bright, do you know that? If they had the power to send you into exile before, imagine what they could do to you now."

"Was the dead man one of theirs?"

"How should I know?" Anton turned toward him. "If you want to be a martyr, be my guest, but be careful of Pavel."

"Why?"

"He bears a huge burden of guilt. He carries it like a yoke."

"He shouldn't."

Anton sighed. "Don't take me for a fool, Sandro. I know what happened. He'll follow you into the jaws of hell if it comes to it. Remember that, please."

Ruzsky shook his head.

"You know what I mean, and don't pretend that you don't. Your desire to take the blame places others in your debt, but you're stubborn and, in these times, that is dangerous."

"So, what do you want us to do?"

Anton didn't answer.

"It was only authorization to move the bodies. We still have responsibility for the overall investigation."

"Well, then it's up to you," Anton said, before walking back into the building. Pavel passed him on the lintel, making his way out into the courtyard.

"Do they frighten you?" Ruzsky asked Pavel.

"It's you they should frighten."

"I won't be their lapdog," Ruzsky said.

"No, well . . ." Pavel shrugged.

"What do you want to do?"

"I don't know. You're the boss."

Ruzsky sighed. "It's still our investigation to run."

Back at his desk while Pavel went to the bathroom, Ruzsky thought of the fear he'd seen in Pavel's face, and even Anton's.

He glanced at the clock, then took out his wallet and removed the photograph of Irina and Michael that he still kept there. He put it on his desk, switched on the lamp, and bent over it. He told himself Prokopiev was dangerous only if he made another mistake. He would just have to be careful. Tackling the thugs of the Black Bands this morning would have been unwise.

Ruzsky stared at the face of his son.

Michael was a handsome boy, with straight dark hair and a solemn face. He was shy, just as his father had been, stubborn and affectionate. When he was difficult—which he had become more frequently as his parents' arguments increased—he would cling to his rebellion tenaciously, only to cry his heart out once it was over.

Irina smiled with an easy, lopsided grin that now completely failed to touch anything within him.

Ruzsky thought of their departure from Tobolsk six months ago. He recalled Michael's desperate affection and Irina's impatience.

He thought of her standing in the tiny kitchen of that house, screaming, "I wasn't made for this!"

Michael would think his father had abandoned him. At only six years of age, it was a terrible conclusion to reach.

Ruzsky stood and, just as he had done at home, rested his head against the damp cold glass of the window.

It was not possible, surely, that a boy could be better off denied a father's love. Wasn't he himself testimony to that?

Ruzsky put his hand into his jacket pocket and pulled out an old printed program from the Mariinskiy Theatre. He opened it to the relevant page and then turned around and placed that over Irina on the desktop, so that Maria and Michael both looked up at him.

He gazed at their faces, allowing his fantasy free rein for a few moments. To have a happy family; was it so much to ask?

Ruzsky noticed the pile of newspapers next to Pavel's desk and he walked over and pulled off the top copy, which turned out to be Friday's *Petrogradskie Vedomosti*. He ignored the war news and flicked through to the theater section. *Romeo and Juliet* in the Mariinskiy, it announced, but there was no reference to her.

Pavel came back into the room and Ruzsky pushed aside the newspaper, scooping up the photograph and the program into his pocket.

Pavel had recovered and his manner was businesslike, but he still had an uncanny knack of perceiving his partner's mood. "You've been dreaming?"

Ruzsky leaned back against the window. "No. But it's not a crime."

"Depends who you are. In my case, no. I dream only of the possible. More vodka, more money, more sex. But with you, I'm not so sure."

"Sex with you? I'm not so sure either—"

"You're a dreamer by nature. You dream of the impossible, I think, and that is a kind of prison."

"Tobolsk was a prison. Without dreams, I'd have been dead from the neck up."

Pavel stared at the floor. "So, where do we go?"

Ruzsky leaned back against the edge of his desk. "The thing is, political murders don't involve someone being stabbed seventeen times."

Pavel didn't answer.

"Do they?"

"It depends on the motive."

Ruzsky left the building five minutes later, and he nearly collided with a man who barely reached his chest. "Sandro!" the man exclaimed. "They let you back!"

Ruzsky recognized Stanislav instantly. The wind had dropped and snow was falling in big, fat flakes, some of which perched on top of the journalist's head.

"They let you stay!" Ruzsky countered. "I can hardly believe it."

"Well, you know . . ." Stanislav shrugged. "Even a sinking ship needs its rats . . ."

Stanislav was a small, lean man with greasy hair, a long nose, round glasses, and oily, pockmarked skin. Pavel called him "the rat" and the name had stuck. He had been a journalist originally. He still called himself one, though he had been employed by the department for more than a decade. His official job was to provide information on the city police's activities to the newspapers—which mostly meant murder cases, since that was all they were interested in—but Ruzsky had other uses for him. Stanislav, more than any of them, was at home in the city's sewers.

"I heard you've got a case for me," Stanislav said, revealing an atrocious set of yellowing teeth. He wore woolen gloves with the fingers cut off.

"Possibly."

"What do you want me to tell them?"

"Nothing. If you have to: Two unidentified bodies found on the Neva. We're searching the missing persons file, but we urge anyone who cannot locate a loved one or colleague to come forward."

Stanislav's eyes narrowed. "I hear they've taken your bodies."

Ruzsky looked over the man's shoulder. He had evidently only just arrived at the office. "How do you know that?"

The rat leaned forward. "As always, my friend, better not to know how I know."

"All right." Ruzsky stared at him. "I need to know who they were. Can you find out?"

Stanislav shrugged, raising his hands to the skies, palms up. He took a step past him and then stopped. "I never thought I'd see you back here, do you know that?"

"Why?"

"Oh, I don't know." He pointed a long, bony finger at him. "But you be careful."

"I've had enough warnings."

"Maybe, but the rules have changed."

Ruzsky frowned.

"Your street investigator, Vladimir, had an assistant a year back. A young army officer, invalided out of the war. Honorable man, like you. He started trying to bring some of those thugs in the Black Bands to account. He wasn't standing for any nonsense." Stanislav's stare was grave with meaning. "He was found in the Moyka with a knife in his back. No one here will tell you that; they don't like to think of it."

"Who put it there?"

"You don't have to ask."

"Was there an investigation?"

"There had to be."

"Who ran it?"

"The Deputy Chief Investigator, Murder."

Ruzsky stared at the man. He wasn't sure what he sought to imply. "I'm sure Pavel did his best."

Stanislav shrugged again. "Maybe. Vladimir helped. He was upset."

Ruzsky stared at the snow falling gently in the courtyard. Vladimir would have been upset. He was a strong man, like Pavel, but equally decent at heart. "Did the Okhrana know who these corpses were?" Ruzsky asked. "And if so, how?"

Stanislav turned back. "How did they know you'd sealed the fate of the man who killed that girl three years ago. You or Pavel, whoever it was."

"Constables gossip. There are hundreds of people in this building."

"Yes, but very few who know exactly what's going on inside the Criminal Investigation Division."

8

The front door of the Mariinskiy Theatre was ajar, and as Ruzsky slipped through into the foyer, he heard the noonday gun being fired from the St. Peter and St. Paul Fortress on the far side of the river.

Ahead of him, two young women stood by the main entrance to the auditorium in animated conversation. He interrupted them with less grace than he intended. He felt, suddenly, the way he had on the ice.

The women looked taken aback. "Who wants to know?" one asked.

"Chief Investigator Ruzsky. City police." Ruzsky fumbled in a pocket for his small, dog-eared identification card, but the girls were not interested. They nodded toward the wooden doors that led into the auditorium.

The door snapped back as he entered and one of the dancers on the stage turned in his direction.

It wasn't her.

Ruzsky's mouth was dry. He pulled the collar of his shirt away from his throat.

He stood beneath the royal box, the blue and gold decor of the auditorium sumptuous even in the semidarkness. At the center of the small group of dancers on the stage stood the ballet master in a blue velvet jacket, bathed in light. He had dark hair and a long mustache. He stepped back to allow his dancers room. "And again," he shouted. "And one and two and *jump* . . . No, no, *no*."

The ballet master became aware of the dancers' distraction and spun around to face Ruzsky. "*Yes?*"

It was a moment or two before Ruzsky acknowledged that the remark had been directed at him. "Maria," he said, "Maria Popova."

"What about her?"

"I was just looking—"

"And who are you?"

"Ruzsky, Alexander Nikolaevich. Chief investigator, city police."

"Has a *crime* been committed?"

"No. I mean, yes. But it's not . . ." Ruzsky began to recover his wits, spurred on by the look of theatrical exasperation on the man's face. "Where is she?"

"So it's a private matter?"

"It's certainly none of your concern."

The ballet master's smile told those around him he understood exactly the nature of Ruzsky's confusion.

"Where will I find her?" he asked again.

"Dressing room number one. Through the side door." The man dismissed him with a peremptory flick of the hand.

Ruzsky walked slowly toward the side exit. He glanced up at the huge gold crown above the royal box and then at the seats his family customarily occupied.

Ruzsky knew where to find the dressing rooms. It was quiet backstage and he stood alone in the dark corridor outside dressing room number one.

He ran a hand through his hair, then rubbed distractedly at his lower lip with his index finger. Now that he was here, he did not know what to do.

A dancer appeared from one of the rooms farther down the corridor. She was in a hurry. "Can I help you?" she asked as she ran past him, toward the stage, but Ruzsky had failed to reply by the time she turned the corner.

He took another pace forward.

He felt the blood pound in his head. He didn't need the ballet master's help to feel he didn't quite belong here.

For a moment, he was transported back to their first meeting at Krasnoe Selo just outside the capital—the site of the summer camps of many of the Guards regiments—shortly before the outbreak of war. On that bright day, the French president had joined the Tsar for an inspection of the serried ranks of guardsmen on a dusty field leading down to a shimmering sea. Ruzsky had forgotten not a single detail. Standing here, he could almost feel the intense heat and smell the acrid odor of burning turf from a distant forest fire. He recalled the sight of the Emperor on his white horse, the stillness in the crowd, and then the cheers rising with the strength of an approaching storm.

Irina had persuaded him that they should accompany his father. After the inspection was over and a sinking sun cast shadows across the gray battleships anchored in the bay, he had been introduced to Maria. They had exchanged only a few words, but as she walked away, in a cloud of dust kicked up by a thousand horses' hooves, she had turned to look back at him, the wide brim of her white hat pushed up and her hand shielding her eyes from the fading sunlight.

Ruzsky took another pace forward. In that moment, his life had been transformed and yet the truth was that he had nothing more concrete to go on than an instinct for her feelings.

He thought of Anton's assertion that she had kept a picture of him on her dressing table and his face flushed with pleasure once more. Was he too late? He knocked.

"Come in."

The adrenaline pumped through him. He put his hand on the door and pushed it gently.

Maria stood on the far side of the room, in front of a mirror, half-turned toward him.

She was tall, with long, dark hair that stretched all the way down the center of her back. She had a petite nose, long eyelashes, rich green eyes, and full, slightly upturned lips.

She was a woman of heart-stopping beauty—talented and womanly and clever—and yet the sight of him made her flush bright red. Her smile was girlish, full of unsophisticated pleasure. "Hello, Sandro," she said, her voice soft.

Ruzsky felt his stomach lurch.

She wore a simple, elegant, cream and gold dress. "You're back," she said.

"Yes."

"You've come home." Her voice was warm.

Ruzsky did not know what to reply.

"You haven't changed one bit," he said.

She gave a tiny smile. "Is that a compliment?"

"Of course."

"You look older."

"And that isn't."

"I don't know. It suits you." She paused, her face serious again. "It's been so long, Sandro."

"A lifetime."

Her cheeks flushed again.

"How was Tobolsk?" Maria asked.

"It was cold."

"You missed Petersburg. City of our dreams."

"And yet it got along without me."

"That's a matter of opinion. I was told that your wife came home."

Ruzsky wanted to ask by whom. "She did, yes."

"I'm sorry for that."

Ruzsky didn't reply.

Maria caught sight of a hole in his boot, then shook her head. "Don't you have anyone to look after you?"

"No," he said with a rueful smile.

It had been intended as a joke, but her face was instantly concerned. Warmth flooded through him.

Maria took a step toward him, then leaned against the dresser upon which she stored her makeup. Her dress was tight and low cut, the swell of her breasts almost sculpted. He caught sight of a single rose in a cut-glass vase behind her, and suddenly imagined another man bending to kiss the smooth skin of her neck.

Ruzsky fought to keep his emotions in check, but it was an unequal battle. He was forty—*forty*—an investigator hardened by more experience than was good for a man; married, betrayed, alone. And yet when he was with her—a girl not much more than half his age—the cares of the world fell away.

Opposite her dresser, a photograph of the male dancer Vaslav Nijinsky as the golden slave—the role that made him famous—took pride of place alongside one of Maria and Kshesinskaya, the prima ballerina *assoluta*. Russia's two best-known ballerinas had their arms draped around each other for the camera. "How is she?" Ruzsky asked, inclining his head.

"Much the same as before." Maria shrugged. "Still collecting Romanovs."

"Perhaps not the best currency in these times."

"The world is at war, Sandro. How many million dead? How many yet to die? Our fantasies count for little."

Ruzsky felt that she was able to look right through him.

"Was it so bad, what you did? To send you away for so long."

Her gaze was intense. Was it hurt that he saw there? Ruzsky sighed. "I helped cause a man's death."

"But he was a terrible man."

Ruzsky stared at the floor.

"And you took the blame, Sandro?"

Ruzsky did not answer.

"So you're the kind of man who will not cheat on his wife, even though she betrays him openly, and who will happily go into exile in order to protect a friend."

"I wouldn't say happily, exactly—"

"An example to us all."

"I'm afraid my father would not agree."

"Is what he thinks still so important?"

"Yes." Ruzsky realized he had said too much. He shook his head. "No." He forced a smile. "Are you rehearsing today?"

There was a shout from the corridor. "Maria Andreevna!" Then another, when she did not respond.

Maria was still looking at Ruzsky. "Something for next month. Two more nights of the Stravinsky and then I go home to Yalta."

"It's a long way, at a time like this."

"My sister is not well. Sandro, I . . ." As she tried to find the words, her face was soft and more achingly beautiful than ever. This was how he had remembered her. "I would like us to be friends," she said.

Ruzsky did not move. His heart banged like a drum. Friends . . . He was not sure if she meant only friends and no more. "We are friends."

Now he saw sorrow in her eyes. Was it longing, or just a deep loneliness that was the mirror of his own? Ruzsky looked at her for a few moments more, but something prevented him from speaking.

"Maria!" the man shouted again.

Maria touched his cheek, her fingers cool on his skin as her eyes searched his. Then she was gone.

Ruzsky stayed rooted to the spot. By the time he had followed her out of the door, she had disappeared.

At the end of the corridor, he stopped.

He could hear the ballet master already barking instructions. "And one and two and *no . . . Again!*"

He waited.

He listened to his own breathing in the silence of the corridor.

After a minute, he continued on his way.

9

It was still snowing heavily as Ruzsky walked across the square toward the Tsarskoe Selo Station, head down and deep in thought. He could see no sign of any police presence, so he assumed the trains must be running today.

The elegant, yellow station took its name from its principal destination; trains from here ran out to the town that was home to the current tsar an hour away. Whenever Nicholas wanted to come to the capital on *his* train, the entire station was sealed off, sometimes all day.

Ruzsky barely registered the long khvost on the far side of the square until he heard shouts and looked over to see a group of soldiers fighting in the middle of the queue.

He hesitated, then began to walk on until he heard the crack of a shot, then another.

A tram rattled past, almost encased in ice, and Ruzsky ran around the back of it, slipping as he narrowed his eyes against the driving snow. A large group of men was fighting—perhaps ten or more and there was another shot. The melee was too confused to tell who was firing, or at what. Ruzsky reached into his pocket for his Sauvage and pointed it in the air. He fired once. "Police! Get back in line."

The men continued to fight. He fired twice more. "*Get back in line!*" he bellowed.

They stopped and, as Ruzsky moved closer, turned slowly to stare at him. Two were on the ground, covered in snow, and got up slowly. All were in long greatcoats, but one at least had large holes in the top of his boots. He was an older peasant conscript with a long, unkempt beard. He had knocked a woman and her son over in the scuffle and Ruzsky stepped forward and helped them to their feet. The woman almost slipped over again, but he caught her. She was dressed in a thick jacket and a scuffy, dark pair of valenki—knee-high rough woolen boots.

He retreated once more, and it was only then that he could see that the line was more than a hundred yards long and stretched all the way around the corner of the block. He couldn't see what they were waiting for. Perhaps, as so often, they did not even know themselves.

"You're waiting for bread?" he shouted.

All of the men stared at him, the snow gathering in their faces. Most of those ahead and behind them were women, wrapped up in head-scarves, so that only their eyes were visible.

He saw himself through their eyes, for the first time in many years. A detested servant of the Tsar. He thought of the article on his desk. No wonder the educated classes feared the mob.

"You're waiting for bread?" he shouted again, wanting to break the mood, but still no one answered him.

Ruzsky walked swiftly along the queue, turning the corner to see that the bakery they waited outside was not even open. He pushed through the middle of the crowd and went to the door, then put his face to the cold glass and peered in. There was no light on inside, but he could see that the shelves were empty.

He turned around. "There's nothing there."

Nobody answered him.

At the front of the queue, a woman waited with her son and an old man they had wheeled on a makeshift wooden barrow. Snow and ice had gathered in the old man's beard and his eyes were beyond caring.

"They said there would be bread later," the woman said. "No one wishes to lose their place in the line."

Ruzsky looked at her for a moment and then turned around and walked back toward the group of soldiers. "It will be a long wait," he said as he approached. "If you must stay, be patient. Fighting serves no one."

But even as he spoke, he felt the patronizing futility of his words.

He stared at them for a moment more and then turned and walked toward the station steps. As he did so, he felt a thousand eyes upon his back.

"Officer!" someone shouted. Ruzsky swung around. The young boy who had been at the front of the queue stood before him. He thrust a piece of paper into his hands.

Ruzsky looked down at it.

"A PROPHECY," it read.

> A year shall come of Russia's blackest dread;
> Then will the crown fall from the royal head,
> The throne of tsars will perish in the mud,
> The food of many will be death and blood.
> —Mikhail Lermontov, 1830.

Ruzsky looked up. They were all staring at him. Even through the veil of falling snow he could see the hatred in their eyes.

He folded the piece of paper, put it into his pocket, and walked away without looking back.

Ruzsky climbed the stone steps to the platform level of the station and emerged onto the concourse. A conductor blew his whistle loudly and the engine closest to him released a burst of steam that billowed out across the platform. Light spilled through the glass panels of the curved iron roof.

Ruzsky walked past the shops selling sweets and cigarettes and noticed how bare even their shelves appeared. Before the war, they'd also have sold pastries and bread, but now there was no sign of either. Only a man standing next to a brazier by the edge of the concourse, selling baked lavasky, the wafer-thin round cakes, appeared to be doing any trade.

Ruzsky grasped the brass rail at the entrance to one of the carriages and swung himself up, slamming the door shut behind him. He took his seat and pushed up the window next to it, a few crystals of snow and ice floating down onto his lap.

On the platform outside, three women in fur coats and hats stood next to an officer in the dark blue and green parade uniform of Her Majesty's Cuirassier Regiment—the Blue Cuirassiers. Next to them, a newspaper boy in a flat cloth cap was shouting loudly in an attempt to sell copies of *Petrogradskie Vedomosti* and *Novoe Vremia* beside a crudely inscribed headline board: "*Western Front: no changes; Rumanian Front: no changes;*

Caucasian Front: no changes. Bravery of Russian Soldiers! Shaliapin Charity Concert to be announced in Moscow."

As Ruzsky watched, the officer stepped over and ordered the boy curtly to be quiet, before moving back toward his companions. He said something to the women and then tipped back his head in laughter as the whistle sounded.

For all his rebellions, Ruzsky could not help sharing his family's prejudice against cavalry officers. The Preobrazhensky was in the Infantry Division of the Life Guards.

He stood and returned to the platform to buy a copy of *Petrogradskie Vedomosti*. He gave the boy a large tip.

The carriage was almost empty, save for a young couple in the far corner staring out of their window. Ruzsky stretched his legs and sank back into the leather seat.

There was another whistle and the train began to move off. The view across the rooftops through dull light and dirty windows appeared endless.

The girl at the far end of the carriage leaned her head affectionately on the man's shoulder. They were young, both of them, possibly palace household staff.

Ruzsky pulled his thin overcoat tight, trying to ignore the cold. He took out his silver case and almost smoked a cigarette, before thinking better of it. He turned the case over and looked at the family crest. Like the Romanovs', it depicted a giant eagle—but single headed.

He closed his eyes. Train journeys always transported him back to his youth and those moments when the family would leave Petersburg and set off for what had been his father's favorite country estate at Petrovo. Sometimes, still, Ruzsky revisited every detail of that journey in his mind: the packing of the household, the excitement that flooded through everyone, even the servants, for days beforehand; the hampers, the first-class compartment, the soporific rattle of the train as it moved slowly south; the horse-drawn troikas that would be waiting at the station two days later and the thrill of that last journey when he, Ilya, and Dmitri would climb down and run through the woods to the house. He could see, even now, the village sparkling through the pine trees as they crested the last hill, the house ablaze with light.

He wondered if he would ever go back.

The train rattled past a frozen lake upon which a boy of six or seven was skating with halting, uncoordinated movements. Ruzsky watched him as he fell and sat suddenly upright, craning his neck to see if he had gone through the ice.

But the boy stood. He dusted the snow from his clothes and began to skate again.

Ruzsky kept his eyes upon him until the train had rattled around the corner of the wood and out of sight.

He picked up his newspaper. There was a long article on the front page that contained the usual fantastic assertions about the progress of the war and a claim that the radical political changes demanded by some would *shatter the foundations of Russian society.*

This was the newspaper Ruzsky's father had always treated as a conservative bible. He flicked through it. A group of criminals had robbed a million rubles from the Mutual Credit Bank in Kharkov, drilling through a wall from a neighboring house.

He put the paper down. Perhaps it was a sign of the times. When a ship hit bad weather, it was every rat for himself.

When he reached the station in the town of Tsarskoe Selo itself, Ruzsky climbed into the back of a droshky and a few moments later the wind was cutting into his cheeks as he was hurried along Sadovaya Ulitsa, past the formal gardens of the Catherine Palace. The weather was much clearer out here, and the magnificent blue, white, and gold baroque facade of the palace sparkled in the sunlight. Above it, the Imperial Standard of the Romanovs crackled in the breeze.

Ruzsky watched a green ambulance with a red cross on its side slide through the gates of the palace. Since the start of the war, a section of the grandest of all the Romanovs' homes had been turned into a hospital for officers.

Not that it had done the ruling dynasty any favors.

Ruzsky smoked a cigarette to hide his nerves. He had been here as a child, when his father had been summoned to a meeting with the present tsar's father, Alexander III, in the Catherine Palace—a rare event since Alexander had preferred his home at Gatchina—but this time Ruzsky doubted he would get past the gate.

Even as the son of privilege, Ruzsky had found the opulence awe-inspiring. So many servants, he had told his mother. Nor could he forget the look of rapture in her eyes.

The droshky slowed as they approached the Alexander Palace and the driver stopped short of the gate. Ruzsky paid and sent him on his way.

He waited for a moment as he pushed the bundle of his own rubles back into his pocket. Two guards stood by the gate. There was a sense of calm within. The emperors did not like to see servants arriving and leaving, he had once been told, so an entrance to the palace complex had been built underground. He was surprised by how ordinary it all seemed. Somehow, given the climate in the capital, he had expected to find hundreds of guards and thick barbed wire fencing.

"Ruzsky, Alexander Nikolaevich, investigator of the Petrograd police," he told the guards, producing his identification papers.

The men were soldiers from the Cossack Escort Regiment, but as he handed over his papers, Ruzsky noticed another man—an officer of the Police of the Imperial Court—watching him from inside the gate. After a few moments, the man, dressed in a long, elegant gray overcoat, slipped out and walked toward him.

"An investigator from the city police," one of the guards explained as the policeman took Ruzsky's identification papers and examined them.

He looked carefully at the photograph, then up at Ruzsky. "It says here you're the chief investigator."

"Yes."

"I don't know you."

"I've been away."

"To the front?"

"No."

The man frowned. "You are still the chief investigator?"

"I suppose so."

"You suppose so?"

"Yes, I am."

"Your papers are out of date."

Ruzsky looked at him, not sure if he was joking. "I apologize," he said, realizing that the officers charged with the Tsar's personal protection had nothing to smile about. "You're quite correct, they are out of date, but I'm conducting a murder investigation."

"Not Rasputin?"

"No." Ruzsky shook his head.

"Who have you come to see?"

"Madame Vyrubova."

"Vyrubova?"

"Yes."

"You have made an appointment?"

"No. I'm afraid not."

The officer looked suspicious. "I'll have to ask you to wait while I telephone."

"Of course."

The policeman retreated to the small wooden box beside the gate, the guards alongside him. Ruzsky walked forward to the railings and looked through to the yellow and white colonnades. It was infinitely more modest than the Catherine Palace, its neighbor.

He turned around, took out his case, and lit a cigarette. It was almost warm now that the sun was out, though his feet were still numb with cold. He bashed them together.

He noticed two faces in an upstairs window of the house closest to the gate. He assumed they were also officers of the palace police, watching the entrance.

The aura of calm was deceptive.

He faced the gate again and watched a gardener chipping ice from outside the steps to the nearest wing of the palace.

Ruzsky thought about the faces of those waiting in the bread queue. Were they really talking about revolution? Now that people discussed it openly, he found himself recoiling from his earlier insistence that change was inevitable and desirable in whatever form. He realized now that it frightened him. He no longer believed that change always made things better.

He thought of the arguments with his father.

If only they had spent less time being so certain they were right . . . but then, the same could be said for the country as a whole.

"All right, Chief Investigator. I'll get someone to accompany you."

Ruzsky was so surprised that he did not answer. The man returned to his box and Ruzsky waited, his hands thrust into his overcoat pockets.

There was a sudden burst of activity as three soldiers ran down from the near wing to open the gate. A long, low black saloon car followed them, the yellow and black imperial flag fluttering over its hood.

It skidded on the ice as it swung out onto the road, affording Ruzsky a brief glimpse of the man inside. The Tsar of all the Russias glanced at him, before settling back into his seat.

One of the soldiers walked over. "I will take you."

Ruzsky heard himself say: "I thought the Emperor was at the front."

The guard gave him a sour look, but did not deign to reply.

They began walking, stepping onto the side of the road, into the snow, where the footing was surer. "How is Petrograd?" the man asked.

"Cold."

"We hear only bad things."

"It will be better when there is more bread."

They rounded the corner of the Alexander Palace and saw a group of children playing beneath the terrace. They were making something from the snow—from here it looked like a house—helped by two men and a woman. As they moved closer, Ruzsky recognized two of the grand duchesses, the Tsar's daughters, and the Tsarevich, his only son.

Ruzsky could not take his eyes from them. Just as with the car a moment ago, it was almost like seeing an apparition. If he'd told Pavel he'd witnessed the Tsar's children playing in the snow—just like any in Russia—the big detective would never have believed him.

It reminded Ruzsky of his own conviction as a child that the Tsar was not in fact a mere man, but a being from another world. It was an impression that he could still not entirely dispel, even though he had once exchanged a few words with the young Nicholas Romanov at a New Year's Day reception at the Winter Palace.

The Tsarevich laughed. He was a pale child, with a thin white face, but there was no sign of the hemophilia with which rumor said he was inflicted. As the guard led him toward the group, Ruzsky tried to tear his eyes away from the boy, but could not.

"Madam Vyrubova," the guard said.

A round-faced woman looked over toward them. She was dressed in a long white coat with a fur collar.

"This gentleman has come to see you. He is the chief investigator for the Petrograd police."

The woman frowned. The two grand duchesses looked at Ruzsky with frank curiosity. They were strikingly beautiful. The men—tutors, he assumed—stopped what they were doing and appraised him also. Both were dressed in long overcoats and suits.

Ruzsky realized he was staring at them as he would at caged animals. He had to force himself to look away.

"I've not seen him before," Vyrubova said.

The Tsarevich looked like his own son. They shared the same gentle solemnity. As he watched, the woman drew the boy to her, but the gesture was proprietorial rather than affectionate.

"I'm new," Ruzsky said, realizing he was required to offer an explanation.

"You're too late."

Alexei slipped his other arm through that of the older of his two sisters. This must be Olga, Ruzsky thought, or perhaps Tatiana. It was many years since he'd seen either of them. They were pretty girls. They projected a luminous innocence. Ruzsky thought of the caricature he had seen on the wall of the office earlier depicting their half-naked mother dancing with Rasputin.

"Take him to my house. I will see him there," Vyrubova said. Her manner was imperious and dismissive. He turned reluctantly and the guard led him away down the central path.

Ruzsky glanced back. The group still watched him.

He was chivied on by the guard. The icy path had been scattered with small stones to give them a measure of grip, but his footing was still uncertain.

The path ran through a long line of trees which stood out starkly against the snowy landscape around them. Ruzsky could see the Catherine Palace to his left and he stopped as he reached the point where the paths leading to both palaces met. He could still see the children playing beneath the curved terrace behind him. The guard chivied him again.

They passed a chapel. "Is that where they buried him?" Ruzsky asked. "Rasputin, I mean."

The guard stopped suddenly, his face severe. "You have no power or jurisdiction here, is that understood?" Ruzsky noticed how red the man's cheeks were from the cold, the capillaries so pronounced that they reminded him of the painted wooden maps they'd studied at school. "This is the home of the Tsar of all the Russias. You will confine yourself to addressing Madam Vyrubova, and no one else."

Ruzsky concealed his irritation at this unnecessarily heavy-handed approach and the man turned around and marched him swiftly down to a small house in the far corner of the park. It was a pavilion that had been transformed into a comfortable, solid residence, with a white wooden fence around its garden and roses curling over the sloping roof of the veranda.

Inside it was neatly, but not lavishly, furnished. The guard left him at the door in the hands of a young housekeeper with pretty dark eyes. She smiled and led him through to a drawing room. He accepted her offer of tea.

The room was bright, sunlight spilling in through large windows. Ruzsky stood with his back to a fire that crackled on the hearth. There was a framed photograph of Rasputin on the far wall with a collection of icons beneath it. Next to it was a picture of Anna Vyrubova sitting alongside the Tsar himself on a thin strip of sand in what looked like the Crimea. The last picture—next to a bookcase—was of Anna surrounded by the Tsar's five children.

Ruzsky took a step toward her desk. It was arranged neatly, a pen and inkwell placed next to a pile of writing paper. On the right-hand side, alongside a small carriage clock, the Tsarina stared out at him severely from an ornate silver frame.

He heard someone coming through the front door and returned to his position in the center of the room.

Vyrubova looked at him for a moment as she entered. "What do you want?"

"I—"

"You didn't come and see us about Father Grigory. If you are indeed the chief investigator, we should have seen you then."

"I have just returned to Petrograd." He shook his head. "And I believe such an important case was always likely to be treated as a political and not simply criminal matter, for reasons that will be obvious to you."

She stared at him. "It has brought shame on our country, and our class."

Ruzsky didn't answer. He wondered exactly what relationship this woman enjoyed with the Empress. Technically, as he recalled, she was a lady-in-waiting, but clearly also much more. This was the woman much of Russia believed to be a lesbian lover of the Empress, and participant in orgies that were variously said to involve both the Tsar and Rasputin.

"If your business is not important," she went on, "then why do you trouble me with it?"

Vyrubova's small eyes were still fixed upon his. He sensed her suspicion, and her cunning.

"The body of a woman was found on the Neva this morning. She was wearing a dress made by Madame Renaud." He paused. "A dress made for you."

Her expression did not alter, but he saw her eyes flicker. "Who was she?"

"That's why I'm here." Ruzsky reached into his pocket for the photographs. He handed her one of the girl's head and shoulders. "I was hoping you would be able to tell me."

Vyrubova took it. She stared at it in silence. "How do you know the dress was mine?"

"Madame Renaud confirmed it."

"How did you know it was one of her dresses?"

Ruzsky was about to explain, but thought better of it. "Do you recognize her?"

"Yes." Vyrubova's face was expressionless.

He waited.

"And?" Ruzsky was beginning to recover his wits enough to find the woman's disdain irritating.

"Her name was Ella."

They heard the front door being opened and shut and a voice in the hall. A few moments later, the Tsarina appeared, dressed in a black over-coat, gloves, and hat, a diamond brooch at her neck.

Ruzsky did not move. After a few moments, he realized that his mouth was open and he shut it. She was taller than he remembered, but there were deep lines around her eyes and her face was harsher, thinner, and more angular than he'd imagined.

For a moment, she stared at him.

The last time Ruzsky had set eyes upon her had been on the day of his arrest. He had been with his brother in the General Staff Building, over-looking a packed Palace Square as the Tsar and his wife came out onto the balcony of the Winter Palace to read a proclamation declaring the Russian Empire to be at war with Germany and Austro-Hungary.

Even now, Ruzsky could recall every detail of that crisp day: the giant crimson drape that hung almost to the ground; the Tsar dressed in the uniform of a colonel in the Preobrazhensky Regiment, his wife in white; the gigantic crowd falling to its knees and chanting the national anthem, "Bozhe, Tzaria Khrani," over and over again, the Emperor raising his hand as he read the proclamation against the great din, his wife bowing.

The swell of emotion had touched even the most cynical hearts. And in the eyes of the young men in uniform around him, what Ruzsky had seen was nothing short of ecstasy.

Now most of those men were dead and the woman who ruled an em-pire stood before him, dressed in black.

His education failed him. He had no idea what he should say if she chose to address him.

"Who is this?" she demanded.

"He says he's a chief investigator from Petrograd."

The Empress snorted in derision, as if he weren't there. "It's not good for Alexei to be out in the cold so long." She spoke Russian with a heavy German accent.

Vyrubova's expression was instantly soothing. "He seems better today."

"He's no judge of his own well-being."

"He wants to be out with the girls."

"I know he does, but that doesn't mean that it is good for him."

The Empress of the Russias turned to him. "What is he doing here?"

Anna Vyrubova handed the Tsarina the photograph that was still in her hand. She studied it for a moment and then looked up again, her mouth taut. "I suppose you think it is our fault."

Ruzsky did not know what to say.

"She was murdered," Vyrubova explained. "It wasn't—"

The Empress looked confused. "Murdered?"

It appeared to be a question for him. "Yes," Ruzsky said, clearing his throat and bowing slightly. "It would appear so, Your . . ." Ruzsky wondered if he should have said "Your Imperial Highness," but, as he considered the question, a hint of resentment at his mother's own fawning approach to the imperial family acted as its own check. Their manner was damned rude.

"It would appear so? Surely you must know."

"Yes . . . That is correct."

"How was she murdered?"

Ruzsky glanced at Vyrubova to see whether he should continue to answer, but received no signal either way. "She was stabbed. Once. The man with her, seventeen times." Ruzsky handed a photograph of the man's head and shoulders to the Empress. She looked at it without expression and then passed it to her companion.

"How did you know she worked here?" the Empress asked.

Ruzsky looked at Vyrubova, but her face was impassive. "I didn't," he said.

Ruzsky thought he saw a slight flush developing in the Tsarina's cheeks.

"Ella worked in the nursery," Vyrubova explained. "And was very fond of the children."

"She was a pretty girl," the Empress said. "But unreliable."

"She was very fond of the family," Vyrubova went on, "and sad to go."

They were silent. Their sudden garrulousness confused him. "If you don't mind me asking," Ruzsky said, "to go where?"

"She was dismissed," the Empress said.

There was another long silence.

"Would it be impertinent . . ." Ruzsky kept his eyes on Vyrubova so as not to rile the Empress. "May I ask why?"

The Empress frowned, tilting her head to one side. "You may not."

"I apologize, Your Highness."

"She stole from us," the Tsarina said suddenly. She sighed. "There was no choice but to dismiss her. It upset the children. She upset the children."

"She was too close to them," Vyrubova added. "To the Little One, to Sunbeam, especially."

The Empress's irritation with her colleague began to show again.

"She was sad to leave here?" Ruzsky asked.

"Devastated. Of course." The Empress seemed suddenly to remember herself. "I did not expect anyone to be here," she told Vyrubova. "Telephone me when you have dealt with this man."

She walked out. They waited, watching her pass the window and the white fence around the garden.

Vyrubova did not look at him. There was an intimacy between them suddenly, as if he had witnessed a domestic scene normally kept away from prying eyes. She stared at her shoes, a rueful smile at the corner of her lips.

"What did this girl . . . Ella . . . steal?"

Vyrubova was evasive again. "Oh, I don't know."

"You don't know what she took?"

"No." She looked out of the window. The Empress was now some distance away. "No."

"Some money?"

"No. I mean, yes. Money."

"How much?"

She turned back, still not meeting his eye. "I don't know."

Ruzsky smiled encouragingly. "You seem to keep few secrets from each other."

"Who?"

"You and the Empress."

"That is not your business."

"No. Of course. I just imagined she would have told you the cause of this girl's sudden dismissal."

"She rules the Empire during the Tsar's absence at the front, commanding our great forces. She doesn't have time to deal with the minutiae of the household. This girl was unimportant."

"But the children were upset."

"They will quickly recover. It is best to be removed from unsuitable influences."

"How was she unsuitable, exactly?"

"Oh . . . I don't know." Ruzsky saw the impatience in Vyrubova's expression, but did not understand why she was making such heavy weather of the lies she was telling. "You must ask the household staff."

"As you wish. May I go over now?"

"No." She was shocked. "You must write. Apply in writing."

"To whom?"

"To the household. To Colonel Shulgin. He deals with such matters."

Ruzsky tried to prevent his exasperation from showing. "Was Ella from Petersburg?"

"No, she wasn't. Yalta or Sevastopol. Somewhere on the peninsula."

"How did she come to be employed here?"

"I have no idea. You'll have to ask the household staff."

"Did you know the girl well?"

"Ella? No. Not at all."

"But you gave her one of your dresses?"

"Yes, but . . . She had not worked here long."

"How long?"

"A few months. Perhaps a little more."

"Did she ever talk about her personal life here in Petrograd?"

"Not to me. I don't believe so. No she didn't."

"Did she have any family or friends that you know of?"

"I've no idea."

"What was her family name?"

"Kovyil."

Ruzsky noted it down. "So you saw her when you were with the children. She was a nanny. To Alexei?"

"She helped in the nursery." Vyrubova's expression clouded. "It was disgraceful. To steal like that. Disgraceful. The Empress has always been most generous."

Ruzsky doubted, from the tone of her voice, that this was true.

"But you knew the girl well. Well enough to give her one of your dresses."

"No. I hardly spoke to her."

"It was an act of great generosity."

"She mentioned how much she liked it one day. It no longer fit me. After she was dismissed, I sent it to her."

"But Madame Renaud's dresses are not inexpensive . . ."

Vyrubova looked at him, assessing him properly for the first time. She took a pace away. "I must go to the palace."

"I would ask you to stay a few moments more," he said quietly.

"I have work to do."

"And I too." Ruzsky's tone checked her. "This girl was walking arm in arm with her lover under the moonlight in the first hours of our New Year. They were viciously attacked. Even in these troubled days, murder must not go unheeded, surely."

She stared at him. He wondered if she had privately expressed such sentiments at the way in which Rasputin's killers had escaped justice.

"Who are you? What is your name?" she demanded.

"Ruzsky. Alexander Nikolaevich."

She frowned. "You are related to the assistant minister of finance."

"My father."

She assessed him with inscrutable eyes. "I cannot help you further."

"*Did* you recognize the man?"

Vyrubova realized she still had the photograph in her hand. She returned it to him. "No."

"He wasn't a member of the household staff also?"

"No."

"You haven't seen him before?"

She shook her head.

"Did Ella ever speak about a male friend, a lover perhaps—"

"I told you. I hardly knew the girl."

Ruzsky breathed in deeply to hide his impatience. "When you say Ella was upset, what do you mean? Did you—"

"It was the Empress who said she was upset. I did not see her."

This was so obviously a lie that Ruzsky found himself getting angry for the first time. "From everything you've said, madam, I find that—"

"I have to go now. The Empress is expecting me." She began to walk away.

"Madam?"

She stopped and glowered at him.

"Could you give me the number of the house to which you sent the dress?"

She looked puzzled.

"You said that you sent the dress to her after she had left."

He thought Vyrubova might explode as she sought a way out of the trap into which she had led herself. "The household staff dealt with it. You must speak to them."

"To Count Fredericks?"

"No, no. He has many more important things to deal with."

"Colonel Shulgin, then?"

"Yes, but you may not do so now. You must make an appointment." There was something close to panic in her voice.

"Tomorrow, perhaps."

"Tomorrow, yes. Tomorrow."

Ruzsky was led back the way he came. The children were still playing with the snow house. Alexei was standing on a block of ice and sweeping snow onto the heads of the two men helping them. He was laughing.

One of the girls threw a snowball at her brother and he threw one back. Ruzsky noticed that the boy dragged his right leg as he tried to run away.

"Keep up," the guard said. "Or I shall be forced to call for assistance."

"The boy tries hard to overcome—"

"It is not your business."

"I don't recall suggesting that it was." Ruzsky thrust his hands into his pockets. "It's a good life here. Quiet. I can see why they hate coming to Petrograd."

The guard looked at him, then turned on his heel. Ruzsky watched the boy sitting on a bank for a few moments more before following. He turned back once and saw that the heir to all the Russias was watching him.

10

By the time he got back to the office, the only light in his department was from Pavel's desk lamp, but Ruzsky noticed that his partner's coat was not on the stand in the corner.

Ruzsky walked over to his own desk. Propped up against the telephone was a letter. He recognized Maria's hand instantly. He tapped it once against his fingers and then tore it open.

My dear Sandro, she had written, *it was so good to see you today*.

Folded into the letter was a ticket for *The Firebird* at the Mariinskiy on the following night.

Ruzsky sat down. He put the letter on the desk and moved it gently to and fro.

He stood again and looked out of the window into the darkness. Was this just an act of friendship? But hope made him want to dance.

"Want to tell me what you're doing?"

Ruzsky turned around. Pavel stood in the shadows just inside the doorway.

"I thought you'd gone," Ruzsky said.

"Russia's most beautiful woman." Pavel took a pace toward his partner. "She delivered it herself. I hope you know what you're doing."

"It's not what you think."

"I'll take your word for it. I should imagine she has many admirers."

"What do you mean?"

"Exactly what I said."

Ruzsky folded the letter and slipped it back into the envelope.

"So," Pavel continued. "How did you get on?"

"You'll never believe what I have to say, so you first."

Pavel raised his eyebrows. "Nothing from the embankment. I spoke to some junior official in the Winter Palace household who assured me it was not possible that anyone could have witnessed anything from an upstairs window."

"We'll go and see him together tomorrow."

"I don't think there's much point. He was quite adamant that the rooms on the top floor are the preserve of the family and none of them were present last night. I don't think he was lying." Pavel yanked his trousers up. "But I've just come from the American embassy, and that sounded promising."

Ruzsky waited. "And?"

"The official we need to speak to has gone out of town and won't be back until the morning, but one of his colleagues said they'd had a report from home six weeks ago asking them to ask us to be on the lookout for a Robert White. An armed robber from Chicago. Said they'd passed it on to the Okhrana. I told them a lot of good it would do them."

"So what does that have to do with the couple on the ice?"

"Someone from the Astoria telephoned the embassy this morning. Apparently, a man calling himself Whitewater checked into the hotel just over a week ago, saying he was a diplomat and writing 'care of the embassy' on the registration form. They suspected him of leaving without paying his bill, because his room was empty and they hadn't seen him for two days."

Ruzsky was silent. "Did you go down to the Astoria?"

"Give me a chance. I'll go first thing. Come on," Pavel spoke with feeling, "I need a drink."

"I can't afford it."

"Neither can I, but there is a place nearby. I've threatened it with closure. They're very cooperative."

Pavel led the way down the darkened stairwell.

Outside, the snow was thick on the ground. The wind had dropped, but the air was still crisp and the night cloudy. Ruzsky's feet were instantly cold again.

"Tell me what happened at Tsarskoe Selo," Pavel said.

"You won't believe it."

"Try me."

Ruzsky smiled to himself. It was hard to believe the episode had not been a figment of his imagination—and yet it had been so ordinary.

"I went to see Vyrubova, but the Tsarina arrived."

"You're not serious."

"On my honor."

Pavel shook his head and Ruzsky did not press it.

"She had horns growing from her head?" Pavel asked.

"Mmm. And she carried a flaming pitchfork."

"No, really, what happened?"

"I went to see Vyrubova."

"She received you?"

"Not exactly. I saw the Tsar depart in his car and then I was taken to her house. We walked past the imperial children, or some of them, playing in the snow. And then the Tsarina arrived."

"Just like that?"

"More or less."

"On her own?"

"Yes."

"No staff, no officials, no fanfare?"

"It was very ordinary."

"No strange priests?"

Ruzsky did not answer.

"And?" Pavel went on.

"Have you ever seen her close up?"

"Of course not."

"She looks very tired."

"Don't tell me she answered questions?"

"The girl's name was Ella and she worked in the imperial nursery. She was originally from the Crimea. Yalta or Sevastopol." Ruzsky watched his feet in the snow. "Vyrubova insisted she'd taken pity on the girl and given her an old dress, but if she cared for her enough to do that, she seemed to me strangely indifferent to news of her demise. The Tsarina forgot herself and began to answer some questions, but they were both evasive and . . . cold. I didn't know what to do; should I ask the Empress of the Russias questions?" Ruzsky shrugged. "And they didn't seem to know whether or not to dismiss me out of hand." Ruzsky thought about the episode for a few paces more. "Vyrubova was obviously lying, or at least not telling much of the truth, but I found it difficult to guess at why."

"What did they say?"

"The girl was close, or so they said, to the imperial children. She was dismissed for stealing. That's as far as I got."

"For *stealing*?"

"Yes."

"Stealing what?"

"They said money, but I'm fairly certain it was something else."

Ruzsky and Pavel waited as a Finnish sled was driven past, its bells jangling, then crossed the street. This side was darker, with no light from the houses and the gas lamps unevenly spaced. Ruzsky's hand closed instinctively on the butt of the Sauvage revolver in his pocket.

"So we know her name, but nothing more," Pavel said.

"I'll telephone the household staff tomorrow and find out who she was and exactly why she was dismissed."

"What about the man?"

"They said they'd never seen him before."

"Were they lying about that as well?"

"I don't know."

"So what do you think did happen with the girl?"

Ruzsky thought about this for a few moments. "I don't know."

Ruzsky and Pavel passed a tall brick building that looked like a warehouse and came to a small door with a white sign above it. Pavel knocked once and it was opened by an enormous man with a round face and a long beard. He nodded at each of them and stepped back to allow them inside. Light, warmth, and music spilled down the stairs.

In the center of the wooden floor of the room above, an old man played a violin with manic energy, two men and two women sweating as they danced before him.

A young gypsy girl led them to a table, returning a moment later with an unmarked bottle and two glasses. She was pretty, Ruzsky noticed, with serious eyes and curly, dark hair that spilled over her shoulders. She smiled at him, then laughed as she leaned forward to touch his arm.

The restaurant was packed. All the tables were full, and a crowd lurked in the shadows behind them. Everyone was drinking from the same unmarked bottles. Prohibition had been introduced at the start of the war, to reduce drunkenness and boost national effectiveness, but had instead robbed the treasury of substantial revenue, reduced the quality of the vodka, and contributed to rampant alcoholism. The fact that expensive wines and champagnes were exempt from the ban didn't do much for social equanimity either.

Ruzsky had heard about these illegal cafés and speakeasies, where people danced and drank to forget the world around them, but this was the first time he had been into one. They'd not existed before his departure.

"They keep this table for you," Ruzsky said.

"A man must have somewhere to relax."

Pavel filled the glasses and they looked at each other over the rim. " 'Sante,' as you would say," Pavel said, before they both drank.

Ruzsky shook his head with the force of it. Pavel smiled and refilled. They drank again.

Ruzsky watched the dancers. The women were voluptuous and fully aware of the hungry eyes upon them. Their dancing was sensual and provocative. Ruzsky dragged his eyes away from the floor, took out a cigarette, and leaned forward to light it in the candle's flame, before pushing the case across to Pavel, who shook his head.

"You're going to go back to Irina?" Pavel asked.

"No."

"Why not?"

"She won't entertain the notion."

"Does she know that you know about her affair?"

"No." Ruzsky had confided in Pavel during a moment of weakness before his departure to Tobolsk.

Pavel sighed. "Isn't that a little perverse?"

Ruzsky didn't answer. His eyes were on the prettier of the two gypsy girls, who was dancing with her back arched, her chest thrust high and forward, her forehead glistening with sweat.

Ruzsky thought of Maria on the stage in the last performance he had seen before his exile, and of her long, sinewy body and graceful movement.

"Why haven't you told her?" Pavel asked.

"Who?"

"Irina."

"About what?"

"That you know about her affairs. That you have known for years."

"I don't know."

"You want to occupy the moral high ground." Pavel was annoyed. "Even if it costs you your boy."

"I want to leave Michael out of it."

"That's not possible and you know it. It's killing you, not seeing him, so tell her, tell your father."

"I don't want her, I've no desire to see my father, and it's not going to cost me Michael. I'm determined that it won't."

"If you say so."

"How is Tonya?" Ruzsky asked. "And your boy?"

"You won't want to know that they couldn't be better."

"I don't begrudge anyone happiness, and especially you." Ruzsky looked at his friend. "I mean that."

"I just want to be at home. All the time. With them." Pavel looked as if he would burst with longing. Ruzsky reached forward and patted his bunched fist.

"The little fellow must be what, four?" Ruzsky always avoided calling the boy Sandro, because, although it was flattering, Pavel's decision to name his son after him had always felt uncomfortable.

"He had his birthday two months ago," Pavel said, smiling at the thought of his son. "He laughs all the time. He always wants to see the joke. He's got a great Russian sense of humor and he's big like a bear."

"Like his father, in other words."

Pavel shook his head. "I don't laugh enough anymore."

"You worry too much."

"And you don't worry enough."

"Go home, Pavel. That's where you should be."

"I want to be with you."

Ruzsky laughed. "No you don't."

Pavel filled both glasses again. "Once more."

They drank. Pavel looked at him. "I shouldn't leave you here."

"This is exactly where you should leave me and you know it. Go home to your wife and child."

Pavel hesitated, staring into his empty glass. "Do you think we should . . . you know, pass on this case. Leave it?"

"Leave it?"

Pavel looked up, a deep unease in his eyes.

"How can we leave it?"

Pavel shrugged. "The Empress, the palace. The Okhrana. I know you saved me last time, lied for me, but I couldn't . . . you know. Tonya wouldn't come to Tobolsk, and these are bad times."

"We broke the law. I was the chief investigator. If anyone was going to be punished, it should have been me."

"Do you think that was what it was about?"

"What do you mean?"

"You think that you were punished because we broke the law?"

"I think Vasilyev wanted to bring the whole department down a peg, show us who was boss in this city."

Pavel shook his head. "Sometimes you're not such a brilliant investigator, after all."

"I don't understand."

"You think he gives a shit about breaking the law?"

"No, but—"

"He's the devil. You, more than Anton, posed a threat. You like digging around in things, you're highborn and disdainful of anyone who doesn't operate on the same moral plain." Pavel raised his hand. "I mean it as a compliment. Above all, you're difficult to control and impossible to intimidate. You're dangerous. And I don't like this case." Pavel leaned back with a sigh. "I don't like it."

"Why not?"

"I just don't. It smells dirty. We should push it on to the Okhrana. They've got the bodies, they're equipped for dealing with that kind of stuff. Why fight for it?"

They stared at each other in silence. Pavel lowered his gaze. "You're thinking what love has reduced me to," he said, reading Ruzsky's mind.

"Of course I'm not."

"I don't mind if you are. They're all I care about, Sandro."

Ruzsky leaned forward to touch his friend's hand. "Of course."

"You think that I think you're emotionally reckless," Pavel went on, "but I don't. We're just different. Or perhaps you've never been in love."

Ruzsky stared at the dancers. "Perhaps."

Pavel stood reluctantly, but Ruzsky could tell he wanted to be at home, and he was determined not to accept charity. "Go on, go."

"Be careful, Sandro."

"I'm not a child."

"I suppose this means we're working tomorrow."

"It's up to you."

"But I know you will be."

Ruzsky shrugged. "It's a Sunday, you have a wife and family. Stay at home. Go to church."

Pavel put one giant hand on Ruzsky's shoulder and then ambled slowly toward the door. Ruzsky watched him go and then turned back to the dance floor and the bottle of vodka. He poured himself another glass.

He was watching the prettier of the girls on the dance floor again when the waitress put down a wooden tray and slipped in beside him. The tray had on it fresh and pressed caviar alongside salted cucumbers and herring fillets. There was a cup of tea with lemon.

The girl looked like the one on the dance floor. They could have been—and probably were—sisters. She was smiling at him, her hand on his knee, her body tilted toward him so that the smell of her cheap French scent caught in his nostrils.

The audience cheered and clapped as the dancers reached a climax. The waitress poured two glasses of vodka, but with her left hand. Her right was massaging his thigh.

They drank and, as he put his glass down, her hand reached his groin. The girl's face was in front of his now, her dark eyes searching his own.

She leaned closer still and her mouth was warm, her hand working beneath the table as the music seemed to get louder and louder.

The woman leaned back, her eyes still searching his. "Come," she said, shifting away from him and taking his hand.

"No," he said.

"You want to come."

"No."

"Upstairs."

"No."

She looked genuinely disappointed. "Your friend has gone."

"And so must I."

She stared at him a few moments more and then shook her head angrily. Ruzsky was too drunk and tired to care. As she marched away from him, he pushed himself to his feet, dimly aware of the eyes on him as he tried to walk steadily toward the door. On the other side of the room, he saw—or thought he saw—Stanislav the rat, watching him.

The journalist immediately turned his back and disappeared past a red curtain. Ruzsky pushed through the crowd and followed him up a dingy staircase beyond. It smelled of varnish, dirt, and cleaning liquid.

He reached a long corridor, with rooms off each side. As Ruzsky walked along it, he heard the unmistakable sounds of copulation. He stopped. "Stanislav?" He wondered why Pavel had brought him here. Was this what he thought he needed? Or was there something else?

"Stanislav?" he called again.

Ruzsky moved slowly forward to the source of the sounds and glanced in through the gap in the door. He saw a girl astride a large man, long blond hair hanging down her back. Whoever it was—and Ruzsky could not see the man's face—he did not see how it could have been Stanislav.

Ruzsky turned around and retraced his steps.

He had not taken his overcoat off inside, and had felt warm for the first time today, but it only served to exacerbate the impact of the cold air as he stepped out into the street. It was snowing heavily again, a new wind whipping the flakes into tiny cyclones. He began walking, head bent, his mind spinning. He knew this was how people died in the winter. They emerged drunk from the warmth, fell over in a dark corner, and froze to death.

On the far side of the street, two likhachy drivers eyed him. It was a matter of honor that the likhach, drivers of the better sprung carriages, with soft rugs and velvet cushions, never touted for or haggled over a fare. There were no droshky drivers in sight—another indication of the kind of place Pavel had taken him to.

Ruzsky kept walking. He tried to shake the vodka from his mind. It was a few moments before he realized that he was not heading back to his apartment, but toward his father's house on Millionnaya.

He passed a doorway and then stopped, his head spinning. He stepped back and looked closer, struggling to focus. There were two of them huddled together. "Anything you like," one said. "Good price."

They could not have been more than thirteen or fourteen. One girl was blond, the other dark, both deathly thin and pale, clinging onto each other for warmth. Their clothes were ragged and their shoes threadbare and holed. "Both of us together?"

On the wall above them and crudely drawn was another depiction of the Empress of the Russias. She lay on her back, her skirt above her waist, stockings visible, her legs wrapped around a half-naked Rasputin whose trousers were down by his ankles. The caricature was graphic and above it was the word *Niemka*—German woman.

For a moment, Ruzsky was paralyzed as the girls tried to appeal to him and then he reached into his pocket, found a few scrunched-up rubles, and thrust them into their suddenly outstretched hands. He stumbled away.

The girls cried out and Ruzsky turned again to see them running toward a car that had pulled over by the side of the road, almost tripping over themselves in their eagerness to reach the open back door. They, like Ruzsky, instantly recognized its occupant.

Ruzsky stepped back into the shadow of the wall. The girls climbed into the car and the door banged shut. The driver revved the engine and the wheels slipped on the icy road as the car belonging to the chief of the Petrograd Okhrana moved off.

Ruzsky caught a glimpse of Vasilyev's square face. He watched until the car disappeared over the canal and then marched on, through Palace Square and into Millionnaya.

He stopped and stared up at the yellow stone facade, the snow settling upon his face. He hammered on the door and stepped back.

A light came on in one of the upstairs windows. At the same time, Ruzsky heard a growl from within and the door was flung open.

11

His father stood before him in a red silk dressing gown.

"I want to see my son."

"You're drunk."

"I want to see him."

"He's asleep."

"Then I want to see him asleep."

The senior Ruzsky's stare revealed the depth of his contempt. "How low can you sink?"

Irina emerged from the shadows, a tiny figure in a white gown, her black hair disheveled and her eyes full of sleep.

"I want to see our son," Ruzsky said.

"He's asleep."

"Then I want to see him asleep."

"Don't make a fool of yourself, Sandro. Any more than you already have." She looked up at her father-in-law, who placed his arm around her shoulder and drew her to him.

Irina murmured, "Give me a minute, Papa."

Reluctantly, the elder man withdrew, turning his back on his son as he climbed the stairs.

Irina took Ruzsky's hand and led him through to the drawing room on the left. It was an oddly intimate gesture. She closed the door behind them. A fire was dying on the hearth.

Irina took a step closer to him. Her mouth was tight, her eyes narrow and without discernible warmth in the fading light. Her hair, which had once been sleek and dark, was shot through with gray.

"You're drunk," she said.

"No."

89

"By doing this, you make it worse."

"How could it be any worse?"

"You lower yourself still further in the eyes of your father."

"That's hardly possible."

Irina gave him a thin smile.

Ruzsky was facing two giant silver candlesticks and a carriage clock in front of a bookcase that stretched to the ceiling. This was his home and yet his wife had succeeded in making it more alien to him now than it had ever been. Her smile was one of victory.

He glanced wearily at the portraits of Dmitri and Ilya. "You said I could see Michael, but when I telephone, you don't come to the receiver. You never return my calls or reply to my letters."

For the first time, she looked shamefaced. Ruzsky realized that it was not merely anger that had been driving her evasiveness. "We thought it—"

"We?"

"Your father thinks Michael would be better away from your influence. I don't—"

"You have talked about it."

"I don't agree with him, but it has been hard for Michael. The arguments, the upheaval. I thought . . . think it would be better if he were allowed to settle for a time, without the upset of seeing you."

Ruzsky thought of his boy upstairs, sleeping peacefully, still unaware of his presence. "I want to see him." He moved toward the door, but she gripped his arm.

"Please don't," she said.

Ruzsky stared into the fire. He thought how much better it would have been to have never been married than to have come to this. "You believe you understand this family," he said. "Our history, and yet . . ." He shook his head. "You know nothing."

"If that's what you want to believe."

"No outsider can truly understand, Irina."

"That's your conceit."

Ruzsky opened the door. His father stood in the hallway, but Ruzsky looked up to see his brother coming down the stairs. "Give me a minute,

Papa," Dmitri said as he took Ruzsky's arm and led him onto the stone steps outside, pulling the door shut behind them.

Dmitri's face was solemn but his eyes sparkled. A smile tugged at the corner of his lips and then they clasped each other. They held on so tight and for so long that when they parted, they were both short of breath.

They stared at each other until Ruzsky grasped his brother again, still harder. "I thought I'd lose you," he said.

They stepped back once more. "You don't look a day older," Ruzsky said. His delight at seeing his brother alive and well began to sober him up.

"I wish I could say the same for you." Dmitri patted his hair affectionately, lowering his voice to a whisper. "If you're not careful, you'll end up looking like the old man."

"How is your arm?"

Dmitri smiled again and raised it. "Strong enough to resist a bear hug from you."

"I'm sorry."

They stood close together, the snow falling silently between them.

"A real soldier now," Ruzsky said. "A veteran. The ancestors would be proud."

"Spare me the judgment of our ancestors . . ."

"You survived," Ruzsky said. "That's all I care about."

Dmitri dropped his gaze and Ruzsky leaned forward quickly to touch his brother's shoulder, his protective instinct not dulled by the years. Relief and warmth flooded through him, but he'd sobered up enough to realize what a fool he was making of himself. "I'll go."

"We'll work something out, Sandro."

"Have you seen him?"

Dmitri hesitated. "He's fine. He's a strong boy. Ingrid helps to look after him."

"How is Ingrid?"

"Still German. She hides away here."

Ruzsky took a step back. "Good night, Dmitri."

"Telephone me. We'll get together."

"Of course."

"I mean it. Tomorrow. We'll have Sunday lunch. At the club. Agreed?"

Ruzsky hesitated.

"Tomorrow. Promise me."

"I'd like that. We have a lot of work. I—"

"Sandro, there is a war on and I'm an officer in His Imperial Majesty's army. If I can find the time, so can you." Dmitri was still smiling.

"Of course," Ruzsky said. "I'll be there."

"One o'clock. Don't be late."

Ruzsky turned his back and began to walk. Suddenly, he wanted to get away. But after a dozen paces, he stopped and turned. The front door was shut, Dmitri back in the warmth of their family home, but he looked up to see Michael in the attic window, the bedroom that had once been his own. The boy's small, dark head was illuminated by a flickering candle. Ruzsky moved closer, urgently, his heart thumping, tears creeping into the corners of his eyes.

The boy was watching him.

Ruzsky raised his hand. He mouthed his name, and the boy raised his own hand in response, his eyes never leaving his father's. And then Irina was behind him, her hostile face replacing his in the window.

She tugged the curtains shut.

Ruzsky turned away, trying to convince himself he had been right not to insist upon seeing Michael. He was drunk. He was a disgrace. Michael would have been embarrassed.

In the night, Michael's face appeared beneath the ice, his cheek pressed against it, eyes distorted by fear, fingers scrabbling silently for freedom.

Ruzsky knelt above him, hammering with his fist against ice as solid as brick until the blood seeped from beneath his nails. Panic gripped him. His body shook. He was shouting for help, but no sound came. And all the time he could see the desperation in Michael's face as he lay trapped beneath him, fighting the current, struggling to breathe . . .

Ruzsky awoke to the sound of rifle shots and leapt from his bed. He was sweating and shaking and not even the intense cold of the darkened room could shake the images from his mind.

Then the room and the city beyond were silent once more.

A dog barked nearby and Ruzsky scratched a patch of ice from the window so he could look out into the night. It was clear now, the moon bright; a new layer of snow lay thick on the street. His breath froze against the glass.

His head hurt. He turned and walked to the door, his boots—he had fallen into bed fully clothed—noisy on the floorboards.

The room that Pavel had rented for him was in a large tenement building on Line Fourteen of Vasilevsky Island, not far from, but much less respectable than, the apartment he and Irina had occupied before his departure.

The rents had gone up and, of course, he no longer had the allowance given to Irina by his own father, so all Pavel had been able to get for the budget Ruzsky had wired him was a small, bare room in a building that stank of cabbage and cat urine. There was a photograph of Michael above the fireplace and a dark wooden dresser along the opposite wall, between two scruffy armchairs.

Ruzsky took out his cigarette case and reached for the box of matches. He lit up and exhaled heavily. He steeled himself for a long night.

He thought of his son's face in the attic window.

At what point, he asked himself, should a man accept that his life had been a failure?

Ruzsky sat down. He cast his mind back to the summer of 1908 when he and Irina had fallen in love. Anton had still been a part-time lecturer in law at the university and Irina one of his students. She had been admitted to one of the special "courses for women" in law, since ladies were not officially enrolled in the university. Ruzsky recalled the long, heady nights in the back garden of Anton's small country home north of the city, the midnight sun bringing a soft glow to faces flushed with vodka and good food.

Ruzsky remembered Anton lecturing Irina on how much her clever paramour was admired in the department, how bright his future, even if it was not the one his father had wished for him.

Ruzsky got to his knees and put a light to the fire that Pavel had laid the previous evening. He sat cross-legged and watched the flames begin to climb from the kindling toward the blackened walls of the chimney.

After a few minutes they died down again, the remainder of the wood too damp to sustain them.

Ruzsky tried to keep the fire alive, but was rewarded only by smoke and a low hiss.

He gave up. He took a full bottle of vodka from his bruised leather suitcase, and placed it on the table beside his bed.

12

Ruzsky awoke to the peel of church bells across the city. He turned over onto his back and listened, his head pounding and his throat dry. It was still dark and he reached over to look at his pocket watch. It was just after nine.

He slumped back and stared at the ceiling. He was cold, but reluctant to move. The smell of damp cabbage from the stairwell was pervasive.

Ruzsky could not help recalling spring Sundays in Millionnaya Street when he would lie in bed with the windows open, listening to the sound of those timeless bells. He thought, too, about Petrovo, where there were no bells, no noonday guns, no shouts, no carriages rattling over cobbles, no horses or soldiers, neither opulence nor squalor—just the silence of the immense Russian forests.

Ruzsky got up, spurred by the recollection that he had once seen Maria in a quiet corner of the Kazan Cathedral on a Sunday morning.

It was a painful process, even for a man used to Siberia. Ruzsky lit a fire in the tiny stove and melted a bowl of ice. After half an hour the water was still only tepid, but he could wait no longer. He washed, shaved, trimmed his mustache with an old, blunt pair of scissors, then dressed and stepped onto the landing.

The stairwell was festooned with clothes hung up to dry, most of which had frozen overnight, and there was not a single light, so Ruzsky had to pick his way down with care. Most of the apartments had been subdivided so that each room was occupied by a different family, but at least no one was sleeping on the stairs this morning. Perhaps it was just too cold.

The stench of the hallway latrines and discarded refuse caught in his throat as he made his way toward the big oak door and stepped out into the chill predawn air of the courtyard. Ahead, two droshky drivers had up-ended their narrow sleds. The nearest was oiling the runners, while the other was packing the inside of his with hay for passengers to rest their feet upon. The horses stood in the corner, beneath one of the slimy, covered wooden staircases that led up to the rooms on the first floor on the other side of the yard.

Ruzsky pulled down his sheepskin hat and crossed the courtyard. A gas lamp glowed dimly through the archway from the street and he nodded to the lanky dvornik—yard porter—who sat in his cubicle by the gate.

He almost fell over the figure crouching in the shadows.

The man was wrapped in a blanket and had a long, unkempt beard, encrusted with filth. He stared up at Ruzsky with hollow eyes.

Ruzsky ignored him, but twenty paces down the street, he changed his mind, turned around, and went back. He pulled the man to his feet, ignoring the indignant shouts of the fat schweizar—the porter—who emerged from nowhere as Ruzsky half carried, half dragged the man up the stairs.

Ruzsky had intended to leave the man inside the entrance to the building, but dragged him instead up to his room and placed him in front of the stove.

Ruzsky straightened and looked at the man as he would a wounded animal. He stoked the fire, sighed, went to his bed and brought back a second blanket to put around the man's shoulders. "What's your name?"

The man just stared at the flame.

"When you are warm, I'd be grateful if you could leave. I have things to do."

Ruzsky waited for a response, but none was forthcoming. He crouched down beside him. "I have work to do. There is nothing here of value, so I will leave you. Please let yourself out when you are warm."

The man continued to stare straight ahead. Ruzsky moved to the door, wondering if he would return to find a corpse.

Outside, he stopped for a moment in an attempt to clear the foul smell of the hallway latrines from his nostrils and then began to walk.

Line Fourteen was close to Maly Prospekt, the seediest of the main three streets that cut across the island. Down at the far end, close to the great massif of the Stock Exchange and the honey-colored buildings of the university, around Bolshoy Prospekt and down to about Line Five, the island managed a faintly well-bred air. But the area around Maly was more or less a slum, run-down ochre-colored houses interspersed between shops with small grimy windows. Most had signs above their doors announcing *Credit not allowed. Do not come in unless you can pay.*

This had never been a good part of the city, but now it was downright depressing. It was close to the narrow streets of the Gavan, St. Petersburg's first port, which lay at the western tip of the island, and, as he walked, Ruzsky brushed past several merchant sailors emerging from the area's seedy pubs.

Maly had no restaurants, but plenty of tea houses. However, even these chaynaya, which had once served basic fare at a reasonable price— before the war you could get a decent fried pot with sausages here for five copecks or so—no longer had anything appetizing to hang in the window. The only activity appeared to be in the secondhand clothes shops which had multiplied along the street.

Ruzsky was hungry, so he walked down to the St. Andrew's Market, which ran in narrow alleys off the back of the cathedral on Line Six, but he was shocked to find that the war had stripped even this colorful quarter of its character.

If Irina had never gotten over having to move away from the south side, she had at least enjoyed helping the servants with the shopping here. It had always been bustling, loud peddlers touting their wares in competition with one another, but this morning a grim silence hung over the tiny square. The only stall holders were families trying to offload secondhand junk in return for a few copecks. In between the piles of old furniture and books, all Ruzsky could find was root vegetables, so he turned around and began to walk in the opposite direction.

He passed a group of students emerging from a café. There were four of them: a pretty girl in an astrakhan cap and three young men in tattered, worn-out clothing. As Ruzsky examined them, their anxious faces brought to mind the phrase put into Judge Porphyre's mouth in *Crime and Punishment*: *"Raskolnikov's crime is the work of a mind over-excited by theories."*

As he reached the waterfront, he saw a few droshky drivers waiting for hire, but he ignored their shouts and continued on past Konradi's sweetshop on the corner, where the servants had brought him and Dmitri to spend their weekend pocket money.

Ruzsky waited for a tram to cross in front of him as he was buffeted by a sudden gust of wind on the Nicholas Bridge. The dawn sun washed the sky a delicate and subtle shade of red. The lamps hissed. Those on the waterfront were the last to be lit and put out.

It was cold, the Arctic wind still whistling down the Neva with startling ferocity. Ruzsky's cheeks stung and his feet grew numb. He recalled running across the bridge to Konradi's and reflected upon the way he still physically shuddered almost every time he thought of his schooldays. As he turned onto Horseguards, he considered, as he often did, how different his life would have been if he'd followed the course prescribed for him.

Would it, in fact, have been easier?

The giant semicircular colonnade of the Kazan Cathedral had been inspired by St. Peter's in Rome, and this morning, as always, there were beggars standing on the steps at its entrance—mostly women with young children. Ruzsky stepped into the relative warmth of the cathedral's interior. It was packed already; small groups stood in front of icons and candles, their heads bent in prayer. Ruzsky bought a candle from the nearest booth and joined a group close to the altar. He lit the candle and placed it in the metal holder, crossing himself as he did so.

The priest's murmured prayers were answered by a choir on the mezzanine floor at the far end of the cavernous hall. Ruzsky breathed out. He did not believe in God, but for as long as he could recall, he had found the church's rituals soothing.

Ruzsky crossed himself once more and then began to wander amongst the other worshipers. All around, pale blue spirals of incense drifted up toward the vaulted ceiling. He walked behind one of the great columns and stood directly before the altar, beneath the great chandelier that hung from the dome.

He searched the faces around him, without success. He was moving toward the darker corners down one wing of the cathedral when he saw her.

Her expression in repose, it seemed to him, had a wistful quality. But a slow smile spread across her face as he approached. "Hello, Sandro," she whispered. "I thought you might come here."

They stood close together, looking at the golden sun above the altar and listening to the priest's mournful liturgy. "I got your note," Ruzsky said.

"You will come?"

"Of course."

Maria was still looking toward the altar. "Perhaps I should not have asked you."

Ruzsky's heart beat a little faster.

"You are chief investigator once more?"

"Yes."

"So we can sleep easily in our beds again." She smiled at him, then gazed back toward the altar.

"We found two bodies on the Neva yesterday. In front of the Winter Palace."

"Who were they?"

"We don't know," Ruzsky said. He recalled Irina's accusation that he never communicated, about anything. "They were badly mutilated."

She turned to him suddenly. "Sandro, I . . ." She was biting her lip and he could see the confusion in her face.

"My wife has left me," he said quickly, before she could go on. "She made her choice."

"It may be that we now live in a world without choices."

"Things change."

"Yes." Maria looked into his eyes. "Things change. But we must stay friends. We can achieve that, can't we?"

"Of course."

She was flustered. "I have to go. You will be there tonight?"

He nodded, not trusting himself to speak.

He watched her go. When she reached the door, she turned once, hesitated for a second, and then slipped out into the cold light.

Ruzsky went first to the duty desk, where the officer that he'd dealt with yesterday sat slumped forward, his face on the report book, fast asleep. His mouth was squashed open and he snored quietly.

"Good morning."

The man sat bolt upright, with startled eyes.

"I'm sorry, sir."

Ruzsky grinned. "It is a Sunday, after all. How long have you been on the night shift?"

"Two weeks. This is my last one."

"Good. You look like you need some sleep." Ruzsky reached for the report book and glanced at the previous day's record of assaults, burglaries, and random acts of street violence. Many more than he ever remembered. "Get me Missing Persons again, would you?"

The officer hurried to oblige.

There were no new entries.

"Nothing there, sir?"

"No."

"Who were they?"

Ruzsky looked at the man for a second. "We don't know," he said.

"Revolutionaries?"

Ruzsky frowned. "Why do you say that?"

"It's what the others think. Out there in front of the palace."

Ruzsky shook his head. He assumed the men had been talking about yesterday's visit from the Okhrana. "I think they're wrong. When's your relief?"

"In an hour, sir. If he's on time."

"Tell him if there is any report of someone missing, I want to be told immediately."

There was a pile of papers on his desk, placed there after he'd left the previous evening. On top was a note from the fingerprint bureau asking for written authorization to begin a search. He filled in the form, ticked the box marked *criminal suspects only*, and placed it in his "out" tray. The one thing common to all departments of the Tsar's government was their insane level of bureaucracy.

Ruzsky looked at his pocket watch. He picked up the telephone ear-piece and waited for a connection. He asked the operator for the line to Tsarskoe Selo and it was answered immediately.

"May I speak with Colonel Shulgin please?"

"Who is calling?"

"Investigator Ruzsky of the Petrograd Police Department."

"What is it concerning?"

"I'd rather explain to the colonel in person."

"One minute, please."

Ruzsky waited and waited, drumming his fingers impatiently on his desk.

"Are you still there?" the voice asked eventually.

"Yes."

"I'm afraid Colonel Shulgin is engaged. He will telephone you later this morning."

"I'd like to speak to him now." Ruzsky was aware of the sharpness in his voice.

"He is otherwise engaged."

"I'll wait."

"He will be engaged for some time."

"This is a murder investigation."

Ruzsky heard the man sigh. "Colonel Shulgin will telephone you later this morning."

"Do you have any idea how long he will be? I have to go out."

"I'm afraid not."

Ruzsky terminated the call. He thought the arrogance of the palace staff in the face of the current popular mood defied belief. He looked at his pocket watch again.

Downstairs, Sarlov was drinking from a tin cup full of strong Turkish cof-fee. There was another corpse on the slab, covered by a single white sheet, folded back at the top. The victim was an old man.

"A drunk," Sarlov explained. "Froze to death."

There was a light on in the corner, but the room was mostly in shadow. The smell made Ruzsky gag, but he didn't recoil. It irritated

Sarlov when detectives were in a hurry to get away. He appeared to prefer the company of corpses to that of humans. There were times when Ruzsky couldn't bring himself to blame him.

"So," Ruzsky said.

"So . . . what?"

"Any further thoughts?"

"I'm thinking about whether you have a cigarette."

Ruzsky took out the silver case and walked around the corpse's head, offering Sarlov a cigarette and then lighting one for himself. They smoked in a silence that was almost companionable. Ruzsky stared at the old man in front of him. His face was as white as marble.

"It's a Sunday morning," Sarlov said. "I'm not officially working."

"I can see."

"You don't know who they are, do you?" Sarlov said. "Or why they were taken?"

Ruzsky pointed with his cigarette. "The girl was called Ella. She worked in the nursery at Tsarskoe Selo—"

Sarlov whistled quietly.

"She was fired, apparently for stealing."

"That's what they told you?"

"Yes."

"But you didn't believe them?"

"I'd hesitate to say that. It was the Empress who told me."

"You spoke to her? She consented to see you?" Sarlov couldn't keep the incredulity out of his voice.

"I wouldn't put it quite like that."

"I was forgetting . . . your fine lineage and noble connections," Sarlov said, with what might or might not have been irony.

"I went out to see Vyrubova," Ruzsky said, "and the Empress walked in during the course of our interview."

"This is the same Vyrubova who is, or was, an intimate of both Rasputin and the Empress?"

"Yes."

"What is the girl supposed to have stolen?" Sarlov asked.

"Money, they said. But I'm not sure I believed them about that either."

"How did she look?"

"Who?"

"The Empress."

Ruzsky stared at the wall. "Tired."

"She stays up late to telegraph the Germans with our war secrets."

Ruzsky didn't react. Rumors had circulated since the beginning of the war that the Empress was feeding secrets to the country of her birth. He looked at the dead couple's effects, which were still piled in the corner. He dropped his cigarette on the floor, stamped on it, and picked up the man's overcoat. "Why didn't Prokopiev take their clothes?"

"He looked at them."

Ruzsky spread out the overcoat. "A cursory glance or a proper examination?"

Sarlov shrugged. "Pretty thorough."

"A few seconds?"

"A minute or more. I don't see what you're driving at."

"What was he looking for, that's what I'm driving at."

"He looked like he was checking there was no incriminating evidence," Sarlov said.

Ruzsky glanced at his colleague. This is exactly what he had been thinking, but he'd not expected the doctor to articulate it. "You said the man was American," Ruzsky went on.

"Possibly foreign," Sarlov said, correcting him.

"We might know by later on this morning, or perhaps tomorrow. Pavel has a lead down at the United States embassy."

Ruzsky looked at the patch where the label in the overcoat had been removed, then turned out the inside pockets. There was still a little dirt there. He faced Sarlov. "Did the girl die instantly?"

"Most unlikely. Why?"

"I can't get a clear view of this. Once we establish both their identities, in what direction should we be looking? Is it a crime of passion, a professional assassination, a family feud? What do you think? I mean, forgetting the Okhrana's behavior for a moment and just considering the crime scene itself." Ruzsky put the overcoat down and turned to the man's jacket. Labels had been removed from the collar and the inside pocket.

Sarlov stubbed his own cigarette out on the corner of the table, then flicked it into the iron wastepaper bin. "I've been thinking about it, too. Let's start at the beginning. I would say the murderer was tall. Take the woman. From what I could see, a healthy incision, but high. Forceful. Overhand." He simulated the action. "Then the man." Sarlov looked at the position he had once occupied on the slab. He pushed his glasses up his nose. His hair was wilder than yesterday. "Stabbed once initially, also overhand and quite high, coming down—remember the cuts on his face." He raised his arm once more. "Then again. And again. And again, and again, and again, and again—"

"I get the picture."

"You see what I'm saying?"

"No."

"The murderer is angry. More than angry. This is a deep, atavistic rage, certainly not the work of a professional assassin. You do not stab so many times to be certain of the man's death. Nor do you plan to do so in the snow, in full sight of the Winter Palace. This isn't some petty squabble over money or . . . something trivial."

"All right, Sarlov. I see."

"Do you?"

"Yes."

"The murderer's anger is directed principally at the man—that is my other point. It is an elementary, but nonetheless important, observation. The murder of the woman is purely functional. There is no anger against her, he just needs to get that done, before he turns to the man. That is why he is here and . . . bang, an explosion of rage. I'm not sure I've ever seen anything quite like it."

"You make it sound like a lover's quarrel," Ruzsky said.

"It could be." Sarlov was interested in drawing conclusions from the medical facts at his disposal, not in dreaming up explanations.

"And the branded star on the man's shoulder doesn't ring any bells for you? You've never seen anything like it before, don't recall hearing of anything similar?"

Sarlov shook his head.

"Can you think of any potential explanation?"

"That's your job. It could be anything."

"What created it, then? What was it made with?"

"As you have observed, it is a branded star."

"An imprint of loyalty to an organization, or group, or society?"

"I don't know."

"A religious sect?"

Sarlov didn't answer. Ruzsky made a mental note to pursue the possibility of a religious connection.

He stared ahead, lost in thought, then turned back to the clothes. The branded star rang a bell somewhere in his mind. Was it in a case he himself had investigated, or something he had read about? He picked up the man's boots. They had tiny holes in both soles, like his own. He caught sight of something on the heel and held them up to the light. "Have you got a magnifying glass?" he asked.

The physician rumbled around in a drawer and then came over, cleaning his glasses and looking up as Ruzsky held both the boots and the magnifying glass to the light. "Do you see that?"

"No."

"The maker's name has been worn down, but you can see something. I think it is 'amburg.' The 'H' has gone. Hamburg. That's where they were made."

Sarlov nodded. "He could be German."

Sarlov took the magnifying glass and returned it to his drawer. Ruzsky examined the man's trousers, turning them inside out. "If the murderer was that angry," he said, "that insane—"

"I did say angry; I did not say mad. Sane men do diabolical things," Sarlov insisted, with some feeling.

"His blood is up and yet, once he is done, the girl is, according to you, probably still alive, bleeding to death on the ice. The murderer bends over her and starts ripping the labels from her clothes. Then he or she goes to the man and does the same. The man's body is covered in blood, which is everywhere, freezing quickly. This all takes time. Five minutes. Longer. It is the middle of the night, but the moon is bright and the danger of being seen must be high. There is no easy escape. You must walk far in each direction to get away from the scene and the murderer has decided that he must leave no prints. It's brutal, methodical, but also amateurish. The murderer goes to the trouble of placing his footprints in those of his victims and then abandons that plan as he gets close to the embankment."

Looking at the overcoat, Ruzsky could not quite believe that the murderer had been able to so thoroughly remove all clues as to the man's identity in a few, rushed minutes out on the ice.

"Do you think he got this coat in Hamburg as well?" Ruzsky asked, holding it up to the light once more.

"Do I look like an expert in international fashion?"

Ruzsky shook his head. "To be honest, no."

Pavel was sitting at his desk. "Progress," he said, holding up a photograph of the male victim's body. "It's the man from the Astoria Hotel. I checked on the way in. And I got hold of the American official. He's waiting for us at the embassy."

Pavel stood. "You've a note on your desk. Another messenger. You're a popular boy."

Ruzsky picked up the envelope and turned it over. It had the seal of his brother's regiment, the Preobrazhensky Guards.

The letter was on thick, yellowish paper.

My dear Sandro, Dmitri had written, *I shall be at the yacht club at luncheon and hope you will join me there. I shall make the assumption that your answer is affirmative, unless you get a message to me by noon.*

Ruzsky sat down and removed from the drawer the roll of ruble notes they'd found on the dead man. He realized that there was more money there than he'd first thought—the outer notes were a low denomination, but there were higher ones within. He leaned forward to count them.

Ruzsky narrowed his eyes. He took out one note and held it up to the desk lamp. He did the same with another and then with the rest. "Come and have a look at this," he said.

The big detective heaved himself from his chair and came around to look at the notes.

"See?" Ruzsky asked, holding two up to the light.

"See what?"

"Here." Ruzsky pointed. It had a series of tiny marks, in black ink, underneath the serial numbers.

Ruzsky looked closer, then at the other notes once more. "Look. They're all in some kind of order. Each note is marked with a minuscule figure in black ink inside the double-headed eagle. By the left-hand beak. You see, one, two, three, and so on. Then each note also has some of the serial numbers underlined with tiny dots."

"That could mean anything. Some teller in a bank fiddling around on a cold afternoon."

Ruzsky spread all the notes out in front of him. He rearranged them in order of the numbers inscribed by the left-hand beak of the eagle. He could see that he was right. "We've got numbers one to fourteen here. So it's a code, and the message has fourteen letters, which are to be assembled in this order. The digits underlined in the serial number must be page references from the code book. If we had that, we could see the message."

13

They found themselves faced with a long wait at the United States embassy over on Furshtatskaya. A fat, middle-aged Russian woman sat behind the reception desk and got more irritated every time Ruzsky went to inquire how much longer the official they sought might be.

He strolled around the entrance hall, glancing as he went at the pictures crowding the walls. The subject of each was inscribed on a brass plaque at the bottom of the frame. There was a watercolor of beach life in California, and another of a town house in Boston. Some government buildings in Washington were depicted in oil, along with a grand plantation house in Georgia and a panoramic view of New York.

He sat down again. The remnants of Pavel's breakfast were still visible in his mustache and on the corners of his chin.

"You smell of herring," Ruzsky said.

"I forgot to tell you. I received a call from Anton when I got home last night. We have to chair a briefing later today."

"For whom?"

"Vasilyev and an official from the Ministry of the Interior."

"Where?"

"Alexandrovsky Prospekt."

Ruzsky's heart sank at the mention of the Okhrana's gloomy headquarters. "You can do it. I don't need to go."

"Oh no." Pavel shook his head. "You want to be back in charge, you do it."

"Do you think," Ruzsky said, "that our corpse was an American intelligence agent?"

"Why do you say that?"

"Think of the banknotes. If they do contain a cipher, an encoded message . . ."

"I still think that's quite a leap."

Ruzsky did not respond. He could see Pavel knew he was right.

"You're seeing conspiracies where none exist," Pavel said. His manner had become defensive again.

"True, but it makes you wonder, that's all. Perhaps it explains why the Okhrana were so quick off the mark. Did you check his room at the Astoria?"

"Inch by inch. There's nothing there."

They sat in silence.

"Nothing at all."

"Come on," Ruzsky said, glancing up at the clock on the wall again.

"I would have thought Tobolsk might have cured you of your chronic impatience."

"I saw Vasilyev last night outside that club."

"And?"

"He was in a car and opened the door to pick up two young girls from the street."

A tall man with small glasses, short hair, and a long, bony nose came through the door opposite them. He had an ungainly walk. "Good morning," he said, speaking Russian with a perfect Petersburg accent. "Abraham Morris. I'm sorry to have kept you waiting."

They introduced themselves.

"Come through," the man said, smiling. His voice was soft and cultured.

Morris led them up several flights of stone steps. His office was on the top floor and it enjoyed a spectacular view of the Neva. His desk was uncluttered. The filing cabinet next to it was covered in what looked like sporting trophies. On the wall, the only painting depicted a white clapboard house overlooking a long, sandy beach.

Morris invited them to sit, then went around to the other side of his desk and pulled over a chair, tugging up his trousers a fraction, just above the knee, as he lowered himself into it. Ruzsky was still staring at the picture on the wall. It had perfectly captured the extraordinary quality of the light. He'd forgotten how much he missed being surrounded by fine paintings.

"Have you been to America, Chief Investigator?"

"No," Ruzsky said, "but I'd like to go. That's a fine painting."

"I'll take that as a compliment."

"It is one of your own?"

The man smiled modestly. He leaned forward. "I telephoned the Astoria a short time ago. You have already been to see them."

"Yes," Pavel said.

Morris took a sheet of paper from a desk drawer. He glanced at it for a few moments, to refresh his memory, then replaced it. He raised his right hand, palm up. "How can I help you gentlemen?"

Ruzsky reached into his pocket for a picture of the dead man.

"Do you recognize him?"

Morris took the photograph and looked at it, pushing his glasses onto the bridge of his nose. "No."

"You have been made aware," Ruzsky asked, "that we are conducting a murder investigation?"

"Yes."

"You don't recognize the man?"

"No."

Ruzsky looked at Morris, whose gaze remained steady.

"This isn't the man you warned the Okhrana about?"

"I don't know."

"My colleague here was informed that you warned the Okhrana to be on the lookout for a man called Robert White, an armed robber from Chicago."

"Correct."

"Is that the same man as the Robert Whitewater who has not paid his bill at the Astoria?"

"It is likely. But I cannot say for certain." Morris handed back the photograph.

"But you don't know if this is him?"

"No, as I've said."

"The man at the Astoria gave his address as care of the American embassy."

Morris shrugged.

"He's nothing to do with you?"

"No."

"His real name, then, is Robert White?"

"He travels under many names. He prefers to amend genuine passports, of which he appears to have an unlimited number." Morris tugged at his trousers and adjusted his eyeglasses once more. "His real name *is* White."

Ruzsky waited for Morris to go on, but the American just continued to regard him with the same level gaze. "Well, who is he, and what is he doing in St. Petersburg?"

"A warning was handed to your colleagues in the Okhrana, as you may know."

"What was the warning?"

Morris studied his feet. "It concerned his presence."

"White was an agent of yours?"

Morris looked up, but didn't blink. "Quite the reverse. He is a criminal and labor agitator of the worst kind."

"A labor agitator?"

"In the steel mills."

"Does your State Department have time to treat all American criminals in this way?"

"Robert White has incurred the wrath of some extremely important and wealthy people."

"What has he done?"

Morris shook his head slowly.

"So you were looking for him?"

"Yes."

"And you found him?"

"We had reason to believe that he was returning to St. Petersburg."

"Why did you have reason to believe that?"

Morris was progressively abandoning any attempt to appear cooperative, but Ruzsky found it hard to fathom why.

"You warned the Okhrana?"

"We asked for more information on White's previous activities here, and those of one of his Russian associates."

"But none was forthcoming?"

Morris didn't answer.

"Who was the Russian associate?"

"You will have to ask your colleagues in the Okhrana."

Ruzsky thought he detected a hint of a challenge in Morris's eyes. He held up the photograph. "Is this White?"

"If not, then he has slipped the net again."

"The man had no identification on him. But our pathologist said he thought it was possible that this man was an American, judging by his dental work."

"I couldn't say."

"Could you get your State Department to send a description?"

Morris looked from Ruzsky to Pavel and back again. He seemed to be assessing them. "Your photograph fits the description."

"So this is White?"

"I didn't say that."

"But then you're not saying anything very much."

Morris stood. "I'm grateful to you gentlemen for stopping by."

Ruzsky did not move. "Why here?" he asked. "Why now? A criminal and labor agitator?"

Morris did not answer. He was staring out of the window toward the Admiralty spire.

"An American with a history of labor agitation in his native country comes to Russia at a time when all the talk is of revolution against the rule of the tsars."

"Mr. White is considerably more interested in crime than revolution." Morris smiled warily. "And your colleagues in the Okhrana are quite adept at keeping watch on political activists."

"So they knew this man was in Petersburg?"

"I informed them six weeks ago, just as I have told you."

"That you believed White was on his way to Russia?"

"Precisely."

"And the Okhrana did not reply?"

Morris shook his head.

"You have heard nothing from them?"

Morris gave them a tight but knowing smile. Ruzsky got the impression he didn't like the Okhrana very much.

"Who did you speak to?"

Morris shook his head.

"Something tells me, sir," Ruzsky said gently, "that there are other things you could choose to share with us."

Morris smiled, his eyebrows arched. "An investigator's instinct?"

"The look on your face."

"It is not my city," Morris said, shaking his head. "Not my country."

"Not the American way."

Morris smiled again. "Not the American way, no." He looked at Pavel and then back at Ruzsky. "Good day, gentlemen. And good luck."

For a moment, in the cold street outside, Ruzsky and Pavel stood in silence, each with their own thoughts, Morris's evident suspicion of the Okhrana hanging between them. "So it was White," Pavel said. His expression was serious.

"Yes."

"Robert White. What do you think he was doing here?"

"I have no idea, but I think Morris probably does."

"He's suspicious of us," Pavel went on.

"Or of the Okhrana, or of the city, or of Russia. He looked to me like a man with too much knowledge, who no longer feels confident of drawing distinctions."

Pavel stared disconsolately at the ground.

"Will you call the Okhrana records office? See if you can get some hint of what they have on White."

"You're joking, right?"

"You might slip through the net. Why would the records library know what the senior officers are doing?"

"You've been away, don't forget. No one does anything over there without authorization now, even the most basic query. Vasilyev's orders."

"Well, try. See what their reaction is at least."

"What are you going to do?"

"I have to go and see my brother."

"Lunch at the club?"

"I've been in Tobolsk, he's been at the front."

"Well, I hope there isn't another murder this afternoon. I'd hate anything to get in the way of your social arrangements."

Pavel walked off. Ruzsky called after him. "Fuck you, too."

Pavel turned around. "Don't forget you've got a briefing to do."

"When?"

Pavel stopped. "In your own good time."

"I think we should try and go back out to Tsarskoe Selo this afternoon."

"If you can fit it into your schedule."

"We'll go out straight after lunch and we'll brief them when we get back."

"Whatever you say, boss. Enjoy your lunch."

"Could you do me one more favor?"

"I doubt it."

"Put out an all stations bulletin. See if any of them have anything on White?"

Pavel turned on his heel and walked away.

14

At the Imperial Yacht Club, time had stood still for more than a hundred years. From the carriages parked outside alongside those for the Astoria, the drivers stamping their feet against the cold, smoking and gossiping in small groups, to the ornate, dimly lit stairwell and the gilt-edged mirrors of the dining room, it had remained resolutely the preserve of the elite within the elite.

Ruzsky walked past the boarded-up German embassy and across St. Isaac's Square, stopping to allow a car to pass. He heard the noonday gun as he reached the grand gray building's front entrance. Parked right outside stood two sleds with the distinctive gold crowns and crimson velvet upholstery of grand dukes of the Romanov dynasty.

The doorman, dressed in the club's blue and gold livery, nodded his head. "Good day, sir. Your brother is waiting in the dining room." For the first time since he'd been sent to Tobolsk, and perhaps for much longer than that, Ruzsky felt like a member of one of Russia's leading families. He took off his hat and overcoat and gave them to the doorman, who bashed a few remaining shards of ice onto the entrance mat and then handed them in turn to a porter standing behind him.

Ruzsky hesitated. He wondered who he would see.

He walked up the curved staircase toward the dining room on the first floor.

The Grand Duke Boris Vladimirovich stood in the hallway, leaning against the wall beneath a huge painting of the Neva at sunset, his portly frame straining the buttons of his uniform. He was talking conspiratorially through a cloud of cigar smoke with a man Ruzsky did not recognize.

The shock of seeing him again made Ruzsky stop dead. He could feel the hairs standing on end on the back of his neck. The Grand Duke noticed him, but made no acknowledgment.

Ruzsky felt the weight of the man's contempt and the color rise in his own cheeks before he had recovered enough to turn away and walk on.

The dining room was full. The clink of champagne glasses carried across tables, and the dust in the air, illuminated by the dull winter sun filtering through the windows, looked like gauze. Everywhere, uniforms groaned with gold braid and medals earned by acts of bureaucratic audacity.

Ruzsky steadied himself for a moment. Anyone who recognized him here would see the disgraced scion of one of the country's leading families, but if they actually appreciated the circumstances he had been reduced to—a dingy one-room apartment around Line Fourteen of Vasilevsky Island—then he'd have been thrown out onto the street.

Dmitri was already seated at the family's favored table at the far end of the room. He was staring out of the window, a tall solitary figure.

Ruzsky approached slowly, studying his brother in a way he hadn't been able to the previous night.

Dmitri's hair was longer, the first flecks of gray creeping into the area around his temples. His face was fleshier than he remembered, though his build was still slight. His eyes were bloodshot; he looked dissolute. He was in the dark green and red uniform of the Preobrazhensky's, but it looked less distinguished upon him than on either their father or uncle.

Dmitri turned around. For a moment, neither man moved.

Ruzsky searched Dmitri's face and saw the same things deep in his brother's eyes that had always been there: love tinged with loneliness, joy at their reunion tempered by the shadows of the past that nothing could dispel.

They gripped each other tight, Dmitri's hands digging into his back. Neither man appeared to want to break the embrace.

They stepped apart again.

"You look terrible," Dmitri said. He had already been drinking.

Ruzsky grinned. "You don't look so great yourself."

They both sat down. Dmitri's eyes were drawn toward the door and Ruzsky half turned to see the Grand Duke entering the dining room, still chomping on his cigar.

"Do you know what the tragedy is?" Dmitri leaned forward, his face earnest, but having lost none of his impetuous, exuberant charm. "Father knows everything. He knows it. In his heart, he understands what is going on, but nothing will shake his faith in the system. He doesn't—or won't—understand that, to the people, Boris Vladimirovich and his kind *are* the system: vulgar, lecherous, crass, whoring, drinking, debt-ridden, and corrupt beyond redemption." Dmitri took hold of his brother's arm. "Please tell me it doesn't upset you."

"What doesn't?"

"You know what I mean."

Ruzsky sighed. "That my wife is having an affair, or that my father turns a blind eye to it because he does not like me, and the recipient of her affections is a grand duke?"

Dmitri shook his head despairingly.

"If it is what Irina wants, so be it," Ruzsky said. "It's only Michael's situation that upsets me."

"The whole thing disgusts me." Dmitri leaned back. "Michael is a *Ruzsky* though, isn't he?"

Ruzsky looked up into his brother's eyes and saw there exactly what Dmitri was thinking—that Michael could have passed for Ilya—even if his words had not intended to convey it. Dmitri immediately looked away.

Ruzsky felt his pulse quicken.

They were silent. The noise in the dining room—the hubbub of conversation and the sound of silver scraping bone china—seemed unnaturally loud.

Ruzsky picked up the menu. The front was embossed with the yacht club insignia and inside, a handwritten sheet had been glued to the board.

A waiter approached, took the white linen napkin from the table, and placed it on Ruzsky's lap. "Something to drink, sir, some champagne perhaps?" He was French. All the waiters in here were.

"Damn right, Armand," Dmitri said loudly, overcompensating for the awkwardness of the moment. "It's a reunion. Brothers back from the dead."

"Dom Perignon?"

"Let me look at the list."

Armand hurried away and returned with it a few seconds later. Dmitri consulted it and then looked up. "Dom Perignon, yes. Make sure it is properly chilled."

"Of course, sir." An assistant scurried away.

Ruzsky stared at the menu. He was crucifyingly hungry.

"*Vous avez choisi?*" The waiter smiled at both of them.

Ruzsky examined the menu with exaggerated care. "The fish and the venison."

"The same," Dmitri said.

Another waiter approached with a silver bucket and their champagne. He opened the bottle and poured it into tall crystal glasses. Ruzsky wondered if his brother was still in debt. Before the war, Dmitri had always eaten here because he was able to use their father's account.

"Begin at the beginning," Ruzsky said. "Tell me what happened."

Dmitri waved his hand dismissively. He lit a cigarette. "What is there to bloody say? Everything you hear is true. Thankfully, I nearly lost an arm, or I'd be buried in six feet of mud by now."

"At least you went. I was being serious when I said the ancestors would be proud."

Dmitri snorted. "Yes, but the point is that I've never consciously chosen to do anything in my whole damned life and you know it. All I've done is take the easy way out, and going to war was the easy route. Not going would have been impossible. You know how Father is. And as to our ancestors being proud, believe me, no one could do anyone proud out there, it's not possible. The war is a disgrace not just to Russia but to mankind and somone will be made to pay for it."

Dmitri's voice had risen an octave and Ruzsky noticed they had attracted a few curious and disapproving glances from a group of older men at the neighboring table. "It's as bad as they say?"

"Bad! Unless you've experienced it yourself, I don't think you could possibly imagine the corruption and incompetence. The Germans are fighting a war, but we're just being massacred. I've seen battalions of our finest troops going into battle against machine guns armed only with revolvers."

"Where did you fight?"

Dmitri sighed. "Father secured me an appointment as aide-de-camp to Bezobrazov."

"What's he now, commander in chief of the Guards?"

"The old man thought it would be good for my career. We started out in Warsaw, then transferred to the southern Lublin front to join the Fourth Army and roll up the Austrian left." Dmitri hesitated, staring out of the window. "That is where we lost most of the Pavlovsky, all laid out in the morning sun, like giant brothers. I found Bibikov, without his head. I only recognized him by his family ring." Dmitri turned to him. "You remember Bibikov from the Corps?"

"Yes."

"Too conscious of himself for you, perhaps. He wasn't a bad sort."

"I know he was a friend."

Dmitri stared at his hands for a moment, then turned back to the window. "From Lublin to Ivangorod, then Warsaw, then Lomja. Back to Warsaw, south to Kholm just as the Great Retreat was getting under way. And so on. We were always short of everything, so I toured the railheads searching for ammunition like a beggar scavenging for food. I pulled a revolver on the commandant of the station at Keltsi and almost shot him. Our men were going to their deaths with solemn faces and a few rifles to share between them and meanwhile all the fat bastards in the rear, friends of Rasputin or some grand duke, were busy lining their pockets. You should look into the eyes of the men, Sandro. It would break your heart. They march to a certain death fully understanding the futility of their sacrifice. When the Germans started using gas, the respirators we were promised in Lomja ended up in Warsaw by mistake and a telegram from headquarters suggested we tell the men to urinate in a handkerchief and tie it around their faces." Dmitri was staring at him now. "And, amongst all this, they are commanded by officers who, with a few honorable exceptions—and they perish soon enough—billet themselves to the rear of the front and visit it only to shout at their men for not polishing their boots—when they are lucky enough to have boots, because I've seen soldiers fighting barefoot."

"How did you get hurt?"

It took Dmitri a few moments to gather his strength. "The Great

Eastern Offensive in July. We were ordered to advance to the section of the front between the Third and Eighth Armies. The idea was to break through at one spot and cavalry charge the Germans." Dmitri took a sip of his champagne. "Actually, a ridiculous plan. I went out as an observer with the Rifle Division. And the section chosen for our attack turned out to be a bog. Brusilov told us not to advance, but our commander knew better, so in we went. Some of the men sank and drowned. And since the Germans were on high ground, the rest were mowed down. We lost more than fifty thousand officers and men and it was my unbelievable good fortune to be cut down in the first arc of fire, before we hit the swamp."

Dmitri stared at the table in silence. He took a gigantic gulp of champagne, then drained the rest of the glass. He took the bottle from the silver bucket and refilled it. "And excuse me for saying it, but Father tolerates the wife of his eldest son having an affair while living under his roof because she is fucking a *grand duke*. All is well and good, then. Boris Vladimirovich. Look at him."

The group at the next table were now staring at them and Ruzsky felt a powerful urge to turn and look at the Grand Duke on the far side of the room, but he resisted it.

"It's *disgusting*." Dmitri drained his glass again. "It is *all* disgusting. But it is all *over*. We are on the edge of the abyss now, there is no question about it, and you should be careful, Sandro."

"About what?"

"You see yourself differently from the way others perceive you. You know you're Sherlock Holmes, but the mob doesn't have the faintest idea who he is."

"The mob? Isn't that going a bit far?"

"No."

Ruzsky shrugged. He thought the champagne was forming his brother's words. "I'll be all right."

"You think so? Do you know that . . ." Dmitri looked ostentatiously around the room. "I'm prepared to make you a very large wager. Your annual police department salary, or more, that at every single table in this room, conversation has already turned to how much longer Nicholas II is going to be the Tsar of all the Russias. Boris Vladimirovich wouldn't give him more than a month. And that's just as a result of the five plots *he's* involved in."

"They always talk."

"It's gone beyond that." Dmitri leaned forward and almost knocked over his glass. "They killed Rasputin for Christ's sake." Dmitri had spoken loudly and now they were definitely attracting disapproving glances. "The woman's lover. And got away with it!"

"Keep your voice down."

"Why? Surely you don't think that is heresy anymore? Look in the faces of soldiers you pass in the street. All those who have been to the front know the truth. The regime is morally bankrupt. Finished. The occupants of this room chit and chat about what will replace it; the rest of the world waits for the whole thing to go up with an enormous bang."

A waiter arrived with their fish. Ruzsky examined it for a moment, turning the plate in his hand. *"C'est bien, monsieur?"*

"Bien sûr." Ruzsky smiled. *"Bien sûr."*

"When was the last time you had anything decent to eat?"

Ruzsky peeled back the skin, then took another sip of champagne. "I don't know."

"You should come around to the house during the day, when Father's at work. One of the servants will feed you."

"Irina is there."

"Of course." Dmitri showed no interest in eating his food. He refilled his own glass once more. "Why is she there, anyway?"

"She enjoys the effect it has on me."

"Surely even she is not that . . ." Dmitri smiled again. "All right, she is that evil."

"How is Ingrid? You didn't really say."

"She is fine. Fine, fine, fine. Always fine. We tolerate each other. We always do."

"She tolerates your wandering still?"

"In a manner of speaking. From time to time, I even wander into the marital bed, though I can't say it is exactly a stimulating experience . . . It's good to see you smile, brother Sandro." Dmitri shook his head. "However, my occasional forays into doing my duty do not seem to have achieved the requisite result. We are heirless, unlike you."

"Another reason why Irina stays at home."

"I still don't understand that. Her own parents are alive."

"But not as rich."

"She is a witch!" Dmitri laughed. Ruzsky had forgotten how much he enjoyed his brother's company. "Burn her!"

The old men at the next table frowned at them again, but now Ruzsky was also enjoying their discomfort. He refilled his own glass before the waiter could reach the bucket.

"Actually," Dmitri said, with a sly smile, "I have acquired another little asset."

"Who is she?"

"That's for me to know and you to speculate about."

"So are you going to tell me, or do I have to beat it out of you?"

"You have my permission to try and drink it out of me." Dmitri raised the champagne bottle. "Another, Armand!" He looked at Ruzsky. "After all, it is not every day you have a reunion with your long lost, deeply loved, elder brother." He held up his glass. "I drink to you, Sandro. The only true Ruzsky among us all. And to the end of the Empire."

This was too much for the men at the next table. Rather than risk a scene, they waved across the head waiter and demanded to move. The only vacant table was right at the back of the room, underneath the picture of the *Standart*. They glowered as they went.

"Pompous farts," Dmitri said. He leaned forward. "They think they're saving us, you know, with all this talk, but we're doomed, and they don't know it."

Ruzsky didn't reply. He finished his fish. "Have mine," Dmitri said, pushing his plate clumsily across the table.

"I'm not that hungry."

"You look thin."

"I never look thin."

Dmitri watched as Ruzsky cleared his plate as well. "So tell me about her?" Ruzsky asked. "This 'little asset.' "

"I know what you're thinking, but it's different." Dmitri waved his finger. "Three years, and no one else."

"Apart from your wife."

"Don't mock. I'm a new man."

"No more carousing until dawn? No more scandalizing society? Just *one* mistress?"

"You can laugh at me all you like."

Ruzsky looked into his brother's bloodshot eyes. "So you're telling me you're in love?"

"It is not, you know, solely the preserve of Sandro the poet."

"Is she married?"

"No. She lost the love of her life shortly before we first met. Off to the war, I suppose."

"She wishes to be your wife or is she happy to be your mistress?"

"She revels in the term."

"Does she know Ingrid?"

"Now you are joking."

"So who is she?"

"It's a secret, damn it."

"I'm not going to beg you to tell me."

"It would make no odds if you did."

"Nothing is a secret in Petersburg. It never has been."

"Well you're the chief investigator. You find out." Dmitri smiled. A wave of hair flopped down onto his forehead. His nose and cheeks were red. "I shall tell you one day."

"I won't hold my breath."

Dmitri looked up. "You know," he said, "I would do anything for her. Anything." He paused. "Have you ever been in love, Sandro? Truly in love."

"I don't know."

"We talked about it so many times."

"You scorned the idea of it, as I recall."

Dmitri stared into his glass, then drained it.

"How are your soldiers here?" Ruzsky asked.

"My *soldiers*?" Dmitri laughed, perhaps pleased that his brother had changed the subject. "They're a rabble, worse than a rabble. Do you know, there is not a single regular battalion in Petrograd. All the units you see are reserve battalions, full of peasants. Every time we go out on a training exercise, I feel this itch in the middle of my back and wonder which of them will shoot me first. It's pathetic, not like the old days at all, but that's what happens if you send Russia's best to be mowed down. Father came to dinner at the mess last week and complained bitterly on the way out about the slovenly way some of the men had dressed and how he'd seen several slouching while on duty." Dmitri laughed. "As I've said, the older generation thinks everything is somehow going to stay the same."

"If things are as bad as you say, what will you do?"

"What do you mean, what will I do?"

"You will leave Petersburg?"

"Of course not. Don't be a fool, man. I've survived the front. What could be worse than that? If it is as bad as we all fear, I will go down in flames, all hands on deck, firing until the good ship disappears below the waves. Armand! Where's our main course?" The waiter hurried away again and Dmitri leaned forward. "The service here is a disgrace." He took hold of his brother's arm. "I'll assist you, Sandro, in any way that I can. I'll bring Michael and we can arrange to meet. Every day, if you like. Ingrid will help. She loves Anton, and anyway, Irina is always out in the afternoons."

Ruzsky felt his cheeks flushing again. Despite himself, the idea of Irina hurrying from the house to spend her afternoons with the bloated figure behind him—no doubt in a suite at the Astoria or the Hôtel de l'Europe—gnawed away at him. He thought of Michael playing alone in the garden.

Dmitri was staring at him. His expression was as he so often remembered it: earnestly seeking approval. Ruzsky locked hands with him and tried to return his desperate affection, recalling Dmitri's distress on the night of their brother's death: the urgency with which he clutched him on the way down to their father's study; the gabbled assertion that he had been too far away to reach Ilusha, and had shouted and shouted in an attempt to stop him.

Ruzsky withdrew his hand. The intervening years suddenly fell away.

"I'll do anything to help, Sandro. Anything at all."

15

Ruzsky was glad of the time alone with Pavel on the train to Tsarskoe Selo. For most of the way, they sat in companionable silence, looking out at the pine forests and fields covered in a thick blanket of snow. Ruzsky watched a woodsman clambering up toward the track. He carried an ax and had a stack of firewood on his back, snow and ice in his beard, and thick leather skins wrapped around his feet and shins.

Pavel was a comforting presence. Ruzsky envied the way he kept his life simple, envied his unwavering loyalty to the people and causes he believed in.

It did occur to him, however, that his friend wasn't quite his old self. He appeared more nervous and defensive, but perhaps it was just a sign of the times.

Perhaps Pavel was right; the case was best ignored. But Ruzsky knew it had moved well past the stage where he could forget it. He'd once told Irina in an argument that the foremost talent an investigator could possess was persistence—to be like a dog with a bone.

Persistence is not a talent, she had replied, and I don't want to be a bone.

"When you're on the run," Ruzsky said, "you surely don't head for the most aggressive police state in the world? If you're an American, I mean, like this man White."

Pavel didn't answer.

"What do you think?" Ruzsky asked.

"You know what I think. It stinks. You know it, I know it. That's why Morris behaved the way he did."

Pavel turned and stared out of the window at the frozen landscape.

―――――

At the Alexander Palace, a servant took their coats and led them into an ornate antechamber. Pavel looked immediately ill at ease. "Don't gawp," Ruzsky whispered.

"It's all right for you. You were born into this."

"Hardly." Ruzsky walked to the windows. The children were skating on the ornamental lake. He could see the grand duchesses, but not the Tsarevich.

The Tsar's daughters were wearing tight-fitting dark overcoats and fur hats. They were hitting a ball to each other across the ice with sticks under the careful watch of two men seated on the bank. Ruzsky wondered how much they knew of the politics of the empire their brother would inherit.

The scene felt more normal to him than it had on his first visit, but Pavel looked dumbstruck.

Although he had once told his father during an argument that it was inevitable, Ruzsky found it hard to imagine life without a tsar.

He turned to see a tall man striding across the room toward them. The head of the palace household was in uniform and wore a monocle, an officer of the old school. To his chest was pinned the dark blue ribbon and silver star of the Order of the White Eagle, marking him out as being of the highest rank of the civil service, not that there would have been any doubt.

"You are Ruzsky?"

"Yes."

"How can I help you?"

"You are Colonel Shulgin?"

"Yes."

"I am the chief investigator for the Petrograd City Police; here is my deputy. One of your employees was murdered three nights ago. Her body was found in the center of the Neva."

"A former employee."

"So I gathered from the Empress."

Colonel Shulgin pursed his lips. "It was most unfortunate and inappropriate that you came to interrogate Madam Vyrubova. You should have approached me."

Ruzsky gave a tiny bow. "My apologies, Your High Excellency," he said, using the correct form of address. "Our inquiries led me to discover that the dress the girl was wearing was made for Madam Vyrubova. I followed my nose."

Shulgin glanced from Ruzsky to Pavel and back again. "Yes," he said. "Unfortunately, I do not believe we can help you in this case. All matters pertaining to members of staff are naturally confidential."

Ruzsky took out and glanced at his pocket watch, to give himself a moment's pause for thought. Shulgin was clearly going to concede nothing easily.

"The girl and her companion were murdered, Colonel. Very brutally." Ruzsky lowered his voice. "In the climate of the times, out there, in front of the Winter Palace . . ." He inclined his head. "And the victim a palace employee. Naturally, it troubles us."

Shulgin eyed them cautiously. "If there was a suggestion of . . ." he chose his words carefully, "*political* motivation, then one would expect to be dealing with the Okhrana."

But Ruzsky could tell from the old man's face that Shulgin had no desire whatsoever to deal with Vasilyev's men.

Shulgin hesitated for a few moments more and then pointed at two stiff-backed chairs pushed up against the wall. He pulled another over from the table in the center of the room. "I have only a few minutes," he said.

They faced each other in silence.

"Ella was dismissed," Ruzsky offered.

Shulgin did not answer.

"If you do not mind me asking, Your High Excellency: why?"

The colonel stared at his highly polished boots. "That, I think, must remain a matter for the palace alone."

"For stealing?"

Shulgin looked surprised.

"Madam Vyrubova told us as much."

"Madam Vyrubova?"

"And Her Imperial Highness."

Shulgin hesitated, clearly still appalled at the way in which Ruzsky had been able to converse with the ruler of Russia, but once again unwilling to dismiss the pair of them. "Stealing. Yes. A disgraceful episode."

"How much money did the girl steal?"

Now the colonel looked confused. "Money?"

"Isn't that what she stole?" Vyrubova had told Ruzsky it was money, even if he had not wholly believed her. Now it looked as if his hunch had been right. Shulgin had frozen and appeared ready to ask them to leave, so Ruzsky changed tack. "The girl worked in the nursery."

Shulgin hesitated again. He was trying to work out how much they had already been told. "That is correct, yes."

A maid in a blue uniform with a starched white front came in with a single porcelain cup on a silver tray. Shulgin took it, stirred its contents with a silver spoon, then put it to his lips.

Ruzsky took the two photographs from his pocket. "These are only head and shoulders . . . The man was stabbed seventeen times, the girl once. The murderer followed them out onto the ice . . ."

Shulgin stared intently at the image of the man. He looked up. "Who was he?"

"We were hoping you might be able to tell us."

Ruzsky watched Shulgin's face for any reaction, but the official simply shook his head. "No, I've never set eyes on him."

Shulgin reminded Ruzsky of his father: obstinate and opinionated, but honest.

"Could you give us a few more details about the girl. When she was employed, where her family lives, and so on."

Shulgin stood. "Give me a minute, please." He marched abruptly out of the room, then returned, holding a file, which he was reading as he walked. He sat down and continued to examine it, flicking through a series of loose sheets of paper until he found what he was looking for. "Ella was from Yalta," he said. "She was twenty-two." He ran his finger down the page. "She started work at Livadia. She was employed to work in the nursery there in the summer of 1910. She would have been fifteen."

"Nineteen ten?"

"Yes. Her father died the following year and her mother moved to stay with her sister here in Petersburg. Ella asked to be transferred."

He turned further pages. "Exemplary record, until . . ."

"Until the theft?" Ruzsky prompted.

Shulgin cleared his throat. "Until then, yes."

"So she worked in the nursery here?"

"Yes."

"What did her duties involve?"

"She assisted in the nursery."

"Looking after the Tsarevich?"

Shulgin didn't respond.

"When he was sick?"

Shulgin flushed. "The Tsarevich's health is not a matter for public discussion."

"Of course not, but as a member of the household staff, and one with such an important role, she would have had access to other sections of the palace?"

Shulgin frowned.

"Presumably, the money she stole wasn't kept in the nursery."

"As I've said, the events surrounding her dismissal are a matter for the palace alone."

"What if I said that the man in the photograph I just showed to you was a notorious American criminal and labor agitator?"

Shulgin stared at him uncomprehendingly. "I do not understand . . ."

"Was she ever seen with the man? Would any of the other palace staff have met him? Who were her friends?"

Shulgin shook his head. "She was a very quiet girl. A labor agitator?"

"Yes."

"An American?"

"Yes."

"What was he doing in Petersburg?"

"That is what we would like to know." Ruzsky leaned forward. "If Ella stole something—a sum of money, or perhaps something else—then isn't it possible, indeed probable, that this man was involved? Assuming that she had never behaved in this way before . . ."

Shulgin stared out of the window, deep in thought.

"What Ella stole is of quite some significance to us, Colonel Shulgin, do you see that?"

He still did not answer.

Ruzsky glanced at Pavel. They waited.

"Ella . . . she was not a bad girl. I did not know her well, but she was quiet, shy, quite solemn. What you have said . . . a man, leading her astray, it would make some sense of her actions. The Empress . . . we were all surprised. Shocked." Shulgin gazed into the middle distance. "The Empress was very cast down by this. It was a sign of the times, in her eyes. With so many difficulties outside the palace, to be betrayed by one of your own staff, from within . . . You understand."

"She confessed to her crime?" Ruzsky asked.

Shulgin hesitated again. "Yes."

"And regretted her actions?"

"I believe so."

"Did she mention the American?"

"No."

"Or any man?"

"No."

"You never heard her refer to him in any way?"

Shulgin shook his head.

"So why did she do it?"

"I have no idea."

"Was she short of money?"

Shulgin's jaw tightened. "As I have said on several occasions, I am not prepared to discuss the circumstances of her dismissal."

Ruzsky leaned forward. "May we speak with other members of the staff? Those who knew her best, in the nursery perhaps?"

Shulgin placed the teacup on the table in front of them. "I will consider your request."

Ruzsky stretched out his hand. "Colonel Shulgin, may I look at the file?"

Shulgin opened the file again and leafed through it, removing several pages before handing it over. "It is of no further use to us."

Ruzsky and Pavel decided to walk back to Tsarskoe Selo Station, but stopped by the railings as soon as they had got far enough away from the gate to be beyond the eyes of the palace police. "What did you make of that?" Pavel asked.

"It wasn't money."

"Why not?"

"I'm just certain it wasn't. Vyrubova *was* lying. If Ella really had stolen money, why not tell us and have done with it? No, she stole something else, much more embarrassing, that Shulgin couldn't talk about."

"Perhaps they had her killed."

"Shulgin? Never. I'd say he is as confused as we are. And he's no fool. He knows how everything hangs by a thread, and he's worried. Three years ago, we'd not have made it through that gate under any circumstances."

"I think you're being too soft on them," Pavel said. "If she stole something embarrassing, who's to say they didn't arrange to have her killed? Maybe they got the Okhrana to do it. Maybe the Empress arranged it herself."

Ruzsky shook his head and opened the file. *Ella Kovyil,* it read, *Born Yalta April 12, 1895. Father Ivan, postal worker, mother Anna, 14 Ilivichi Street. Employed June 29, 1910. References: schoolteacher Mme Ivinskaya, father Ivan Alexandrovich (former NCO, Preobrazhensky Guards 1890–1906).*

"That's why she got the job," Ruzsky said. "Her father was in the Preobrazhenskys. He must have retired to the Crimea."

Unmarried. Employment record: summer 1910, assistant in nursery at Livadia, and summer 1911. Autumn 1911, requested full employment and transfer to Tsarskoe Selo. Assistant nanny with special responsibility for Tsarevich. Remains in Post.

Somebody had written, by hand, at the end of the first sheet: *Reliable. Category One.*

Ruzsky showed this to Pavel. "Categorizing staff by loyalty," he said.

"Yes, I suppose so."

Most of the rest of the file was given over to Ella's evaluations, which had been completed in December every year since she had reached Tsarskoe Selo. They were written by hand, never stretched to more than a paragraph, and signed at the bottom by Shulgin himself, alongside the palace seal.

Performs her duties adequately, the first sheet read, *and is in possession of a cheerful manner. Claims to have formed a strong bond with the Tsarevich and has expressed a desire to concentrate on looking after his needs . . .*

Ella can be somewhat careless over detail (and other nursery and household staff have had occasion to complain of poor moods and sloppy manners), but is considered reliable and honest . . .

Shy character, well suited to work in the nursery . . .

Time off is spent with mother in Petersburg . . .

Continued employment and security clearance granted.

In the evaluation for 1915, he noticed the line *acquaintance of Father Grigory.* The next year, Shulgin had written: *spends time with Rasputin and Vyrubova, at cottage here, but also in Petrograd.*

The last sheets contained details of her salary. She had begun earning ten rubles a month in Livadia, the Tsar's palace in the Crimea, but her pay had not risen much over the years and remained low right up until her dismissal.

Pavel had been reading the notes over Ruzsky's shoulder. "It's good to know someone is paid less than us," he said.

"Why give us this?" Ruzsky asked.

"What do you mean?"

"The details about Vyrubova and Rasputin. He removed several pages from the file, but he left this one in. Why?"

"I don't see what you're driving at."

"I think Shulgin was trying to help us, as far as he feels he can." Ruzsky held up the file. "He didn't have to give us this at all, and he made a point of removing several pages. Therefore what we have, we have for a reason." Ruzsky looked down again. "He has given us her background, and he's linked her to Rasputin and Vyrubova."

Ruzsky turned the page. The last sheet contained an address for Ella's mother in Petrograd.

"Something tells me," Ruzsky said, "that Ella was the real victim."

16

Ella's mother lived in a squalid tenement building in the Alexander Nevsky Quarter, but the door was locked and her neighbor told them she worked nights and had only just gone on shift.

Ruzsky and Pavel hurried back on foot to the department through the darkened, snow-covered streets, but when they got to the office, there was a note on Ruzsky's desk saying that a briefing had been fixed for Vasilyev at Alexandrovsky Prospekt at six. They were already late.

They got a droshky to take them over the ice-packed Troitzky Bridge. The spire of the St. Peter and St. Paul Fortress, bright in the moonlight, was a visible reminder at the heart of the city—as the place where the regime's enemies were confined—of the power of the man they were heading to meet.

As they disembarked outside the dimly lit entrance to Alexanderovsky Prospekt, they heard a dull mechanical roar and turned to see a green liveried car sliding to a halt behind them.

The nearside door opened and Vasilyev stood for a moment on the running board, his outstretched arms and wide black cloak making him look like a bird of prey.

He stepped down and began to stalk toward them with the slow, deliberate gait that Ruzsky recalled so well.

Vasilyev drew level and stopped. His hair was short and deep crow's feet at the edge of his temples led down to hooded, pale blue eyes that were washed out with too much knowledge. A man who could look the devil in the eye without blinking, Anton had once said. He had a pronounced scar on the right side of his forehead.

"Chief Investigator," he said. His voice was low and measured. "Welcome back."

Vasilyev led the way up into the gloomy hallway. Just as in their own headquarters, a reception desk faced them. The corridor was full of newspaper sellers and cabbies and tramps—men from the External Agency, or the Okhrana's street surveillance division. As Vasilyev walked in, their conversation became instantly subdued.

They marched down the long corridor behind him. Ruzsky glimpsed giant black presses in noisy operation as they passed the print room. He saw several leaflets scattered on the floor, but read only one headline: *Vermin of Russia*. The Okhrana's notorious anti-Jewish propaganda machine appeared to be in full swing.

Ruzsky glanced at Pavel, who was staring straight ahead, determined to avoid any chance of confrontation.

They walked into the elevator and the attendant pulled back the cage, pushed the button, and stood ramrod straight as they ascended to Vasilyev's office; it did not stop at any other floor.

Anton was already at the round wooden conference table, alongside Maretsky. There was a bespectacled official next to him—perhaps the man from the Ministry of the Interior—whom nobody bothered to introduce and who avoided Ruzsky's eye. Next to him sat Prokopiev, in a shirt and thick leather suspenders.

Vasilyev's protégé might have been wrought in his image. They were physically different—Prokopiev was tall and lean, where his master was stocky and short—but they had the same hair color, cropped close, and a similar intensity in their eyes that gave no hint of warmth or humanity. Prokopiev was head of the Internal Division, the section of the Okhrana responsible for running agents within organizations hostile to the state.

As they sat down, Pavel leaned toward Ruzsky. "Be careful," he whispered.

"Would you care to share your thoughts with us, Deputy Chief Investigator?" Vasilyev asked. He was standing behind his desk, with his back to a tall window that afforded an astonishing view of the fortress, and the frozen river beyond.

Pavel flushed.

"He told me to remember to be respectful," Ruzsky said.

"Ah," Vasilyev responded. "No need to stand on ceremony."

The chief of the secret police moved a round metal weight from some papers and shuffled them to the center of his desk, before walking over to the bookcase and leaning back against it. Above him hung a line of religious icons and pictures of the Tsar and Tsarina. Vasilyev took a silver case from the inside of his pocket. "Cigarette, anyone?"

No one answered. Ruzsky studied him. He was immaculately turned out, from his neatly groomed mustache to his highly polished shoes. His manner was precise and meticulous, and he still had the habit of obsessively removing small specks of dust from his waistcoat as he spoke.

"Would you like some English tea?" Vasilyev asked. It was a question to all of them, but directed at Ruzsky.

"No."

"Your father is well?"

Ruzsky hesitated. He wondered if the question was designed to humiliate him. "I believe so."

Vasilyev lit his cigarette. He held it away from his body, so that the ash did not fall upon his suit. "Anton Antipovich has told me a little, but perhaps you would care to expand. You found two bodies on the Neva. Who were they?"

Ruzsky scrutinized the table in front of him. It was inconceivable that Vasilyev had called the meeting in ignorance; he wondered how much he already knew, and how little he could get away with telling him. "You have the bodies," he said caustically.

Vasilyev betrayed no visible reaction. "But you have still been working on the case, is that not so?"

"The girl was called Ella."

"Her family name?"

"Kovyil."

"Kovyil?" Vasilyev frowned and glanced at Prokopiev. "Does that sound familiar?"

Prokopiev shrugged, but Ruzsky could see that it was a charade. They both knew precisely who she was. "She worked in the nursery out at Tsarskoe Selo," he said, since he was certain they must know that, too.

"You should have informed me immediately that the girl was a palace employee."

"We only found out this afternoon," Ruzsky lied.

"And the man?"

"As I said, you have the bodies."

"We wished to ascertain that the murder was not the work of a political assassin."

"And have you done so?"

"Indeed we have. But I repeat. It is your belief, is it not, that the course of the overall investigation remains under the jurisdiction of the Petrograd City Police Department."

To buy himself time, Ruzsky pulled out his own cigarette case and lit up. "We believe the dead man was probably an American called Robert White."

Ruzsky watched Vasilyev's face for a reaction.

Apparently unperturbed, Vasilyev drew deeply on his cigarette. "An American?"

"So it would appear."

"How did you discover this?"

"Sarlov thought he might be, from his dental work. So we went to the embassy and asked."

"And they confirmed it?"

"Yes."

"How could they be so sure?"

"They were looking for him."

"Looking for him? Here?"

Ruzsky watched his opponent. "He was a criminal and labor agitator."

"A labor agitator?" Vasilyev turned back to Prokopiev. "Ivan?"

Prokopiev shrugged again.

"You've never heard of him?" Ruzsky asked.

Prokopiev blinked, but did not feel the need to reply.

"You've spoken to Shulgin?" Vasilyev asked. He clearly knew that they had.

"Yes."

"What did he have to say?"

"Ella worked in the nursery at the Alexander Palace. She was from Yalta. Perhaps you remember her?" He noticed a muscle twitch in

Prokopiev's cheek. "I believe you were chief of police in the city at the time, and Ivan your deputy?"

"Why should either of us remember her?" Prokopiev asked.

"No reason."

They were silent. The man from the Ministry of the Interior stared at his notepad. Ruzsky needed no further evidence that the city's overall chief of police, Prince Obolensky, was no longer in control. In the deteriorating political climate, all power had passed to the man in front of them.

"Go on," Vasilyev said.

"Ella was dismissed for stealing."

"Stealing what?"

"I don't know."

"Money?"

"Probably."

Vasilyev was now standing with his back to them, staring out of the window.

"The man had a small branded star on his right shoulder," Ruzsky said.

The official from the Ministry looked up and scribbled something on the notepad in front of him. But Vasilyev remained unmoved.

"In addition to which, the killer went to considerable effort to strip them of anything that might identify them."

"So you *are* saying it was a political crime," Vasilyev went on.

Ruzsky shook his head. "The man was stabbed seventeen times . . ."

"But the girl was a palace employee." Vasilyev's tone was emphatic.

Ruzsky glanced around the room. Anton shifted nervously in his seat. Pavel stared dead ahead.

Vasilyev took a pace forward. "Thank you, gentleman. That will be all."

For a moment, nobody moved, then Pavel stood, looking relieved.

"A word in private, Sandro," Vasilyev said, as he turned to leave.

The others filed out, but the man from the Ministry of the Interior stayed where he was. He seemed to relax a little, leaning back in his chair.

Vasilyev still had the remains of the cigarette in his hand. He stubbed it out in a big silver ashtray on his desk then lit another. He picked at his suit. "It is difficult," he said, "isn't it, when we cannot be certain of the victims' identity, especially in these times, when our manpower is stretched so thin?"

"Criminal investigations are rarely as straightforward as we would like them to be."

"But times have changed, Sandro. Our concerns are so . . ." Vasilyev spread his hands, "broad. I think we could view this as a lover's argument. A man, a woman . . ."

"So, they killed each other?"

"Don't play the fool with me, Ruzsky." Vasilyev chose his words carefully. "I had a telephone call this morning, from the Alexander Palace. From the Empress herself. You can, perhaps, imagine my dilemma." Vasilyev stubbed out his cigarette, in a manner that hinted at the anger bubbling under his cloak of self-control. "Or could if you weren't so damned *arrogant*."

Ruzsky fought hard to keep his voice level. "This is a murder. A criminal case, and therefore under the jurisdiction of the chief of the city police, according to the dictates of the Ministry of the Interior." He paused. "There is no sign of political motivation. As soon as there is, we will pass over the evidence we have accumulated to this department."

Vasilyev glared at him.

"Will that be all?" Ruzsky asked.

"There are other matters that require your attention, I'm sure."

"But none as important."

"So the Tsar is no longer to be obeyed?" Vasilyev's voice was like velvet. "Is that what you think?"

"I think that now, more than ever, there is a need for justice."

Vasilyev's face darkened. "It is the Tsar or the mob, Ruzsky. You would do well to remember that."

Ruzsky turned away. He could almost feel the fury at his back, propelling him down the corridor.

17

At the headquarters of the Petrograd City Police Department, they were waiting for him in Anton's office. Ruzsky sat down heavily, staring at the picture of Napoleon's retreat on the wall opposite. He could see that the others were nervous and apprehensive.

"He invited me to close the case on the grounds that it had proved impossible to establish the identities of the victims," Ruzsky said solemnly.

No one replied.

"He said he had received a call from Tsarskoe Selo, and that I must understand his *dilemma*."

Pavel leaned forward. "Do you think that's true?"

"Why wouldn't it be?"

"Shulgin seemed concerned to me, and uncertain, rather than hostile."

They considered this. Ruzsky looked into the eyes of his colleagues. They wanted to appear defiant, but none could entirely hide their fear.

Anton sighed deeply. "Vasilyev is a powerful and dangerous enemy, now more than ever."

"But still not omnipotent."

"I'm not so sure." Anton suddenly looked old. "It has a pleasing hint of irony about it, don't you think? In the dying hours of the regime, we loyally carry out the tasks assigned to us in the name of a tsar that none of us believes in, while those who once professed fanatical loyalty to the absolute monarch now prepare themselves for the moment when he is no longer with us."

"I don't understand," Ruzsky said.

"What do you think our friend Vasilyev has been doing these past weeks?"

"I can't imagine."

"He's been a very, very busy man. Meetings and telephone calls. Reading telegrams and letters. Those to him and those intercepted. He speaks to the generals, the politicians, and the grand dukes. He even talks to the revolutionaries." Anton raised his hand. "You won't believe it, but trust me, he does. How can I manage this for maximum advantage, he asks. He could stay loyal to the Tsar, as he claims, but he knows it's moving beyond that. Change is coming, so which way is it going to blow and how can he be seen to assist it? Strikes, demonstrations, protests; the appearance of disorder. He can orchestrate them all. The generals and politicians and grand dukes could then claim they were forced to take resolute action. But, of course, if Vasilyev and his agents get it wrong . . . then who knows what could happen?"

"He just told me that the choice was between the Tsar and the mob."

"And he is right."

"If he is that preoccupied, then why bother to interfere with us?"

They sat in silence again. None of them could answer this.

"It doesn't smell good," Pavel said. "They were warned this American was coming back. And when he does, he gets seventeen stab wounds for his trouble."

"And yet," Ruzsky went on, "we cannot get away from the fact that, to all of us, their deaths still feel personal."

They looked to Maretsky. He examined his chubby hands. As a professor of philosophy at the university, he had developed a passionate interest in the criminal mind and had been brought in by Anton—after his disgrace—on a part-time basis to assist in investigations. Shortly afterward, Vasilyev had seen the value of his work and had requested—or rather, they believed, coerced—his assistance too. "I see only files," Maretsky said, "and sometimes individuals. I would be the last person they would tell."

"What do you think lies beneath this case?"

"I don't know. I've never heard of White or the girl. Never seen any paperwork on either of them. But then, if it was something they wanted to keep from you, I wouldn't see it either."

"Why have they warned us off?"

"I don't know."

"Did they—"

"Sandro, I can see the questions. I just don't have the answers."

They glanced at each other. Pavel seemed suddenly less than pleased at the idea of being one of a band of brothers, but there was warmth in Anton's eyes.

"We cannot easily trace the American," Ruzsky said. "So we must begin by following the path of the girl. If any of you want to stay officially neutral, then now's the time to make that clear."

There was an awkward silence.

Pavel got to his feet. His face was strained. He came level with Ruzsky, raised his head, looked apologetically into his eyes, and then slapped him so hard on the back that he almost choked. "God, Sandro," he guffawed, "you're a pain in the ass."

Pavel went home and Ruzsky retired gratefully to his office. He shut the door, switched on his lamp, and sat behind his desk in the half-darkness.

He extracted the ticket Maria had sent him for the ballet from his pocket, and glanced up at the clock. It was almost eight; the performance had already begun.

He stared at the ticket, put it down, moved it from one side of his desk to the other.

He reached for his "in" tray.

On top was an internal envelope containing a note from the fingerprint laboratory; they needed a formal signature of authorization before examining the prints from the dagger.

Ruzsky put the form down, dipped his pen in the inkwell, scrawled, *Is this bureaucracy really necessary?* and put it back in the envelope and readdressed it.

Next was a thick sheaf of telegraphs responding to Pavel's All Russias bulletin.

There were only three that showed any promise. The Moscow City Police had made two sightings of an American wanted on suspicion of espionage, theft, and affray who traveled under the name Douglas Robertson.

Kazan reported that a Canadian traveling under the name Robert Jones had failed to pay his hotel bill in August 1914.

The most encouraging was from Yalta. *American wanted*, it read, *in connection with armed robbery, October 1910. Fits description. More details upon request. Detective Godorkin, Yalta 229.*

Ruzsky leaned back, rested his feet on the edge of the desk, and stared at the small religious icon hanging on the wall.

He imagined Ella as she might have been while alive. He pictured her as shy and timid; the American, aggressive and manipulative. A pretty royal nanny and a thieving brigand; it was an unlikely romance.

The minute hand on the clock moved with a loud clunk.

Ruzsky headed downstairs. The machines in the communications room were idle. The solitary operator was drinking coffee and reading his newspaper.

Ruzsky handed him the three telegraphs and asked him to get onto Moscow, Kazan, and Yalta for further details.

Back in his office, Ruzsky glanced at the clock again, though he had been acutely aware of the time all evening.

He sat down, pulled open the drawer, and took out the roll of ruble notes that had been removed from the dead man's pocket. He spread them out in order of the numbers outlined on the left-hand side of each note.

He stared at them, looking for a flaw to the theory he'd shared with Pavel. If you assembled the notes like this, you got the order of the letters. The numbers on the right could refer to a page and line number. But he could get no closer to breaking the code without knowing what had been used as the key.

Ruzsky shifted the paperweight to and fro, deep in thought.

He noticed that a figure had crept into the doorway and was leaning back, watching him. "Only a rat moves that quietly," he said.

"Only a fool allows himself to be burned twice."

Stanislav swung in through the door and sauntered over to Pavel's desk. He perched on the end of it, his short legs not quite reaching the floor. His leather boots were in as advanced state of disrepair as Ruzsky's own.

"Did you talk to the newspapers?" Ruzsky asked.

"I tipped one or two off."

Stanislav was sober, but he looked tired, his thin face yellow with in-grained dirt. "Was that you last night?" Ruzsky asked.

Stanislav didn't answer. He was stroking his stubble and looking at the floor.

"Up to something you'd rather I didn't know about?"

The journalist still didn't reply.

"So, what are you trying to tell me?"

Stanislav took out a packet of cigarettes, lit one, and threw the pack over toward Ruzsky, who sent it straight back.

"How did Prokopiev know about the bodies?" Stanislav asked.

"I have no idea. Probably from one of the constables."

"That's a coincidence."

Ruzsky frowned.

"That's what you said last time," Stanislav said. "You—or rather Pavel, with your agreement—put that pervert in the cell at the end of the corridor and told his fellow inmates what he'd been up to. When I asked you who told the Okhrana, you said probably one of the constables. But Prokopiev was here within an hour of the man's death."

"I still don't see your point."

"Almost without exception, we now have a different set of constables. So, one hour after the bodies are brought in from the ice this time, Prokopiev is around to remove them."

"So?"

"They knew. Someone high up is singing down the wire."

Ruzsky did not respond.

"In another time, maybe that wouldn't matter, but you took three years in exile and Vladimir's man wound up in the Moyka with a knife in his back. It's not a game anymore."

They were silent. The clock ticked loudly on the wall and Ruzsky glanced at it.

"Spell it out," he said.

Stanislav shrugged. "If I had the answers, I'd tell you."

"I've got to go."

Ruzsky got up and put on his coat, slipped the ballet ticket into his pocket, and walked briskly along the corridor.

By the time Ruzsky arrived, the intermission had begun. The first-floor lobby was thronged with theatergoers discussing the performance, the hubbub rising toward the curved ceilings as liveried waiters, balancing silver trays, weaved through the throng. The men were dressed in white ties and tails, the women long dresses and gloves, diamonds glittering in the light spilling from the chandeliers.

Here, outside the dress circle, tradition dictated that theatergoers walk slowly around the edge of the room, arm in arm.

Ruzsky hesitated at the top of the stairs, momentarily dazzled by the finery on display. Petersburg and Russia really were two different countries. This city was as sophisticated and European and rich as most of Russia was backward, remote, and poor. The salons of the capital and the endless pine forests of the interior bore no relation to each other, and he belonged wholly to neither world.

He glanced at his ticket and then at the signs directing him up to the top floor.

As Ruzsky turned back up the stairs, his father's booming laugh stopped him in his tracks. His family had spilled out of their box and into the corridor. The landing was crowded, but not enough for him to credibly pretend he had not seen or heard them. He found himself propelled across the rich red carpet behind the dress circle boxes. They were drinking champagne, clustered around a low wooden table laden with bottles in silver buckets. Ruzsky's father stood at the center of the group.

Dmitri's German wife, Ingrid, was at his shoulder. She was coldly beautiful, long blond hair framing a neatly formed, perfectly made-up face. She had a petite nose and a small mouth, her personality so naturally shy and reserved that Ruzsky had rarely been able to penetrate much beneath the surface. But her kiss tonight was warm and her eyes sparkled as he stepped away from her. Was it, he wondered, just the natural empathy of betrayed spouses?

Dmitri stepped down from the box, his face flushed. "Sandro," he said, glowing with pleasure. Vasilyev was behind him, followed by Irina.

"I believe you know one another," Ruzsky's father said stiffly, gesturing toward the chief of the Okhrana.

"Yes," Ruzsky said, stunned by the man's sudden presence in the bosom of his family. "Yes," he said again, "I believe we do."

Irina was staring at him as Dmitri stepped forward and hugged him so tight his ribs almost cracked. "The prodigal returns," he said, turning toward the silent company. "Come on," he said. "This ridiculous feud cannot go on forever."

Dmitri's tone was laced with jollity, but it carried an unmistakably serious plea. He stood next to his brother, an arm around his shoulder, the two of them facing the assembled company.

Ruzsky found it impossible to avoid Vasilyev's hooded gaze.

Irina's face was flushed red, her eyes barely concealing her anger at his presence. Perhaps the Grand Duke was close by.

"Sandro must join us," Dmitri exclaimed. "A benchmark performance." As Ruzsky saw the hurt in Ingrid's eyes, he realized how drunk his brother was.

They remained silent. Vasilyev continued to stare at him with intense, unblinking eyes. Ruzsky tried to summon enough energy to retreat with grace, but found himself catching his father's eye. Just for a moment, beneath the severe frown, he thought he saw his expression soften. "Sandro must join us," he said. "Of course."

Dmitri stepped away from him and lit a cigarette, looking suddenly sober.

Ruzsky cleared his throat. "No." He saw relief in Irina's eyes, regret in Ingrid's. "No, it's a kind offer. Another time, perhaps."

"You're here anyway," his father said.

"Yes, but I'm . . . on duty, in a manner of speaking."

His father glanced at Vasilyev.

"One must take time to relax, Sandro," Vasilyev said, but his unyielding glare belied the soothing tone of his words.

"Of course." He looked at his father, whose face had not quite returned to the hostile set of previous encounters. "Have a good evening."

Ruzsky did not look back as he climbed the stairs. He slumped down into his seat at the far end of the front row with some relief, and gazed down at the empty stage. He was very high up here and it was pleasantly warm.

He only became aware that the performance was about to resume when he realized that the seats around him were once again full. The orchestra was warming up discordantly.

Ruzsky glanced down at the royal box. He could see the Tsar's brother Grand Duke Michael in earnest conversation with Teliakovsky, the director of Imperial Theatres, and Count Fredericks, minister of the court.

The lights faded, the lavishly embroidered stage curtain was raised, and the overture began.

Maria appeared, in pure white against a startling blue backdrop, and her presence was as intoxicating as it had been when he had first watched her here, all those years ago. A young girl next to him craned her neck for a better view, her face alive with excitement.

Ruzsky forced himself to relax, sitting in the semidarkness, far above the stage.

She was tall for a ballerina. Her long, willowy body moved with such supple grace that nothing she did, no step she took, no pirouette or twist, ever seemed less than perfect. He watched her in a daze, oblivious to the music, or the onlookers, or even the careful choreography of the dance itself. He allowed himself to wallow in the sensation of being close to her.

But, as he watched, he was suddenly gripped by doubt. Only a fool would wait three years for a man who had let an unfaithful wife stand in the way of their fragile chance of happiness.

Ruzsky tried to stem the growing tide of dismay and self-reproach, but without success. He stood and pushed his way along the row, to a chorus of disapproval from those around him.

Outside, as he turned the corner of the stairs, he almost knocked Ingrid over. He grabbed hold of her to steady both of them and as he looked into her eyes, Ruzsky saw the depth of her hurt.

"I'm sorry," she said.

He stepped back. "No . . ."

They both stared at the floor. Ruzsky wondered what his brother had done or said on this occasion.

"You are . . ." He could not think of what to say. It was obvious that she was too upset to join her husband below.

"You're leaving?" she asked.

"Yes." He could see that her assumption was he'd been upset by the exchange with his father. "I have work to do," he went on. He moved past her on the stairs.

Ruzsky wondered if he should offer words of comfort, but a natural sense of decorum restrained him. Whatever the cause of her unhappiness, she was his brother's wife. "Have a good evening," he said.

"Yes."

Ruzsky walked down the stairs. At the corner, he looked over his shoulder and saw that she was still watching him. He raised his hand briefly—intended only as a gesture of support—and then was gone.

18

Ruzsky waited next to the canal that ran along the rear of the theater. It had started snowing again. The visibility was poor in the glow of the widely spaced gas lamps, but it was warmer tonight.

The last of the audience was making its way out of the Mariinskiy, some heading for sleds or carriages, some on foot. There was the occasional burst of laughter as they went, but then the street grew quiet.

The stage door opened and a familiar figure appeared. The chief of the Petrograd Okhrana adjusted his fur hat and hesitated briefly before moving into the darkness.

Ruzsky ducked into the shadows until the rhythmic crunch of Vasilyev's departing footsteps could no longer be heard.

Ruzsky wondered what his family was doing. He walked over the bridge, hands in his pockets.

He leaned against the railing and looked down at the icy canal.

It was a few moments before Ruzsky realized that she had left the theater and was heading away from him. Light flakes of snow gathered in her hair.

He almost called out, but thought better of it and took off in pursuit.

He touched her arm when he caught up with her, and she spun around. "Sandro!" Relief flooded her face.

"Are you all right?"

"Yes. You gave me a fright."

"Who did you think I was?"

The stage door banged shut and two men hurried toward them. Ruzsky recognized one as the ballet master with whom he'd crossed swords the previous day. "You'll catch your death of cold," he told her, in French.

"*Ça ne fait rien,*" she responded.

"*C'est qui?*"

"*Un ami.*"

The man took a pace closer and eyed Ruzsky. "We have something to eat and some vodka at home." He pointed down the canal, in the opposite direction. "Just there, number 109."

"*Je suis fatiguée,*" Maria said.

Ruzsky recognized the man now as the legendary Fokine.

"You're going home?" he asked Maria.

"Yes."

Fokine smiled. "Well, be good."

He turned around and, with his companion, walked briskly away. Ruzsky felt his face reddening.

They turned and began to walk in the direction of the St. Nicholas Cathedral. "What did you think?"

"Of Fokine?"

"Of tonight."

"Oh, it was good."

"Good?" She laughed, kicking fresh powder up around her. Her mood was suddenly much lighter. "*Good*, Sandro?"

"All right, very good."

"*Very* good?" She had walked a few paces ahead and faced him now, laughing. She scooped the snow up into his face. "Very good?"

"Astounding."

"Astounding?"

"You're Russia's finest prima ballerina, what can I say?"

"*One* of Russia's finest."

"Such modesty . . ."

"You were bowled over by the scale and ambition of the choreography, or the physical perfection of the dancers. You—"

"All of the above."

"I wager you don't even like the ballet."

"On the contrary."

"Don't you mean *au contraire?*"

"What's so funny?"

"I bet you were asleep."

He grinned. "If only I had been."

"It was that boring?"

"Tedious beyond words."

They were beside the cathedral now, its golden domes towering above them.

"My father used to take me to the ballet," Ruzsky said quietly.

"Now there is a story."

"Mmm . . ."

Maria looked into his eyes. The snow fluttered slowly down between them, big flakes melting as they touched her cheeks. His feet were cold, but he had no wish to hurry.

He turned his face toward the sky.

Maria began to walk again, half turning to examine her footprints in the snow. "You went with your father, alone? Just you and him?"

"Yes."

"What about your brothers?"

"I don't know. Perhaps he thought they were too young."

They crossed another bend in the Griboedov Canal and walked past the covered market. Ruzsky glimpsed figures huddled inside its entrance, seeking shelter. "Poor devils," Maria whispered.

Ruzsky took a few more paces. "Do you know Vasilyev?"

"Of course. Of him, anyway."

"You don't know him personally?"

She frowned. "No. Should I?"

"I just saw him leaving the theater by the stage door. I wondered if you had known him from Yalta?"

"He's an admirer of a colleague," she said. "Poor girl."

Maria's apartment was on the top floor of a faded yellow building just beyond the Nicholas market. It was not far from where she had lived four years ago.

Maria did not ask him to come up, but nor did she turn to say good-bye at its entrance.

They climbed the stairs slowly. Ruzsky watched as she found her key and placed it in the lock. He had to resist the temptation to reach forward and brush the snow from her hair.

They stepped inside. Maria turned on a lamp by the door.

Ruzsky's throat was dry.

She led him down a narrow corridor to the drawing room, their leather boots noisy on the wooden floorboards. He could hear the water squelching from the holes in his own.

Maria lit a candle above her writing desk, slipped off her coat, and threw it across the end of a chaise longue.

She wore a white dress, and he caught a glimpse of stocking above her boots. On the wall beside her was a painting of the bay at Yalta, at sunset.

"Are you still planning to go home?" Ruzsky asked, glancing at the picture.

"Tomorrow night."

"It will be warmer."

Maria shrugged.

"It was a wonderful place for a holiday," Ruzsky said.

"Then come again. I'll show you around."

Ruzsky looked at her. "One day, I'd like that."

"One day, I would too."

"It's a long way. Perhaps more than two days with the railways in the state they are."

She did not answer.

Ruzsky cleared his throat. "How did you get a ticket? They say the khvost at the railway bureau is five-deep."

"I have a friend at the Ministry of War."

Ruzsky could not stop himself wondering what kind of friend.

"Would you like some vodka?" she asked.

"No. Thank you, no."

"Whiskey? I have some bourbon in the dresser."

Ruzsky shook his head, then changed his mind. "I'd love one."

Maria shook out her long dark hair. It was a simple gesture that still had a devastating effect on him. She gathered it again at the nape of her neck as she went to the dresser and picked up the single glass and what was left of the bottle of American whiskey.

Ruzsky knew few people who drank bourbon. It was Dmitri's favorite, but hard to come by these days, he imagined, even in Petersburg.

Maria handed him the glass. "I'll make us some tea also."

"I should go," he said.

"If you wish . . ."

He didn't move. They looked at each other for a few moments before she walked down to the kitchen.

Ruzsky sat on the chaise longue between the bookcase and the fireplace, his heart racing again. He looked about him. On the wall opposite was a framed poster, in dark red, advertising her first performance as a prima ballerina at the Mariinskiy Theatre, in *Swan Lake*. The year was 1911.

Ruzsky stood again, walked to the window, and looked down at the street below. It was deserted but for a sled standing by the iron railings, its driver hopping from one foot to the other to keep warm.

Ruzsky turned. The fire had been laid and he reached into his pocket for some matches and stepped forward to light it. It caught quickly and he sat back on the rug, watching the flames. He didn't hear her return.

"I've been hoarding fuel," she said. "They say the bakeries don't have enough to keep their ovens working."

Maria put down a silver tray and unloaded its contents: a silver teapot, milk jug, and sugar pot, and two china cups and saucers. Ruzsky watched her pour the tea through a strainer.

Maria returned to the kitchen once more and brought back a plate of English biscuits. He took one, then sipped his bourbon.

"How do you survive, Sandro?"

"What do you mean?"

"You said your father had cut you off without a ruble, and I don't get the impression much has changed."

"I have my salary."

Maria raised her eyebrows. "You're a Ruzsky."

"So I survive. Like others do."

"By not eating. You look thinner. It doesn't suit you."

He ignored her. Maria looked at him seriously. "You should leave Petersburg."

"I've done that. Tobolsk was not an improvement."

"I'm serious. You may see yourself as the guardian of justice, but for all that, you are a policeman."

"I'm a detective."

"You expect the mob to care?"

Ruzsky remembered what Dmitri had said, and the hostile faces outside the bakery. He leaned back against the chaise longue. She was looking at him, as if in a trance, her mind somewhere else. "You know what really saddens me?" he said. "The way everyone assumes change is going to make things better."

"You have changed your tune."

"You were the radical," he said.

"Well, everyone is a radical now."

Ruzsky stared into the fire.

"So, what of the two bodies you found on the ice? The girls were asking."

Ruzsky looked at her. He liked the idea that they had been talking about him. He wondered if it was true that Maria had kept a photograph of him with her during his exile.

"Still a mystery," he said.

"I like mysteries."

"We could swap."

"Sandro the ballet dancer? I'm not sure."

"I'd be perfect. Apart from the boots." He raised one foot. "No. Perhaps you're right." Ruzsky took another sip of the bourbon. His natural instinct was not to talk about the case, but he did not want to repeat the mistake he had made with Irina. If need be, he would force himself to communicate. "The girl was from Yalta, as a matter of fact. Ella Kovyil. Ever heard of her?"

She smiled and shook her head. "Yalta is small, but not that small . . ."

"No, well—"

"What was she doing here?"

"Ella was an imperial nanny."

Maria tilted her head in surprise. "An imperial nanny?"

"Yes."

"Why was she killed?"

"We don't know."

"A lovers' quarrel?"

Ruzsky shrugged.

"Who was the other one?"

Ruzsky hesitated. "An American."

"What was he doing in Petersburg?"

"We don't know."

"So you don't know much, really."

Maria glanced at the clock and the smile instantly left her face. She hesitated for a moment and then stood. It dawned on him that he was expected to leave. He felt suddenly disoriented.

He stood opposite her, staring into her big, dark eyes. "I'm sorry, Sandro," she said softly. "It's just . . . I'm sorry."

"For what?"

But her eyes told him everything he needed to know. Her loneliness was the mirror of his own, and her apology was for the opportunity they had lost.

Ruzsky turned and walked slowly out into the corridor.

"Sandro?" She was at the door. "Thank you, for coming tonight."

They looked at each other for a moment more and then Maria closed the door.

Ruzsky stood, rooted to the spot.

He forced himself to turn and walk down the stairs.

Ruzsky took a few paces down the street outside, then stopped. He looked up and saw her face in the window.

He set his head down and began to move away. It was a moment before he recognized the figure hurrying down the snowy street toward him, his face flushed with alcohol and expectation.

Ruzsky could hear his brother's voice in his head: *Actually, I've acquired another little asset.*

He turned on his heel and slipped into the shadow of a doorwell.

He watched every jaunty, carefree step his brother took.

Ruzsky waited, listening to the sound of Dmitri pounding up Maria's stairwell. It had stopped snowing and the night was uncannily still, the footsteps echoing like rifle shots.

He crossed to the far side of the street and looked up at her window.

Just for a moment, he caught a glimpse of both of them before Maria unfolded the shutters and blocked out the night.

Ruzsky did not move, his eyes fixed upon the darkened window above.

In his barren room a short time later, Ruzsky tried to sleep, but could not. He tossed and turned until he could stand it no more. He stood to dispel the images and paced around the silent room, turning to the window and the deserted, snow-covered street for solace, or at least distraction. He heard a dog bark again.

Ruzsky placed the tips of the fingers of his right hand against the window and waited until they grew numb.

He walked to his suitcase and pulled out his last bottle of vodka. There was no trace in the apartment of the tramp he had rescued this morning, except a lingering smell of decay.

Ruzsky upended the bottle. He gulped down the harsh liquid within.

Oblivion came quickly. His head swam, but even the fire of the vodka in his belly could not extinguish his fury. He raised the almost empty bottle above his head and smashed it against the edge of the dresser next to the door, slashing the palm of his hand.

He looked at the blood oozing from his skin, but could feel nothing. He staggered toward his bunk and fell, face first, out cold.

But if Ruzsky achieved sleep, peace eluded him. He found himself returning to the lake at Petrovo, the images that assaulted him stark against a clear, blue sky. He could see the ice cracking and feel the freezing water and then he was down—plunging back into the darkness, his arms flailing as he sought Ilusha's outstretched hand.

He could hear the dull swish of his movements in the water and the sound of the bubbles ascending as the air escaped from his lungs. He could see, through the shimmering surface, his father's long hand stretched out toward him.

And then he had turned away and was flailing in the darkness once more.

Ruzsky kicked and swam, down and down. But all that touched his grasping fingers were the weeds and all that he could hear was the beating of his own heart.

Ruzsky closed his eyes and began to shout, the pain searing his soul.

He looked up. He could see the light slicing through the surface and his father's hand pawing at the water. He felt the lake wrapping him in its icy embrace.

He could no longer summon the will to resist. He slipped farther and farther away, the hand that trembled on the surface receding. Until at last, he was enveloped in water the color of night, and with it, a kind of peace.

The banging had risen to a crescendo in his dream long before it woke him. Ruzsky had been curled up beneath his blankets like a fetus, and only reluctantly stuck his head out into the night. The gash in his hand was painful, his throat was dry, and his head pounded like a locomotive. The empty bottle of vodka beside him shimmered in the moonlight.

Someone was thumping insistently on his door.

"Who is it?" he yelled.

Ruzsky heard a muffled cry, so he pulled back the covers and dived for his overcoat. As he walked across the room, he pulled out the Sauvage revolver. He winced as he gripped it with his injured palm. By the door, he considered turning on the light, then thought better of it. "Who is it?"

"It's me."

"Who's me?"

"Don't be an ass."

Ruzsky pulled the bolt back and left Pavel to push the door open. The pain in his head seemed suddenly to explode.

"Get dressed," Pavel said.

"It's the middle of the night."

"We have another body."

19

The victim lay crumpled in the shadow of the arch.

They were not far from the Mariinskiy Theatre, next to the Lviny Most, the Lion Bridge, a well-known haunt for lovers. It was about six in the morning, the city around them still shrouded in darkness.

Ruzsky was standing next to one of the white stone lions, wondering how he could avoid going down onto the ice. His injured hand still throbbed gently. "Do you want us to bring him up?" Pavel asked. "He was pushed over from the parapet."

Ruzsky looked around him. The path was too well trodden to trace any footprints. "All right."

There were three constables, the same men who'd been on duty when the bodies had been found on the Neva. They listened to Pavel without enthusiasm and then walked down onto the ice behind him.

Pavel bent over the body. One of the constables glanced up toward Ruzsky.

The chief investigator muttered a curse and then walked down to the ice. The Griboedov Canal curved to the left here, its frozen surface ghostly in the light of the gas lamps. As he stepped onto it, Ruzsky twisted involuntarily and slipped. He struggled to control his breathing. Gradually, he became aware that he was under the scrutiny of the constable closest to him. Ruzsky lowered his head and marched toward the body.

The man lay curled up, his body frozen. "Shit," Ruzsky said. He waved to indicate that the constables should move back, then he took hold of the corpse with his good hand and dragged it out into the moonlight.

He bent down again.

For all his experience, he felt his stomach lurch. The man had been stabbed so many times in the neck, his head had almost been severed.

The blood had frozen and crystals of ice had collected in his mustache and along his eyebrows.

"Christ," Pavel whispered beside him.

The man had a young, lean face and yellow teeth. Ruzsky guessed that he would only have been marginally more attractive in life than he now appeared in death.

He pulled back the man's overcoat. There were no markings on it, and at first, he thought the body had been systematically stripped again. In the right-hand pocket he found a disordered fistful of banknotes.

Ruzsky riffled through them, holding them up to see if any had been marked in the same way as the American's, but they had not. In the middle of the bundle was a return rail ticket from Sevastopol to Petrograd, issued from an office in Yalta. The card for the first leg of the journey had been stamped three days ago at Sevastopol, so the man must just have arrived in the capital.

Ruzsky tried the other pocket. He pulled out some identity papers. They appeared to be genuine. "Boris," Ruzsky said. "What does that say?"

"Molkov," Pavel said, scrutinizing it closely. "Or Markov. Markov."

"Yalta. Thirty-four years of age."

Pavel pulled the coat back farther to be sure there were no other wounds. "Almost certainly the same killer, wouldn't you say?"

Ruzsky didn't answer. He took two paces back and scanned the buildings overlooking the canal. They were residential apartments or houses, backing onto the Conservatory. "More chance of someone having seen here," Ruzsky said.

"Not at that time in the morning. He's been dead several hours, at least."

Ruzsky looked at his pocket watch. It was almost seven. He wondered if the man had already been dead when he had left the theater with Maria.

"This time," Pavel said, "the killer wasn't stalking his victim."

"An arranged meeting?"

"Don't you think so?"

"Yes, but it's a strange time to choose."

They heard a group of horses whinnying and turned to see a green Okhrana sledge pulling up. Prokopiev jumped down before it had stopped and strode toward them. He vaulted the side and landed squarely on the ice—a silly, theatrical gesture. "Thank you for your assistance, gentlemen. We shall take over from here."

Prokopiev's shirt was open at the neck, as though he had, himself, just gotten out of bed. He looked at them with his head titled down a fraction, and, in the dark, it had the effect of making his stare still more intense. Two other Okhrana men leaned over the bridge above them.

Ruzsky slipped the dead man's identity papers and the wad of money into his overcoat pocket. Prokopiev was too busy preening himself to notice.

"By order of the interior minister," Prokopiev said.

"What is?"

"We'll deal with the case."

The two groups glared at each other. "Is there something I'm missing?" Ruzsky asked. As he spoke another sledge rounded the corner and drew up in front of the Lion Bridge. The chief of the Okhrana climbed down and strode toward them. He wore a fur hat. He stepped awkwardly onto the ice, before turning to face them. The moonlight made his face seem older, the lines exaggerated and his skin bloodless. He nodded once. "Good morning, gentlemen."

No one replied.

"We need more constables, I see."

It was a moment before Ruzsky realized that this had been an attempt at humor. "Yes," he said.

"What is the situation?"

Ruzsky frowned. "What is what situation?"

"You have discovered another body and the constables have reported that the killing was aggressive?"

"Something like it."

"*Something* like it?"

Ruzsky looked at the dead man. "It's similarly savage." He glanced at the constables, each of whom avoided his eye.

"So the same killer?" Vasilyev asked.

"Possibly. Or someone who wants us to think that."

"You can go home now," Vasilyev said. He'd spoken so quietly that it was a moment before Ruzsky grasped what had been said.

"What did you say?"

"Ivan will deal with this."

Pavel tugged at Ruzsky's arm. "Isn't that Anton's decision?" Ruzsky asked. "Or does the Okhrana have an interest in the case we should know about?"

"The same frenzied attack," Vasilyev continued smoothly. "We should have let Ivan deal with the couple on the ice."

"And why is that?" Ruzsky asked. Pavel tugged at his sleeve again.

"Ivan has many agents at his disposal, Sandro. A member of the imperial staff . . . it must have been the work of terrorists."

Ruzsky hesitated. He was about to go on. He wanted a confrontation, but he could sense Pavel's nervousness. He made them wait. "Good luck," he said finally, before clambering back onto the bridge.

"Will they get Sarlov to do the autopsy?" Ruzsky asked when they had turned the corner.

"I don't know."

"We should get him out of bed and explain what has happened."

"What's that going to achieve?"

"Forewarn him, Pavel."

"We should just leave it."

"And how did they find out so quickly?" Ruzsky went on, ignoring his partner. "Which one of the constables is in their pay?"

"Calm down, Sandro."

Ruzsky stopped and stared at his colleague.

"All right," Pavel said, "but let's slow down, can we? And by the way, you look terrible." Ruzsky wasn't surprised. He pressed his eyes into their sockets. His head was pounding. "I don't understand," he said.

"Understand what?"

"When they took away the bodies from the Neva, why didn't they just assume control of the case? It doesn't make any sense to me. Their actions aren't consistent."

Pavel didn't answer. "What happened to your hand?" he asked.

"Oh." Ruzsky looked at the rag he had bound around his palm. "An accident with a vodka bottle."

"You should be more careful, my friend."

20

Back at his desk, Ruzsky picked up the telephone earpiece and asked the operator to put him through to Dr. Sarlov at home. It rang repeatedly.

"Yes?" The pathologist sounded sleepy.

"We've had an incident with the Okhrana."

"I don't want to know."

"Another victim. Same kind of attack. The head was almost severed. They have removed the body. Will you still do the autopsy?"

"I have no idea."

"If you do—"

"Consider who is listening," the doctor said, before abruptly terminating the call.

Ruzsky sat back. He sorted through the telegraphs he'd received the previous night. He reread the one from Yalta. *American wanted in connection with armed robbery in Yalta, October 1910. Fits description. More details upon request.* He picked up the receiver again and asked to be put through to Detective Godorkin.

The line went dead, but he held on.

Ruzsky heard a loud crackle, as though someone were screwing up newspaper next to the mouthpiece. "Detective Godorkin, please," he shouted again.

"Godorkin here," a voice said calmly. The line was suddenly clear.

"Detective Godorkin?"

"I am he."

"This is Chief Investigator Ruzsky, Petrograd City Police."

"Chief Investigator. I was trying to contact you."

"I don't know how long the line will last," Ruzsky said, "so let's dispense with the niceties. We've got three dead bodies, including two from

Yalta; a girl from the palace called Ella Kovyil who was murdered with her American boyfriend on the Neva, and a Boris Markov."

"I see."

"What can you tell me? Could the American have been the one you are searching for? His name was White . . ."

The line faded again and Ruzsky cursed.

It came back, but Ruzsky only caught the end of a sentence. "I missed that," he shouted.

"Robert Whitewater," Godorkin said.

"Whitewater?"

"Yes. That was his name. An American . . ."

The line disappeared again. Ruzsky tried repeatedly to get another connection, but without success. He sat back in the chair as Pavel walked in with a newspaper under his arm. He threw it across the desk at Ruzsky. "Page three."

It was a copy of *Novoe Vremia* and Ruzsky flicked past the advertisements on the front page and scanned the inside of the newspaper. The article was a factual account of the discovery of the original bodies on the river and only the headline—*Blood on the Neva*—exhibited the sensationalism for which the paper was known. It did not give either Ella's or the American's name. The last line posed the question: *In these difficult times, is a killer on the loose in Petrograd?* The piece alongside it followed one woman's daily struggle for survival while her husband was fighting at the front. *While the rich drown in excess*, it said, *the struggle of the poor gets daily more impossible.*

The news item at the top of the page appeared under the headline *Further explosion of crime; Petrograd's streets more dangerous than ever.*

Ruzsky glanced up at the clock. It was almost time for the morning conference. "Are we going?" Ruzsky asked.

Pavel shrugged.

Ruzsky stood and took his coat from the stand. Through the open door, he watched Vladimir rolling into the room opposite. The *Investigator, Street Crime*, was a barrel of a man, no taller than Ruzsky's shoulder, but with the strength of an ox. He trailed a young assistant—a new one. He caught sight of Ruzsky, altered course immediately, and charged across the room toward him. "Here's trouble," he said, loud enough to be heard downstairs. "Welcome back."

They clasped each other. "This is my new assistant"—Vladimir indicated the young man standing awkwardly in the doorway—"Constable Shavelsky." Shavelsky's handshake was firm, his grip making Ruzsky wince, though the constable appeared not to notice. Ruzsky wondered whether he knew of the fate of his predecessor.

"So," Vladimir said, "they finally let you come home."

The fat detective took out a cigarette and offered one to both Ruzsky and Pavel, but not his assistant. He lit his own when the others declined, and smoked it with one hand in his pocket, looking out toward the secretaries who had begun to take their places at the desks outside, steam rising from mugs of tea alongside their giant black typewriters. They leaned forward in their chairs, gossiping. "How was Tobolsk?" Vladimir asked.

"Cold."

Vladimir shook his head. "He should never have let you go."

Ruzsky remembered the last morning conference before his exile, when Vladimir had launched a vicious attack on Anton for not fighting harder to protect him.

"They're keeping you busy, I see," Ruzsky said, holding up his copy of *Novoe Vremia*.

In response, Vladimir held up the sheet of paper in his own hand. It listed a series of crimes and incidents. "Last night alone."

"Deserters?"

"Deserters, the desperate. Serving soldiers sometimes. Our friends in the Okhrana. Another three Jewish properties burned last night."

Ruzsky put his coat on. "How do you handle that?"

"We take a look. If it is them, which it usually is, we leave it. What choice is there?" Vladimir turned around. "Are you coming to the conference?"

"Not today," Ruzsky said.

"What happened to your hand?"

"A small accident." Ruzsky raised his hand, took off the rag, and threw it into the bin in the corner. A little blood was still oozing from his palm.

Ella's mother lived on the top floor of the tenement block and it was a slow climb. Pavel wheezed heavily.

They stopped for a moment to catch their breath, surrounded by clothes which had been hung up to dry on lines crisscrossing the landing. A thin trickle of water ran down the stairs, forming a pool by their feet. There was an overpowering smell of urine.

The door closest to them opened and a young girl appeared. She had wild black hair, hollow cheeks, and staring eyes. She wore high boots and stood with her feet close together, watching them. There were six or seven people at least in the gloomy room behind her, lying in bundles on the floor.

Ruzsky started walking again and Pavel followed him. At the top, they saw that the trickle of water on the stairs had come from thick ice around the windows, some of which was beginning to melt.

Pavel ducked under another line of frozen washing and knocked on the door at the far end of the corridor.

They waited.

"Who is it?" a voice asked.

"Madam Kovyil? City police."

There was another pause and then the door was opened by a tiny woman who barely reached Pavel's waist. She smiled at him nervously and stepped back to allow them to enter. "This is Chief Investigator Ruzsky," Pavel said, as if he himself was unimportant.

The woman forced herself to smile. "My husband once served under—"

"My father. Or perhaps my uncle." Ruzsky grinned and clasped her wrist with his left hand. "Sandro."

She placed a small, cold hand in his and tried to hold her smile in place.

She looked up at him with hollow eyes.

"Madam Kovyil, I'm afraid I have to tell you that . . ."

But he could see she already knew. From the palace, he assumed. From Shulgin, probably. She began to cry and Pavel was at once next to her, ushering her into a chair close to the fireplace and holding on to her arm until she had recovered her composure. Ruzsky wondered how long ago she had been told.

"I'm sorry," she said. "I'm so sorry."

"There is no need to apologize, Madam Kovyil," Ruzsky responded.

"Anna. Please call me Anna."

She pushed herself forward in her chair. She seemed even frailer than when they had arrived. "Would you like something to drink? I'm afraid I have no vodka, but tea perhaps?"

Ruzsky and Pavel both shook their heads. The room was small and neat, but the fireplace was too clean to have been used at any time in the recent past, and if she ever heated any kind of pot, they could both see it was a rare event.

The only light in the room emanated from one small window, covered in frost. Ruzsky stood and peered at the photographs on the mantelpiece. The first was of Anna and her husband on their wedding day, the second of him in the regimental uniform of the Preobrazhensky Guards, and the third of Ella at age fourteen or fifteen. As Ruzsky had imagined, she had a shy, sweet smile, like her mother.

"She was your only child?" Ruzsky asked.

Anna nodded once and then slowly and with dignity, placed her head in her hands. Pavel gripped her shoulder once more.

She composed herself and looked up. "I'm sorry," she said again.

Ruzsky returned to his seat. Even in this light, he could see that its cover had been carefully stitched together. Like everything else, it spoke of a threadbare respectability.

"This is a terrible time, Madam . . . Anna, I know, but if you feel strong enough to answer questions, we'd greatly appreciate your assistance."

Anna nodded. "Of course."

"We don't believe Ella's murder was an isolated incident."

Anna stared at him with unseeing eyes. Her face was narrower than Ella's, and if, as the photograph suggested, she had once been beautiful, her features had been ravaged by age and cold and poverty.

"I told your colleagues," she said quietly. "But if there is something else—"

"Our colleagues?"

Anna frowned. "Yes."

"Which colleagues?"

"They came this morning, just a few minutes ago."

"Did they give their names?"

"No, they just said they were from the police department."

"Was it they who told you of your daughter . . . of Ella's death?" Ruzsky asked.

She shook her head.

"You were informed by palace officials?"

"Yes."

"Yesterday, or the day before?"

"The day before. On New Year's Day, in the evening."

"Colonel Shulgin came to see you?"

Anna did not respond, but he could see that this had not been the case. Ruzsky looked around. There was no telephone. Had they sent a messenger?

They had informed her by letter?

Ruzsky looked at Pavel and then back at Anna, unable to conceal his disgust at her treatment. "What did they look like, the men who came this morning?"

"The man in charge was tall. Like you, but bigger. He had short hair and poor skin and a large . . ." With long bony fingers she indicated a pronounced nose. "He didn't tell me his name."

Ruzsky glanced again at Pavel. "And what did he want?"

"There were four of them. They asked questions about Ella and . . . some others."

"Which others?"

Anna sighed and stared at her hands. "Some I didn't know."

"Did they give names?"

"I can't remember all of them."

"It would help if you could recall one or two, Anna."

She was overtaken by confusion. "Were they not policemen?"

"Not really, no."

"Who were they?"

"Government officials." Ruzsky glanced at Pavel again. "Okhrana. I don't think they would be interested in finding your daughter's killer."

Anna kneaded her hands. Ruzsky hoped he'd not frightened her into silence. "They asked about Ella's friend."

"The American?"

"Yes." Anna looked up, pleading with them.

Ruzsky showed her the photograph. "This man?" He was on the point of apologizing when he saw a hint of satisfaction in her eyes.

"He was charming, of course, but I didn't like it. He was so much older than her. He . . ." She trailed off.

"He manipulated her?" Ruzsky suggested.

"I wanted her to marry a man like her father, like my . . ." Anna shook her head. "He was such a good man, so loyal, to the Tsar and to us."

"Where did Ella meet her friend, Anna? Here in Petersburg?"

Anna shook her head. "At home."

"In Yalta?" Ruzsky felt his pulse quicken.

"Such a long time ago now. I thought she had forgotten him."

"She met the American on a holiday, or before you moved here?"

"Yes. That's why I left. I wanted to get her away. But I didn't know."

"You didn't know that they remained in contact?"

"How could I? She never told me. I thought perhaps she would have met some nice man at the palace, which would have been so much more . . . appropriate. I always asked her about it and she said no, there was no one, that she was devoted to the Tsarevich and to her work . . ." Anna stopped again, frightened that she had revealed something she was not supposed to.

"We know your daughter worked with the Tsarevich," Pavel said. "We have been to the palace. They spoke very highly of her."

Anna seemed relieved. "She was a good girl. Such a good girl."

"You met the American in Yalta?" Ruzsky asked.

"Only once." Anna sat forward and pushed the scarf back from her head. She appeared stronger now, bolstered by hostility to her daughter's lover. "That summer, he came to the house, just after Ella's father had died. He was charming." She shook her head again. "I don't know what it was. He was so much older than her. She was just a young girl."

"Did you sense that your daughter—"

"I'm not a fool, Chief Investigator. I knew that they were lovers, but I thought that it was an infatuation that would run its course. She said that he'd encouraged her to apply for a job at the royal palace and I thought she would soon forget him."

"He encouraged her?"

"Yes."

"He encouraged her to get a job at Livadia?"

"Yes."

"This would have been . . . what year exactly?"

"Nineteen ten."

"How old was she then, Anna?"

"She was fifteen."

"Did Ella tell you why he'd encouraged her to apply for a job at the royal palace?"

Anna didn't understand the significance of the question. "Her father had died," she said defensively. "It was a difficult time for both of us, of course. Ella was at that age . . . she wanted to find her own feet. It was understandable."

"But the American specifically encouraged her to get a job in the imperial household?"

"My husband had been in the guards. He had always hoped she would find employment at Livadia, but . . ."

"She had initially been reluctant to work in the imperial household?"

Anna stared at her hands. "She was just a young girl."

"She didn't like doing her father's bidding?"

"A lot of people filling her head with silly ideas." Anna smiled. "We dealt with it. After the move to Petersburg, it was so much better."

"Silly ideas?" Ruzsky asked.

Anna did not answer.

"Revolutionary ideas?"

Anna looked worried again, until she realized that her daughter's death had absolved her of any need to fear this point at least. She sighed. "It was different in Petersburg," she repeated.

"White was a revolutionary and Ella was influenced by him?"

"My husband would not allow discussion of politics in the house. They . . . he and Ella argued in the last year of his life. It upset him greatly."

"She met the American in revolutionary circles in Yalta?"

Anna looked at Pavel and then back at Ruzsky. "I don't know about that, but I didn't like him. After my husband died, I wanted to move away. It would be good to begin again. It was my gift to him."

"To your husband?"

"Yes."

"He had been very worried about Ella?"

"She would never have brought the American to the house when her father was alive."

"Did the American ever explain what he was doing in Yalta, Anna?"

"Traveling, he said." Anna shrugged contemptuously. "Just traveling. That was all he said. Ella told me his father was a millionaire from America and he liked to travel to other parts of the world. He boasted that he had no need to work."

Ruzsky could see how the the poor, respectable Kovyils must have hated the charming interloper who had bewitched their daughter with strange ideas and the prospect of another life.

"Did you meet any of Ella's other friends from the same circle?"

"From the same circle?"

Ruzsky tried to remember the name of the man they had found at the Lion Bridge this morning. "Boris Markov? Perhaps just Borya?"

"I don't know."

Ruzsky dug the man's identification papers from his pocket and showed her the dark, smudged photograph. But she just shook her head.

"Who did the men this morning ask you about?"

Anna looked at him blankly as she handed back the papers. "I'm not very good with names."

"What did they want to know?"

"If Ella had brought him home, and whether I had met him."

"The American?"

"Yes."

"And had you, this time?"

Anna's face quivered briefly before she recovered her composure. "How could I know she had taken up with him again?" She shook her head. "I thought he was on the other side of the world, where he belongs."

"Did she bring him here?"

"No, but I knew he had come here."

Ruzsky could tell he was upsetting Anna, who once again stared at him in a kind of trance. He crouched down in front of her. "Anna, can you think of anything over the last few months that would give us an indication of why someone would want to kill Ella?"

Anna looked at him, tears welling up in her eyes. "She was a loving girl, Officer, so loving."

"When did you last see her?"

Anna turned to the photograph of her daughter on the mantelpiece and the religious icon hanging above it. "Last Sunday. She always came to see me on a Sunday. It was her day off and she would catch the train into town and we would go to church together."

"And what happened last Sunday?"

Anna stared at the wall. The silence dragged on, but Ruzsky did not wish to push her.

"It was just a Sunday," she said. "Like all Sundays."

"You went to church?"

"She was so happy, Officer. That smile, I wish you could have seen it. She was such a pretty girl."

"Why was she so happy, Anna?"

"I thought she was just . . . happy. To be with me. To be close to the Lord. Such a fine, clear, bright day; the city so beautiful. I felt happy too; happier, I think, than on any day since I came here. It was wonderful to see her so bursting with joy."

"What did you do?"

Anna shrugged. "We came home. She had brought us some food. She was a kind girl."

"Did she tell you any special reason why she was so happy?"

She couldn't hold her emotions in check any longer. She suddenly collapsed, burying her face in her hands, thin shoulders heaving. Pavel held her. "It's all right, Anna," he said quietly. "It's all right."

Ruzsky took hold of her arm and squeezed gently. She was all skin and bone.

They waited until the convulsions had stopped and then stepped back and averted their eyes while she composed herself. She took out a handkerchief and blew her nose. "I cannot bear the thought of it, do you understand?" she said simply. "Those Sundays were my life."

Anna wept once more.

"We're intruding," Ruzsky said. He stood. "Perhaps we could come back another time."

"No, please." She wiped her eyes again. "I would like to help." Anna put the handkerchief away. "Please ask me whatever you wish."

Ruzsky sat down. "Was there anything unusual about that Sunday, Anna? Did she say or do anything out of the ordinary?"

"There was an argument, that's all I can think of. Not even an argument."

"What about?"

"She asked me a question and I was offended."

"What did she ask you?"

"It was unlike her. And I said her father would have been disgusted."

"What did she ask you?"

Anna stared at Ruzsky. She was uncertain again. She glanced at Pavel for reassurance and then steeled herself. "She asked me whether I thought it was possible that the Empress and Rasputin had enjoyed intimate relations. Whether they had been lovers."

"Why do you think she asked that?"

"I don't know."

"Surely, Anna, your daughter, more than anyone, would have been in a position to know the answer to that question."

Anna shook her head sorrowfully.

"Do you think she was seeking reassurance for something she already suspected?"

"Someone had been poisoning her mind."

"There have been many rumors. You must have heard them."

"The work of revolutionaries. What do they want, these people?"

Ruzsky rose again and moved to the mantelpiece. "Anna, your daughter knew Rasputin. On the records kept by the household staff, it is said that she met him both at the palace and in Petersburg."

Anna stared at the floor. "She would never have consorted with such a man."

"By all accounts, he was able to cure the Tsarevich of his bouts of hemophilia, or so the Empress believed. That would have encouraged Ella's approbation."

Anna did not answer.

"Did she give any intimation as to why she was asking you the question?"

Anna shook her head.

Ruzsky glanced at Pavel, then took a pace forward. "We must go. Thank you for your assistance." He leaned forward to touch her shoulder. She did not stand to see them out.

As they stepped out into the corridor and pulled the door gently shut behind them, they heard her begin to sob violently again.

They listened for a few moments, wondering whether to go back in and try to comfort her once more.

"God in heaven," Pavel said, as they began to walk away.

21

Downstairs, the sun was so shrouded by cloud that it was difficult to tell day from night. The wind whistled along the narrow alley between the tenements, and the few people out on the street moved quickly, their heads bent.

A funeral procession rounded the corner. Four men dressed in black carried a coffin draped in a simple scarlet cloth. Behind them came a group of women huddled together against the cold and holding their veils to their faces as the wind worried at their billowing robes. Alongside them walked three soldiers in dirty gray overcoats and woolen hats.

Ruzsky and Pavel waited as the procession passed, the only sound that of boots crunching in the snow. None of the mourners met their eye.

Ruzsky thought of the soldiers he had seen going off to the front on the day of his departure for Tobolsk three years ago. Then, the capital had been full of khaki-clad men marching with grim but determined faces.

Now only the politicians claimed the war could be won; defeat was in the face of every man in uniform.

For a moment, after the small cortege had turned into an alley and disappeared, the detectives gazed after it, both deep in thought. As they turned back, they saw a man huddled in the front of his cab at the far end of the alley, clutching the reins to his chest as his horse shifted restlessly. Once he saw that they were looking at him, he turned the cab around and moved off.

It came as a shock to Ruzsky, though he knew it shouldn't; they were being watched.

"A ruble for whoever's first to spot the next one," Ruzsky said, but Pavel wasn't smiling.

"Just ignore them," Ruzsky said. "If they've got nothing better to do—"

"But they have," Pavel said.

They had breakfast in the canteen. It was the first working day of the New Year, and it showed.

Pavel got a full tray of cold meat and pickled cucumbers; Ruzsky made do with Turkish coffee, since the vodka had killed off his hunger. They went to sit in the far corner, so that they would not be overheard.

"I knew Rasputin would come back to haunt us," Pavel said.

Ruzsky offered him a cigarette and they smoked in silence, glancing occasionally at the other diners.

"Why would Ella ask her mother that question?" Pavel asked.

"A guilty conscience."

"I don't understand."

"Ella was a shy, somewhat naive girl," Ruzsky said. "She knew little of life outside the palace and the respectable but dull world of her parents. For all her talk of revolution, she never quite comes to terms with what her American has asked her to do."

"To steal something?"

"Something personal."

"To do with Rasputin."

Ruzsky nodded. "It starts to make sense of things, don't you think?"

"And he has justified it to her on the grounds that the Empress and Rasputin are lovers. So what did Ella steal?"

"A diary?"

"If it had been a diary, she'd have been thrown into the darkest dungeon of the fortress over the river."

"Perhaps they don't know for sure what she stole."

"Then how did they know she'd stolen anything?"

"I'm not sure," Ruzsky said. "But I think we should try Shulgin again today. See if we can talk to some of the people Ella worked with." He stubbed out his cigarette. "What were Prokopiev's men doing there? I don't understand why he would be asking Ella's mother questions to which we assume he already knows the answers."

Pavel gestured toward the street outside. "I can understand why they might want to take over the case, but why would they want to watch us?"

Ruzsky shook his head.

"The country stands on the brink. And they have the time to watch two Petrograd city policemen going about their business?"

Ruzsky looked around the room. "We should go to Yalta," he said.

"Good idea. I need a holiday." Pavel wasn't taking him seriously.

"Everything leads to Yalta. We'll go tonight."

The color drained from Pavel's face.

"You don't wish to come?"

The big detective looked up. "It's up to you."

Anton and Maretsky came in. Anton was smoking a cigarette and raised it in greeting as they went to get a cup of coffee. Ruzsky and Pavel watched their progress in silence until they came to join them.

"So they're officially taking over the case," Anton said, as he sat down. "I just got a call from the Interior Ministry." He took off his glasses and placed them on the table, rubbing his forehead and eyes as Ruzsky had done. He stubbed out his cigarette on the top of the hardwood table, throwing the butt onto the floor beneath their feet, and lit another. Anton's eyes were bloodshot and he looked the way Ruzsky felt.

They sat in silence. None of them wished to take the matter further.

Maretsky was drinking hot water, which steamed up his glasses as he bent over it. He slid the mug to and fro, restlessly.

"We're going to Yalta," Ruzsky said. "Tonight."

"Why?" Anton asked.

"The man we found this morning was from Yalta," Ruzsky went on. "Ella was from Yalta. We think the dead American is wanted for armed robbery in Yalta."

No one spoke.

Ruzsky leaned forward. "I don't particularly want to live in a world where the chief of the Okhrana can do whatever he likes. Do you?"

Maretsky and Pavel both stared at the table. Anton shook his head. "We already live in that kind of world, Sandro."

"Well, we shouldn't just accept it."

No one responded. Maretsky shook his head slowly. Ruzsky looked at his colleagues. He knew what they were thinking—that he, of all of them, had nothing to lose. All that had awaited him upon his return from Tobolsk was a cold wife and a son whom he couldn't see. He tried to block Maria from his mind.

Maretsky, by contrast, had a family, despite the incident with the student. Anton had a daughter on one of the university courses for women who would not want her fellow students to know her father was a policeman—even one in the city police. And Pavel had Tonya and his boy, who were, as he so readily admitted, all he cared about. But Ruzsky was reluctant to let go.

Anton's lips thinned. "This isn't the time for a crusade. They've made it official. We can't ignore that."

"Since when has doing our job been a crusade? We've got three bodies and at least one killer. That makes it a murder case. That's what we're here to do."

"It *was* a murder case, now it's a series of atrocities carried out by a suspected revolutionary cell. And if you don't believe me, call the Interior Ministry."

"Revolutionaries don't stab their victims seventeen times."

No one responded.

"Let's ask ourselves some questions, then. Why do the Okhrana want this case? Maretsky?"

The professor continued to stare at the table.

"Maretsky? You work with them. You don't think this was the work of revolutionaries, do you? And what are the Okhrana doing?"

The professor looked up. His face was strained. "I go over there when I have to. I do not work with them."

"Well, what do you—"

"Do you know why you were sent into exile?" The professor's eyes flashed at Ruzsky through his dirty round glasses. "Because he didn't know what to make of you. He was still feeling his way then. You're highborn. You had connections. You were an unknown quantity. Better to play safe and get you out of the way. But it's all changed, Sandro. You've seen him up close. You know that."

Ruzsky thought of Vasilyev at the ballet, in the midst of the family that had largely disowned him. "I see nothing behind his eyes."

"Precisely. We're not talking about exile to Tobolsk anymore."

They contemplated this in silence.

"He's a chief of police, not God," Ruzsky said.

"We're not here to give you a sense of purpose," Anton responded.

Ruzsky felt his face redden.

"The Okhrana have taken over this case. There is nothing we can do about it."

"We could take it up with the Interior Ministry." It was a weak argument and he knew it.

Anton shook his head. "Vasilyev can pick up the telephone and call the palace anytime he chooses."

"But the palace doesn't like the Okhrana," Pavel said quietly. He smiled at Ruzsky, his earlier faint heart apparently forgotten.

Anton sighed.

"They can't punish us for continuing to amass information on a murder case," Ruzsky went on.

"Of course they can."

"We can say we were still seeking to assist them."

"They can suspend us, dismiss us, send us to where you've just come from. Or worse."

To Ruzsky, Anton suddenly seemed terribly tired. It was as if he had given up, not just on his work, but on life. It was hard to recall the witty, outspoken man who had kept them laughing for hours during those evenings at his country home overlooking the Gulf of Finland.

"They have removed us from the case. Categorically. Explicitly," Anton said. "They left no room for me to claim a misunderstanding. I'm going to have to ask you to desist from any further inquiries."

"But why?" Ruzsky asked. "That's the question. Why are they so determined to block us?"

"That may be the question, but it is not one to which we have to find an answer. My instructions are clear. It would have been difficult to get to Yalta, anyway. You've heard what it is like."

Anton stood. He did not meet Ruzsky's eye. He turned and walked out. Maretsky followed him.

"So now we are two," Pavel said once they'd gone. "Well done."

22

The train out to Tsarskoe Selo moved slower than ever, the rhythmic hiss of the steam engine and the gentle rattle and roll of the carriages sending Pavel to sleep. He rested his head between the seat and the window, his mouth wide open.

As he looked out at the snow-covered landscape, Ruzsky could not imagine ever leaving the country of his birth.

"What are you thinking?" Pavel asked. His head hadn't moved, but his mouth was shut and he'd been watching him.

"Nothing much."

"A girl?"

They pulled out of the trees and Ruzsky leaned closer to the window. It was so dirty and the landscape here so monotonous, it was hard to distinguish snow and sky from the grayness of the pane.

"Is it love?"

Ruzsky didn't answer.

"Who is it?"

Ruzsky shook his head.

"The ballerina?"

"No," Ruzsky lied.

Pavel whistled quietly. "She's beautiful. I wouldn't blame you. What will you do?"

"Nothing."

"I don't believe you."

"Believe what you want."

"Love has a habit of overcoming most obstacles," Pavel said.

Ruzsky looked out of the window. Two young boys in thick winter coats stood on top of the bank, waving at the passengers. Ruzsky waved back.

"Sometimes the obstacles are impossible to overcome," he said.

"But you don't really believe it. That's your secret."

Pavel smiled, but Ruzsky could not respond. He had a sudden, vivid image of Maria and his brother naked in front of her fire, the soft light dancing over their bodies.

He stared out of the window again.

"Now what are you thinking?" Pavel asked.

"That I wish you would shut up."

"I'm here to torment you until you talk."

Ruzsky attempted a smile. "Nothing profound. About Russia. About home."

Pavel searched his face. "Did you ever think of escape?"

Ruzsky thought of the ice cracking, of the water's embrace. "And leave Michael in the hands of the Grand Duke?"

Pavel nodded ruefully. "I could never live anywhere else."

"Neither could I."

Pavel straightened. "Perhaps you could take him with you. I'm not saying you wouldn't miss home—you do miss it—but whatever it was that happened in your . . . well, you know. You could go."

"You sound like my nanny."

Pavel took that as a compliment, though it wasn't necessarily meant as one. "We've known each other a long time."

Ruzsky didn't answer.

"It's been a privilege to be your friend."

Ruzsky frowned. "Am I missing something?"

"I like things to be said. I don't like them to be hidden, you know that."

Ruzsky turned to the window again.

"Do you enjoy your job, Sandro?"

"What do you mean?"

"Exactly what I said."

"This is a strange series of questions."

"You're an idealist; you didn't have to work—"

"Neither true, alas."

"You could have made up with your family, if you'd wanted to."

Ruzsky didn't answer.

"I started out as a constable—I had very little choice—but I enjoy what I do. I was just thinking about it . . ."

Ruzsky leaned forward to interrupt. "I don't know where this is leading us, Pavel."

"I've always assumed that I understood what made you do this job, but I've never asked."

"Yes. I suppose the answer is yes. I enjoy what I do, but you're wrong about a lot of things. I don't think of myself as an idealist."

"Why not?"

"Because what you see as idealism, my old friend, I know to be obstinacy. It's not the same thing at all."

Pavel pressed his forehead against the cold glass of the window. "What will become of us?"

"We'll be all right."

"Do you think so?"

"Yes."

"I don't. Not anymore."

"What are you worried about?" Ruzsky asked.

"About Tonya. About my boy."

"They'll be all right. If anyone, it is you who should worry."

"Exactly. And where would they be if something happened to me?"

"I'd look after them."

"Would you?" Pavel's eyes glistened.

"Of course. I'd steal one of my father's paintings."

Pavel looked uncertain for a moment, then grinned sheepishly. "Very funny, Sandro," he said.

At the Alexander Palace, they were shown through to the same anteroom and told to wait. Ruzsky walked to the window and looked out at the frozen lake, but there was no sign of the imperial children. A skein of mist curled around the trees in the distance and stretched out across the ice.

"This is a bad idea," Pavel said again.

Ruzsky did not respond.

"Just because we didn't see them watching us on the way here doesn't mean to say that they weren't."

Ruzsky turned. "Shulgin doesn't like the Okhrana, or at least the Petrograd Okhrana, and I think the feeling is mutual. We'll see what happens."

"It's crazy to come here."

Ruzsky shook his head. They'd had this argument three times already.

They heard footsteps and turned to see the guard who had brought them. "Come with me," he said, without grace or ceremony.

Their coats were returned to them in the hallway. "Are we not to receive an audience?" Ruzsky asked with equal curtness.

"Please come with me." The guard turned on his heel and led them out, past the columns at the front of the palace and the two curved archways, to the far wing.

The door swung open and they were admitted by a tall houseboy in a bright red and gold uniform. Two others stood behind him; a fourth took their coats.

He took them up two steps and marched them down a long corridor.

"What's going on?" Pavel whispered.

"These are the family quarters," Ruzsky said.

Their footsteps echoed. Martial paintings lined the walls. Ruzsky's eye was caught by a giant portrait of Nicholas I on a white charger. A shrill peel of laughter rang out from somewhere on their left.

They were led past two large golden urns and into a formal room decorated, too, in red and gold. They stood for a moment at its entrance, flanked on either side by a phalanx of white marble busts, beneath a vast tapestry of Marie Antoinette and her children.

The houseboy invited them to sit on an upholstered, gilt-edged sofa, between two inlaid grand pianos, then withdrew. They listened to his footsteps receding.

"What's going on?" Pavel whispered again.

Ruzsky was staring up at Marie Antoinette. He turned to Pavel and put his finger to his lips. He mouthed: "Empress," and pointed to the open door on the far side of the room.

They heard more footsteps in the corridor.

Shulgin entered, scowling. "You did not telephone."

"Please accept my apologies, Your High Excellency," Ruzsky said quietly, knowing that the colonel's performance was not entirely for their benefit.

"That does not—"

Shulgin stopped as both Ruzsky and Pavel became aware of a figure standing in the shadows beyond the doorway.

"What do they want, Shulgin?" the Tsarina asked.

"They are investigating the death of Ella Kovyil, Your Majesty."

"I asked, what do they want?"

"They wish to speak to some of the household staff who worked alongside her. I have told them already, on a previous occasion, that this is a matter that requires discussion with other senior members of staff . . ."

The Tsarina stepped forward into the doorway. She wore a black dress, with an oval mother-of-pearl brooch pinned to the neck.

"I saw you before," she said to Ruzsky. "Two days ago."

"Yes, Your Majesty."

Ruzsky stood and made a small bow, then gave a sidelong glance at Pavel, who was sitting with his mouth open. He snapped upright and did the same.

"What do you want now?" she asked.

"They fear a conspiracy," Shulgin said, his tone dismissive. "Some political skulduggery."

"Is this true?" the Tsarina demanded. She looked at them for the first time, concentrating her attentions on Pavel, but her gaze was neutral, neither censorious nor inquisitive.

"It is one possibility," Ruzsky said.

"Then it should be a matter for the Okhrana."

"If it pleases Your Highness."

"*Is* it a matter for the Okhrana?" She made no attempt to conceal her impatience.

"Yes."

"Then why are they not here instead of you?"

"I don't know, Your Majesty. Perhaps they will be."

The Tsarina hesitated. "You give swift answers, Detective, and yet I do not believe them."

Ruzsky did not respond.

"Why have you not found Ella's killer?"

Ruzsky looked at Shulgin, whose expression now appeared to carry more than a hint of apology for his mistress's haughty manner. "We are working tirelessly, Your Highness," Ruzsky said evenly. "But our resources are few. As I'm sure you are aware, the city has known better times."

"What do you mean by that?"

Ruzsky immediately recognized his mistake. "The war, Your Majesty; a strain upon us all, but especially on your good self."

"The Tsar is returning to the front," she said. Perhaps realizing this had little relevance, she added: "We will prevail." It was said with finality, but she did not move.

Shulgin coughed nervously. They all examined the highly polished floor.

"Why do you think Ella was murdered by a revolutionary?" the Tsarina asked.

"It is only a theory," Ruzsky said, not wishing to contradict her.

"Tell me about it."

Ruzsky glanced at Shulgin again, but was given no lead. The colonel was still staring discreetly at his boots.

"Your Majesty, Ella's lover, the American, was a notorious agitator."

"An American?"

"Yes."

"What was he doing in Petrograd?"

"We don't know."

"You have spoken to the Okhrana. To Vasilyev, to that other tiresome, arrogant man . . ." She snorted in distaste.

"Ivan Alexandrovich, ma'am," Shulgin said.

"Prokopiev. Yes. Have you spoken to them?"

"We have." Ruzsky answered.

"What do they have to say on the matter?"

"I believe they were informed some weeks ago that the American would be returning to the capital."

The Tsarina looked at him sharply. Her eyes had narrowed. Ruzsky knew that he was playing with fire, but had been unable to resist. "Who told you that?" she asked.

"The American embassy."

"The American embassy? That ridiculous man . . ."

"A Mr. Morris, ma'am," Shulgin offered.

The Tsarina stared at Ruzsky. "You don't seem to have achieved very much, Investigator . . ."

"Ruzsky."

"Ah, yes. Your father is the assistant minister of finance."

The Empress seemed on the verge of making some dismissive remark, but thought better of it. "So am I to understand that a member of the imperial household was stabbed in the center of our city, and yet you know nothing of who killed her, or why?"

"We believe that the American may have had something to do with whatever it was that she stole from you."

"Who told you that she stole from me?" The Tsarina glared at Shulgin.

"With respect, you did, Your Majesty," Ruzsky said. He could no longer recall if this was true, or whether he had first learned of Ella's alleged crime from Anna Vyrubova, but he wanted to see if he could catch the Empress off balance.

"You must try harder," she said, before turning on Shulgin. "This is an absolute disgrace. Speak to Vasilyev and—"

"I was under the impression that it had already been done," Ruzsky said.

In the uneasy silence that followed, he could see that the Tsarina was caught between fury at the interruption and curiosity as to what he had meant.

"We were led to believe," Ruzsky went on, "that the palace considered it in the nation's best interests that the matter be given . . ." Ruzsky caught Pavel's eye. He looked as if he was about to faint. "We were under the impression," he said carefully, "that the palace had dwelt upon this matter, and did not consider it an item of high priority."

Shulgin again became the focus of the Tsarina's infuriation. "What's this?"

"I have no idea."

"What do you mean?" She turned back to Ruzsky.

"Exactly as I said, Your Highness. But I must have been mistaken. I apologize. You wish the matter to be given the highest priority?"

"Of course. An attack on one of our members of staff? What could be more important than that?"

Shulgin breathed in deeply as the Empress retired. For a moment, they were all co-conspirators, but his reserve quickly reasserted itself. He took a step back, as if to distance himself from the exchange that had just taken place.

"Please wait here for a moment," he said.

23

It was almost an hour before he came back—during which time they had more or less sat in silence—and when he did so, his manner was off-hand. It took Ruzsky a few moments to realize that this was from anxiety rather than irritation.

Shulgin, he decided, as they followed him down the corridor, was not a bad sort. He reminded him even more forcibly of his father.

Their coats were again returned and they were led back across to the library, where a silver tray with a samovar upon it awaited them, between two low chairs and a long settee, covered with crimson velvet and gold piping. "Please have a seat," Shulgin said, before disappearing.

They did as they'd been instructed and looked around. It was a beautiful room, less ornate and therefore somehow more intimate than the antechamber they'd just left. A fire burned on the hearth between two enormous bookcases filled from floor to ceiling with leather-bound volumes. In the center of the room, there was a giant globe with a three-dimensional, topographical map of Russia similar to the ones he had been taught with at the Corps des Pages. It stood beside a grand piano. Ruzsky had an almost irresistible desire to go and play.

"Could you please explain what in hell is going on?" Pavel asked.

Ruzsky shook his head. "I have no idea."

Shulgin reentered the room, accompanied by a man in a sailor's uniform and a young girl of about Ella's age. The man looked resentful, the girl shy and nervous. They both sat awkwardly on the chairs, while Shulgin took his position on the long settee. He leaned forward and poured tea, though only Ruzsky accepted the proffered cup.

"These are two of Ella's colleagues from the household staff," Shulgin explained. "They knew her as well as anyone."

Ruzsky waited in vain for them to be introduced and then leaned forward to offer his hand to the man, who took it reluctantly. He seemed about to open his mouth when Shulgin intervened. "I don't think there is any need for you to know their names."

Ruzsky sat back down.

"For their own safety," the colonel added.

"Of course."

Ruzsky dug a notepad and pencil from his jacket pocket. He turned to the girl. "You knew Ella well?"

"Quite well, sir, yes."

"You worked alongside her in the nursery?"

The girl glanced at Shulgin. Her vulnerability made her seem even prettier than she'd first appeared.

Shulgin nodded and she turned her anxious eyes back to Ruzsky. "Yes," she said.

"Did you know her from Yalta, or from here in Petersburg?"

"Just here, sir. I'm from Moscow."

"You've never been to Yalta?"

"No, sir."

"How long have you worked at the palace?"

"About two years."

"I served with her father," Shulgin said. "Her background is second to none."

Ruzsky ignored the interruption. "You both looked after the Tsarevich?" he asked. "You and Ella?"

"I worked with Ella," the sailor said.

Ruzsky swung toward him. "You looked after the Tsarevich together?"

"Yes," the man said.

"Did you know Ella before she came here?"

"No. I'm from Petrograd."

"How long have you been working at the palace?"

"Three years. Before that, Kronstadt; before that, the Barents Sea." It was said without pride, almost like a prisoner rattling off the length of his sentence.

"You liked Ella?"

"Of course. Everyone liked her."

"You were lovers?"

Shulgin almost choked on his tea. "Investigator, I must warn you—"

"No," the man said. His gaze was steady.

"Ella already had a lover?"

"So she said."

"Did she say who?"

"I knew he was an American, someone she'd met at home."

"What did she say about him?"

"Nothing. Not to me, anyway."

"Nothing?"

The man shrugged. He had a wide, strong face and held himself well. His naval uniform was immaculately pressed.

"She was secretive?" Pavel asked, suddenly finding his voice.

"About him, yes."

"What about other friends?" Pavel asked.

The sailor shook his head. "She went to see her mother on Sundays. She wrote letters. That was all. She led a quiet life and didn't deserve to have it ended like that."

"Few do," Ruzsky said. He turned toward Shulgin. "Do you have any of her letters, or other belongings?"

The colonel shook his head.

"Did she ever talk about politics?" Ruzsky asked the sailor. He knew neither wished to be here, or to help their former colleague.

"Not to me."

"Not to you, or not at all?"

"Not to me." A muscle was flexing in the man's cheek. Why was he so angry?

"To others?"

"I can't say." The sailor shook his head.

Ruzsky turned back to the girl. "And you, mademoiselle?"

"Not to me. No, of course not."

"Why of course not?"

"This is the imperial household, Investigator," Shulgin said.

"Did you ever hear her discussing politics with others?" Ruzsky asked the girl.

"No, sir."

"Did you know that her American lover was a well-known revolutionary criminal?"

"No, sir." Her shock was genuine.

Ruzsky addressed the sailor. "You?"

"No."

"But you knew that she went to see Rasputin in Petersburg on her days off?"

It took Shulgin a few moments to react. "That is a confidential matter," he said. "And no business of other members of staff."

"But you knew?" Ruzsky asked the man.

"She had the good sense not to broadcast any relationship . . . friendship," he corrected himself.

"Why do you call it good sense?" Ruzsky asked.

The sailor did not answer.

"This has no bearing on the investigation," Shulgin said again. "I really must ask you—"

"Tell us about her last few days," Pavel said.

The sailor leaned forward, placing his elbows on his knees and rubbing the palms of his hands together. "What do you want to know?"

"Was there anything different or unusual about her behavior?"

The sailor shook his head and then looked at the girl.

"No," she said.

"She was very happy," the sailor added.

Shulgin stood. "Chief Investigator, a word, please."

As they stepped outside, Ruzsky said: "There is no point in allowing us to meet with these people if you are going to prevent us asking them any pertinent questions."

"*Remember where you are*," Shulgin whispered.

"I can see exactly." Ruzsky looked down the corridor. "Now, do you want to find out who killed your girl or not?"

"We shall call the Okhrana," Shulgin said.

"Be my guest, but they are utterly unsuited to anything that might require a modicum of patience to unravel."

"You have your father's arrogance."

Ruzsky hesitated. "How well do you know my father?"

"He was in my year at the Corps des Pages." Ruzsky realized that, despite his own lowly office, Shulgin had deliberately accorded him from the start the respect due someone of a similar background. "I can't have you rampaging about in there—"

"They're as stiff as boards."

"They're nervous."

"That's not the reason, and you know it. You want us to get to the bottom of this, or we'd not even have got through the door this morning. And so, by the sound of it, does the Empress. What is it? You don't trust the Okhrana?"

"You have not served your cause well."

"Did you telephone the police department after our first visit?"

Shulgin looked at him with incredulity.

"After we first came out here to see you, did you telephone the department to request that the investigation be dropped?"

"Why would I do such a thing?"

"We humble members of the city police," Ruzsky said, "were led to believe that the Empress herself did not wish the investigation into Ella Kovyil's death to proceed."

"That's preposterous. Who told you that?"

"Your friend Mr. Vasilyev."

Shulgin glanced down the corridor in the direction Ruzsky had a moment before. A weary resignation seemed to replace his confused frown. He removed his monocle and tucked it into the pocket of his immaculately pressed uniform.

"It would be better if you were not there while we talk to them," Ruzsky said.

"That's out of the question." Shulgin raised his arm to indicate that they should return.

Ruzsky resumed his seat and leaned forward. "A few final matters, if you would be so kind. Did she . . . did Ella talk about the American's return?" He had been looking at the sailor, but now turned toward the girl. "Mademoiselle?"

"She was very happy that Robert . . . Mr. White had come back. She received the news that he would be, several months ago in a letter."

"Did you ever meet Mr. White?"

The girl shook her head. "No, sir."

Ruzsky looked at the sailor. "How did you find her over these past few months?" He made a conscious effort to soften his tone. "You must have seen her every day. Was there anything you noticed that would help us, anything unusual?"

"She was moodier. One minute very happy, the next withdrawn."

"Did she give any hint as to why?"

"I thought it was . . . women's matters."

The girl nodded. "One minute she would . . . talk about it, I mean. She would say something like, 'Natasha, he is coming, he really is.' And then she would say, 'Natasha, I don't know what to do, but he is wonderful.' When I asked her what she meant, she would say, 'It is nothing.' She received many letters, addressed by the same hand; one or two a week in the last months. They are placed on a table outside the kitchen. She would fall upon them and no matter how late she was, or what other duties awaited her, she would race up to her room and stay there for half an hour, sometimes more."

"There were . . . *incidents*," Shulgin said.

"She loved the boy more than anyone," the sailor snapped back. Ruzsky saw for the first time that the man's anger was directed against his superior.

"She harmed him?" Ruzsky asked.

"She raised her voice, that was all," the sailor said. "The boy was unwell, it was not his fault, but we are all under pressure."

There was an awkward silence.

"How did she behave in the last day or two, immediately before the incident that caused her dismissal?" Ruzsky asked.

They both shook their heads.

"She gave no sign of being under any additional strain?"

They didn't respond.

"So what exactly happened?"

"Chief Investigator—"

"I'm not asking what she stole, but how she was caught," Ruzsky told Shulgin. "Surely we can be informed of that."

"One of the footmen found her in the Empress's study," Shulgin said. "Naturally, he had no choice but to inform me, and I the Empress. It was not a place she was entitled to be."

"What was she doing there?"

"The footman in question said that she started in a guilty manner when discovered."

"She was at the Empress's desk?"

Shulgin had taken out his monocle again and was staring at it. "I don't see how this can have any direct bearing on the case."

"So she didn't steal anything?" Ruzsky asked.

Shulgin looked at him. "The Empress believes that she did."

"What?"

"I'm afraid—"

"What on earth could this girl have been looking for in the study of the Empress of the Russias?"

"I don't know." Shulgin could no longer conceal his own exasperation. "I simply do not know."

"The Empress told you she had stolen something, but not what? I thought you said Ella readily confessed to her crime."

"She didn't steal anything," the sailor said.

"Then what was she doing in there?" Ruzsky said.

"We have taken this as far as it can sensibly go." Shulgin stood. Neither of the others now met Ruzsky's eye.

As soon as they had been let out of the wrought iron gates, Pavel breathed an enormous sigh of relief. "Christ," he said. "Has Tobolsk done something to your mind?"

Ruzsky did not respond. He took out and lit a cigarette.

"Going on with the investigation is not exactly sane, but that was pure madness."

Ruzsky stopped. "It gives us a degree of protection. Don't you see that?"

"No."

"That was the most bizarre interview we have ever conducted. Correct?"

"Indisputably."

"They are completely in the dark. They're suspicious of the Okhrana and Vasilyev."

"That may be, but it's not going to help us. We're just caught in the middle." Pavel pointed at him aggressively. "You have taken us into the middle of a minefield, and you know it."

"If the Okhrana has been following us this morning, then now they'll know that they have to tread carefully."

"Rubbish. We've just increased the stakes in a game whose rules we don't even begin to know. And we're still no nearer to working out what in the hell is going on." Pavel's face was flushed. "Tell me what that was all about."

Ruzsky shook his head. "I don't know."

"You're damned right you don't know. We're invited into the family apartments. The woman who rules us is lurking in the doorway like some kind of ghost. It is all completely unreal. She asks us whether the Okhrana are involved. She doesn't know what's happening beyond her own doorstep?"

Ruzsky raised his hand. "But Ella did steal something."

"The sailor man denies it."

"But as you say, they're worried. Very, very worried. Worried enough to entertain the notion of interrogating a couple of lowly city police-men, and then allowing us to interview members of the household. Is that normal? Hardly. And a few months ago it would have been unthink-able."

"So we go crashing in like a couple of ignorant peasants—"

"That girl stole something important."

Pavel stared miserably into the distance.

"It is the only rational explanation for that episode. They can't admit she stole something, let alone what it was, but they don't trust the Okhrana. Or at least, they were talking to us as a way of finding out how the investigation is proceeding."

Pavel shook his head. Farther down a cab driver stood by his horse, waiting for a fare.

Ruzsky had never seen a droshky waiting there before.

There was a young, dark-haired boy standing in the far corner of their of-fice, looking out of the window.

For a moment, Ruzsky felt a surge of excitement. "My boy," Pavel bellowed as he bounded over and took his son into his arms.

A woman appeared next to him. "Sandro," she said, embracing him warmly.

He held her. "Tonya."

Ruzsky stepped back. She was thinner, her blond hair framing a face that seemed more careworn than before he had gone away. Her lips were pinched and her cheeks hollow and in another woman it would have had the effect of making her look mean, but Tonya had always possessed an air of fragility. She gave him a shy smile.

"What do you say to your uncle Sandro?" Pavel said. He still had his son in his arms.

"Hello, Uncle Sandro." The boy was younger than Michael. He had long eyelashes and big blue eyes and, apart from his hair, was the spitting image of his mother.

The sight of him, the innocence in his voice, made Ruzsky's heart lurch.

It was insane. He had been back more than forty-eight hours. Why had he not seen his boy?

Tonya picked up a suitcase and put it on Pavel's desk. "A holiday in Yalta!" It was a poor joke and, when she turned to face Ruzsky, he saw clearly the fear in her face. "You will look after him, won't you, Sandro?"

"I was rather hoping it would be the other way around."

"I don't trust him to look after himself." Whatever confidence Tonya had projected a few minutes before had vanished.

"He'll be fine," Ruzsky said. "I'll see to it he's kept out of trouble."

"I can tell, even on the telephone, when he's uncertain about something."

"Tonya—"

"Please, Sandro." Her eyes burned. "You will look after him, won't you?"

"Of course."

"Tonya . . ." Pavel's face softened further as he took his wife into his arms and drew their son into the narrow gap between their bodies. Ruzsky stood, transfixed, then turned and quietly withdrew.

24

There was a low archway to one side of the front door to the house in Millionnaya Street, and beyond it a gate into the garden. Ruzsky slipped through and climbed the stone steps that led up to the lawn. He saw Michael immediately, but there was a woman with him, so he ducked instinctively back into the shadows. It took him a few moments to realize that the woman was Ingrid.

They were building a snowman, and Michael was perched on a wooden chair, leaning forward to work on the eyes and mouth.

They were both dressed in dark overcoats, but neither was wearing a hat. Ingrid's long blond hair had shaken loose down her back, and shone in the dim light. Ruzsky suddenly wanted to reach out and touch it.

Michael concentrated on scooping holes carefully in the center of the snowman's head, until he got bored and threw a handful of snow at his aunt. Ingrid roared and chased him around the garden as he shrieked with laughter. After allowing him to escape repeatedly, she caught him and rolled him in the snow until he was in hysterics.

She straightened and caught sight of Ruzsky. "Stop, Liebchen, stop," she said, blushing. "It's Papa."

For a moment, Michael stood rooted to the spot. Then he ran headlong into his father's outstretched arms. Ruzsky hugged his son so tightly that Michael groaned with the pressure.

"Papa," Michael said, his eyes shining as Ruzsky released him, but then he looked down, suddenly unsure of himself.

"It's all right, my boy."

"Where have you been?"

"I've been . . . working."

Michael looked at him solemnly. "Mama said you didn't want to see us."

Ruzsky stared at his son in silence, then gathered him into his arms again. "You know that's not true, don't you?"

Michael nodded, but Ruzsky mourned the fact that the look of playful innocence he had radiated during the game with his aunt a few moments before had vanished from his face.

Ruzsky walked over to Ingrid. She adjusted her hair nervously. "I'm sorry, Sandro. I didn't see you."

"Why should you apologize?"

"It was just a game."

"Of course. We can play on." Ruzsky put Michael down, inclining his head toward the house. "Is . . . ?"

Ingrid shook her head.

"Out all afternoon?" Ruzsky said.

"I don't know," Ingrid answered. "She never says."

"Let battle commence," Ruzsky said. He built himself a small wall, scrabbling around in the snow and glancing across to where Ingrid and Michael were preparing their ammunition. Once or twice, he caught the look of bewilderment in his son's eyes, but sought to divert it by chasing him around the garden. They collapsed in the corner and Michael stuffed snow in his father's shirt and over his hair and face as Ruzsky giggled and screamed for help. Ingrid stood above them, her face flushed and chest heaving. She was smiling and Ruzsky thought again that she was even more beautiful than he remembered.

He wrestled with Michael until he was cold and knew his son must be, too. He cried, "Enough," and stood, tossing Michael over his shoulder and striding toward the house. Michael wriggled with delight, then lay still, his head pressed against his father's, a small hand clutching the back of Ruzsky's collar.

Outside the kitchen, Ruzsky unpeeled Michael's overcoat, scarf, and boots. The boy watched him warily. As Ruzsky hung his son's coat on the low hook by the kitchen door, his nostrils filled with the aroma of baking bread and he was overcome by a wave of nostalgia.

He took Michael's hand and pushed open the kitchen door with his foot. Katya was bent over the oven. A young assistant he didn't recognize eyed him nervously while Katya fussed over the baking tray. When she straightened and saw him, there was a hint of anxiety in her eyes too, but she quickly smothered it. "Sandro," she said, beaming, as she bustled toward him and put her round, red face against his.

Before he had had a chance to respond, she had begun to fuss over Michael. "You're freezing cold, young master," she said. "Look at the state of you!"

Michael glanced at his father and rolled his eyes. Ruzsky smiled.

"You need a cup of hot milk," Katya said as she returned to the stove and pulled across a pan. "Would you like some English tea, Master Sandro?" She glanced at Ingrid, who was standing behind them. "Madam?"

"Why not?" Ruzsky said, turning.

"Your father is here," Ingrid blurted.

Katya bustled across the room. Ruzsky sighed quietly. How they all jumped to the old tyrant's tune.

"Why is Grandpapa always angry with you?" Michael asked.

Ruzsky knelt down and lifted his son onto a side table. "It's a long story."

"Mama says that Grandpapa won't let you into the house, but I asked Grandpapa about it and I told him it was unfair, because it is your house, too."

Ruzsky forced himself to smile. "And what did he say?"

"He said he would think about it."

"I'm sure he will."

"I love Grandpapa. Some people, like the servants, say he is frightening, but he doesn't frighten me."

"I'm pleased to hear it."

"He gave me a wooden train set and we play with it together."

Ruzsky put his hands in his pockets and breathed in deeply, trying to hold on to his smile. Once, his father had liked nothing better than to join his eldest son after a day's work, building a train track on the floor of his bedroom.

"You must like playing with Auntie Ingrid," Ruzsky said.

"Yes, I do. Auntie Ingrid is kind. She always plays with me. Mama never does."

Ingrid unselfconsciously stroked Michael's hair. "That's not true, Liebchen."

"It is true." Michael's face had become sorrowful. "She is always busy." He looked at his father. "Why don't you live with us anymore, Papa?"

Ingrid looked embarrassed. "I'll go."

"You don't have to." Ruzsky took his son's hand. "I'll explain in a minute. We'll go upstairs and play together. Would that be all right?"

"Yes!" Michael jumped off the table. "We can build a big train track!"

"In a minute. Have your milk first."

Michael walked over to Katya's side and the housekeeper hugged him to her as she had Sandro when he was a boy, his head resting upon her ample thigh while she finished warming the milk. She reached up and took down a large mug from the shelf. It had a familiar picture of Peter the Great on one side holding a hammer and the dates of the city's bicentenary: 1703–1903.

"Is it true, what he says?" Ruzsky asked Ingrid.

"I honestly don't know, Sandro."

"She ignores him?" he whispered.

"He misses you."

Ruzsky closed his eyes for a moment. Should he try and patch up some kind of relationship with Irina for Michael's sake? Would she allow it? Could he bear it? He thought of their violent, bitter, loveless rows, of her screaming at him, teeth bared.

"I don't know what one can do," Ruzsky said. "Perhaps you should be grateful you don't have children."

"I would never be grateful for that," Ingrid said, and Ruzsky saw the deep sadness in her eyes.

"I'm sorry."

She smiled. "There is no need to be sorry."

"What will you do?"

Now she laughed, and although her laughter was brittle, it brought light and warmth to her face. "What *can* I do? A German in wartime Petrograd. I'm a prisoner."

"It can't be that bad, surely."

"These last few months . . ." Ingrid shook her head. "My accent is still strong."

They both watched Michael sitting at the table with Katya, drinking his milk.

"I am pleased that you are back," she said, quietly. She spoke slowly and carefully, and Ruzsky felt his face reddening. "Will you live together again? With Irina?"

"We couldn't afford to," Ruzsky said. "Not in the style she would insist upon, anyway. Irina's parents are embarrassed by me and will only entertain the idea of her without me. As for my own father, you know the situation well enough."

"I'm sure Dmitri could—"

"No." Ruzsky turned toward her and smiled. "It's not possible anymore."

Ingrid gazed at the floor. "Have you seen Dmitri?" she asked.

"Yes."

Ingrid still did not look up. "Did . . ."

It was painful to watch her struggling with herself. "I'm sorry," Ruzsky said, without thinking.

She raised her head. "Did he tell you?"

"No."

"It is common gossip?"

Ruzsky wished he could ease the desolation he saw in her eyes. Had she not known of his brother's reputation before? Was it only Maria that she was aware of? Her pain fueled his own. "I do not believe so," he said kindly.

"Then how—"

"I guessed."

She did not believe him. "Dmitri has been arguing with your father."

"What about?"

"I don't know. But it puts him in a foul temper."

For a moment, they stared at each other, then Ruzsky walked over and bent down by his son. "Come on, my boy. Shall we build that train track now?"

As he left the room, Ruzsky turned and saw Ingrid with her head down, her hands over her eyes.

The house in Millionnaya Street was almost dark. Ruzsky led his son quietly past the door of his father's study. Like their home at Petrovo, the walls here were filled with portraits and banners from the family's martial past. The floors were covered with rich red rugs from central Asian campaigns, and the mantelpieces laden with strange and exotic artifacts—masks, daggers, even jewels.

They turned the last corner and, still hand in hand, climbed the narrow stairs to the attic.

At the top, Ruzsky hesitated. To the right of the landing, behind a door that was now shut, had been Dmitri's room when they were both children. Ilusha had shared it with him, because he hadn't liked sleeping alone.

Ruzsky stepped toward it.

"Come on, Papa," Michael said.

Ruzsky felt the nerves tauten in the base of his stomach as he depressed the metal latch.

"Grandpapa says that room will be for Dmitri's son."

Ruzsky pushed open the door, ducked forward, and opened the curtains. Gray light filtered through the dust that hung heavily in the air.

The two wooden box beds were still in place under the lee of the sloping roof. Ilusha's tattered elephant lay on his pillow. A painted wooden soldier in the uniform of the Preobrazhenskys stood guard at the end of his bed. On a shelf, a black-and-white photograph of Ilusha, flanked by two short brass candlesticks, made the alcove seem like a shrine.

On the other side of the room, above Dmitri's pillow, was the box in which all his toy soldiers were stored, arranged neatly by regiment. His tattered polar bear was sprawled across the lid, its head drooping.

"Grandpapa doesn't like me to come in here," Michael said quietly.

Ruzsky stared at Ilusha's elephant. One ear had fallen off and his trunk had been loved almost out of existence. Its one remaining eye was fixed upon him.

"Grandpapa doesn't like me to come in here," Michael said again.

Ruzsky put his hand around his son's head and drew him closer, then bent down and picked him up, holding him tight, the boy's head resting upon his shoulder.

"I love you, my boy."

"I love you, Papa."

Ruzsky carried his son back out onto the landing, pulling the door gently shut behind him. He lowered Michael to the ground and let the boy lead him into his bedroom. An electric lamp spilled across the floor, which was littered with bits of train track and other wooden toys. Ruzsky saw his own bear sitting above Michael's bed, also now a shadow of its former self. He picked it up, smiling.

"I always sleep with him," Michael said. "And my bear, of course."

Ruzsky felt the tears creeping into the corners of his eyes.

"What happened to Uncle Ilusha, Papa?"

Ruzsky wiped his eyes.

"Are you all right?" Michael asked.

Ruzsky sat down next to his son and breathed in. "Did anyone ever tell you that you look like your uncle Ilusha?"

"Does that mean I'm going to die too?"

"Of course not." Ruzsky leaned forward and started gathering together the pieces of track. "Of course not," he said again.

"How did Uncle Ilusha die?"

"It was an accident."

Ruzsky began to concentrate on assembling the track, and soon Michael was doing the same. The sections were beautifully made, and easy to fit together. There was a station, three bridges, a group of wooden houses, and a sprinkling of pine trees. The houses had been modeled on the village at Petrovo. There was even a replica of the big house itself, which Ruzsky set on top of a papier-mâché hill.

While Ruzsky assembled the track, Michael put the train together and began to push the engine around, imitating the sound of escaping steam as the wheels turned.

Ruzsky was working on the signal box when he looked up to see his father standing in the shadows by the doorway. He seemed to tower above him.

For a moment, Ruzsky tried to think of something to say, but couldn't, so he returned to what he was doing.

The silence grew.

Did the old man expect him to stand and be polite? Did he expect him to apologize for coming to his own home to see his own son?

Michael was steering the train around the other side of the track, oblivious to any tension, as if having his father and grandfather alongside him was an everyday occurrence.

The old man sighed and then squatted down and took the signal box from Ruzsky's hands. He looked at it for a moment and then slotted it together and placed it by the side of the track. He reached over, picked up the roof of the station building, and slotted that into place too, before gathering up all the people from the box beside him and placing them in position on the platform. There was a stationmaster, a newspaper seller, several passengers.

"No wounded soldiers," Ruzsky said.

The old man grunted. His lined and distinguished face was solemn, the tension visible around his eyes.

"Why were you arguing with Dmitri?" Ruzsky asked.

"That woman will be the death of him."

"Which woman?"

"You know damned well which one."

Ruzsky flushed with embarrassment. He wondered if Dmitri's affair with Maria really was common knowledge in the city.

The Colonel—as they had sometimes called him—examined his toy figures closely, then rearranged them so that the passengers were more obviously waiting for a train. "The world's gone mad," he said.

"Mad enough for you to be entertaining a man like Vasilyev at the opera?"

Ruzsky hadn't intended to be this provocative, but his father didn't flinch. "Vasilyev is a monster, but I don't know if he is a necessary or a treacherous one."

"Don't hold your breath."

"I won't, but this is a time of moral relativism."

"What are you talking about, Grandpapa?" Michael asked. He had sat back on his haunches, his hand still protectively over the train, his face creased by confusion.

"What indeed?" Ruzsky's father asked.

"Mama says that you hate each other."

There was a long silence. Ruzsky rearranged some of the pine trees into a small coppice in front of the house. "Then Mama, on this occasion, is wrong," his father said quietly.

Ruzsky didn't dare meet the old man's eye. He watched him check his gold pocket watch and then twist in his direction. "She'll be back in a minute," he said softly.

Ruzsky nodded and straightened, but his father got to his feet first and took a step back toward the door. "Have a few moments more in peace." He took another pace away. "Come again . . . won't you? Sandro?"

"Of course, Father."

The Colonel hesitated for a moment longer. Ruzsky turned away, his heart beating fast, and, a few seconds later, he heard the sound of his father's retreating footsteps.

25

As the night train to Moscow prepared to pull out, Ruzsky and Pavel watched the last burst of activity on the platform from the red velvet window seats of their second-class compartment.

A pair of swarthy Tartars selling shashlik competed volubly with two Chinese touting illegal hooch in tin bottles. The last of the third-class passengers bustled past, clutching straw baskets and clumsy bundles. A newspaper boy running the length of the train, his wares held aloft to display the headline, was suddenly lost in a cloud of steam that billowed from the engine.

As the steam drifted slowly along the platform toward the rear of the train, all Ruzsky could see were soldiers in long greatcoats. Some were sitting on benches, others standing and talking in small groups, a handful lying crudely bandaged, on stretchers. They didn't appear to be in a hurry to go anywhere.

But then, the train was already full of soldiers. Ruzsky and Pavel shared this compartment with four of them—rough peasant conscripts, uncommunicative and sullen, from south of Moscow, on their way back to the ancient capital. There were others in the corridor who had not found a berth, but showed no signs of disembarking.

"The country's like a military camp," Ruzsky said.

"You're policemen?" the man next to Pavel demanded.

They didn't respond.

"I thought so. I can smell it."

The man nodded curtly at his colleagues. He had big, full lips and a greasy, unshaven face. He put his boots up on the seat opposite, forcing Ruzsky to move his own legs out of the way. He ignored the provocation and turned back to the window. It would be better after Moscow, he told himself. Most of the soldiers would disembark there. The train on to Yalta would be more or less empty.

Ruzsky stretched out his own legs toward Pavel. The train lurched. The steam engine behind them hissed violently as it began to turn the giant iron wheels.

Despite the circumstances, Ruzsky found it hard to contain his excitement. As the train departed, he recalled how Dmitri and Ilya would stand with their noses pressed against the glass, waving to the servants who were staying behind to look after the house on Millionnaya Street.

Just as quickly as it had come, the thrill of those memories melted into something more melancholic. In every sense, the journeys to Petrovo were a part of history now.

They were gone forever.

The train gathered speed, pulling out of the Nicholas Station and gliding through the moonlit spires of the city.

The moon was bright until they reached the suburbs, and then it was suddenly engulfed in a bank of clouds and the world around them was swallowed by the night.

There was a single dim light in the compartment, but Ruzsky was happy to evade the scrutiny of his companions. "When will we see it again?" Pavel asked.

"See what?"

"Home."

"We're going to Yalta, not the moon."

"Thanks for your understanding."

"You're going to Yalta?" the man opposite asked, pausing in the process of lighting a cigarette.

Ruzsky didn't answer.

"Running away?"

Ruzsky leaned forward and offered his hand. "Sandro."

The soldier opposite stared at Ruzsky, smoking nonchalantly, until the offer was withdrawn. "Officer class," he said. "But not your friend." He grinned. He had almost no teeth.

Pavel shook his head and leaned against the window. Ruzsky glanced at his pocket watch and then closed his eyes. He had not checked the passenger lists before they'd embarked—partly because he couldn't think of an excuse to give Pavel—but he had climbed up onto the train brimming with confidence that she would be on board.

Her presence was like a magnet; it took a conscious act of will to remain seated.

Ruzsky tried to put her out of his mind. He listened as the soldiers opened a bottle of vodka and began to drink. They didn't offer any to their traveling companions, but didn't talk much amongst themselves either. When Ruzsky opened his eyes briefly, the man opposite was staring at him. Pavel started to snore gently.

Ruzsky listened to Pavel for a few moments, then could contain his impatience no longer. There were still soldiers in the corridor outside, as surly as those in his compartment. They allowed him to pass reluctantly, and his passage was a slow one.

Most of the blinds in the compartments had already been drawn, so Ruzsky had to knock on a succession of doors and open them, nodding to passengers within when he saw that she wasn't there.

He worked his way down the train. About fifty percent of the billets were occupied by soldiers, and they packed the corridors until Ruzsky reached the first-class carriages.

Here, a conductor stood on the inside of the door, barring entry, and was reluctant to open it even to speak to him. Ruzsky tried putting his weight against it, but it was locked.

He began to gesticulate at the man, but the glass was thick and the rattle of the train loud, and the conductor looked away from him.

Ruzsky pulled out his identification papers, placed them against the glass, and then hammered hard to force the man to turn around. "Police," he shouted.

Reluctantly, the guard unlocked the door and let him through, looking warily behind him to be sure he was on his own. As soon as he was past, the conductor slammed the door shut and locked it again.

It was quieter in here, and warmer. The curtains had been pulled shut all the way along the corridor. The conductor's face was visible in the dim glow of an overhead lamp.

"Maria Popova," Ruzsky said, and the man pointed down the corridor, without needing to consult the passenger list in his hand.

"Next carriage. At the end," he said. "Cabin number eight."

Ruzsky strode down the richly carpeted corridor and through the door into the next carriage, his nerves sharp again.

He breathed in. It was a relief to have left the soldiers behind.

He knocked.

"Who is it?"

Ruzsky did not answer.

"Who is it?" she called again.

"It's me, Sandro."

He waited. A thin sheen of sweat gathered on his forehead.

The door was pulled back.

There was no light in her eyes; she was not pleased to see him. His heart pounded faster. "I thought I would find you here," he said.

Her gaze remained steely.

"I have business in Yalta," he went on, aware that he was trying too hard to fill the silence that hung between them. "I am on the train with my partner and I recalled you saying you would be traveling south tonight."

"I suppose you had better come in," she said. She stepped back and sat down.

Ruzsky shut the door and seated himself opposite her. She wore a long, navy blue dress, buttoned with pearl studs high around her throat. Her dark hair spilled over her shoulders and down to the swell of her breast.

There was a single reading lamp, with a red lantern, casting shadows across the walls and ceiling, and the drawn blinds behind it.

Maria reached up to the leather suitcase on the rack above him, stretching on tiptoes as she removed a bottle.

She poured a large measure of whiskey into one of the glasses on the table by the window and handed it to him. She filled another for herself, then replaced the cork stopper and slipped the bottle under her pillow.

"Thank you," Ruzsky said. His voice felt as if it were coming from someone else.

They both drank.

Maria lifted the blind closest to her and stared out of the darkened window, but because of the light inside, he knew it was impossible for her to see anything.

"So many soldiers on board," Ruzsky said. "All ill-mannered."

"Wouldn't you be, if you'd been fighting with the Tsar's army?"

"Probably."

They sat in silence, each avoiding the other's eye. Ruzsky sipped his whiskey, then took out his cigarette case and offered her one. She declined, so he slipped it back into his pocket.

He thought she had never looked more beautiful.

Maria shut her eyes. Ruzsky watched a pained expression take hold of her face and then relax its grip again.

He listened to the steady rattle of the wheels on the iron rails beneath them.

"Have I done something wrong?" he asked.

Maria opened her eyes, but continued to stare out of the window. "No."

"You seem . . . angry."

"It was foolish," she said, almost inaudibly, "to think that we could be friends."

"Why?"

"You know damned well why." She turned on him. Anger burned brightly in her eyes. "What are you doing here?"

"I thought that—"

"What kind of fool do you take me for?"

"I made a mistake."

"I'll say you did." Maria faced the window again. "I'd have waited for you until the end of the world, Sandro, if you could have given me just the faintest breath of hope."

"I could not . . ."

"Compromise?" She shook her head. "No. Of course not. I know. It's not in your genes."

"I had a wife and a one-and-a half-year-old son."

"A wife who is a liar and a cheat."

"And a son who looks up to her as a mother."

"Well, where is she now, Sandro?"

"I know I made a mistake."

"You wouldn't lower yourself."

"Don't be absurd."

"You didn't touch me." She was almost shouting now. "Your sense of honor would not allow you even to *touch* me. Your wife fucked like a whore that . . . *disgusting* man—and others—and yet you would not—could not—bring yourself to touch the woman you professed to love."

"I was . . . I wanted you so much . . ."

"You were right!" Her face was strained to breaking point, her eyes wet with tears. "You were right not to touch me."

"If I'd known—"

"What? That I would become your brother's mistress? His whore . . ."

Ruzsky swallowed hard. "Don't talk like that."

"Does it disgust you, Sandro?"

Ruzsky found that he was holding his breath. He shut his eyes. "I made a terrible mistake."

"You made your choice, and now we can both pay for it. Does it disgust you to think of him touching me? To think that he can do as he wishes with me?"

"Stop it."

"Does it disgust you to think of him naked beside me, inside me? Your brother—"

"Control yourself."

"And now it is too late."

He looked at her and saw the emotion swelling in her eyes and in her breast, then breaking like floodwater. She curled herself into the corner of her bunk, her body racked by fierce convulsions. He moved instinctively to her. "Maria," he said, but she pushed him away.

"Get away from me," she screamed.

There was a knock at the door. She did not reply. "Are you all right, madam?" the conductor asked. Ruzsky moved back to his seat.

"Yes," she said weakly.

"Please open the door so that I may ascertain that you are not being threatened."

Maria did not move. The conductor turned the lock and pulled the door back. He glared at Ruzsky, who avoided his eye. Maria was wiping the tears from her cheeks.

"Is this gentleman upsetting you, madam?"

"No, Officer. It is all right."

"He's not from the first-class compartment."

"It's all right. Truly. He's a friend."

The conductor eyed Ruzsky suspiciously. "There are all kinds of bad sorts on the train," he said. "I only let him in because he showed me police papers. I'll check them again if you wish."

"It's all right, Officer, honestly. I know the gentleman."

The conductor hesitated. He shot an admiring glance at Maria and then reluctantly withdrew. "If you need anything, Miss Popova, please don't hesitate to call."

"I won't. Thank you."

The conductor pulled the door shut and relocked it from the outside. Maria closed her eyes and for a moment looked composed, before starting to shake once more.

"Maria, please—"

Ruzsky was leaning forward, but she had raised her hand to prevent him coming closer. She switched off the lamp, and the landscape beyond the window sprang instantly to life, illuminated by a bright moon in a cloudless sky.

"You really don't understand, do you?" she asked.

"Understand what?"

Maria's anger had gone, and in its place Ruzsky saw only regret. It was worse. "You would not compromise," she said. "But I did."

Ruzsky's eyes pleaded with her.

"And you don't understand why, do you?"

"I—"

"I'm your brother's mistress because I loved you." Maria rested her head against the window. "I'm your brother's mistress because you would not bend. And now that you will, *my* compromise has put love beyond our reach." She turned back to him. "Don't you see?"

Ruzsky could not answer. He shook his head, as if to try and deny what they both knew to be true. "Christ," he whispered.

"I'm sorry, Sandro," she said.

"No," he muttered.

"I've hurt you . . . I'm sorry."

Ruzsky did not move, attempting to lose himself in the rhythmic beat of the pistons. "Do you love him?" Ruzsky bit his lip. He had not wanted to ask the question and did not wish to have an answer.

Maria looked up. She wiped her eyes.

"I'm sorry. I shouldn't have asked."

"I'm very fond of your brother, Sandro."

"Fond?"

"I'm moved by him; by the sadness in his heart, and by his devotion to you . . . I am nothing more than an adornment for him. I know that he will never really be in love with me . . ." She sighed. "I do not believe he can love—really love—another."

"Why not?"

"Because he does not love himself."

"I don't understand," Ruzsky said.

"Oh, Sandro . . ." She seemed to look right into the depths of his soul. "I think you understand better than anyone."

Ruzsky waited for her to continue, but she did not.

They sat quietly together in the dark. From time to time, the moon disappeared behind a stand of pine trees, then burst out again, making brilliant the snow-covered fields, and washing her troubled face with light.

"Why him?" Ruzsky asked at length. "Of all people, why him?"

Maria's head rocked from side to side. Her hands rested upon her lap. "I have told you already," she said. "Because, at his best, he is like you." She gave him a look of almost infinite sadness. "And because I can't have you."

They listened to the sound of the train and watched the changing patterns of light and shadow as it carved its way across the landscape. They were silent for a long time.

"What do you want of me?" he said.

"I don't know anymore."

He watched her face.

"It is too late for us," she said. "But it doesn't change the way I feel."

Ruzsky swallowed hard. His throat was dry. "Should I go?"

"No." Her voice was just a whisper.

"Do you want me to stay?"

Maria did not answer immediately. "Can we escape from the world, just for a moment? Just for a heartbeat?"

She turned and lay down on her bunk, her head on the pillow.

Ruzsky watched her face.

He waited.

One long, elegant arm stretched out toward him in the moonlight.

He watched, transfixed, marveling at the cool perfection of her fingertips, desperate for her touch.

He moved across the compartment and lay down beside her, his arm over her waist, his lips brushing the nape of her neck.

She lay quite still, her breast barely rising and falling as she breathed. At length, she turned toward him, her lips close to his, her eyes searching his own. "Are you nervous, Sandro?" she whispered.

"Yes."

With her thumb and forefinger, she smoothed the lines on his temples, then gently caressed his cheek.

Her lips were parted, her breath warm.

"So many wasted years," she said.

"Maria, I cannot—"

"Don't punish me," she said, placing a finger upon his lips. She brushed his eyes closed, and then smoothed his brow. "Just rest, Sandro. You need to rest."

They lay side by side. The compartment was warm. He wished he could stay here forever.

26

Maria's cheek was resting on his shoulder and he thought that she might be sleeping.

He listened to the sound of her breathing.

On the train journeys he had made with his family, he and Dmitri had always occupied the top bunks in the same compartment and lain awake deep into the night, listening to the train rattling south.

"I love to listen to the sound of the train at night," she said. "The snow outside, the warmth within. It makes me feel safe."

Ruzsky did not move. He didn't want to do anything to break the spell.

"Do your parents still live in Yalta?" he asked.

"No."

"Where did they move to?"

Maria did not answer.

"You said you were going to see your sister."

"Yes."

Ruzsky sensed he was skating on thin ice, but needed to continue. "Why don't you ever talk about your past?" he asked.

"For the same reason that you don't."

"Are your parents in Petersburg?"

"No."

"So you moved up alone?"

"They died a long time ago."

Ruzsky hesitated. "I'm sorry," he said.

Maria slipped away from him, onto her back. She gazed up at the ceiling.

"How old were you when they died?"

"Young. But old enough to remember how wonderful they were, which should make it better, but only makes it worse."

"What—"

"It was an accident."

Ruzsky watched the shadows crossing and recrossing her solemn face. "Who looked after you?"

"My uncle."

"Is he still in Yalta?"

"He's dead now, too."

"Were you fond of him?"

"Of course. He was a good man."

Ruzsky sensed a reservation in her voice. "But it was still—"

"His wife never wanted us."

"Is she alive?"

"Yes."

"Will you go to see her?"

"No."

"Where is your sister now?"

"In a sanatorium."

"What happened to her?"

There was a long pause. "I don't know," Maria said. "I don't know."

Maria closed her eyes. He recognized the cold, brittle place within her all too well.

In the darkness, he could feel his love growing and deepening. He reached over and held her to him. For a moment, her fingers dug into his shoulders as she hugged him and then she let go.

"Did your—"

"Sandro. I don't want to talk about it anymore," she said. "Tell me about Petrovo. Tell me about the house there."

"Why do you want to know about that?"

"Dmitri won't talk about it. And yet it's such an important part of you both."

Ruzsky contemplated her request in silence. It was many years since he had consciously thought about Petrovo, and yet it was so intimately enmeshed in the fabric of his existence that he didn't need to. The house, its atmosphere, its history—he carried it with him all the days of his life. "What do you want to know?"

"Paint me a picture."

Ruzsky was silent again. What harm could it do, just to describe the house?

"It's tall," he said, "with a series of ornate pillars along its facade, but not too grand. Inside, it was a family home, with fireplaces as big as my father, and rugs, military portraits, and souvenirs gathered by the Ruzskys over the years, from campaigns in the Caucasus, the Far East, and Europe. There were sabers and lances and primitive, rusting muskets, and banners and giant silver plates. There was a shaded veranda all the way along the front of the house where we used to spend the summer evenings . . ."

Ruzsky stopped.

"Go on."

"I—"

"Please go on, Sandro . . ."

Ruzsky twisted away from her. Recalling long-suppressed memories made him feel as vulnerable as he had as a child. "In the summer, my mother would sing. She had a lovely voice and we would join in, even my father; the sound carried across the valley. Sometimes, my father would go into the drawing room and play the piano. I would sit with my feet over the edge of the balcony, my toes brushing the top of the thick lilac bushes that surrounded the house."

Ruzsky was silent for a minute, perhaps more.

"One year, when our time there usually came to an end, Father and Mother said we wouldn't be returning to the house on Millionnaya Street until the end of the following summer. A whole year at Petrovo. I was about twelve, and for us boys, it brought unexpected joy. No school. Father hired a tutor, but it was still a magical time. Every day, after lunch, we would go out and play in the woods, in the snow. We made camps, staged battles, played on the ice, all the things that young boys do."

Ruzsky ground to a halt. He had a vivid memory of them all skating on the lake, their breath billowing in the chill air as they chased each other around the island in the middle.

He could recall the sound of their laughter and the swish of the blades cutting across the ice.

"It's as far as Dmitri gets."

"What is?" Ruzsky asked.

"His story always stops in the same place. When Ilusha was still alive."

Ruzsky closed his eyes. She caressed his brow and then placed a soft hand against his cheek. "It's all right, Sandro," she whispered. Then, "We should go back . . ."

"Go back where?"

"The house is one day's ride from Mtsensk, isn't that so? On the way to Yalta."

Ruzsky swung his legs over the edge of the bunk, and sat there with his back to her.

"You cannot run away from it forever, Sandro."

"I'm not running away from anything."

"You both are."

"And you're the expert on the pair of us."

Ruzsky immediately regretted the sharpness in his voice.

"I'll come with you," she said.

"Why?"

"I told you." Maria raised herself onto one elbow. "Because you need to go. And because I want to escape from the world. Just for a moment. It's all changing, Sandro . . ." Maria lay back down. "You asked me why I'm going to Yalta. I want to see my sister. I want to make sure that she will be cared for, no matter what happens to me, or to Russia. But first, I want to escape."

As he returned to the second-class section of the train, Ruzsky pulled the door shut and heard it being locked behind him. A soldier slouched in the corridor, his back to him, smoking a cigarette. As Ruzsky squeezed past, he saw that it was one of the men who had been in their compartment earlier. He hesitated for a moment, but the man quickly averted his eyes.

It took him a further twenty minutes to pick his way through the sleeping bodies that now lined the corridor. When he reached his own compartment, the blinds had been drawn against the moonlight.

Ruzsky waited for a moment for his eyes to adjust to the darkness. He saw that one of the top bunks was empty and he put a foot on the ladder and swung himself up onto it.

He lay still. One of the men was snoring. He didn't think it was Pavel.

Ruzsky turned on his side and tried to make out the shape of his friend.

"Where in hell have you been?" Pavel asked.

"I'm sorry."

"These men haven't seen a woman for months. I've been lucky to escape with my virtue intact."

"Don't flatter yourself."

Pavel grunted. "Some friend you are. After the revolution, I'm not sharing a cell with you."

"Even revolutionaries need policemen, Pavel. You should remember that."

Pavel grunted again.

"Are they asleep?" Ruzsky asked.

"You can hear them."

"I think they're still watching us."

"Here on the train?"

"Yes." Ruzsky turned over. "We'll talk about it in the morning."

Ruzsky awoke late. By his watch, it was almost ten and there was no sign of Pavel in the compartment. His bunk had been folded away.

Only two of the soldiers were still there, smoking in silence with their legs resting on the seats. They didn't acknowledge him.

Ruzsky swung around and stared out of the window. It was a poor day, snow driving across the wooded landscape reducing visibility to no more than twenty feet.

He rolled off his bed and landed with a thump by the door. He adjusted his coat, making a point of trying to establish eye contact with the soldiers. They both avoided it.

Ruzsky found Pavel at the far end of the carriage, looking out at the snow. There were fewer soldiers here now, so they had room to stand and converse in relative privacy.

"You should have woken me," Ruzsky said.

"So that you could join me staring out of the window?"

Ruzsky pulled out his silver cigarette case. Pavel declined. Ruzsky took one and lit up.

"So, where did you get to?" Pavel asked.

Ruzsky sucked deeply on his cigarette, then blew the smoke against the glass. "Nothing interesting."

"That's for me to judge."

"I saw someone getting onto the train," Ruzsky said.

"Or knew she was going to be on it."

Ruzsky raised an eyebrow.

"I could get quite insulted sometimes, by you treating me like a simpleton."

Ruzsky looked at his friend apologetically. "Do you mind if I don't tell you? Not yet, anyway?"

"I had a feeling this trip wasn't entirely straightforward."

"We're going to Yalta because we need to."

"A happy coincidence, then?"

Ruzsky didn't answer. "There are two of them in our compartment." He glanced over his shoulder. "Last night, I went right to the other end of the train and one of these goons followed me all the way. They're not soldiers."

Pavel's eyes narrowed. "What did he think you were going to do, jump off the train?"

"Seriously."

"They're following us all the way to Yalta?"

"That's what it's beginning to look like."

Pavel turned back to the window. "What do you want to do?"

"Nothing. I'm just telling you."

Pavel glanced down the corridor. A group of soldiers was sitting on the floor, playing cards.

"I have a favor to ask you," Ruzsky said quietly. "Beyond Moscow."

"What is it?"

"My family home. Petrovo. It's on the way—more or less."

"I thought this was a murder investigation." Pavel's tone was not amused.

"It will take a day, that's all."

"Why now?"

Pavel looked at him and Ruzsky could see in his eyes that he knew the answer, just as Maria had understood his state of mind better than he had himself. Everyone was experiencing the unsettling effect of the winds of change. "I was thinking about Ella last night," Pavel said.

Ruzsky didn't reply.

"She didn't deserve to die like that."

"No one does."

"You saw the grief in her mother's face."

"That's why we're going to Yalta."

"Some of us in our own time."

Ruzsky frowned.

"Who's to say who will be next?" Pavel asked. "The man at the Lion Bridge . . . Are we any closer to understanding why these three people have been killed?"

Ruzsky looked away. He wrestled with himself as he recalled the image of Ella's body on the slab in Sarlov's laboratory. Pavel was right, but he knew it would not dissuade him.

"You can be very stubborn, Sandro."

"I'm sorry."

"You don't really need to apologize. It's a virtue as well as a vice."

"I'll be a day behind you. Two at most."

"I'll come with you. I'd like—"

"No." Ruzsky looked at his partner. "I need to go alone."

Pavel was hurt. "How long will you really be?"

Ruzsky leaned back against the window. "It takes twenty-four hours in a troika, but I can make it in twelve with a good horse. I'll be two days behind you, at the outside."

Pavel's expression softened. He placed a big hand on Ruzsky's shoulder. "I understand. But be quick."

"Will you be all right?"

"I'll be fine. But I'm worried about you. What if there are bandits or deserters? You're too weak to defend yourself without me."

Ruzsky smiled. "I'll just stay out of trouble."

27

The train pulled into Mtsensk just before dawn. Ruzsky lay on his bunk, not moving, listening to the hiss of steam and the subdued voices on the platform.

He checked his watch. It was just before six.

The blinds in their compartment had been drawn, but the station lights penetrated the interior sufficiently to allow Ruzsky to see Pavel's face. The big detective was staring at him.

Ruzsky looked at his watch again. Most station halts lasted ten minutes. Rarely more, never less. They had been standing here for two, so far.

There was a shout from farther down the platform. Ruzsky wondered if Maria would change her mind.

He glanced at his watch once more, then turned, nodded at Pavel, and swung off the bunk. As he emerged into the corridor, Pavel was half a step behind him, as they'd agreed. Ruzsky walked into the toilet, looked back, and saw his partner leaning against the door to prevent anyone leaving. Pavel nodded at him once more.

Ruzsky closed the door and looked at himself in the mirror. Now that he had committed himself, he had second thoughts. He splashed water onto his face.

The soldiers had been swapped in Moscow and this group appeared to be less vigilant. Pavel was convinced they were from the Moscow Okhrana; Ruzsky thought they were a replacement team from Petersburg. Either way, they must have been told that the two of them were bound for the Crimea, and they appeared to be fast asleep.

Ruzsky heard the conductor's low whistle and he opened the door of the toilet. Pavel was still there and he shrugged as Ruzsky turned the corner. He opened the door, stepped down onto the snow-covered platform, and then shut it again as quietly as he could. He walked swiftly through the drifting snow toward a darkened side entrance to the station.

As soon as he was out of sight, Ruzsky looked back. The train was pulling away and there was no sign of anyone scrambling to get off.

Once it had gone, he stepped out into the dim light. He watched the stationmaster disappearing back into the warmth, leaving the platform deserted. Ruzsky went to the waiting room, then the station entrance, but could see no sign of her. He returned to the center of the platform, glancing one way, then the other. He turned to face the drifting snow, letting it gather on his face.

She had changed her mind and the disappointment was crushing.

Ruzsky glanced around him once more. There was little doubt that he was the only passenger who had disembarked.

The stationmaster caught sight of him through the window. He replaced his hat and came back out into the cold.

"You got off the express?" the man asked. He was assessing Ruzsky carefully, trying to marry his demeanor, which would clearly indicate noble birth, with his tatty overcoat and boots, which did not.

"Yes."

"I'm sorry, I didn't see you. Are you expecting someone, because there is no one here."

"I'll need a good horse."

"You're with the lady?"

Ruzsky turned around and saw her emerging from the shadows at the far end of the platform, carrying a single suitcase and shrouded in the swirling snow.

It was two hours before the horses arrived, but when they did, Ruzsky acknowledged that the stationmaster had been right; they were worth the wait.

The road was passable until they reached the start of the pinewoods about fifteen versts from the station. Here, they led their horses through a thick snowdrift as the sun peeked above the horizon amidst the tall, thin pine trees. It was no longer snowing, and the sky was now clear. Their breath hung on the still morning air.

Beyond the snowdrift, the road down to the river was clearer again and they cantered toward it. "It's hard to believe," Ruzsky shouted as he led his horse through what was now little more than a stream, "but this is sometimes difficult to pass in summer."

Ruzsky recalled hanging off the back of the troika, by their luggage, alongside his brothers.

"I can believe it," she said. Maria took off her hat and shook out her hair. She was smiling, her cheeks flushed. "You look as if you were born in the saddle. I thought you were a city boy."

"I learned in these woods. Our stable boy taught us all bareback. At one point I wanted to run away and join the circus."

The road on the far side of the river was steep and winding, but at the top there was a long stretch across some high ground, between peasant fields. Up here, the wind had blown the deep snow off the road and Ruzsky and Maria let the horses go, icy air cutting through their coats and whipping their cheeks, snow flying up into their eyes and mouths. The freedom was exhilarating, and by the time they reached the end they were both out of breath.

"There is an inn not far from here," Ruzsky said. "We can stop for breakfast."

"Let's press on. The horses are fit. We can stop later."

Ruzsky turned his mare so that they were alongside each other, then, without warning, and without letting go of his own reins, he jumped horses, landing behind her. Her mare started briefly, but Ruzsky had performed the maneuver so expertly that the shock was minimal. He curled one arm around Maria's waist, his face against her neck, her hair against his cheek.

Maria laughed and leaned back against him.

Ruzsky wedged the reins beneath his knee and used his free hand to brush aside her hair so that he could kiss her. She reached back and laced her fingers in his.

They were moving with the rhythm of the mare's progress, both at ease in the saddle. The rising sun was a bright orange disk that shimmered through the narrow pines.

Ruzsky listened to the steady thump of the horses hooves in the snow. He began to hum quietly.

"What is it?" she asked him.

"I've no idea. Mother used to sing it to us."

Maria listened to him. He could see that she was smiling.

"What's so funny?" he asked.

"Not funny, joyful. Memories."

"Of what?"

She sighed. "Of our summers. Of the azure blue sea and skies bright like joy . . ."

"Pushkin."

"So your tutors did not neglect you, Sandro. We had a big white house overlooking the bay, with a long, sloping lawn. My father was the governor and my mother renowned for her beauty and her voice. In the summer, she would sing after dinner in the garden. Kitty and I would listen from the upstairs window when we were supposed to be asleep."

"Your father was the governor?"

Maria did not reply.

"I didn't know that." Ruzsky waited for her to continue and when she did not, he asked: "What do you remember of your mother?"

"Of my mother?"

"Yes."

"Why do you ask that?"

Ruzsky shrugged. "Piecing together the jigsaw, just as you are."

Maria thought deeply for a minute or more. "Everything. Every little detail. Every expression, every act of kindness. If I believed in God, perhaps I could believe it was his doing, but I don't and it wasn't."

"How long was your father the governor for?"

"Some time."

"You were close?"

"Who is it that you were traveling with?" she asked. "Another detective?"

"Yes. My deputy, Pavel."

"Also the son of a noble family?"

"No. He used to be a constable."

"What did you tell him?"

"To wait until I got there. We were being followed."

"Why?"

"I don't know." Ruzsky thought back to the other night, when he had arrived at the ballet. "Who invited Vasilyev to that performance? He was with my family."

"Your father, I imagine."

"Did Dmitri say so?"

She turned to face him. "Does it matter? I have no idea."

Ruzsky pulled her closer and gently eased her head back onto his shoulder. "No, it doesn't matter."

They were silent again. He thought about how quickly she shied away from a discussion of anything personal, and how rapidly she moved from fragile melancholy to prickly defensiveness.

"How long did you tell Pavel you would be?" she asked.

It was after nightfall by the time they neared Petrovo. Maria was fit and a natural horsewoman, but both she and her horse were tiring. They'd rested and fed themselves and the mares at an inn just after lunchtime, and as it had grown darker, their progress had become slower. Ruzsky had expected to be there by eight, but as they stopped at the crest of the hill he checked his pocket watch to discover that it was past nine.

Her skin was pale in the moonlight.

"Are you all right?" he said, reaching out to touch her arm.

"I'm fine."

"Only another few minutes. We'll soon be able to see the lights through the trees." Ruzsky pressed his heels against his horse's flanks. The path was gentler now, but there were no lights. To begin with, he thought he must have misjudged the point at which he would be able to see the house, but the farther he went, the more unsettled he grew.

For a terrible moment, he wondered if the house was no longer there, if it had been burned down or destroyed in one of the peasant rebellions, and his father had not known how to tell them.

And then he saw a light and began to make out the shape of it, nestled in the corner of the valley. Of course, on every previous occasion he'd arrived here, a welcome had been prepared, every light on, torches burning around the gardens and along the driveway.

28

Petrovo loomed out of the darkness. As Ruzsky reached the beginning of the short driveway, a bank of clouds cleared overhead, and the white facade glimmered in the moonlight.

The house hadn't changed, though it seemed smaller than he remembered.

Maria came up alongside him. "It's beautiful."

For a moment, and to his surprise, Ruzsky felt a twinge of bitterness. All this should have been his.

The drive and hedgerows had been well maintained, but as he dismounted by the big front door, Ruzsky saw, even in the darkness, the results of his family's neglect. The brass had not been polished, and paint was peeling off the door and windows beside it. Inside, the shutters had been closed and there was no sign of light.

Ruzsky took hold of the knocker and hammered it hard three times.

They waited.

Ruzsky began to walk around the edge of the house.

He stood on the veranda, under the sloping glass roof, looking down to the lake.

Ruzsky walked ten paces backward down the slope, so that he could look up at the house. The shutters on the first floor were closed too, but he could see a light on in the attic.

He ran back around to the front of the house and hammered hard again. "Hello," he shouted. "It's me, Sandro!"

He felt like a child, his excitement tinged with fear. He wanted everything to be the same. "Hello!"

He hammered again.

A light came on, peeking through the shutters.

"What is it?" he heard a voice demand.

Ruzsky felt his spirits surging. "Oleg, it's me, Sandro!"

"Sandro?"

"Yes!"

Ruzsky waited impatiently as the bolts were pulled back inside. He heard the big lock turn. It seemed to take an interminable amount of time and then Oleg stood before him, in his nightgown, a candle in his hand.

They stared at each other.

"Master Sandro?" Oleg took a step closer. "Is it really you?"

There was a moment of hesitation, even awkwardness, and then Sandro walked forward and into Oleg's arms, the candle tumbling to the floor, the room plunged once more into darkness.

For a former sergeant in the Preobrazhenskys, Oleg was surprisingly slight, but when he stepped back, Ruzsky still saw the steel in his eyes. He bent down, picked up the candle, lit it again, and handed it back. "This is Maria," he said.

Oleg raised his candle in order to get a better look at her. His face, Ruzsky thought, was thinner and more lined. "Maria?"

"Popova."

If Oleg knew of her relationship with Dmitri, he gave no sign. "Welcome," he said.

Ruzsky moved through into the central hallway, and looked up into the shadows of the dome. A wooden staircase gave access to the first-floor gallery, from where he and his brothers had spied on his parents' guests through the balustrade. Three tattered military banners on long poles hung down from the balcony where an orchestra had sometimes played. All around him, lurking in the darkness, were Ruzsky's ancestors, grim-faced in military uniform. "Do you think they ever had fun?" Ilusha would always ask when they were standing here.

Ruzsky walked on into the drawing room, which ran the length of the veranda. Oleg and Maria came in behind him, the light from the candle casting flickering shadows across his father's prized collection of rare and ancient texts. Ruzsky ran his finger along them, disturbing a thick layer of dust.

He touched the leather chair by the door and turned the globe beside his father's writing desk. Next to it was a bust of Ruzsky's great-grandfather, who had become ADC to Alexander I and traveled to Paris with him, after Waterloo.

Ruzsky reached the window and pulled back the shutters, allowing the moonlight to stream across bare floorboards. He turned the key, shoved open the glass door ahead of him, and stepped out onto the snow-covered balcony.

Ruzsky slipped his hands into his pockets. He thought of those long summer evenings: Father at his desk, Mother at the piano, the three of them playing on the grass or lying on the veranda, legs swinging against the lilac bushes.

He found that he was staring at the tree on the hillock by the lake. It was impossible, in the darkness, to make out the tiny gravestone.

"We didn't know you were coming, sir."

Ruzsky turned around. He could see the compassion and concern in Maria's eyes. "I didn't know I was coming."

"How is your father?" Oleg gave him a toothless smile.

"He's fine."

"And Dmitri?"

"Dmitri survived the front, that's the main thing. He's back in Peters-burg now." Ruzsky caught Maria's eye. "He's fine. Where is the good Mrs. Prenkova?"

Oleg looked down. He shook his head. "She passed away, Sandro. Some years ago now."

Ruzsky felt his face flush. "I'm sorry. They didn't tell me."

Oleg looked up again. His eyes were hollow. "You must be ravenous! Come downstairs."

As they walked through the hallway, Ruzsky guessed that the house's decline had begun in earnest with the death of Oleg's wife. She and Katya were sisters from Petrovo who had married local boys and seen go on, under the Ruzsky family patronage, to become noncommissioned officers in the Preobrazhenskys before entering his father's service. It was the way things had always worked.

As they descended the back stairs to the kitchen, the light from Oleg's candle flickered across the lattice of cobwebs that hung from the ceiling. Since he was taller than Oleg, one caught in Ruzsky's hair.

"You should have warned me," Oleg said. "You should have warned me."

There was no electric light in the kitchen—there never had been—but in the winter darkness, the cavernous room had always been brightly lit by huge torches. Oleg hurriedly lit two more candles as Ruzsky peered through the gloom. More cobwebs tethered the line of enormous copper pots and pans to the shelf beside the range.

He pulled back the wooden bench from the long table, for Maria to sit.

"You should have warned me," Oleg said again as he disappeared into the larder. He returned with some bread—old and stale—and a hunk of ham and of cheese.

Oleg placed the food in front of them. In the awkward silence that followed, the truth of Oleg's life here dawned on Ruzsky. The old man was alone, scraping a marginal existence amongst the cobweb-shrouded ghosts of their past. He had been forgotten by the family.

Ruzsky looked at the meager fare. He wondered how long this would keep Oleg.

"It must be lonely here on your own," Maria said.

"A boy from the village comes to help with the garden." He pushed the bread across to them. "The Colonel sometimes sends word."

It was a lie and Ruzsky knew it, but said for Oleg's benefit, he guessed, rather than his own. To accept poverty and neglect was one thing, to lose respect for the family you'd served for more than half a century, quite another. "Has he been down to visit?" Ruzsky asked.

"Not for a time."

"Not since before the war?"

Oleg pretended to have to think hard. "It's been a time. A few years, maybe. It is the war, of course."

Ruzsky knew his father had been here since Ilusha's death, but he thought that his visits had been nothing more than an attempt to prove something to himself, and so had eventually petered out. Dmitri had once told him that in the year before their mother's death, both parents had eradicated the house and its memories from their minds, but the old man still refused him the chance to take it over and restore it. "It's like a living tomb," Dmitri had told him. "And I think that's the way he wants it to remain."

Ruzsky thought of his mother. He remembered the cold accusation in her eyes on the morning after Ilusha's death.

Ruzsky took a hunk of bread. Maria cut herself some ham. Oleg was trying to assess her with a subtlety he had never possessed.

"You've come far together?" he asked.

"We were on our way to Yalta," Ruzsky said. "We found we were traveling companions." Ruzsky wondered if Oleg would tell his father about his visitors, but he doubted it.

"All the boys in the village have gone," Oleg said. "You remember Kirill?"

"Of course. He rode bareback, like a maniac," Ruzsky told Maria. "He was the son of the foreman at the glassworks, and he loved to taunt us with his superior ability. Ah, Kirill . . ."

"Killed. And two of his sons. And many more. What's the news from Petersburg. Will we win?"

"All the talk is of revolution again."

Oleg looked at Maria. He did not seem to know whether to disapprove of her or not. His own personal code considered infidelity—even a hint of it—an abomination, and yet he could hardly fail to be affected by her beauty. Even in the dull light of this basement, she seemed to sparkle. Ruzsky watched as the old man sought a way of tactfully framing the questions to which he wished answers.

Oleg stood. He waved his hand. "It was bad enough last time. They know if they come to the house, I'll shoot 'em. What have I got to live for?"

"Have you had trouble?"

"We've had trouble, once or twice. When did it start before? In 1905? I can't remember. She was alive then. Tanya, I mean. There were some at the door. She stayed in her room. Shouted at me not to go down. I said I'd blow their heads off if they took another pace forward."

"Who were they?"

"Thugs."

"From the village?"

"No." Oleg shook his head vigorously. "No, no. One of them was, a bad boy. He was dismissed from the factory for stealing. This house belonged to the people—that's what he said! He must have led the others here. I heard some of them were from Tula, but I don't know how they got this far."

"What happened?"

"They left us alone, but I heard they burnt the Shuvalov house to the ground."

Ruzsky shook his head. He was shocked. He'd heard of such things, of course, but did not expect them here.

"And assaulted the servants. Killed the butler!" Oleg was obviously proud of his success in defending their property. His face softened. "I'll leave you, Master Sandro. I know you will want to look around. There are sheets on the bed in your parents' room on the first floor." His expression remained suitably opaque. "And in the guest room."

Oleg lit a candle for them and then walked slowly to the door. "I've done my best, sir," he said, turning to face them.

"Of course, Oleg."

"I'm sorry for . . ." He thought better of it. "Good night, sir."

"Good night."

29

Ruzsky walked slowly around the ground floor, the candle in his hand and Maria beside him. There were cobwebs in each nook and cranny and dust upon every surface. In the dining room, the silver candlesticks and salt and pepper cellars were still on the table, as if waiting for the family to sit down to dinner. Ruzsky opened the shutters, allowing the moonlight to spill into the room. "We used to eat as a family in the summer, all of us together, with these doors open and the sun streaming in."

Ruzsky pushed open the double doors to the library. He pulled back the shutters here too. "The rest of my father's collection of books. And his father's. If you want a rare or unusual text, it's probably here." Ruzsky patted the dust off the top of a leather armchair.

A shaft of moonlight fell upon the giant portrait that hung above the fireplace and Ruzsky stood in front of it. "Your father?" Maria asked.

"My grandfather. They looked very alike."

"All three of you do."

Ruzsky looked at the face above him. "They were both tyrants, in their own way."

"Did you know your grandfather?"

"He died when I was five. We had come down here to see him and he passed away in the room upstairs." Ruzsky's brow creased. "It was like a giant weight had been lifted from my father's shoulders. That night, I heard him laugh for the first time."

Ruzsky continued to stare at the dour, imperious face of his grandfather. "For a few years, he was a completely different man."

"Is he buried here?"

"There is a graveyard beyond the walled garden. My father has never been there, but I have."

He turned to face her.

"Is your mother buried here also?" she asked.

Ruzsky shook his head. "No. In Petersburg."

"Dmitri never talks of her."

Ruzsky tried not to react to the mention of his brother's name. "No, well . . ."

"He says your father believes she died of a broken heart."

"It was a claim he once made."

"Is it true?"

"No."

"Why is it that you do not talk of her?"

Ruzsky stared at the portrait of his grandfather. "I don't know."

Maria waited for him to continue. After a long silence, he did so. "She was afflicted with a deep melancholia, even before Ilusha's . . . Sometimes, she stayed in her room all day." He put his hand to his forehead. "She suffered from terrible headaches."

Ruzsky looked at Maria again. "Perhaps my memory plays tricks, but after we left here that last time, she never embraced me again."

"Where should I sleep, Sandro?"

Ruzsky did not respond.

"I'm tired," she said softly. "And this is your home."

"Of course." He cleared his throat. "Of course."

Ruzsky led her through the hallway and up the stairs. He walked swiftly down the landing, past the orchestra gallery and his parents' bedroom, to those reserved for guests. Oleg had lit a candle and placed a bowl of warm water in the first of the rooms. He'd also pulled back the covers. Ruzsky patted the bed with his fist and a cloud of dust rose into the air. "I'm sorry," he said, glancing up at the ceiling, where the wallpaper had begun to peel, the spreading damp visible even in this light. "Will you be all right?"

Maria moved slowly toward him. She took his face gently in her hands, her eyes searching his. She kissed him once, with soft, warm lips, then wrapped her arms around him and pressed him to her. "Thank you for bringing me here, Sandro."

She released him and stepped back.

Ruzsky hesitated.

Maria did not move. He saw compassion and regret in her eyes. Was that all?

He turned and walked to the door. He looked back.

"Good night, Sandro," she said.

"Good night."

Ruzsky stepped out, pulled the door shut, and took two or three paces down the corridor.

He stood in the darkness, his mind clouded and his heart pounding.

He waited.

He walked a few more paces and then stopped again. This corridor stripped away time. He felt a tightness in his chest. He was back at the night of Ilusha's death, when Dmitri had clung to him by the door of his room, here, just before he had been summoned to his father's study.

Ruzsky remembered every inch of that journey.

He remembered the warmth of the fire, the look on his father's face, and his own terror as the reality of his emotional exile dawned upon him for the first time.

He could hear his mother's cries, and Dmitri's echoing silence as he had tried to recount his father's words.

Ruzsky shivered. He found himself at Dmitri and Ilya's door.

The room was empty. The two beds were still there and the old chest of drawers, but everything personal had been removed: Ilusha's collection of bears that had occupied half the bed, Dmitri's sword that had hung on the wall, the regimental flag above the door.

Ruzsky was as still as stone. He realized that he had wished to bathe in these memories, and even this had been denied him. He moved toward the shutters and pulled them slowly back.

The lake was white in the moonlight. Ruzsky felt his eyes drawn along the ice, toward the top of the slope on the far side, to the place where a small black stone stood in a clearing beneath the trees.

He turned and looked across the corridor toward his own bedroom. The door was shut.

He hesitated for only a moment before opening it. If his father—or perhaps even his mother when she had been alive—had stripped his brothers' room, then he was certain they would have done the same to his own.

He was right, but the disappointment still tugged at something within him.

There was a blanket at the end of the bed where his toy bear had once slept, and Ruzsky lay down and covered himself with it, his boots hanging over the end of the mattress.

He closed his eyes.

All Ruzsky could see and all he could feel was the ice-cold water against his clammy skin, his arms and legs swirling helplessly.

He was drowning, eyes bulging and lungs empty. He was trying to breathe, but could not.

They were watching him. His father, mother, Dmitri . . . they were standing there impassively, watching him die.

Ruzsky felt the searing, wrenching pain in his chest.

This was his punishment, and would be for all eternity.

"Sandro!"

The slap awoke him, but it was a moment before his surroundings began to coalesce. She was above him; it *was* her. It was Maria, her face soft and beautiful and etched with concern; Oleg behind her, a candle above his head.

"Sandro?"

He felt paralyzed. He became aware that he was soaked in sweat.

"Sandro?"

"Yes . . ."

"You were screaming."

"I was drowning . . ."

"Screaming and screaming. We couldn't wake you."

"I'm sorry." He looked into her eyes. "I'm sorry."

Maria turned toward Oleg. "It's all right, Oleg. I'll look after him now."

Oleg hesitated for a moment and then nodded. He looked at Maria with compassion and then handed her the candle.

They listened to his footsteps recede.

Maria put the candle on the side table and then leaned back over him. She put a warm hand against his frozen cheek.

Ruzsky looked at her. He thought that it might be love he saw in her eyes.

Maria blew out the candle, then slipped onto the bed, pulling him toward her, cradling his head on her breast.

They lay still in the darkness.

"Everything's going to be all right, Sandro," she whispered.

"It will never be all right."

"It will. Believe me."

She tightened her grip on him.

"My sister cried out," Maria said. "But I could not stop her."

Ruzsky listened to the sound of her breathing.

"I could never cry out," Maria said.

30

As the cold fingers of dawn crept through the shutters, Ruzsky slipped out of bed, crossed to his brothers' room, and looked out over the gardens.

Very little had changed. The hedgerows appeared overgrown, but everything was covered in a thick layer of snow, so it was hard to tell. Nothing moved by the lake. The ice seemed intent on squeezing the life out of the island at its center. The rowing boat that they had used as children had been discarded by the jetty.

Ruzsky watched as the mist cleared, grudgingly making way for the hazy outline of the sun.

At length, he turned and walked quietly back to his own room. He squatted down and watched her sleeping. She lay on her front, her face to the side and her lips slightly parted, her hair fanned across the pillow.

He watched the rise and fall of her back.

He reached forward and brushed a few strands of hair from her cheek. She did not wake.

Ruzsky slipped along the landing and down the wide stairs.

Oleg was dusting the busts in the hallway. "You weren't made for this, old man," Ruzsky said.

"Someone has to do it." Oleg looked up at him. "When the war is over you'll all be back, and the Colonel will want to know why I've let the place go."

Ruzsky was moved by the old man's stubborn hope that the old days would return.

"I'm sorry," Ruzsky said. "The horses. I didn't—"

"It's all right," Oleg snorted. "I've not taken leave of my senses."

"I'll . . . if she wakes, I've gone out . . . just for a walk."

"As you wish."

Ruzsky opened the big front door and strolled out onto the driveway. It was much lighter now. He could see the decay in the woodwork of the windows.

Ruzsky made his way slowly down to the stables. The roof here was in much better condition and he recalled Dmitri once telling him it was the last money his father had agreed to spend on the place.

Ruzsky checked on the horses and then moved down the corridor between the stalls and unlocked the double doors.

The family's troika and sledge stood before him, exactly as he remembered them. He ran his hand slowly along the solid wood front of the sledge and then leaned over to feel the leather of the forward seat. The woodwork was painted red and gold. The bells which they had attached to it at Christmas hung on the wall, alongside a couple of spare wheels for the troika and an array of leather harnesses. Ruzsky gave one a tug. The leather was still supple.

He turned. Oleg was watching him.

"Still the same," Ruzsky said.

"Still the same."

Ruzsky leaned back against the sledge. "Do you remember how Dmitri liked to drive it?" He thought of them all in the back as the horses charged down the hill toward the gates.

"He was a fine horseman, your brother," Oleg said. "Always was, even as a boy." He shook his head. "No discipline for learning, but a natural."

"We should hitch it up and go down to the village."

"We could do that," Oleg said, but Ruzsky could sense the hesitation in his voice.

"Well, perhaps we should ride down, anyway."

Oleg didn't answer.

"You don't want to go?"

Oleg avoided his eye.

"What is it? We're not welcome? Is that it?"

"There are a few bad . . ." Oleg shook his head. "One or two of the young ones. Some of those who used to be employed at the works."

"Used to be?"

"Didn't get on with the new owner."

Ruzsky stepped away from the sledge. "What new owner?"

"Your father sold the glassworks, Sandro."

"When?"

"Before the war."

Ruzsky stared at him. He could scarcely believe it. The employment provided by the factory—and the benevolent way in which the family ran it—had been the bedrock of the social fabric of the entire area.

"I'm told the man was offered the house as well, but did not want it."

"He was offered the house?"

Oleg was still embarrassed. "So they say."

"Who was it?"

"From Moscow. It's all changed, Sandro."

Ruzsky glanced up at the old muskets along the wall above him. "Have you still got a working rifle?"

Oleg shook his head. "No good to me. My eyes."

"But you've got one?"

"In the house. You never know when the swine will come back."

"Come on, then, let's see if we can find ourselves some lunch."

They walked out into the sunshine and Ruzsky waited by the edge of the house for Oleg to get his rifle. When he returned with his old blue hunting coat, they walked down to the end of the drive and turned onto the path that led up the hill.

Oleg did not ask him why they avoided the much quicker route beside the lake.

They climbed up through the silent pine forest, the snow on the path so thick in places that they were almost stopped in their tracks. They reached a fork, where the path to their left led directly back to the lake and the garden. Ruzsky stopped and took the rifle from his friend and the three bullets that he offered. "Better shoot straight," the old man said, grinning.

"Why change the habit of a lifetime?" Ruzsky smiled.

"Mmm. Always a fine shot." Oleg raised a bony finger to the sky. He had taught all three boys to hunt. "The best. You'd have made a fine soldier, better than your brother."

Ruzsky looked at the sun glinting through the trees. It was much warmer today.

They walked on and stopped in a clearing a hundred yards farther up. Oleg was short of breath as they looked back down toward the house. Ruzsky pushed a bullet into the breech and closed the bolt.

They waited.

The forest was silent.

"A hare would do," Ruzsky said.

He walked on, cresting the hill and emerging into the larger clearing where his father had helped the estate workers build the tree house.

Ruzsky had secretly hoped that this remnant of their childhood, at least, had survived, and his disappointment was unexpectedly bitter when he saw that it had gone. There were a few fallen pieces of rotting wood, but nothing more.

He rested the rifle on his shoulder.

"What happened to the dogs, Oleg?"

The old man shook his head.

Ruzsky sighed deeply. He saw movement on the other side of the clearing. "Deer," he whispered.

Ruzsky and Oleg stalked the deer for an hour before they got a clear shot. Ruzsky took it through the heart.

Oleg went back to get one of the horses to drag it home and Ruzsky hunted on alone, roaming through the silent forest, the sun upon his face. An hour or more later, he returned to the tree house clearing, sweating from the exertion. He wiped his brow and looked around him.

The only sound was the drip of melting snow falling from the pines.

Ruzsky walked to the far side of the clearing and then back down the path. He stopped a few yards short of the point at which he knew he would get his first glimpse of the house.

Past and present merged, just as they had in the corridor last night. It was not memory that overpowered him, but the pervasive sense that he was rooted in a place and time that he had never left.

He began to walk faster and then broke into a run, the sun still bright above him, the house dancing through the trees. Ruzsky took the right-hand fork, running hard through thick snow.

He reached the garden, breathing heavily. Maria stood on the veranda. Ten yards from the jetty, he stopped. He could see the boat. He could see the island.

Ruzsky took another step, his feet leaden. He looked at the ice. He turned and walked up the slope, toward the line of trees.

Ruzsky found himself slowing down again, as if trying to force his way against an invisible wind. He could see the stone.

He pushed his legs forward until he was standing in front of it, his head bent. He read the name, in gold, and saw the small mound of snow and the dead flowers in the vase.

Ilya Nikolaevich Ruzsky
7.6.1882–3.4.1889
Beloved son

Ruzsky knelt and prayed. He had an image of his brother's impish smile and recalled the way they had indulged him and fought for the right to be his protector in any battle.

He remembered Ilusha's kindness at Christmas and the thoughtful way in which he would construct his own presents for his brothers with the help of Oleg or one of the other servants.

Ruzsky fumbled in his pocket and pulled out a tiny wooden snuff box that Ilusha had made for him over that last winter. He kissed it once, rubbed his thumb across its smooth ebony top, and then slipped it back into his pocket.

He stood, wiping a tear from the corner of his eye.

He leaned down and touched the gravestone.

"I miss you." Ruzsky began to weep gently, hanging his head. "Oh God, how I miss you."

He waited until the tears had stopped and then wiped his eyes once more and turned around. He walked back toward the house. Maria watched him, but he did not acknowledge her.

He crossed the veranda, stepped into the drawing room, and then walked up to Ilusha's room on the floor above.

He climbed onto Ilusha's bed by the window and curled into a ball.

31

Maria stood in the doorway. Ruzsky would have found anyone else's presence grotesquely intrusive, but he straightened and leaned back against the wall.

Maria sat down on the bed beside him. "What happened?" she asked.

"It was spring," he said. He breathed in deeply. He had never recounted or explained any part of this before, not even to Irina. "Father told us not to play on the ice. We used to skate all the time in winter, but we had never been here during spring and he told us that once the weather was warm, the ice became thin, even if the lake still appeared to be frozen. He told all of us, but especially me. I was the oldest and he believed that carried a special responsibility. 'Make sure that your brothers don't go on the ice, Sandro.' "

Ruzsky stared at the opposite wall. "My father and some of the estate workers had built us a camp on top of the hill. We'd been there all morning—the three of us—and we were coming back for lunch. We reached the lake. I realized I had forgotten my jacket, so I told them to go on home and I would catch up."

Ruzsky breathed in deeply. He stood and walked to the window.

"I went back to the tree house and I got my jacket. I was running down the hill. The air was quite warm and I noticed that wild strawberries were beginning to emerge from the melting snow. The forest was silent. Completely silent. And then I heard his cry. Just a brief, startled yell. For a moment, I stopped, paralyzed. Then I ran, tearing through the trees as I heard Dmitri's shout for help."

Ruzsky could almost see Dmitri now, standing there beside the lake.

"I came into the clearing and I saw it all. I didn't pause. I ran out onto the jetty. Dmitri was paralyzed. I went on my belly and crawled onto the ice. I was shouting at Dmitri to get help. And then Ilusha slipped away and I stood and ran toward him and the ice gave way and it was still so cold and somehow I knew that . . ." Ruzsky stopped. "Ilusha couldn't swim, you see."

Ruzsky stared at the lake. "It is deep and I dived. It was dark and I held my breath and held it and held it."

Ruzsky looked over at his brother's gravestone.

"I was tired and cold. So cold."

"And there was a moment when you wanted to go with him . . ."

Ruzsky did not answer.

"I could see Father's hand outstretched toward me," he said, "and I knew that by taking it, I would never escape."

She stood behind him, her arms around his waist, lips soft against the nape of his neck. "Ilusha would not have wanted an older brother who was a coward."

"But that is what I am."

"No." She tightened her grip. "No, you're not."

Ruzsky tried to control his breathing.

"Why did Ilusha go onto the ice?" she asked.

He remained silent.

"And why didn't Dmitri stop him?"

Ruzsky still did not turn around. "What does it matter?"

"Because you hold yourself responsible."

"Because I am responsible." He stared at the side of the lake where Dmitri had been standing. "Perhaps Dmitri was doing something else."

"What?"

Ruzsky cast his eyes across the garden to the clearing. "Perhaps he did not think that the ice would break."

"But why did Ilusha go onto it if your father had told you not to?"

Ruzsky shook his head. His mind felt numb. "I don't know."

"Did he often disobey your father?"

He shook his head once more. "No. Not about something like that. As good as gold, we always used to say." Ruzsky turned to her. "Why could you not cry out?"

"For the same reason that you can't, except in your sleep."

"Your parents?"

"My father was killed in an accident, my mother died of grief. I saw her face in the doorway of my room and I knew. I knew. And I promised myself I would never allow myself to be hurt again."

They were standing inches apart, her eyes upon his. Her breasts rose and fell, her breath warm upon his face. "And I hurt you?"

She did not answer, but he touched her face, a cold hand against warm cheeks. She pressed it to her, resting her head upon his chest.

They rode hard against the setting sun that afternoon, weaving through the woods before picking up the road to the house from the village in the gathering darkness.

Ruzsky brought his horse alongside hers and once again jumped across.

Maria leaned against him, one hand cupping the back of his head, the skin of her neck soft against his lips.

Ruzsky curled his arm more tightly around her waist.

"Hello, my wounded soldier," she said. She turned around gently and placed her moist, warm mouth against his. She arched her back, a palm against his cheek. "No one has ever loved you before, have they, Sandro?"

He did not answer.

Maria turned around again and they rocked with the motion of the horse all the way back to the house, the sunset washing the horizon a blazing red.

Oleg was waiting for them at the front door to take the horses. Ruzsky could tell from his eyes that he knew, but there was no hint of censure. "A fire is laid in the drawing room, Master Sandro, the venison cooked. I shall leave it to you," he said. He glanced at Maria. Their faces were flushed with exertion and excitement.

Inside, they discovered that Oleg had lit a fire in both the drawing and the dining room, where the table was laid as it always had been, groaning with silver, the venison arranged on a giant salver at its center.

Ruzsky shut the door behind them and then she was in his arms, with sudden, passionate urgency. He lifted her against the door as her lips sought his. She tugged at his belt, one hand around his back, the other seeking him, pulling at his trousers until he was free and then melting into him, her face against his shoulder, her warm breath upon him.

"God, Sandro," she said.

She traced his neck with her fingertips, her mouth warm as he held her, their bodies fused gently together. He walked with her to the great bear rug in front of the roaring hearth and, without parting, he sank to his knees and placed her very carefully onto the ground.

He moved over her, his face inches from her own.

Her eyes melted as she watched him.

Ruzsky reached down and ran a hand across the top of one of her silk stockings, tugging at her suspender belt and then feeling the smoothness of her skin.

Maria pushed him gently onto his back.

Ruzsky began to unbutton her dress and she helped him, then shrugged it off, raising herself up, her knees either side of his waist, her hair brushing his face as she bent over him.

Never taking her eyes from his, Maria lowered herself against him, straightening her legs. She kissed him gently, as his hands reached for the curve at the top of her long legs. He pushed gently against her clenching muscles and lay back.

Her back arched, her hair dusting his knees, her breasts high and proud. In the firelight, her skin seemed luminous.

Ruzsky ran his hands gently up her thighs, over her hips, and across the flat, muscular plain of her belly.

She lifted herself up, waiting as she looked into his eyes. She was smiling at him.

Then she lowered herself down again gently, slowly, almost agonizingly. Ruzsky shut his eyes as the pleasure threatened to burst within him.

They lay that night in front of the fire, wrapped in the bearskin rug. Ruzsky did not sleep, reluctant to concede a moment to the dawn. He listened to the sound of her breathing, her long, warm body half across his. He was as content as he had ever been.

Fatigue stalked him and he slowly succumbed, until the sleep of a few hours gave way to the day of their leaving.

Ruzsky listened to the birds as the light crept into the room and the shadows shortened. He would not move until she stirred.

32

Ruzsky stood before Ilusha's stone one last time. He thought of his brother's smile and prayed for his happiness. "Rest in peace," he said, and even as did so, against his best intentions, he found a tear once again rolling down his cheek.

He turned away and walked toward the house. On the veranda, he glanced back one last time and raised his hand, before stepping into the drawing room. "Goodbye," he whispered. "I'm not sure we will see each other again."

Inside, Ruzsky composed himself for a moment and then strode on into the hallway. Through a window, he could see Maria and Oleg with the horses.

He glanced up at the banners and balustrades above him, his breath visible on the air even in here. For a last moment, he tried to recapture something of the happier memories of those past summers, but they proved elusive.

He walked out of the front door without looking back.

Oleg saw that his eyes were red, but made no comment. Ruzsky put a foot into one of the stirrups and swung himself up onto his horse. "You'll look after him, won't you, Oleg?"

"Always, sir."

"Perhaps the rest of my family will be down this summer?"

"Perhaps. The Colonel will let me know well in advance, I'm sure. There's work to be done. You've seen that."

Ruzsky reached down to shake the old man's hand and he saw that there were tears in his eyes, too. He took hold of Oleg's shoulder. "They will be down before too long, whatever happens," Ruzsky said.

"Of course, Master Sandro. As soon as the war ends."

Ruzsky straightened and nudged the horse forward. "Good luck, Oleg."

"And to you, sir," he shouted. "And to your lady friend!"

Ruzsky set the horse down the snow-covered drive. He rode her hard up the hill beside the house and only stopped as he reached the top of the path. He turned for one last look.

Oleg stood on the veranda, a tiny figure against the house's grand facade. Ruzsky thought he saw the old man raise his hand once and he responded, only to be left wondering if it was just his imagination.

Ruzsky swung back. Maria was looking at him with an intensity that seemed to him to be something like love. She smiled faintly in response to his gaze.

"To a new beginning," he said, "for both of us. You agree?"

She gazed at her horse's mane.

Ruzsky fired his horse up the hill with a shout, determined not to look back again. He reached the crest and slowed the horse to a walk on the icy descent, only glancing over his shoulder when he was sure that the house was out of view.

Maria was behind him, deep in thought, her long hair and much of her face concealed in a wide fur hat.

As he headed down the hill, he tried to keep the past at bay. Sandro the protector, Dmitri had always called him. The guilt, when it returned, was like lead in the pit of his stomach.

33

Throughout the journey, Ruzsky had watched the excitement building in Maria's eyes, but as they crossed the Crimean isthmus under a clear blue sky, she seemed more than ever like a little girl on the final leg of a long journey home. Her bag was packed and she gazed endlessly out of the open train window, the warm breeze of Russia's subtropical paradise on both their faces.

The night had transported them to another world. The previous evening, they had pulled down the blinds on sleeting rain and mile upon mile of bare brown fields, fringed by straggling birch trees. This morning, they had opened them to a flood of sunshine, fruit trees in full blossom, and a bay as blue as fallen aquamarine.

Below, the town of Sevastopol stood perched on a barren rock, narrow streets leading down to a wide harbor. Overhead, black and white gulls circled. Out in the still waters of the bay, two gray battleships lay at anchor, the Russian national flag twisting lazily from their sterns.

Ruzsky had his own memories of holidays here. They'd come twice to see an aunt who had a modest palace not far from the Tsar's own in Yalta, but his recollections, though warm, were vague and misted by time.

The conductor knocked and poked his head around the door. "Everything all right, mademoiselle?" He looked at Ruzsky suspiciously, as he had throughout the journey.

"Yes."

"A couple more minutes. You'll arrange your own transportation on to Yalta?"

"Yes. Thank you."

The conductor eyed Ruzsky again. "You don't wish me to arrange it for you?"

"No. Thank you."

The conductor retreated.

The train wound slowly down the last hill. Ruzsky glanced at Maria, but she did not respond. If her excitement had grown as the journey had progressed, so too had the distance between them. Her manner was still warm, but the farther south they had traveled, the more she'd retreated into herself.

He told himself it was the natural melancholy of a return to her own past.

"You will go straight to the sanatorium?" Ruzsky asked.

She continued to stare out of the window.

"What is it called?"

Maria looked at him. The distance between them was solidifying, but he could not tell why. Once again, he suppressed a momentary sense of alarm. "The Tatyana Committee Convalescent Home." She turned back to the window.

The train jerked twice as the brakes were suddenly applied and then pulled very slowly into the station, the porters waiting on the platform disappearing in a huge cloud of steam. Maria was instantly on her feet, her small leather case in her hand until Ruzsky wrested it from her.

He followed her down onto the platform, a warm breeze on their faces. She disappeared into the cloud of steam too, and he hurried after her.

The platform was busier and bigger than he remembered. A large group swarmed forward in front of him to greet a friend or relative disembarking from the train and Ruzsky lost sight of her again.

He halted. He could not see her ahead, so he looked back and, just for a second, as the steam floated down the length of the platform, he saw a man standing at the far end whom he could have sworn was Ivan Prokopiev. Ruzsky took a step toward him, but the man appeared to realize that he had been seen and slipped from view, into the crowd. Ruzsky looked about him once more and saw Maria emerging into the sunlight by the exit.

When he caught up with her, she looked startled and, for a split second, examined him strangely, as if she had no idea who he was, just as she had done outside the theater in Petersburg. "Sandro," she said.

"Are you all right?"

"I'm fine. Why?"

He shook his head. "Can you wait a moment?"

Maria was squinting.

"There is something I need to check," he said.

She didn't respond.

Ruzsky retraced his steps back to the platform. It was still crowded with passengers and porters, escaping steam and the hubbub of voices.

Ruzsky wove his way through the crowd. An elderly man selling lemonade in old bottles sat next to a group of conductors talking in a small circle. There were a couple of soldiers, but the atmosphere was different from that in the big cities farther north. The air was warm, sunlight filtering through the glass roof onto the platform. Some people around him were in shirtsleeves.

Ruzsky reached the point at which he thought he'd seen Prokopiev, but there was no sign of anyone. He walked through the exit, squinting too as he stepped out into the sunshine. A fly landed on his cheek and he waved it away. A group of small boys leaned against the station wall, playing a game with what looked like primitive musket balls instead of marbles. He asked them if they had seen a tall man with short hair leaving the station by this exit, but they looked at him uncomprehendingly. Perhaps it was his accent.

Ruzsky went back onto the platform and returned to the relative shade of its central section. Shafts of sunlight illuminated the dust in the hazy air. Ruzsky gave a brief description of Prokopiev, but although the men at least appeared to understand him, they all shook their heads.

Ruzsky gave up. He scoured the platform as he returned to where he'd left Maria.

But when he reached the road, she wasn't there. He waited for a few minutes and concluded she had probably gone to excuse herself.

Ruzsky took out his cigarette case, then returned it to his pocket. He closed his eyes and enjoyed the feel of sunlight upon his face.

Time stretched out. He waited ten minutes or more, then checked his pocket watch. Confusion gave way to very mild irritation.

Ruzsky returned to survey the platform once more and then came back out into the sunshine. Almost all of the passengers had gone.

He tried to relax, but a tiny kernel of doubt had entered his mind.

On the far side of the road, a lone troika driver was still waiting for his passengers. Ruzsky wandered slowly over and asked him whether he had seen a tall and beautiful dark-haired woman carrying a simple leather case. Although the man's accent was thick, Ruzsky understood from his answer that he was certain he had. She'd climbed onto a car with two men and driven up the hill, in the direction of Yalta.

Ruzsky argued with him, but the man was emphatic and then curtly dismissive. Ruzsky turned around. There were two more automobiles waiting in a rank outside the station—no doubt to ferry rich bankers from Moscow to their homes on the coast. He reached into his pocket, pulled out a wad of money, and began to count it.

The driver said the journey would take three hours in a car—much quicker than the last time Ruzsky was here—and the first hour consisted, as he recalled, of a comfortable journey across the dusty plain past occasional monuments to ancient battlefields.

After that, they wound up through valleys and golden hills to the gray gateway of Aie Petri miles above the sea. As they passed it, Ruzsky began to feel sick and grew tired of the interminable twists of the descent, past crowded Tartar villages and great white villas with stone-walled gardens and baby cypress trees.

Their journey was slowed by the many simple Tartar pony-trap carriages, but eventually Ruzsky caught sight of the bay of Ghurzuf and the white town huddled untidily along the shore, brilliant in the midday sunshine.

He pulled himself upright as the cab wound slowly down toward the bay. It was just as he remembered it: an azure sea beneath cloudless skies. In more than just a geographical sense, this elegant town was a long way from the Empire's frozen capital. A two-day journey transported one to a different world.

Ruzsky asked to be dropped off at the top of the hill and, with his bag on his shoulder, he strolled briskly down narrow alleys, past colorful Tartar houses, to the seafront.

The Oreanda Hotel, with its giant blue awning, faced the promenade and Ruzsky had fondly imagined that they would be able to claim they were on police business and insist on staying here for nothing, but the hotel was smarter than he recalled and he doubted the wisdom of this plan as he walked through its cool, airy hallway to the reception desk.

In front of him, a swarthy man in a dark red and gold uniform was talking to a colleague next to a tall palm tree. A fan turned on the desk. The man ambled forward, smiling. "Can I help you, sir?"

"I'm here to check in. Chief Investigator Ruzsky from Petrograd."

"Yes, sir." Ruzsky had wanted the attendant to be impressed, but he wasn't. "Your colleague told us you would be arriving."

"Is he here?"

"I do not believe so. I have not seen him this morning." The man turned and examined the rack behind him for Pavel's key. "He must have taken his key with him, sir."

"Is there a message?"

The attendant shook his head.

"Which room is he in?"

"Number eleven. Next to your own."

Ruzsky filled out the form he was given and took possession of his key. He waved away the offer of assistance from the porter and climbed the wide stone steps to the first floor. He knocked on the door of number eleven, but there was no answer, so he slipped into his own room. It was large and airy with a small balcony overlooking the sea. It had dark wooden floors and a large, four-poster bed. Ruzsky stepped onto the balcony. Even though it was only one floor up, the breeze seemed stronger here.

Ruzsky put his hands in his pockets and gazed out over the shimmering water. Above him, craggy mountains rose majestically toward the sky. It was the most romantic place in the world, and the thought left a dull ache in the pit of his stomach.

Ruzsky slipped back inside and tried to turn his mind to the job he had come here to do. He shut the windows, then sat at the desk and wrote Pavel a note on the headed paper the hotel provided, the sun streaming onto his face.

Outside, he knocked once more on Pavel's door to be sure he was not there and then slipped the note beneath it.

34

The chief of police in Yalta's tiny station was a more important post than this leafy, sun-kissed town might otherwise have merited, on account of the proximity of the Tsar's summer palace at Livadia, a car or troika journey up the hill.

Godorkin was still older than Ruzsky had expected. He was tall and lean, with wavy brown hair and a clean-shaven, narrow, but pleasant face. He had steady eyes and a relaxed air and held himself like the former military officer that Ruzsky soon learned he was. He'd come here for the weather, he said. His family was from outside Odessa. There were sketches on the wall depicting officers of the Ataman Cossacks regiment on horseback, and photographs of five children on his desk. Godorkin was not, Ruzsky was relieved to conclude, Vasilyev's man.

He sat, legs crossed, behind a wide teak desk. He lit a cigarette and offered Ruzsky one.

As he sucked in the smoke, Ruzsky tried to imagine Vasilyev sitting in that chair and wondered what kind of ambition could drive a man from such serene and peaceful surroundings to the frozen back alleys of the nation's capital.

"Did you know Vasilyev?" Ruzsky asked.

"Met him once. Years ago. There have been two other chiefs between us. And three governors." He leaned back in his chair and smiled, blowing a plume of smoke up toward the roof. "The weather didn't agree with them." There was a quiet knock and Godorkin's plump secretary bustled in with a tray and two cups of tea. She smiled shyly and withdrew.

Ruzsky considered asking about Maria's father, but thought better of it. Perhaps later.

Godorkin leaned forward and pushed a sheet of paper across the desk toward him. "Your colleague left this list with us, just in case we could come up with something else, but I'm afraid we haven't."

It was a note of the victims in Petersburg in Pavel's handwriting: *Ella Kovyil. Robert White/Whitewater. Boris Markov.*

"As I told your colleague," Godorkin said, "Whitewater is on our wanted list. That's why I responded to your telegram."

"Wanted for what?"

"Armed robbery. He is suspected of having held up the train from Simferopol to Kharkov."

"Recently?"

"In 1910."

Ruzsky frowned. "Not on his own?"

Godorkin shrugged. "He had accomplices, of course."

Perhaps it was his imagination, but Ruzsky sensed that the genial detective was embarrassed. "It was before your time?"

"Yes, I'm glad to say." Godorkin leaned forward on his desk, suddenly every inch the army officer. "There's no excuse for it. Just because a case is old, it doesn't mean that it should be forgotten." He leaned back again, waving his arm. This was clearly not the first time he had been exercised by this subject. "It's damned difficult getting to grips with old cases when there are no files."

"Why are there no files?"

"Lost. Missing. No paperwork written up. Who knows?"

"So there is no file on this armed robbery?"

"A file exists, but the paperwork within it has been lost."

Ruzsky shook his head. "Shouldn't the case have been handled in either Simferopol or Kharkov?"

"They say it was dealt with here."

"Why?"

Godorkin shrugged. "I don't know."

"I'm sorry, but I'm confused," Ruzsky said. He sat up straight. "How did you know about Robert White's involvement if there is nothing in the file?"

Godorkin sighed. His expression told Ruzsky that the exact same things had been explained to Pavel. "White's name was on our wanted list. The details that I gave you are all that we have. The case notes from the file itself are missing."

"So what was stolen?"

"A sum of money, I believe. Several thousand rubles. The case has been inactive for some time. I only took over in September last year, so it was well before my tenure. I went in search of the file when I received your telegram."

"Vasilyev was the chief of police at the time of the robbery?"

Godorkin's gaze was steady, but wary. He appeared to be assessing whether he was being led into a trap, but whatever it was he saw in Ruzsky's eyes, it appeared to win his approval. He relaxed. "That is correct," Godorkin said.

"His investigation?"

Godorkin shrugged.

"His file."

"I've no idea."

Ruzsky turned to face the window. He watched a sail being hoisted on a white racing yacht. "Strange," he said. "Vasilyev has a reputation for efficiency." He turned back to face Godorkin. "You said that you knew both of them. White and the girl, Ella?"

"She was a sweet little thing. I knew her father."

"Were you aware that Ella began an affair with this American, White, in the summer of 1910?"

"I was with the military liaison department at the embassy in France at that time. I hadn't seen Kovyil for some years when he died."

"He wouldn't have approved. Or so his wife said."

"Of an American criminal? Hardly."

Ruzsky stood and watched the yacht tack across the center of the bay. The wind seemed to have slackened and the craft brought itself around slowly. "What brings a man like that halfway across the world?"

"Yalta is famous, Chief Investigator. Perhaps you shouldn't underestimate our appeal."

"Perhaps not." Ruzsky sat on the sill. The cigarette had gone out in his hand—he'd barely smoked it—and he threw it out of the window.

"What is the connection between this office and Livadia?"

"That I can't discuss."

"You vet staff?"

"We have, in the past. If they're local. Sometimes they come from far-ther afield."

"Who do you deal with there?"

Godorkin smiled. "Your friend has beaten you to it. He left here yes-terday to go straight up to the palace."

"You must have a list of political suspects. The Okhrana supplies you with information?"

"A certain amount is disclosed to enable us to ascertain that any local individual has no inappropriate political involvement, but normally we know them well enough to be sure."

Ruzsky faced him. "Would you mind if I spent some time in your file room?"

Godorkin looked astonished, but not insulted. An honest man, Ruzsky thought.

If Godorkin's intention was to regularize the station's affairs, he hadn't be-gun with the filing system.

Indeed, there was no system to speak of. The filing cases were kept in a gloomy, dust-laden room in the basement. There wasn't even an elec-tric light. Ruzsky shuddered. This place reminded him uncomfortably of the station in Tobolsk.

"Help yourself," Godorkin said, with heavy humor, lighting a candle and thrusting it into his hand. "What are you looking for?"

"I don't know precisely. Other cases around that time. Names that are familiar to me from somewhere else."

Ruzsky hoped he would not be offered any assistance. He wanted to be alone. "Broadly," Godorkin said, "cases are filed by order of year, start-ing at the beginning of the century on the left here. Any personal files are at the far end of the room, in alphabetical order. I've achieved that much. Shout if I can be of any assistance."

Godorkin coughed once and then slowly climbed the stairs. Ruzsky walked down toward the far end of the room. There was a small grille here for ventilation that let in a thin stream of light. Beneath it stood a desk. Ruzsky brushed the dust from its surface. He retraced his steps and found a ledge upon which to place the candle so that he could use both hands to work through the files.

Godorkin was right. The files had been sorted through recently, because the layer of dust upon some of the cases was thinner than around the rest of the room. Ruzsky found 1910 and took all the files for that year down to the desk under the grille. There were about five large piles. Quite a lot, he thought, for a small provincial town, however important.

All of the files had the nature of the crime to which they related inscribed on the front, along with the date upon which it had been said to have taken place. The date the crime had been reported was also recorded. Most, though not all, files were annotated in the same flowing hand. Ruzsky had seen only one detective upstairs in the main room on the ground floor, but he looked about seventeen—much too young to have been working here seven years ago.

The crimes were mostly incidental. Petty theft, vandalism, the odd affray, some domestic violence. It took Ruzsky about an hour to work through all the files and he reached the end with a sense of disappointment. He supposed that he'd hoped White's name, or Markov's—or even Ella's—might have cropped up in some other context.

He began on the files relating to political suspects or criminals.

They were not strictly in alphabetical order, so he ended up going through the whole shelf. There was no reference to any of them.

Ruzsky sat back down at the desk. He watched the dust dancing in the shaft of light still angling through the grille. He checked his watch. He had arrived at Sevastopol shortly after breakfast and it was now almost three o'clock in the afternoon. He was hungry.

He began to sift through the files for 1909. The task was beginning to seem pointless, but instinct told him that these people could not have passed through Yalta without coming to the attention of the authorities.

And if White had robbed a train, he had certainly not acted alone.

There were fewer files for 1909, but they were no more illuminating. Ruzsky was close to giving up when he saw a small, discarded pile on the top shelf. He brought the chair from the other end of the room.

There were ten files, covered in dust. He carried them back to the desk. The top file had the words *Black Terror* written in the same flowing hand on the front. He opened the buff cover and sifted through the loosely bound, yellowing pages within.

A feeling of unease crept slowly through him.

One name appeared three times. The last entry was for August 11, 1910.

The Black Terror was one of many revolutionary groups that had sprung up at the end of the last century to concentrate on assassinating luminaries of the regime. This small and, by the look of the notes, loosely affiliated cell had been formed on January 12 of that same year by a Michael Borodin, according to the statement of a well-known Bolshevik from St. Petersburg. The police had had an informant on the inside of the group, because the date and venue of each meeting was recorded alongside a paragraph or two describing what had transpired.

Ruzsky ran his eye over one of the entries again. The reports must have been written by the informant's police contact.

July 12. Dumskaya Hotel. Present: Borodin, the American White, Ella Kovyil, Constantine Markov, Olga Legarina, Maria Popova.

Ruzsky stared at her name, struggling to take it in. *Maria Popova.*

Meeting called to order by Borodin. Further discussion of possible assassination of Governor of Odessa. Markov agreed to travel to Odessa, to research Governor's movements. Popova expressed view that Chief of Police in Odessa perhaps better target. White spoke of the need for money to carry out revolutionary tasks. Raised possibility of robbing a bank in Odessa, Sevastopol, or Simferopol in order to raise funds. All agreed on necessity of this type of action.

Ruzsky's mind swam. He stood, transfixed. *Popova expressed view that Chief of Police in Odessa perhaps better target.*

He sat and stared at the grille, his vision blurred.

There was bile in the back of his throat. A revolutionary? A murderer? He thought of the softness of her skin and the gentle sadness in her eyes. It wasn't possible.

But who were the men she had left the station with this morning?

Had she been watching *him*? Is that why she had come to Yalta?

No, it had been her suggestion. She had told him she was returning before they'd discovered Markov's body on the Lion Bridge.

Ruzsky read through the entries again. Half of him still did not believe the evidence before his own eyes.

He tapped his fingers against the pages. Why did the reports come to a halt on August 11?

Ruzsky toyed with the idea of keeping what he'd found to himself, but he decided that it could do no harm to discuss it with Godorkin. The chief of police sat at his desk, a cigarette burning in the solid silver ash-tray, a blind flapping idly against the window.

Ruzsky placed the file in front of him. "Have you got the folder for the train robbery, even if it is empty?"

Godorkin was already reading. He opened the cupboard beneath him, took out an empty folder, and handed it to Ruzsky. *Simferopol–Odessa train robbery*, it read. *August 31, 1910*.

Godorkin looked up.

"The entries cease," Ruzsky said, "roughly two weeks before the train robbery, of which they make no mention."

"Yes."

"I assume it takes longer than two weeks to plan a crime of that kind."

Godorkin nodded. "I should imagine so."

They were silent. Both men stared out of the window. There were two yachts in the bay now, and they crossed each other, their sails a startling white against the sea.

"Ella Kovyil got a job in the royal household up at Livadia," Ruzsky said. "How did she manage that, if the department here was doing the vet-ting?"

Godorkin did not reply. The answer was obvious to both of them. "Someone must have called a halt to the surveillance," Ruzsky said, forc-ing home the point. "After the robbery, Vasilyev makes sure the case is handled here, but goes nowhere. Eventually, the notes are removed and disposed of. If there was an investigation, that is."

Godorkin still did not reply.

"Did you know the Popova family?" Ruzsky asked. "Wasn't her father the governor?" He tried to keep his tone and expression neutral.

Godorkin shrugged.

"I think the girl must have been the agent. Nothing else would make sense. Her father died some years before?"

The policeman didn't respond.

"You didn't know him?"

"No."

Ruzsky stood. He felt suddenly profoundly uneasy.

35

Ruzsky strolled back down the winding alley to the promenade. He had established from Godorkin that the Tatyana Committee Convalescent Home was on the other side of the hill, overlooking the next bay, but even if Maria had gone there to see her sister, neither the prevailing atmosphere nor Ruzsky's state of mind encouraged haste.

He needed time to think.

He stopped and leaned against the wrought iron railings. A group of small boys was throwing stones on the shingle beach below, trying to land them in a small pool of water they'd dug in the sand. Farther down, a man was selling cold drinks from a cheerful red and white stall.

Ruzsky straightened. He crossed the road and walked into the hotel lobby. He climbed the stairs to the first floor and knocked on Pavel's door. There was no answer. He cursed under his breath. It *was* unlike Pavel not to have left a note. Beside him, in the corridor, a palm tree fluttered in the breeze from an open window.

Perhaps his departure from the train had upset his old friend more than he'd imagined. Ruzsky rubbed his hand hard across his face and groaned inwardly. He supposed it had been a typically selfish gesture. He walked toward the stairs again. He needed that cheery, gregarious face now.

The Moorish palace at Livadia was cut from almost translucent white stone. Ruzsky was admitted to the grounds by the security guards at the gate and told to wait in the sunshine beside the front steps. He squinted heavily, shading his eyes as he watched one gardener clipping a hedge while another scrubbed the stonework around the fountain. The garden, like so much of Yalta, was green even at this time of year, packed full of the distinctive narrow firs and tall palm trees.

The man who came to meet him was exceptionally tall and lugubrious, but without the military bearing Ruzsky had grown to expect in palace officials. He stooped slightly, as if weighed down by his long, drooping nose. He was thin almost to the point of emaciation, and superior to the point of being immediately irritating. A much lesser individual, Ruzsky judged, than Shulgin at Tsarskoe Selo. "You are the investigator?" the man said, his voice so soft that it was hard to hear.

Ruzsky nodded expectantly as he listened to the clip-clip-clip of the shears behind him.

"How can I help you?" He had not bothered to introduce himself.

"And you are?" Ruzsky asked.

"I am the chief officer of the household."

"You have, I'm sure, already spoken to my colleague."

The man inclined his head. "I do not believe so."

Ruzsky frowned. "He came here yesterday, direct from the police station. A big man, with a generous beard. Investigator Miliutin. Pavel Miliutin."

The man shook his head, his confusion genuine.

"Perhaps he spoke to someone else?" Ruzsky asked.

"That's not possible. I was here all day. If he had called, the guards would have sent for me."

Ruzsky was silent. He turned to face the sea and watched the gardeners at work again. He wanted to leave now, but suddenly had no idea where to go. Pavel must have been onto something. He must have followed a lead.

"How can I help you?" the man asked, and now his supercilious manner annoyed Ruzsky.

"Ella Kovyil."

The official frowned again.

"She used to work here. Her father was a noncommissioned officer in the Preobrazhenskys. She was taken on as a nanny to the Tsarevich in the summer of 1910."

"It may be."

"It may be, or it was?"

Perhaps the man sensed Ruzsky's unease. His patronizing manner melted away and his face grew more serious. "It was."

"You were here?"

"I recall the girl, if that is what you mean."

"Tell me about her."

The man tilted his head a fraction and appraised his interlocutor properly for the first time. "You have come a long way, Chief Investigator. What is the nature of your inquiry?"

"Ella was found with a knife in her chest in front of the Winter Palace on New Year's morning. Her companion was cut to bits."

The man did not react. His expression was sober, but neutral.

"Did you know when you employed her that she was a member of a revolutionary organization?"

Now the lugubrious bureaucrat looked as if he had seen a ghost.

"She was part of a cell of the Black Terror that met regularly through the spring and summer of 1910, at different venues in Yalta."

"I don't believe it."

"But it's true." Ruzsky was enjoying his power to shock, even if he wasn't enjoying much else. "The question that I have is a simple one. Who was responsible for vetting her before she took up her post in the nursery here?"

The man shook his head. "She was only here a short time. I could never have—"

"Who was responsible for ensuring she had the correct security clearance to take a job working in close, daily contact with the heir to the throne? The chief of police in the town, isn't that so?"

"She was from Yalta," the man answered defensively. "She'd lived here all her life. We naturally assumed that if there was anything amiss, then it would have come to the attention of the chief of police. And of course, Mr. Vasilyev is now . . ." He trailed off, not wishing to offer a criticism.

"The information that I have just given you," Ruzsky said, "was gleaned from Mr. Vasilyev's files here in Yalta."

The official stared out to sea. He pressed his finger against the skin above his lip, as if smoothing an imaginary mustache.

Ruzsky left him. He wanted to find Pavel. He wanted to find Pavel *now*.

On the journey down the hill, Ruzsky rested his head on the back of the horse-drawn cab and gazed up at the unblemished sky.

The path was dusty and the cab threw up a cloud behind it which was blown gently across the rocky scrubland.

He considered the possibility that Ella had once been a police agent, but could not see it. The girl of his imagination, and of her own mother's description, was too timid for such a thing. And yet, she'd continued in her doomed love affair against the wishes of her family, and had stolen something intensely personal from the most powerful woman in Russia—or had tried to.

The cab stopped in front of the hotel and Ruzsky climbed down into the street. He paid the driver and noticed as he did so that a different man sat behind the red and white stall on the promenade. He seemed to be consciously avoiding his eye, even though the street was almost deserted.

Ruzsky put the change in his pocket. He watched the group of boys he'd seen earlier climb the steps from the beach and walk off in the direction he'd just come from.

Ruzsky patted the cabbie's horse. The man at the stall still didn't look at him.

He turned around and moved slowly into the lobby of the hotel.

He knew people were watching. Everyone seemed suddenly too busy. The air of indolence had been replaced by one of unnatural industry. Only the palm trees still swaying in the gentle breeze bore witness to the hotel's normal, relaxed atmosphere.

Ruzsky approached the desk. The clerk gave him a frozen smile.

Ruzsky heard himself ask if his colleague had returned, but now, when the man shook his head, Ruzsky could see that he was lying.

The world seemed to turn more slowly. Ruzsky felt the screeching in his ears that he remembered from the day of Ilusha's death—and the sense of everything around him disintegrating.

He watched his boots as he climbed the stone steps.

The first-floor landing was deserted, the window still open, another palm swaying in the breeze. A fan turned on the ceiling above him.

Ruzsky crossed the wooden floor toward Pavel's room. He saw the gold number eleven on the big green door and heard his own knock, though he could barely feel the impact on his knuckles.

There was no reply.

He knocked again.

Ruzsky hammered harder. "Pavel."

He waited.

"Pavel!" he shouted.

He reached inside his jacket for his revolver. "Pavel!" he bellowed again.

The corridor and the room within remained silent. No one had come to investigate the source of the shouting.

Ruzsky put his shoulder to the door and shoved. He stepped back and kicked it. He tried again with his shoulder and it suddenly gave.

The room was dark, thick, embroidered curtains tightly drawn.

Pavel Miliutin lay facedown on the bed, a naked arm trailing along the floor.

Ruzsky did not move. The silent breeze cooled his face. His head spun and he pushed himself forward. He opened his mouth to shout, but no sound came out.

He reached his friend and heaved him roughly over, pitching him onto the floor.

The sunlight spilled onto his face. Pavel opened his eyes. "Sandro?" His breath reeked of vodka.

Ruzsky stood up, gave him a firm kick, and then slumped down on the bed. He saw the bottle of vodka on the floor beside him. "You idiot," he said.

Pavel heaved himself up, frowning heavily. He rubbed his eyes. "Why didn't you answer the door?" Ruzsky asked.

"What time is it?"

"Time I got a new deputy."

"Be my guest." Pavel frowned again. "What happened to the door?"

"You didn't answer when I knocked. Everyone in the lobby was be-having as if they knew something that I didn't."

"They've been like that for days." Pavel yawned and rubbed his fore-head again. "They know we're being watched."

Ruzsky strode forward, tore the curtain back from the window, picked up his revolver from where he had dropped it, and stepped out onto the balcony. The red and white stall on the promenade had disap-peared.

The street was deserted, the light rapidly fading.

Ruzsky waited, but there was no sign of life. Even the waves seemed quieter.

He came back into the room. The last of the sunlight illuminated Pavel's creased face.

They both heard the quick footsteps of someone running in the street and Ruzsky looked down to see a man in a dark suit—young, with long hair—sprinting with his arm stretched back behind his shoulder.

For a moment, he was paralyzed, his eyes on the black cylinder as it left the man's hand.

Ruzsky took two quick paces and hit Pavel, knocking him to the floor as the bomb thumped against the wooden frame of the balcony door and then fell to the ground.

There was a moment's silence.

The explosion sucked the air from the room, filling it instead with a deafening roar.

Ruzsky moved his arms first and was relieved to find he could feel the broken glass around him. He tried to push himself to his feet and was able to do so without any pain. He could find no signs of injury, save for some blood on his face.

He put his hand against the wall to steady himself.

Pavel was staring at him, his face white. "All right?" Ruzsky asked, but his ears were ringing.

Ruzsky turned and leaned against the wall.

The curtain still twisted in the breeze, but the windows had been shat-tered, along with the woodwork of the door. Pavel pushed himself to his feet. It was clear to both of them that they had been saved by the way the bomb had bounced back off the window frame before exploding, the force of the blast twisting the balcony's iron balustrade.

Ruzsky walked toward the door across broken glass, but Pavel moved swiftly to intercept him, a giant hand upon his shoulder. "Where in the hell do you think you're going?" he bellowed. Pavel had small specks of broken glass in his beard.

"Let's find him."

"No." Pavel shook his head and it was clear he was not going to let go. "They'll be waiting for us."

"If we catch the man, we can find who sent him."

"We know who did." Pavel prized Ruzsky's gun from his hand and shoved it into his own pocket, then wedged the door shut as best he could and manhandled Ruzsky across the room. He pushed him into the chair and sat himself on the bed.

They watched the red sun sink slowly toward the bay. The wind was still fresh, the world around them quiet.

There were hushed voices in the road outside.

"No one is coming," Ruzsky said.

Pavel did not answer.

The voices died away and only the sound of the waves disturbed the peace.

"No one from the hotel has been up," Ruzsky said.

Pavel still didn't respond.

"Nor Godorkin."

Pavel stood. He took out his own revolver and handed Ruzsky's back to him, then brushed the glass from his clothes and beard.

"What should we do?" Ruzsky felt disoriented. He was conscious of how rarely he had looked to Pavel for a lead.

"They're waiting for us," Pavel said. "So we're not going to give them the satisfaction of wandering out." He moved toward the door. "I'll have a look around. You stay here."

Pavel pulled back the broken door, his footsteps receding rapidly in the corridor. After he'd gone, Ruzsky took out a cigarette and smoked it.

The night brought a chill to the air, but he didn't move. Moonlight crept through the shadows, the smoke melting into it.

He wondered where she was.

Ruzsky heard footsteps in the corridor and forced himself to concentrate. He stood and moved as quietly as he could into the darkest corner, facing the door.

The man was moving fast, with steady, straightforward steps. The door was pushed back and Pavel's bulky figure silhouetted against the light.

"I can't see anyone," he said. He moved over to the wall to look out of the window. "There is an alley which we can reach from the balcony on the first floor of the far wing."

A shot rang out, the bullet thumping against what was left of the woodwork around the window and then ricocheting inside. Pavel slammed himself back against the wall.

Ruzsky stood. Without a word, he tugged at his partner's coat and began to drag him in the direction of the door. "We'll gain nothing by staying."

Pavel led the way down the corridor outside, into the darkness of the opposite wing. One of the long windows at the far end was creaking gently in the breeze and Pavel reached it and looked down at the alley below. "Swing from the balcony, drop, and then run. I'll go first."

"No." Ruzsky pulled him back roughly. "You watch."

Ruzsky glanced up and down the lane. On the far side, a tobacconist's sign swung from a long wooden pole.

He stepped out onto the balcony, swung himself over, and landed quietly in the dust. The sea glinted in the moonlight and the only sound was the gentle roll of waves onto the shore.

He crossed to the other side and watched as Pavel jumped.

Ruzsky pointed down the alley to indicate the direction they should go and then led the way, trying to keep to the shadows. He glanced around the corner. Light spilled from the back of the hotel in a wide arc.

Ruzsky left the shelter of the wall and began to walk away. He heard a shout and then a shot. He ducked his head and ran, turning to check that Pavel was still with him.

He pounded over the river, swung left onto Yalta's fashionable Pushkinskaya and then right into a narrow alley that led off it. He slowed as he ran up the hill into the warren of Tartar houses.

They rounded another corner and Ruzsky pulled Pavel to the ground beside him.

They looked back down the slope, breathing heavily.

Two men in dark suits and fedoras dashed into the light. Ruzsky aimed carefully at the first.

He fired once and watched the man fold. The other ducked into the shadows and shouted for assistance.

Ruzsky pulled Pavel to his feet.

They ran again, the alleys getting narrower and steeper, all criss-crossed by lines of washing.

There were more shouts behind them. Pavel hissed, "Stop," his voice low but hoarse. Ruzsky waited while his partner regained his breath.

A window opened above, the alley bathed in light as a woman came to the window. She saw them standing in the darkness opposite and heard the shouts of their pursuers. She stared at them for a moment and then pulled the shutters closed again.

"Come on," Ruzsky said.

They moved at a slower pace, but the warren of alleys gave them the advantage. At the top of the hill, Ruzsky led them across the road and into the shelter of a cypress tree.

They sat against its trunk, trying to catch their breath. Pavel's forehead glistened with sweat. Ruzsky watched the road.

They heard a horse whinny and then saw a cab race up the hill to the crossroads.

In the moonlight, they could both clearly make out the figure of Ivan Prokopiev climbing out of the cab, the sea shimmering behind him. He was wearing a long black cloak and stood with his hands on his hips, facing the alley up which they had just walked. The horse breathed heavily from the exertion, snorting into the night air.

Two of their pursuers emerged.

"No sign," one said, in response to Prokopiev's barked question.

"Impossible," Prokopiev snapped. "Go back."

The men swung around reluctantly and began to jog down the hill. Prokopiev waited for a few minutes and then turned around. Ruzsky wondered whether he had sensed their presence, but they were well hidden.

They listened to the sound of the cicadas.

The secret policeman got back into the cab, standing tall as he looked down over the town. Then he sat and barked at the driver to continue along the straight road ahead, disappearing in a cloud of dust.

Neither Pavel nor Ruzsky moved until he was out of sight.

They stood in silence. Ruzsky considered lighting a cigarette, then thought better of it.

"Which way?" Pavel asked.

"Hold on a minute."

"What's the point in waiting? They'll be back."

"We're well hidden."

Neither man spoke.

Ruzsky closed his eyes and tried to gather his thoughts. The peace of the night was beguiling.

"I have something I need to do," he said eventually. "We can walk over the hill, then get transport from there in the morning. Or you can stay here, and I'll come back to get you."

"What is it that you need to do?"

"I need to find someone."

"Why?"

"I'll explain when we get there."

"Explain now. Don't tell me it has to do with the girl."

Ruzsky didn't answer.

"Sometimes—"

"I found the names of our victims in Godorkin's files," Ruzsky said. "I looked through all the paperwork for 1910 and found nothing. So I tried by name and still drew a blank. Then I found the political files. All three of our corpses were part of a cell of the Black Terror here in Yalta."

"The assassins?"

"Yes."

Pavel shook his head sorrowfully.

"The files detail meetings through the spring and summer of 1910. There are six names in the reports: Ella, the American White, Markov—"

"The one we found by the Lion Bridge?"

"Yes. Then a man called Borodin, another woman, and Maria Popova."

"Your Maria?"

"Maria Popova, yes."

Pavel was silent. They stared at the crossroads. A crude sign had the word *Yalta* in one direction and *Sevastopol* in the other.

"She is a revolutionary? An assassin?"

Ruzsky did not respond.

"So, what did they do, this group?" Pavel asked.

"In the file that I saw, they were engaged in planning a train robbery. All surveillance was called off two or three weeks before it happened and there are no further references to that or anything else in the file. After it, the records come to an end."

"So where is Maria Popova now?"

Ruzsky sighed heavily. His desire to strike out on his own was overwhelming, but he knew Pavel would never accept it. "She said she was going to a sanatorium to see her sister." Ruzsky eased himself gently to his feet, leaning against the tree trunk.

"Did she say which one?"

"Yes."

Pavel stared out to sea, deep in thought. "Did you know she was going to be on that train?"

Ruzsky hesitated. "Yes."

"Did she ask you to join her?"

"No."

"Did she know that you would be coming to Yalta?"

"No."

Pavel looked at him. "If this sanatorium exists, what makes you think she'll still be there?"

Ruzsky shrugged.

"Sandro," Pavel said, "come on."

"What do you mean?"

"She's one of them. She has lured you down here into a trap. If she gave you the name of this sanatorium, who is to say they won't be waiting for us when we get there?"

"I'll go alone."

"That's not the point." Pavel's voice was gentle and full of compassion. "I understand how you feel, but please face the facts as they are."

"I know how it might look," Ruzsky said softly, "but it's not like that."

"Love is blind."

Ruzsky shook his head. "I understand what you say and why, but it's—"

"It's about faith."

"Yes."

"Well . . . I trust your judgment. More than anyone's," Pavel said.

"Why don't you stay here. I'll—"

"From now on, we stick together. What was Borodin doing in Yalta?"

"I don't know," Ruzsky replied.

"This is the same man . . . the Bolshevik?"

"I assume so."

"Well, what about the American. What was he doing here?"

Ruzsky shook his head.

36

The sanatorium stood high on the hill overlooking the bay and Ruzsky and Pavel watched its entrance closely as the red dawn stole through the trees around them.

A nurse in a starched white apron with a cross on her chest wheeled an officer in uniform out of the wide doorway and slowly down the gravel drive. On the still morning air, Ruzsky heard a terrible, hacking cough from inside the hospital's entrance.

They could discern no sign of Prokopiev's men, but Ruzsky found it difficult to concentrate on the possibility of danger. If Maria had no sister here, as Pavel suspected, she was a liar and he'd been played for a fool.

Ruzsky stood. He nodded at Pavel and walked down the grassy bank to the curved stone porch. The sign next to the entrance announced that this was the *Yalta Convalescent Home*, but a newly painted one above the reception desk bore the title *Tatyana Committee Convalescent Home*. A large icon hung on the wall next to it.

The charitable initiatives of the Tsar's second daughter still had a long reach.

The elderly porter summoned a nurse. She was a stiff, formal woman in her fifties or sixties with dark hair pulled back from her forehead and tied behind her neck. Ruzsky realized that he must look disheveled and scruffy. He had not shaved and could feel the fatigue behind his eyes.

"Popova?" she said, in response to his inquiry. "No. We have no one of that name."

The nurse frowned in response to the desolation he could not keep from his face. An intense blanket of loneliness enveloped him. "Who are you, may I ask?" she went on.

Ruzsky responded slowly, pulling the papers from his pocket. "Chief Investigator Alexander Ruzsky," he said quietly, "Petrograd City Police Criminal Investigation Division."

The nurse looked at his papers, examining the photograph and then checking his face. She handed them back. "You are a long way from home, Chief Investigator." Her voice and expression were sympathetic, as though she sensed something of the scale of his anguish, if not its cause.

He did not respond. It was not possible, he told himself, that the emotion of those days at Petrovo was an illusion.

It still felt utterly real.

"What is it that you seek?"

Ruzsky felt suddenly, crushingly tired. He wondered if he should leave immediately; was this another trap? He scanned the lobby and looked over his shoulder toward the bank where Pavel was hiding. He could make out nothing amiss.

"What is it that you want?" the nurse repeated.

"We were looking for a woman called Maria Popova," Ruzsky said. "But it is no matter."

"Why do you seek her?"

Ruzsky saw that she was curious. "I'm conducting a murder investigation."

"Is she a suspect?"

It was an odd question. "No."

The nurse looked at him steadily. "I don't know a Maria Popova," she said. "Did you expect her to be a patient?"

"No."

"A nurse, then?"

"No, not a nurse. She came down to Yalta from Petrograd to see her sister. She told me the girl was a patient here."

Ruzsky saw a flicker of recognition and his pulse quickened.

The nurse shook her head carefully. "We have no one called Popova."

"But the name is familiar to you?"

"No."

Ruzsky waited.

"The woman I seek," he said, "is tall, with long dark hair. She is strikingly beautiful. She—"

"We have a Catherine Bulyatina. She has a sister named Maria who came to visit her from Petrograd yesterday."

Ruzsky's spirits rose. "Bulyatina?"

"Yes."

"Catherine Andreevna?" Ruzsky asked. Maria's patronymic was also Andreevna. It was too much of a coincidence. They must share the same father. One or other had changed her surname. "The girl here is Catherine Andreevna?"

"That is correct, yes. Kitty."

"Is she here now? Might I see her?"

"No. I'm afraid that will not be possible."

The woman's eyes were steely. Despite his fatigue, Ruzsky tried to summon up the energy to be charming. "We have come a long way . . ." He sought her name.

"Eugenia Sergeevna."

"Eugenia Sergeevna," he repeated, smiling. "It is a sad case. A young woman and her lover stabbed on the frozen river Neva."

"I'm sorry for it."

"It would help—"

"You said the woman is not a suspect."

"No." He inclined his head. "No, no, she is not. But she may be at risk."

Eugenia Sergeevna hesitated, her eyes narrowing. "You would not come all this way for such a reason."

"She has information that may place her at risk."

"Information that you want?"

Ruzsky did not know what answer to give. His relief that Maria had been telling the truth was clouding his mind. "Yes."

She seemed satisfied that he had conceded. "It is a long journey," she said to herself. "Difficult in these times." What she meant was that the reason for such a trip must be compelling. "Why could she be at risk?"

"The victims were colleagues of hers . . . friends."

"Friends?"

"Yes."

She hesitated for a moment more, then shook her head. "Maria Bulyatina returned to Petrograd last night."

"Are you sure?" Ruzsky tried to keep the disappointment from his voice. But it did not matter, he assured himself. She had come here to see her sister, just as she had told him.

"I'm certain."

"Would it really not be possible to speak to Kitty? Under your supervision, of course."

"No, I'm afraid not. Her health is . . . fragile."

"Miss Bulyatina must love her sister a great deal," Ruzsky said quietly, "to come such a long way for only one day."

The nurse appraised him carefully. "The war has changed many things, Detective, but not love."

"Perhaps especially not that."

"Perhaps. To make such a journey . . . yes, it is a mark of love. Sadly, it was not—" She checked herself. "I must be getting back to my work. I'm sorry we cannot be of more assistance."

Ruzsky was taken aback by the sudden change in her mood. "Would you ask Kitty if she would speak to me?"

"No." She shook her head. "I'm afraid that would not be appropriate."

"Have you known the family long?"

"No," she said.

Eugenia Sergeevna had half turned away, but something was causing her to hesitate. "Maria Bulyatina is truly at risk?" she asked.

"Yes."

"Why?"

Ruzsky thought carefully before responding. This was not a woman to be fobbed off with half-truths. "A group of people she was once involved with . . . some time ago, here in Yalta, has become the target of a killer. Three have been murdered already, in Petrograd. So far as we can tell, the group had only three other members. Maria was one of them."

"What kind of group?"

"A . . . political group."

"Revolutionaries?"

He hesitated once more. "Yes."

"Bolsheviks?"

"It is not clear."

Eugenia considered this and then shook her head. "She did not strike me as that type of girl."

"No."

"You know her?"

"A little."

Eugenia shook her head. "It's not possible."

Ruzsky did not answer. It was heartening to hear someone so formidable echoing his own judgment.

"You wish to arrest her?"

"No."

"You are a policeman, however."

"But not an agent of the Okhrana."

Eugenia's nose wrinkled involuntarily and Ruzsky thought it a revealing gesture. If you wanted to know the depths of opprobrium the Imperial Crown had fallen to even in the eyes of ordinary, decent, middle-class Russians, it was only necessary to mention the name of the Emperor's secret police. It was more respectable to be a revolutionary, no matter how violent.

The woman assessed him for a moment more. "Very well, Chief Investigator. Kitty may choose to tell you what she wishes. It is a decision for her. I will say no more than that."

She spun around and led him out of the door and past a neatly tended lawn. Ruzsky tried to keep pace with her. "The sanatorium has been renamed," he said.

"Funds were provided."

"From the Tatyana Committee?"

"There are some officers here."

As Ruzsky rounded the corner of the terrace, the sight of her stopped him in his tracks.

Maria stood in front of the steps down to the lower part of the garden, by a long line of tall palm trees, looking out over the sea. She was dressed in white, fringed by the rich dawn light, long, dark hair tumbling down her back.

Eugenia Sergeevna was still walking toward her. "Kitty?" she asked.

The woman turned. It was not Maria at all, but the likeness was striking: the same eyes, the same hair and cheeks—the same soft skin delicately lit by the dawn sky.

Ruzsky opened his mouth to introduce himself, but no sound came out.

The look in her eyes was different. It was distant, almost ethereal. But in all other respects she was so like Maria they could have been twins. "Kitty," Eugenia said softly, "this is Chief Investigator Ruzsky from Petrograd."

The girl offered her hand, her eyes upon his face. She tilted her head to one side, smiled, and then sat down on the wicker chair behind her. "Hello," she said, her response delayed, as if her mind only worked very slowly. She stared out toward the sea, still smiling, her face tilted up toward the early morning sun.

Eugenia leaned forward. Her face radiated concern. "The chief investigator was asking after your sister, Maria."

Kitty looked at him for what seemed like an age, her guileless stare as unself-conscious as that of a child.

"He has come from Petrograd," Eugenia went on. "He is trying to help your sister."

"My sister?"

"Yes, my dear."

Kitty shook her head very slowly, frowning. "No . . . that is not possible."

Eugenia's face was gentle but commanding. "He is trying to assist her, Kitty."

"No . . ." She shook her head. "That is not possible, Eugenia Sergeevna."

"My dear . . ."

Without warning, Kitty crumpled into a ball, clutching her knees and resting her head upon the side of the chair, tears creeping into the corners of her eyes. Ruzsky had to force himself to remain seated.

Eugenia gently touched her hand. Ruzsky noticed the scars on Kitty's wrists.

The only sound was the distant murmur of the sea.

"My dear, she came to see you yesterday," the nurse whispered again.

"No . . ."

"She traveled all the way from Petrograd."

"Did she?" Kitty sounded as if she wanted to believe it.

Eugenia glanced at Ruzsky.

"But I do not have a sister, you know that, don't you?" Kitty turned toward Ruzsky and he saw now that she was the victim Maria had fought to prevent herself becoming.

"I understand," he said.

"Do you?"

"I believe so."

Kitty scrutinized his face with greater interest. "Who is it that you seek?"

"A Maria Andreevna."

"It's a common patronymic."

"Yes. Of course."

"What has she done, this Maria Andreevna?"

"Nothing."

"Then why do you seek her?"

"Because I fear for her safety."

Ruzsky waited patiently.

"I have no family," she said. "Ask anyone here."

"How long have you been in this hospital, Kitty?"

She did not answer.

"Your sister or . . ." Ruzsky stopped as she tightened her lips in protest. "This Maria Andreevna came a long way to see you."

Kitty's face was still.

"Do you know why she came?"

Ruzsky watched Kitty struggling with herself.

"What did she ask you?"

"I do not have a sister," she repeated.

"What did this Maria Andreevna ask you?"

"I don't remember."

Ruzsky waited for her to expand, but she remained silent, staring at the line of palm trees that fringed the sea. "You came here after your parents died?"

A tear formed in the corner of her eye. The nurse leaned forward to touch her arm.

"You lived in a white house overlooking the sea," Ruzsky said softly. "Isn't that so? With neatly tended lawns, open windows, and a mother with the voice of an angel."

Tears rolled down Kitty's cheeks. She bowed her head. Ruzsky had an overwhelming desire to comfort her, but he remained seated.

Eugenia forced Kitty to stand and placed her head upon her shoulder, her face concealed by long dark hair. She stroked Kitty's head gently until her sobbing eased. "It's all right," she said. "It's all right."

Ruzsky stared at the ground with regret, then stood. "I apologize, madam."

Eugenia looked at him, her expression sympathetic, then took Kitty's hand and led her slowly across the terrace.

At the doorway, Kitty stopped and looked back, strands of hair blown across her face. Then she followed Eugenia inside.

Ruzsky waited. It was a few minutes before the nurse returned. She sat down and straightened her uniform again. "Would you like some tea, Chief Investigator?"

Ruzsky did not respond. He felt as though he had damaged something priceless. "I'm sorry," he said. "I did not fully understand."

"She has blocked the past from her mind, Detective. The last twenty-four hours have been . . ." Eugenia's voice trailed off.

"She is here because she harms herself?"

"Yes. And because she is too fragile to cope in normal society."

"And she has never acknowledged her family?"

Eugenia shook her head. "I cannot say that Kitty has never acknowledged her family, only that she does not do so any longer. Maria's visit was . . . difficult. She stayed only a short time."

"Were you privy to what they discussed?"

"No. Maria asked to be left alone with her sister. Afterward, they were both . . . well, I do not think it was easy for either of them."

"Did Kitty talk about it?"

"No."

Ruzsky took out his silver cigarette case and offered it to her. She hesitated for a moment, before reaching forward to take one. Ruzsky lit it and watched as she sucked the smoke into her lungs, momentarily relaxing. The act transformed her. "You have worked here long?" he asked.

"Eight months."

"You're from Yalta?"

"No. I worked in field hospitals before."

"Whereabouts?"

"In different places. Galicia, close to the front line." She looked at him with pain in her eyes and saw that he understood.

"How long will you stay?"

"I leave at the end of the month. To return to the front."

Ruzsky saw the concern in Eugenia's eyes; the girl was to lose a protector.

"Kitty will stay here?"

"She will be well looked after," Eugenia said, without appearing to be convinced by it.

"You discussed her situation with Maria?"

"Yes, of course." She sucked heavily on the cigarette again.

Ruzsky tried to ascertain the cause of her apprehension. "Maria was concerned? That is why she came all this way?"

Eugenia looked at him. "She came to say goodbye."

Ruzsky felt the color drain from his face.

"She did not say as much to Kitty, of course, but that is what she told me. She promised to wire money, but what can we do?" Eugenia shrugged hopelessly. "I did my best to reassure her, but could not make the promise that she asked for. I cannot stay any longer. All of the staff move on, it is the way of things. How can we know who will be here in five months, let alone five years? Kitty is still young. God willing, her life will be long."

"I don't understand. Why did she come here to say goodbye? Where did she say she was going?"

"She did not explain. Maria said only that she wanted to settle things, to be sure that Kitty would always be all right. She was very sad. She was crying. 'But if there is a revolution,' she kept saying, taking my hand, 'what then? Can't you stay? Who can I find who will always be here?' "

"Why did she say that?"

"I don't know."

Ruzsky shook his head. "What did she mean about wiring the money?"

"This is a private sanatorium, Chief Investigator. The Tatyana Committee pays for those officers who are recovering here, but other patients' fees have to be met from personal funds. Kitty was only moved here a short time ago and Maria came to see that she was well cared for. She wanted to give us enough money in one transfer to ensure her sister would always be looked after here, but . . ." She shrugged.

"It would be a sizable sum."

Eugenia didn't answer.

"Kitty's parents are dead?"

"Yes."

"They were—"

"I don't know the details."

"Would it be possible, do you think, to see Kitty's personal file here. It would be most—"

"No. We could not do that." Another nurse had come onto the terrace and was waving at Eugenia to indicate that her presence was required. She stubbed the cigarette out beneath her foot and then brushed the ash from her white blouse.

"It would be helpful to ascertain whether she has other relatives."

"Maria said she had no other family members here."

"So Kitty never talks about her past, her family . . ."

"Chief Investigator . . ." The nurse shook her head. "I would like to help, but there is nothing I can tell you." She stood. "I'm sorry." She offered her hand. "Good luck."

As they shook hands, Ruzsky saw once again in her eyes the strain caused by too great an acquaintance with tragedy. The nurse who had appeared so strong and calm in the hallway within was agitated now. She hurried away.

Pavel was waiting at the top of the bank, beneath the shelter of a tall fir tree. Ruzsky crouched down beside him and, for a moment, they faced each other in silence.

"She wasn't there?" Pavel asked.

"No, she was." Ruzsky looked back down toward the entrance to the sanatorium and saw Kitty's face in the window above the doorway. She was watching him, her nose pressed to the glass. Pavel saw her too.

They watched her, but she did not move.

"I need to go back into the town," Ruzsky said.

"Sandro—"

"Just for a few more hours."

"Sandro, come on." Pavel stood, imposing in his bulk. "Maybe Maria was telling you the truth, but she's still a revolutionary. Groups like Black Terror used to blow officials like your father to the four winds."

"I know, but—"

"Please. Think about it. Prokopiev's men will be crawling all over the town. We have found what we came in search of: all of the victims were revolutionaries. The question is what were they doing returning to Petersburg. What had they gathered for? If the murders are the key to something bigger, the answer is not here. This is a trap. Don't you see it?"

"But why were they killed?"

"I don't know, but the answer is in Petersburg."

"Why do you assume that?"

Pavel frowned. "Well, why did they come back? The American, the man we found at the Lion Bridge . . ."

Ruzsky was still staring at Kitty. He thought of the nurse's assertion that Maria had come to say goodbye.

He clung to the fact that Maria had been telling him the truth about her sister.

Had she wanted him to come here? Had she wished him to meet Kitty?

Pavel put his arm gently around Ruzsky's shoulder and led him away.

As they walked down onto the drive, Ruzsky looked back once more at the entrance to the sanatorium.

Kitty was still there, her hand resting against the glass, as if waving goodbye.

37

Pavel and Ruzsky stood side by side looking out of the tiny, dirty, barred window at the spires of Russia's capital, which were indistinct against a pale, lifeless sky.

They did not converse, because, even at this speed, the transport carriage proved an almost total bar on audible forms of communication.

They'd made the assumption that the station at Sevastopol would be watched, so had gone to Simferopol instead and waited many hours before boarding a train bound for Moscow. From there, only troop trains had been moving. In all, it had taken a full two days to get back home.

This goods wagon was all they'd been able to find and they'd passed the last section of the journey to Petrograd in extreme cold and discomfort, the noise ensuring they were barely able to exchange a word.

It was instructive, Ruzsky thought, that this carriage was empty. Why wasn't the government using it to bring food into the city?

They jumped down from the wagon as it rolled into the Nicholas Station and clambered over to the edge of the track. Ahead of them, amidst clouds of steam rising to the glass and iron roof of the station concourse, a lone conductor furled and unfurled his flag. An engine hooter roared, but the train on the platform did not move.

Ruzsky and Pavel slipped through a narrow passage between two wooden warehouses, the pungent aroma of engine soot and rye bread carried on the breeze. As they passed the low entrance to one of the warehouses, Ruzsky stopped. Every inch of his body ached.

The rye bread was in a tin bucket just by the door, but the air was now thick with the smell of cheap tobacco and putrefaction. There was a cough, quickly answered by another. Ruzsky stepped forward and peered into the gloom.

Inside, there were hundreds of wounded soldiers on makeshift pallets laid down on the freezing mud. One or two stood, smoking, but most were lying down in an eerie silence. The men stared at him. There were more coughs.

Ruzsky turned around. Outside, a railway worker was walking in their direction, a giant metal mallet over his shoulder. He wore a quilted winter coat, with a sheepskin hat pushed back from his forehead. He, too, was smoking, the cigarette hanging from his lips.

Perhaps Ruzsky's face framed an unspoken query, because the man answered: "They said they were moving them to Moscow."

He spat his cigarette out and continued on past them toward the tracks. "Prisoners of war," he shouted. "Escaped from the Germans and treated no better than animals!"

Ruzsky and Pavel tipped themselves over the edge of a low iron fence and trudged down the snowy embankment to the road beyond. The country was falling apart. He couldn't help recalling the ecstasy in those faces in Palace Square as the Tsar read out the Declaration of War.

War was not an instrument of foreign policy. It was a national disease.

Icy winds cut through their overcoats as they mingled with the crowds moving down Ligovskaya. Ruzsky waved at a droshky driver waiting outside the station. Eventually, the man saw them and snapped his reins to bring his horse to attention, swinging the small sled around. "Ofitserskaya Ulitsa, twenty-eight," Pavel instructed him as they climbed into the back.

"Forty-five copecks."

The vanka turned around. He had a thick, black beard and the hollow eyes of an alcoholic addicted to the worst kind of moonshine.

"You are joking, right?" Pavel asked. Vankas always haggled, but his quoted price was at least double the going rate. This wasn't the game.

"It's far."

"It's a mile at the most."

The man was still looking at them. "I know the building. I don't carry pharaon in my cab."

Ruzsky and Pavel stared at him. *Pharaon* was an insulting street slang name for policeman, usually reserved for members of the Okhrana. They were shocked both by the man's audacity and by the fact that he appeared to include them in the same bracket.

Ruzsky leaned forward. "Twenty copecks says you'll take us."

The man spat noisily into the snow beside them and turned around. They set off down the Nevsky in silence.

Ruzsky thought the capital surpassed itself in bleak grayness, snow and sky melting into each other, the city's inhabitants bundles of rags hurrying to be out of the wind. One of the single-story buses pulled by a team of horses had veered into the course of a tram and there had been a minor collision which they had to work their way around. The passengers of both were shouting at the bus driver.

As they came close to the wooden pavement, Ruzsky saw a small group of students coming out of Filippov's bakery. There were three girls dressed in the distinctive wide green robes of seniors at the Smolny Institute and two boys in the uniforms of cadets at the Corps des Pages. The sight of them brought back instant and vivid memories. For some reason, Ruzsky recalled rounding the corner of the washroom to see his brother Dmitri suspended naked from a chain, upside down, while some of the senior cadets beat him with leather whips.

He had been thinking of his brother on the journey home, nagged by lingering guilt at his liaison with Maria.

Ruzsky had fought to free his brother on that winter day at the Corps des Pages. The cadets had been seniors and the fight had proved the final nail in the coffin of his military career.

Ruzsky turned away and saw that Pavel was watching him. His expression was quizzical, but when Ruzsky frowned, he just shook his head and looked away.

The sled swung past the Kazan Cathedral and slithered along the banks of the frozen canal. Ruzsky buried his face in the collar of his jacket and pulled his sheepskin hat down over his eyes. He could feel the stubble on his chin scratching against his neck and his bones ached from the relentless rattle of the iron goods vehicle.

He'd found himself fantasizing about vodka. He looked again at Pavel. His partner's eyes now carried the same message they had throughout the journey: *How the hell did you get us into this?*

As Pavel paid off the cabbie outside their office, Ruzsky hurried into a lobby so silent they could have heard a pin drop.

The entire department had gathered to hear Anton address them and Ruzsky was confronted by a sea of solemn faces.

They stood loosely in groups. It seemed that almost everyone in the department was present: cooks, transport boys from the stables, secretaries and typists, even the cleaners. There was tension in every face.

Maretsky stood next to Anton. He had clearly seen Ruzsky come in, but avoided his eye, staring at the floor and playing with his pocket watch. Vladimir and his assistant stood a few feet away. Only the journalist Stanislav appeared to be absent.

"Thank you all for coming," Anton said. He had his fingers in his waistcoat pocket, his jacket pulled back, a confident stance that failed to conceal his nerves. "First a piece of unwelcome administrative news, which most of you will already be aware of and will certainly not surprise you: all leave has been canceled for the foreseeable future. This applies to every member of the department and is by direct order of the minister of the interior." Anton's face softened a little as he shifted his weight onto one leg and then back again. "I know it is some years since many of you had any leave and quite a number have made requests in the past few weeks." He lowered his voice. "We will look to ensure leave entitlements are taken once the war is won and the current uncertainty brought to an end."

Anton surveyed the room. "On a more positive note, I can confirm I have approved an order to allow all members of staff in each department to pick up one loaf of bread every second day from the canteen here after six in the morning. I hope this will do something to alleviate the circumstances that I know many of your families have found themselves in."

Anton cleared his throat. "As to the reason for calling you together again like this, I am instructed to inform you that this afternoon, approximately ten thousand workers from five armaments factories in Vyborg will come out on strike. Shortly after dark, they will gather outside the gates of the Symnov factory. There will be an inflammatory speech and then, most workers imagine, they will disperse.

"In fact, they will be led over the Alexandrovsky Bridge and then toward the Winter Palace, where the leaders will attempt to incite the crowd to the point where bloodshed is again inevitable. It is the intention of the Okhrana that they will be intercepted long before they reach Palace Square and strongly discouraged from attempting such action again."

Anton stared at the floor. They all knew exactly what he meant.

"I have been asked by the Ministry to *draw* this to your attention, firstly to be on the lookout for any peripheral troublemakers. We all know there are those who try to take advantage of any disorder, however well controlled, to engage in everyday criminality. And secondly, the Ministry, or rather the Okhrana believe that some of the most notorious agitators have slipped back over the border and returned to Petrograd. So, I am asked that you all check the suspect bulletins and sharpen your eyes. Report any sightings, at any time, anywhere, direct to me."

Anton took a pace forward. "Are there any questions?"

The speech had not invited questions and there were none. Anton walked toward the stairs, the crowd ahead of Ruzsky parting to allow him through. It was only as he stopped next to him that Ruzsky realized Pavel was beside him. "I'd like to see you two, please."

They turned and followed.

Anton passed the secretaries outside his office without acknowledgment and turned to shut the door behind them. He ran his hands through his hair. "An explanation, please."

Maretsky slipped into the room and shut the door again. Pavel leaned back against the wall, Anton the desk. Ruzsky did not move.

"I don't need this," Anton went on. "I know exactly where you've been, by the way." He went around to the other side of the desk and slumped into his chair. He threw his glasses down and then pressed his hands into his eyes. "What have you got us involved in? Do you have any idea how many times the palace has rung me? Colonel Shulgin has called twice, every day, without fail. The *Empress* would like to know, Anton Antipovich, how the investigation into the death of the girl Ella Kovyil is progressing? Where are the two detectives who came out to Tsarskoe Selo? They are in *Yalta*? What are they doing in Yalta?" Anton picked up his glasses again. "Then Vasilyev telephones. He'd like to speak to the chief investigator, please. That isn't possible? Why is it not possible? He has taken a few days leave? But all leave is canceled by direct order of the minister of the interior. Why have they disobeyed regulations?"

"Vasilyev knew exactly where we were."

Anton flicked his glasses with his hand, sending them flying onto the floor. Pavel picked them up and put them back on the desk.

"He tried to have us killed," Ruzsky added.

Anton stared at the depiction of Napoleon's retreat from Moscow.

Ruzsky took out and lit a cigarette. Pavel shook his head when offered the case, as did Anton. "We found a file in Yalta," Ruzsky said. "It contained details of the activities of a small cell of the Black Terror. Six individuals in all, three of whom are the corpses we have here. Vasilyev kept the group under surveillance until three weeks before an armed robbery, then nothing."

"I don't understand. What are you saying? The implication is . . . you think Vasilyev . . . what?"

"It's possible he was involved with the group in some way, or became involved. I cannot say exactly what transpired."

"And the three corpses we have here were all members of this group?"
"Yes."

"So what happened to them?" Anton asked. "What were they doing in Petrograd?"

"It appears they had gathered here for some purpose. We don't yet know exactly what it was."

"Who are the other three?"

"A man named Borodin. Michael Borodin."

"He's a Bolshevik."

"Yes. A woman named Olga Legarina."

They were silent.

"And who is the sixth?" Anton asked.

"We don't know."

Pavel looked at Ruzsky sharply. Ruzsky instantly regretted the lie, but found himself unable, or unwilling, to correct it.

"You don't know?"

"The name was impossible to read."

"Did you bring the documents with you?"

Ruzsky shook his head. "No."

Anton stared at the glasses in his hand. He rubbed his forehead and Ruzsky could see the immense strain in his eyes.

"We have three bodies," Ruzsky said. "Before long, we may have more."

"What evidence do you have for that claim?"

"The American was stabbed seventeen times. Markov almost had his head severed. Three of the group have been murdered, but three remain."

"They're revolutionaries," Anton said.

Ruzsky imagined Maria's body sprawled on the ice as Ella's had been, a knife wound to her chest. He recalled the fear in her face on the night he had followed her outside the Mariinskiy.

Anton seemed to make a decision. He pulled his seat to the edge of his desk and reached for the telephone. "We have to go and see Vasilyev."

"Vasilyev?" Ruzsky asked.

"Shulgin is with him. They telephoned me about an hour ago. They want all of us to go over; Maretsky and Sarlov, too."

"I can't," Ruzsky said, standing. "I have—"

"Sit down, Sandro," Anton said. "You're not going anywhere."

Pavel, Maretsky, and Ruzsky waited in their office for Sarlov to arrive. Maretsky stood by the door, smoking, while Ruzsky and Pavel began to sort through the paperwork that had accumulated in their absence.

Ruzsky found a thick wad of internal memorandums, a few more—belated—responses to the All Russias missing persons bulletin he had posted, but nothing that related directly to the case. He opened the drawer and took out the roll of banknotes they had found on the dead American. He sifted through them again, carefully examining the numbers that had been marked.

"Did you come up with a translation of that inscription?" Ruzsky asked Maretsky.

The little professor frowned.

"I gave you the knife. It had an inscription on the side."

"Oh, yes. I . . . er, I gave it to a former colleague at the university."

"Who?"

"Professor . . . Egorov."

"What did he say?"

"He's out of town today. He promised to call me tomorrow."

There was an unusual degree of hesitation in the professor's voice. Ruzsky leaned back in his chair. "You know Borodin?"

"Of course."

"He's a Bolshevik or a Menshevik?"

"Oh, a Bolshevik. A colleague of Lenin's over the years."

"You've discussed him with the Okhrana?"

"No, no." Maretsky shook his head. "Too sensitive."

"So in their definition, he's a revolutionary, not a criminal."

Maretsky shrugged. "It has never been discussed, Sandro."

Ruzsky held up the role of banknotes. "Do the Bolsheviks use ciphers?"

"What do you mean?"

"These numbers on the banknotes."

Maretsky shook his head to indicate he did not understand.

"I think these numbers could represent some kind of code. Have the Bolsheviks used ciphers to communicate in the past?"

"I don't know . . . yes, I'm sure."

"Would the money have been sent to him by mail? Would it have been left for him somewhere? How is it done?"

Maretsky shook his head again.

"What about the reference book? He would have carried it with him in his luggage?"

"They will almost certainly go into a library to decode anything they receive. It's safer."

As Ruzsky thought, Maretsky knew more about this subject than he wanted to let on. Pretty much all revolutionaries, so far as he knew, used some kind of cipher to communicate. Since the Okhrana intercepted and checked most letters, it was the only reliable means of relaying a message in secret.

"If Borodin is the leader, he would have chosen the code reference book?"

"Perhaps. I don't know."

"The American must therefore be able to go into a library and decode a message sent by his leader. Correct?"

Maretsky shrugged.

"Are you sure he could not have kept the reference work on him?"

"There would be no security in that."

"So he might have received a new message anywhere. He would have had to go to a library to decode it?"

"I suppose so."

"He might have picked up a new message here. When he arrived, perhaps?"

"Perhaps."

"An English text in a Russian library?" Ruzsky asked.

"Who is to say it was an English text? White must have spoken Russian." Maretsky did not understand what his colleague was driving at.

"You would commonly find English texts in a Russian library, but not Russian texts in an American or European one."

Maretsky thought about this. Despite himself, he was being drawn into the conversation. He put his glasses back on and stared at the floor, deep in thought.

"Major works of English fiction," Ruzsky suggested.

"Perhaps." Maretsky shook his head. "The Bible's too complicated—too many different editions and they wouldn't have an English Bible in Germany or France. Academic books . . . hard to think of too many that you could guarantee you'd find everywhere."

"So which author would he choose?" Ruzsky said.

"I see your train of thought, but it's an impossible task."

Sarlov put his head around the edge of the door. "Come on. He wants to go."

38

On the top floor of the Okhrana's headquarters, the dull afternoon sun fringed Vasilyev's head, his office silent but for the ticking of a clock on the far wall.

The chief of the secret police stood with his hands clasped behind his back, his shoulders hunched, his squat, round body blocking light from the window.

"Good day, gentlemen," he said.

Ahead, about eight or nine chairs had been assembled in a circle. Colonel Shulgin was already seated, and next to him, the assistant minister of finance, in a dark morning suit. Prokopiev stood behind them and Ruzsky knew instantly that he and Vasilyev were gauging his reaction to his father's presence.

Ruzsky nodded toward Shulgin, then his father. "Your High Excellency," he said. He sat and the other members of the city police took their places on either side of him. Shulgin shuffled his papers, glancing through them as if to refresh his memory.

Vasilyev and Prokopiev followed suit. As they did so, Ruzsky caught his father's eye and saw the deep unease that lurked there.

Ruzsky adjusted his overcoat. He had his revolver in one pocket and the police department crime scene photographs in the other and both were digging into his ribs.

"Gentlemen," Vasilyev said, surveying them carefully. "We know why we are here. Perhaps the chief investigator would like to tell us what he has discovered?" The head of the Okhrana took a white handkerchief from his pocket and dabbed his face. Ruzsky detected the scent of cologne.

Vasilyev ran a finger across his forehead, along the line of his scar.

"We have continued to investigate the case," Ruzsky said carefully. "By express order of Her Imperial Majesty."

The room was hushed, but Ruzsky saw a muscle flexing in Vasilyev's cheek. "You have been to Yalta?" he responded.

"Yes."

"And what took you there?"

Ruzsky looked at the pale blue eyes, as steady and inanimate as crystal. "We had reason to believe that there was a connection between all three murder victims."

"And did that prove to be correct?"

Ruzsky looked at Prokopiev, then Pavel. "Yes," he said, "it did."

"Perhaps you would like to give us a few more details?"

Ruzsky hesitated. Prokopiev, he calculated, would have spoken to Godorkin in Yalta. They must know exactly what he'd discovered. "The victims were all members of a cell of the Black Terror."

Vasilyev glanced at Shulgin, then his father, and Ruzsky sensed that this was all for their benefit. "You once kept them under surveillance," he added.

No one responded. Ruzsky realized that Shulgin and his father were already aware of this fact. "The American," Shulgin said, turning toward Vasilyev. "From . . ."

"Chicago," Vasilyev responded.

"Yes. How did he first meet the girl Ella? How did he come to be in Yalta?"

"White's mother bore the maiden name Kovyil."

Ruzsky frowned. Was it the case that even Mrs. Kovyil had been lying to him? Hadn't she given the impression that the American had been a stranger?

"So, White's mother was originally from Yalta?" Shulgin asked.

Vasilyev nodded.

"How did she end up in Chicago?"

"She met a sailor."

"White and the girl Ella were *not* lovers then?"

"They were cousins. That doesn't stop them being lovers."

Shulgin considered this. He looked at the papers in front of him.

"We were told by the Americans," Vasilyev went on, "that there are some influential people back at home who would have liked to talk to White, had they been given the opportunity. Executives of a large steel company for one."

"What did he do to them?"

"He kidnapped one of the men's sons," Prokopiev interjected, "a boy of six, then cut him into small pieces and delivered him to their door in a canvas sack."

Prokopiev turned toward Ruzsky. Was that intended as a threat?

They were silent again. Ruzsky's father stared at the table.

"This Friday," Shulgin said. "In three days. That is . . ."

Vasilyev nodded gravely. "That is what our intelligence would suggest."

Ruzsky wanted to ask a question, but held his tongue.

"We expect it to begin on Friday?"

"Friday or Saturday, yes."

"What to begin?" Ruzsky asked.

Shulgin turned to face him. "It is of no import to the investigation."

"But how can we—"

"It is not." Shulgin's tone was emphatic. "There is intelligence to suggest that antisocial elements will try to stir up trouble at the end of this week. It is not your concern." Shulgin turned back to face Vasilyev, indicating he would brook no further discussion. Ruzsky wondered why he had chosen to bring the subject up. Was Shulgin deliberately trying to make him aware of something? "And this man . . ." Shulgin went on.

"Borodin," Vasilyev responded.

"Yes, still no sign?"

"No."

Shulgin sighed. "The murders." He turned toward Ruzsky. "Were all three committed by the same man?" His tone had grown impatient.

Ruzsky deflected the question to Sarlov. The pathologist sniffed and pushed his glasses up to the bridge of his nose. "Yes," he said, "I would say so."

"Could you expand, Sarlov?" Anton asked. Ruzsky formed the impression, as he glanced at him, that his superior had been aware of the exact direction this conversation would take.

"I cannot say for certain." Sarlov took off his glasses and began to use them to make his points. "I did not see the body from the Lion Bridge, but from a conversation with my colleague, I should say it is likely that all three victims were stabbed by a man of a similar height. More than six feet tall. The particular nature of the wounds"—Sarlov indicated with his glasses—"is the same in each case."

"The murderer was a man?"

"Without doubt."

Ruzsky's father leaned forward. "If the dead are revolutionaries, as you say, then the question as to who is killing them is immaterial, isn't it? Their deaths can hardly be considered a matter of the gravest concern."

"We do not wish to give the impression that the state is indifferent to murder," Vasilyev said, with heavy irony. It was a reference to Rasputin's aristocratic killers and the Tsar's lenient treatment of them. Shulgin did not react.

"The savagery of these murders makes them a cause for public concern," he responded evenly.

They all looked at Ruzsky.

"What do you think lies behind these murders, Alexander Nikolaevich?" Vasilyev asked.

The chief of the Okhrana stared at him, his head bent forward. Ruzsky remained still, refusing to look away. Were the murders the work of this man? Had he been settling old scores?

"Thank you for your time, gentlemen," Vasilyev said. "Naturally, we will need to continue to work together."

It was a moment before Ruzsky realized that they were expected to leave. As they did so, Shulgin and his father remained seated.

Outside, Ruzsky began walking swiftly away, but Pavel caught up with him.

"Sandro," he said, out of breath. "I know what you're going to do."

Ruzsky did not answer.

"If these murders are about what happened in Yalta, then you think she will be next."

Ruzsky stopped.

"In any case, what was that all about?" Pavel's face was earnest and well meaning and Ruzsky's affection for him swelled again. He took out his cigarettes and offered his friend one.

They smoked them together, side by side, moving their feet against the cold and watching the group of their colleagues fifty yards away.

Anton, Maretsky, and Sarlov were waiting for their sled outside the gloomy entrance to the Okhrana's headquarters. They, too, were huddled together and Ruzsky got the impression they were ignoring the pair of them.

"Why have they changed their tune?" Pavel asked. "The Okhrana, I mean."

"They haven't."

"Then why do they want us to cooperate?"

"They don't."

"So what was that all about?"

Ruzsky watched Anton, Maretsky, and Sarlov getting into the sled. They did not look around. "I'm not certain."

"Do you think Shulgin has forced them to cooperate?"

"No."

"Why not?"

"Because that's not how Vasilyev works. He's the spider. He spins the webs."

Pavel seemed disheartened again by this. Perhaps he had genuinely believed the investigation might be entering less stormy waters.

"I think we were there for Shulgin's benefit, all right," Ruzsky said, "so I would guess the Empress told him to call the meeting."

"Why was your father present?" Pavel asked.

"I'm not certain. It may be that Vasilyev asked him to attend." Ruzsky stared after the departing sled. "Perhaps it was an attempt to intimidate me. If you recall, my father did nothing to try and prevent me being exiled to Siberia. Vasilyev knows we don't get on." Ruzsky glanced over his shoulder. "No one watching us. If Prokopiev and his thugs didn't manage to eliminate us in Yalta, will they try again?"

Pavel did not answer. He was staring at his feet.

"Should we be frightened, Pavel?"

"I don't know, Sandro."

Ruzsky took a long drag on his cigarette and then exhaled violently. "Christ," he said.

39

Fokine was onstage at the Mariinskiy, his voice echoing around the empty auditorium. Ruzsky and Pavel stood beneath the golden splendor of the royal box, the double-headed eagle of Imperial Russia looking down upon them.

Fokine pointedly ignored them for a few minutes. Ruzsky kept his temper.

"*Yes*," Fokine said, at length.

"I need a word."

"I'm busy."

"So am I."

"You're the detective?" Fokine asked, knowing perfectly well who he was. The other dancers were looking at him with ill-disguised contempt.

Ruzsky breathed in silently.

"Can't it wait?" Fokine asked, a hand upon his waist.

"No."

"I know what it is about."

"Then it will not take much of your time."

Fokine turned around. "I'll be down in a minute—"

"Get down here. *Now*," Ruzsky snapped, and the tone of his voice made Fokine swing around sharply.

The choreographer hesitated for a moment, in shock, before moving across the stage swiftly. One of the younger dancers sniggered.

Ruzsky took hold of Fokine's arm and moved him through a door beside the orchestra pit. Pavel, who had been standing behind him, followed quietly. The corridor was dark, the man's ghostly face dimly lit by the lights from the stage. He had a big nose and red lips, which he pursed together when frightened. "Where is she?" Ruzsky asked.

"Where is who?"

Ruzsky stared into his eyes. "Do you want a spell in the Lithuanian Castle?"

"Don't be absurd."

Ruzsky gripped his arm tighter. "Do you have any idea what they would do to a man like you?"

"Let go of me."

Ruzsky dug his thumb and forefinger into Fokine's arm until he squeaked. Pavel took a step closer, as if preparing to intercede.

The choreographer wriggled, so Ruzsky released him, took out his heavy revolver, cocked it, and placed it against the bridge of Fokine's nose. "I'm afraid I don't have time to be polite."

"I have no idea where she is."

"I think differently."

"Why should I—"

"I think you know."

Ruzsky pressed harder.

"All right." Fokine raised his hand and pushed the gun away. He was shaking, a thin sheen of sweat clinging to his forehead. "You'll find her at the Symnov factory today."

"The Symnov factory?"

"Yes." Fokine wiped the sweat from his forehead with the sleeve of his velvet jacket. "There is a strike. That is where you will find her."

The Symnov factory loomed like a giant in the half-darkness, its tall brick chimneys towering above them.

Ruzsky was jammed inside a tram, the air warm with the heat of bodies, despite the cold outside, steam gathering in the windows. Pavel was two feet away and they eyed each other warily.

The trolley bell rang and they joined the crowd getting off opposite the factory.

It was not yet five, but it was already dark, the moon bright as the crowd flowed toward the gates and the mass of people gathered beyond them. There appeared to be an equal number of men and women—solemn, unyielding faces staring at them as they pushed through.

Ruzsky and Pavel were shoulder to shoulder. "Why don't you go home?" Ruzsky hissed into his ear, but the big detective ignored him.

A group of strike organizers stood at the gates, controlling the flow of people, and Ruzsky forged his way toward one. He was a tall man with short hair and round glasses—a student, Ruzsky thought, rather than a worker.

"Identification," the man demanded.

Ruzsky shook his head. He was a couple of feet ahead of Pavel now.

"You've no papers?"

"I left them behind."

The man assessed him. "Then you'd better make sure the Okhrana don't get their hands on you."

He was allowed through into the factory yard, where perhaps as many as a thousand people had gathered.

Ruzsky became acutely conscious of the police photographs and revolver digging into his ribs. He cursed himself for not disposing of them.

Ruzsky surveyed the crowd, trying to get his bearings.

He looked back and saw Pavel showing some papers to the man at the gate. Perhaps he had got himself issued a set that did not list his occupation.

One group of men had gathered around a brazier. Ahead, light flickered on the stone steps leading to the factory entrance.

Pavel joined him and Ruzsky found his concern eased by his friend's grim determination. They slipped through the crowd, trying to scrutinize faces in the distance, while avoiding those close by. Wherever they went, they appeared to attract hostile and suspicious glances.

After ten minutes or more, Ruzsky stopped in one corner of the yard. He took out and lit a cigarette, then offered one to Pavel. They smoked in silence, listening to the expectant murmur of conversation.

Ruzsky saw her emerge onto the steps. She looked around, then disappeared again. Ruzsky threw his cigarette to the ground and began to walk toward her. He looked back to check that Pavel had not followed him and saw the warning in his friend's eyes.

The light on the steps came from flaming torches bolted to the walls. Ruzsky followed her into the half-darkness of the central hall.

A man stepped forward. His demeanor was much more aggressive than that of the guard at the gate. "Yes?"

Ruzsky pointed at the stairwell ahead of him. "I was with the woman who just came through."

"Who?"

"The woman who just passed."

"What is her name?"

Ruzsky frowned. "Maria. Maria Popova."

The guard relaxed a little. He came forward and Ruzsky saw that he had a revolver in his right hand. "Papers."

"I don't have any. I just told the man at the gate."

"You have no papers?"

"No."

The man was confused.

"You're with Popova?" he asked again.

"Yes."

The guard nodded for him to continue and slipped back into the shadows.

Ruzsky walked up the staircase to the landing on the first floor. A small group stood in an alcove, gathered around a man who leaned against the wall with his hands in his pockets. He was tall, good-looking, and well groomed, his dark hair short and his features neat, lean, and angular. Torchlight bathed his face as he listened to the woman beside him. Ruzsky was certain that this was the last member of the group in Yalta, Michael Borodin.

The man's eyes flicked to the right. He stared at Ruzsky.

Maria swung slowly around. Her expression did not alter. She was a stranger to him.

"Yes?" Borodin asked.

Ruzsky took a step forward. Their eyes bored into him. He thought of the guard at the bottom of the stairs and the thousand hostile faces in the courtyard below.

"I . . ."

Maria stared at him, her look now every bit as hostile as the others'.

Ruzsky could feel the muscles in his face starting to twitch and a low pain gather in the pit of his stomach.

"Who are you?"

Borodin did not move, but he did not need to.

Maria offered no hope or acknowledgment. Ruzsky did not move. He could not think.

"Who are you?" Borodin asked again, with greater force.

"I am Alexander . . ." Ruzsky's voice was weak. He could think of no believable explanation for his presence, nor any means of escape. He had told the guard he knew Maria Popova, but if he made the same mistake here, she would denounce him.

He took an involuntary step backward. The stares grew still more hostile. They could sense his confusion and taste his fear.

The hallway was silent but for the hissing of the torches.

Ruzsky watched, helpless, as Michael Borodin reached inside his coat.

"Alexander is a friend," Maria interceded.

Borodin lowered his hand slowly.

Her eyes never leaving his, Maria approached Ruzsky, took his arm, and led him gently forward to the edge of the group.

Borodin stared at Ruzsky. He had a fierce, unblinking gaze. "Who is he?"

"He's in the Ministry of War. Sandro. Sandro Khabarin."

"What is he doing here?"

"I invited him."

"Why did you invite him?"

"He wished to become one of us."

"Why does he wish to become one of us?"

Maria looked at Ruzsky. Her eyes carried the most potent warning. Now they were bound together in danger and his heart swelled in gratitude. "We cannot wait any longer," Ruzsky said. "Everyone must play their part."

"We cannot wait any longer?" Borodin's eyes flicked to the hallway and then back again. "Why can we wait no longer?"

"Things cannot go on as they are. Even the Tsar's servants know it."

"And you *are* a servant of the Tsar?"

"We all are."

Borodin tilted his head fractionally, his scrutiny unbroken. He took his right hand from his pocket and slowly scratched his cheek. Ruzsky could see the bulge in his overcoat and was certain that he was armed. "What does the servant of the Tsar wish to do about it?"

"It is too late for anything but revolution."

Borodin smiled. "But that has always been so."

"Perhaps."

"I question whether an official of the Tsar, with soft hands and a softer mind, is prepared to sacrifice himself for our cause. Why not join the liberals, with their many lunatic schemes?"

Ruzsky did not answer.

"Do you question that, Maria?"

"No."

"No?" Borodin turned to face him again. "She is confident. We trust Maria, perhaps above all people. But should we trust you?" Borodin looked into his eyes. "Should we trust the man with soft hands? What would you do for the revolution, Khabarin?" He smiled. "Would you kill a man?"

"Of course."

"Would you kill a friend at your Ministry of War, another enemy of the state?"

"Yes."

Borodin turned to the others. "A man who will kill his own comrades?"

Ruzsky stared at him.

"But you wish to impress us. And not too much. I like that." Borodin's eyes searched Ruzsky's own. "Very well. A friend of the ballerina is a friend to us all."

Borodin turned back to the group. The man next to him was thin and, like the student at the gate, wore tiny round glasses. His teeth were poor and his hair dirty. The woman on the other side of him could have been his older sister; she, too, looked like she had seen neither soap nor water. Her lank hair hung down to her waist, a cloth cap in her hand. Once, she might have been almost pretty, but her face was lined and careworn, her teeth rotten. The pair were resentful, Ruzsky could see, not of him but of Maria and the way their leader instinctively responded to her.

There was a fifth member of the group and when he stepped forward into the light, Ruzsky could see that he was just a boy. Sixteen at most.

"As soon as Michael has finished speaking," the older woman went on, "he will make the announcement. Then we will go."

"Come," Borodin said, with sudden urgency. He turned and marched away down the corridor, the torch above his head. They climbed another stone staircase and onto an iron gangway that ran the length of the factory. Borodin walked quickly, the torch splashing light onto the machines standing idle beneath them. Their footsteps echoed in the cavernous space.

Ruzsky was at the rear of the group, Maria just ahead of him.

Borodin led them into a room on the far side of the building. There was a clock on the wall and four desks, all facing tall windows with views across the factory floor. A shelf in front of them was laden with boxes of tools of every description: wrenches, hammers, spanners.

It was cold in here, too.

Borodin swung around to face him.

"Let's talk about your friend a little more, Maria."

"He looks like a police agent," the older woman said, her mouth tight.

Ruzsky tried to keep his breathing even, his face calm.

"An official inside the Ministry of War? It was too good an opportunity to miss." Maria smiled at him. "I—"

"What is his name again?"

"Khabarin. Alexander Khabarin."

"How senior is he?"

Maria turned.

"Grade seven," he responded.

"How did you meet him?"

"I was given his name and address by a friend in Moscow. I was told he was loyal and decent and"—she looked at him significantly—"I have not been disappointed."

"Why have you not mentioned him before?"

"He needed to be convinced."

"No revolutionary should need to be convinced."

Maria did not flinch. "He can provide details of the movements of soldiers and other information that might prove useful. He's strong and brave."

This last remark was directed at Borodin, in apparent admonishment of some other members of the group. Ruzsky understood that she was using her own personal standing with the leader to appeal over the heads of the others.

Borodin took a step forward. His face was dark and unyielding and his every movement suggested a violence barely suppressed. "Why now?" Borodin asked.

"I told you already," Ruzsky responded.

"Where were you educated?"

"My parents were teachers at the Kirochnaya."

Borodin nodded, understanding the significance of the name. It was an officers' school and explained his aristocratic bearing.

"He still looks like a police agent," the woman said.

"I found him, Olga, not the other way around," Maria's voice was still controlled. If she shared his fear, the way in which she contained it was extraordinary.

Borodin turned to the others. "Maria is right. We cannot allow ourselves to be *paralyzed* by mistrust, isn't that so, Andrei?"

The boy looked startled. "Of course."

"But it would be naive to imagine they don't try to infiltrate us, wouldn't it?"

Andrei realized he was required to respond. "Yes, Michael."

"Do you think they have succeeded?"

"I don't know. I mean, no, they have not."

"And yet I wonder. This man Maria has brought . . . It appears she sought him out. The ones we have to watch most carefully are those who have sought us, don't you think?"

"Yes."

"Factory workers could be unreliable, couldn't they, those who approach us to be involved in our work?"

He hesitated. "Yes, they could be."

"Or students."

Borodin had returned his hands to his pockets, his black overcoat drawn back. He wore a smart suit beneath it, a silver watch chain strung across his waistcoat.

"Yes," the boy said.

"Students worry me especially, Andrei."

Ruzsky saw the boy's Adam's apple move violently as he swallowed.

"You're a student, Andrei."

Andrei didn't answer.

"Tonight, for instance, we have plans. Plans that only people in this room know about. People in this room and, I'm told" — he looked Ruzsky straight in the eye — "the police."

They were silent.

Olga glared at Maria. Ruzsky edged closer to her, but she betrayed no fear, her expression steady, her attention on Borodin. Andrei was farthest away from the torch and his breath was visible on the cold air.

"The police are expecting us." Borodin took a step back toward the shelf full of tools. "Do you think it should stop us, Andrei?"

"No. I don't know."

"The Cossacks are waiting. Aren't you frightened of them?"

Andrei did not answer, his face white in the half-light.

"Or are you more afraid of being discovered?"

The only sound was the rasp of the boy's breathing.

"Just a few more days, Andrei."

The boy swallowed violently.

"By Saturday, our task should be complete. Do you think they know about us?"

Andrei did not respond.

"Answer me!"

"I don't know." Andrei blinked rapidly.

"What about our friend the American? What about Ella? What about Borya? Who is killing them, Andrei?"

"I don't know, Michael." The boy was on the edge of tears.

"Did the police kill them? Are they picking us off one by one before we can reach our goal?"

As the boy shook his head, Ruzsky moved a fraction and felt the photographs pressing against his chest. He felt a bead of sweat gathering upon his forehead.

Borodin turned toward him, as if sensing his fear. "Perhaps the police are watching us, Khabarin. Perhaps they are trying to infiltrate us?"

Ruzsky did not answer.

"An official at the Ministry of War befriends a pretty girl. She vouches for his loyalty, perhaps in ignorance of his real purpose."

Ruzsky could feel the sweat run down into the corner of his eye. He tried not to blink.

"They use an agent to try and get close to us. It would be their way, would it not?"

The question was directed at him. "I don't know."

"You don't know?" Borodin shook his head. "Then you appear to be less of an expert on the workings of your own government than I think you are."

They were silent again. Borodin's eyes never left his. "An infiltrator," he said softly. "What should we do with such an enemy in our midst?"

Borodin turned away, half shielding the torch. Ruzsky listened to the sound of the boy's breathing, hoping it drowned out his own.

The eyes of the group flicked from Ruzsky to the boy and back again. Maria watched Borodin.

The torch hit the ground. The flame flared, casting nightmarish shadows as Borodin grabbed a wrench from one of the boxes and turned, his arm above his head. Ruzsky saw his eyes glint as he walked purposefully back toward him. He felt the ice crack beneath his feet, and knew that this time, no one would be able to save him.

Ruzsky saw the terror on Andrei's face for a split second before the wrench struck the center of the boy's forehead.

Blood spurted into the air.

Andrei fell, but Borodin was onto him even before he hit the ground, his arm rising and falling. They listened to the sound of the wrench pulverizing flesh and bone.

At last, Borodin straightened. The boy's head was half lit, but unrecognizable, almost indistinguishable from the pool of blood and pulp that lay beneath it.

Borodin breathed heavily. He began wiping the blood from his face with the back of his hand, but it only smeared it further. He bent to pick up the torch.

"Get me a cloth, some water," Borodin snapped.

Nobody moved.

"Get it," he snarled.

Maria moved first and broke the spell. Olga followed quickly after her.

Ruzsky stood opposite Borodin, whose breath still rasped from the exertion. He took out a white handkerchief and began to clean his face.

He tried to wipe small particles of Andrei's skull from his shirt and coat.

Maria returned with a bowl of water and a cloth. She put the bowl down on the shelf and began to attend to Borodin like a maidservant, washing his face and hands, before trying to remove the stains from his clothes.

Ruzsky felt the blood pounding through his brain.

"You still want to be part of this, Khabarin?"

For a moment, Ruzsky did not respond to his assumed name, but he recovered. "Now more than ever," he said.

"You can report the death to the police, if you wish."

Ruzsky stared at the revolutionary. He thought that only a man with an intimate relationship with the police would dare to behave like this in front of a stranger, but he held his tongue. "Change has casualties. It could not be otherwise."

Maria bent over and wiped the blood from the silver chain of Borodin's pocket watch. Ruzsky felt the muscles twitching in his jaw as he tried to hide his revulsion at the way in which she was attending to him. He tightened his overcoat, the tip of his revolver pressing into his chest.

Could he have stopped the boy's murder?

Was this the man who had repeatedly stabbed the American and almost severed Markov's head at the Lion Bridge?

Borodin turned toward him. "You don't flinch from the sight of blood?"

Ruzsky stared at Andrei's corpse. Olga and the other man took an arm each and dragged it away to the far corner of the room. Ruzsky heard a thump as they rolled Andrei up against the wall.

"Why aren't you at the front?" Borodin asked. Maria was concentrating again on his collar.

"I work in the War Ministry."

"Don't you want to do your patriotic duty?"

"I'd rather not die for the Tsar, if it is all the same to you."

Borodin smiled. He took hold of Maria's hand.

They followed Borodin out onto the steps, Olga holding the torch aloft beside him so that the crowd could see his face. For a moment, Ruzsky stood behind him, but he saw Maria slipping away and he followed her to a corner where they would be less conspicuous.

As she turned, Ruzsky expected to see some kind of recognition or warmth in her face, but all he received was a blank stare. The woman who had saved his life only moments before was again a stranger.

"Good evening, comrades," Borodin's voice boomed. His face shone. Ruzsky realized that Andrei's death had not just been a performance for Alexander Khabarin's benefit. Borodin had enjoyed every minute of it. He couldn't dispel the image of Maria kneeling before the revolutionary, wiping the blood from his cloak.

"Which of us here is not hungry?" Borodin demanded of the now silent onlookers. Ruzsky noticed a soldier ahead of him on the far side of the steps, leaning against the wall of the factory.

"Which of us here hungers for enough bread to eat, to feed their families, enough fuel to warm their home, enough . . ." He was drowned out by the roar of the crowd.

"Bread," he went on, when the crowd had quieted. "That's what I promise you, comrades. Bread, and peace."

There was another roar.

"How many have you lost in our great patriotic war? Papa's war. Mama's war, though who knows which enemy Mama is fighting . . ." The crowd began to shout its approval again, but he quieted them with a sharp cut of his hand. "We have all lost. Fathers, brothers, husbands. Each and every family has lost a soul, and for what have we been forced to make these terrible sacrifices? So that Papa and Mama could sit at the knee of their unmentionable priest?"

He scanned faces in the crowd, his head twisting one way and then the other.

"It is not men and women who go to the front, but a silent army of the damned, forced to their deaths like cattle. Without rifles, without purpose, without hope, while Mama is paid by the enemy to starve our families to death.

"We see train after train of the wounded arriving at the Warsaw Station day after day after day. We see the hungry eyes in the slums, we see the corrupt officials in their carriages and the parasitic merchants and aristocrats who wanted this war for the greater glory of the Empire, well I say enough. *Enough!*"

Borodin was silent.

"This is our country too. We want our land back. We want our people back. We want bread, we want *peace!*"

The crowd began to shout its approval, but Borodin once again demanded silence with a wave of the hand.

"Now, we can wait no longer. We the people, the workers, demand change. We demand a government that can deliver peace, that can give us bread so that our children do not starve while we slave to provide the armaments to protect their empire. Tonight we demand a new beginning. This is not simply a strike. This is a message we wish to send to the heart of the government of this country. To Papa, to Mama."

Borodin smiled as he once again used these as terms of abuse.

He waited.

"Tonight we march to the palace. Like our brothers and sisters did before us. And we will send a message to the government and the world that we will take no more." He paused once more and then leaned forward. "Do the police and soldiers dare stop us from passing, comrades?"

"No," chanted hundreds of voices in unison.

"Comrades, it is better for us to die for our freedom than live as we have lived until now."

"We will die!"

Ruzsky looked at Maria, but her face was stony, her lips tight, her eyes fixed on the man at the top of the steps.

Ruzsky glanced about him and took in for the first time the composition of the crowd. He saw railwaymen in uniform and workers from the tramcar depot in knee boots and leather jerkins, better-dressed civilians from white-collar jobs in long overcoats and groups of what he would have said were no more than children, pockets of schoolboys and girls. "Do you swear to die?" Borodin demanded.

"We swear!"

"Let the ones who swear raise their hands . . ."

Borodin swept down the steps and through the crowd, pushing forward toward the gates. Maria followed, Ruzsky half a step behind her.

He turned to see Pavel making his way toward him, his eyes wide with alarm. "Slowly," he seemed to be saying, but as Ruzsky forged ahead through the factory gates, the big detective was swallowed by the crowd.

The moon was bright. Around him, in every face, Ruzsky saw determination and anger as the protesters cascaded out into streets. He walked by Maria's side.

She still would not meet his eye.

Ruzsky brushed past a group of schoolchildren; would they not be siphoned off from the march?

And then Borodin was once again alongside them. He had put on a fur hat. He leaned toward Ruzsky. "Do you fear the police, Khabarin?" he asked quietly.

Ruzsky shook his head.

"Do you fear the Cossacks?"

He did not answer.

"If blood is shed, then it will be to the greater glory of our revolution, isn't that so?"

Ruzsky still did not respond.

"People do not care anymore, do they? Desperation is the force we need." Borodin touched his shoulder. "Can you fire a rifle?"

"Yes."

"Then I will find a use for you."

Borodin swung around the front of them, so that he was next to Maria.

He whispered in her ear and then dropped back. Ruzsky wanted desperately to know what he had said.

As they passed the barracks of the Lithuanian Regiment, a group of soldiers hurried to the iron railings to cheer them on. "We're with you," one shouted. "Show the dogs," another called. As they walked along, more soldiers came to the railings. A few started to sing the first bars of "La Marseillaise" and the song was taken up by the crowd.

There was a shot from inside the compound and a series of barked orders from the officers.

Ruzsky was swept on.

Half a minute later, there was another shot. Ruzsky began to wonder if this was the beginning of the end.

Was this revolution? What plans had Borodin sought to involve him in?

The strikers were silent as they marched over the bridge. Across the river, the city's ornate and classical domes were swathed in moonlight.

Occasionally, one of their number would cough, but otherwise the only sound was of hundreds of feet crunching against the snow-covered ground.

Maria had been pushing forward, so that now they were once again nearing the front of the crowd. There was more space here and Ruzsky caught up with her. "What happened—"

She turned to him, her eyes blazing. "I never asked you to get involved," she hissed.

Ruzsky took hold of her arm, but she shook it free. He looked around to be sure that others had not witnessed the gesture, but saw only grim concentration; they expected the worst.

As they came to the far side of the bridge, the protesters wheeled right. Ruzsky turned to see if Borodin was still watching them. He heard muffled cries.

The snow had shielded the sound of the horses' hooves and the Cossacks were close, approaching fast, heads low and sabers raised.

For a brief moment, it was unreal and almost beautiful: the dark horses against white snow and moonlight glinting off swords held high above the soldiers' heads.

They thundered silently toward the marchers, snow flying up around them.

The protesters were suddenly still. There was a single cry and then others. The crowd began to break up at the back. There was a high-pitched scream as the horses reached them and Ruzsky saw the first lightning flash of a saber striking down.

The panic spread in an instant, like wind on water, and Ruzsky was a prisoner of a chaotic, uncontrolled mass. He was almost knocked down, but he used his strength to hold himself upright against the swell. He took hold of Maria and moved forward, pushing through the chaos around him. She did not resist.

White, fearful faces flashed past his eyes as he focused on the broad expanse of Liteiny Prospekt, stretching away into the distance. Maria gripped him, her face wild. "You're a fool," she said.

Ruzsky turned and saw that a horse and rider were almost upon them.

In a split second, they would be dead.

Ruzsky could not move.

Then he was pushed violently. For a moment, as he was tumbling toward the flailing hooves, he knew that she had propelled him to his death.

But as he hit the snow, he rolled over in time to see Maria take the full force of the collision, her body like a rag doll. The rider was thrown forward, the horse whinnying as it skidded to its knees.

Ruzsky heard more gunfire, and screaming all around him. Ahead, a group of infantrymen were kneeling in the snow, firing volley after volley above the crowd.

Maria was lying flat on her back. He bent down and took her in his arms. Her eyes were open, but her face was as lifeless as a statue.

Ruzsky ran. He careered into the side of a horse and heard a curse, but kept charging down Liteiny Prospekt.

He heard another volley of shots and more screams. He ran faster, slipping and crashing onto his back as he reached the corner.

As he rolled over, Ruzsky saw a Cossack lash out with his whip against the head of the woman who had been running alongside him. She collapsed.

Ruzsky lay still. They were encircled by three horsemen who were eliminating moving figures one by one until they were just so many black stains upon the white earth. Ruzsky could hear people crying for help. He raised his head and looked back toward the bridge. There was no crowd now.

A young girl had climbed to her feet and was running toward where they lay. A Cossack circled her, shrieking like a banshee, the glint of steel above his head before he slashed down across the girl's face, cutting it open from the eyes to the chin.

The Cossack yelled again, punching the air with his saber.

Ruzsky edged forward and touched Maria's alabaster cheek. He heard the thunder of hooves and half turned, but the horse passed within inches of him, kicking snow into his face as its rider sought another figure fleeing for the cover of a nearby house.

Ruzsky stood again and scrabbled for Maria in the snow. She felt pitifully slight, her head lolling back against his arm.

In the distance up ahead he saw a private carriage still waiting outside one of the huge houses, a world away from the gunfire and screams.

Ruzsky ran toward it. He slipped, almost fell, but regained his footing and ran on, the sounds becoming distant echoes as he focused on his destination.

He heard the thunder of a horse's hooves again and turned. The rider was close, bent for the strike, and Ruzsky stopped suddenly and swerved toward the iron railings of the houses alongside them.

The Cossack swung his whip down, but missed. He spun the horse around, turning on the smallest circle Ruzsky had ever seen, and charged toward them again, his long whip raised high above his head, his saber bouncing up and down at his side.

Ruzsky stood with his legs apart, Maria in his arms, offered up like a sacrifice. He breathed in deeply. "Police!" he yelled. "I'm a police officer!"

He saw the shock in the rider's eyes and the sudden uncertainty as he lowered the whip and veered away, almost crashing into the railings.

"City police!"

"You shouldn't be here!" the Cossack shouted. "You shouldn't be here!" He waved his hand and then wheeled away.

For a moment, Ruzsky stood with his eyes closed, swaying with relief.

He tipped himself forward and stumbled into a run, focusing on the carriage ahead once again. When he reached it, he almost threw Maria onto its floor. "The Hospital of St. George," he shouted.

The startled driver snapped the reins. "Quick," Ruzsky shouted. "She's badly hurt." He knelt over Maria. He checked her pulse and then bent his face low over her own to check that she was breathing.

He couldn't see any blood, but looked carefully around her scalp, her ears, and her neck. He bent down. "Don't go," he whispered. "I've only just found you. Please don't go."

She didn't move. Her face was still and cold to the touch.

40

A crowd thronged the entrance to the hospital. Two orderlies carried a patient on a stretcher out of a motorized ambulance, shouting at the wounded to allow them passage. Ruzsky swept Maria into his arms and jumped down into the snow, trying to push his way through the crowd. "Let me pass," he shouted.

"Wait your turn!" a woman in front hissed. She turned, half illuminated by the gas lamp high on the wall above the great wooden doors at the hospital's entrance. She had blood streaming down her face.

Ruzsky swung around, so that he was walking backward. He shoved hard, using his height, weight, and strength to push through the jostling, cursing crowd. He glanced down at Maria, but she hung lifeless in his arms.

There were two soldiers at the entrance to the hospital, trying to keep people back, but he pushed past them into the hallway.

Inside the cavernous reception area, the wounded were lying on the floor in all directions alongside soldiers from the front for whom no bed had been found. There was no one behind the reception desk and nurses in dirty blue and white uniforms, with a red cross on the chest, darted through the lobby trying to avoid cries for help.

The orderlies who had been carrying the stretcher lowered it to the floor in the center of the room and began to shout for assistance. The body of the injured woman was covered with a dark blanket, but her head jerked violently from side to side.

Ruzsky looked down at the woman in his arms. "Maria?" he whispered. But she did not open her eyes.

Ruzsky moved to the far corner and laid her down gently. "I'll find a doctor," he said.

He ran through the enormous wooden and glass doors to the ward beyond, the fetid smell that assaulted him so violently unpleasant that he almost gagged. The room was full of the dead and dying, mostly soldiers covered in putrid, leaking bandages. There were many beds, but the injured were laid out on the floor between them and even in the aisle in the middle of the room.

This part of the hospital had once been a school and the tall windows and high ceilings ensured that it was freezing cold, despite the crush of human bodies. Ruzsky saw that several panes on the window closest to him had been broken. Few of the injured had blankets.

He ran forward past the hollow faces of the wounded—mostly peasants with long black beards, many of whom were unlikely to be leaving here alive and returning to their families in the Russian hinterland.

A patient began to scream at the far end of the room and Ruzsky caught sight of a doctor bending over a struggling soldier, trying to restrain him. After a few moments, the medic turned away.

"Doctor?" Ruzsky asked.

He looked up. He was a young man, a boy even, no more than twenty or twenty-one, but his face was as haggard and lined as that of someone twice his age, his eyes glazed with exhaustion. "Doctor, I need your help."

The man stared at him.

"I need your help."

"Everyone does."

"Please, could you come this way."

"I have work to do."

"It will only take a minute."

"Please wait your turn!"

After his explosion, the doctor looked as if he might cry. He put a hand to his face and rubbed his eyes, swaying unsteadily on his feet.

"Just one moment of your time, Doctor."

"One moment," he repeated, "my life is measured by moments."

Ruzsky took his arm and began to lead him carefully down the center of the room. Briefly, it looked as if it might work, but the doctor soon rebelled against the way in which he was being maneuvered.

The doctor released himself from Ruzsky's grip, turned around, and began to walk away in the opposite direction. Ruzsky ran after him. "Please, Doctor."

"No!"

Ruzsky swung around in front of him. "Please. For Christ's sake, don't make me beg."

"There are hundreds of patients."

"But none like her."

A glimmer of humanity flickered in the doctor's exhausted eyes. "You'll have to wait your turn."

Ruzsky did not respond and the doctor rocked gently on his feet. "Fine. Where is she?"

Ruzsky turned and led the man down into the hallway. Maria lay on the floor, her eyes closed. He knelt down and touched her cheek.

The doctor knelt also.

"Doctor!" an old woman shouted from the other side of the hallway, but he ignored it. Ruzsky noticed that most people around them were waiting with quiet dignity and he felt ashamed, but unrepentant.

"What happened?" the doctor asked, as he took Maria's pulse.

"The full impact of a horse," Ruzsky said.

The doctor listened to her chest and then began to check her body with his hands, starting with her head and neck and shoulders and then moving down her chest. She opened her eyes, wincing as he touched her ribs, her face suddenly distorted by pain. She did not make a sound. Relief flooded Ruzsky.

"Any blood?"

He checked her clothes to answer his own question.

"Was she knocked out?"

"Yes," Ruzsky answered.

"For how long?"

Ruzsky looked at his watch. "Twenty minutes," he answered. "Perhaps twenty-five."

The doctor held up three fingers.

"Three," Maria answered weakly.

"Now?"

"Five."

There was a piercing, haunting scream from inside the ward ahead of them, the roaring bellow of a wounded lion, but it had no impact whatsoever on the doctor. He covered each of her eyes in turn, checking the response of her pupils to light. He straightened. "Shock," he said. "Take her home, keep her quiet. If the pain doesn't lessen, bring her back."

And before he had even finished his sentence, the doctor had mentally moved on. He stood and stared into the middle distance, oblivious to the cries for help all around him. Ruzsky saw a young boy lying on the floor on the opposite side of the hallway. He was painfully thin, his skin yellow and body wasted. He was with his mother and they both just stared at him.

Ruzsky bent down and scooped Maria into his arms. As he walked toward the exit, she leaned her head against his shoulder, her breath warm against his face.

Ruzsky let her down gently by the door to her apartment and supported her as he fumbled for the keys.

Once inside, he lowered her slowly onto the chaise longue, then took the sheepskin rug from the floor, laid it over her, and set about making and lighting a fire.

As it began to take, he turned to see that she was looking at him.

Ruzsky sat by her feet and they both watched the flames in silence. He moved closer, took her pulse, and then placed his hand against her forehead. He held up three fingers.

She did not respond.

Maria looked up at the changing patterns on the ceiling. The fire crackled loudly. Her skin glowed a soft, honeyed yellow.

"Are you in pain?"

She still did not answer. She closed her eyes.

Ruzsky waited, watching the firelight flickering on her face.

When she had drifted off to sleep, her chest rising and falling rhythmically and without apparent discomfort, he allowed himself to relax a little.

Ruzsky stood and glanced around the room, from the potted plant in the corner, to the theatrical posters and Parisian street scenes that adorned the walls. The richness of the decor had somehow become gloomy.

He made his way slowly to the window, glancing over his shoulder to be certain she was still asleep.

Outside, a cold wind whipped at the snowflakes and wind rattled the windows in their frames. Ruzsky wiped the condensation from the glass. Down below, the street was deserted.

He walked to the dresser, opened the front of it, and took out the bottle of bourbon, pouring himself a large measure, which he drank in one gulp. He tipped his head back in pleasure and relief. The desire to get blind drunk, so familiar from his time in Tobolsk, was overpowering. He poured himself another glass and drank that, too.

Maria lay still, her head tilted to one side.

Ruzsky thought about the boy at the factory, and wondered what had happened to his body.

Ruzsky moved to Maria's desk and stood before a bundle of letters, an inkwell, two or three fountain pens, and a blotting pad.

Ruzsky glanced across at her once more, then untied the gold ribbon around the letters.

He began to sift through them. Most were notes and instructions from the Mariinskiy, some from Fokine, others from the theater's administration department, formally offering her roles and discussing her salary. Ruzsky was surprised to see how little she was paid.

He reassembled the pile in the same order and retied the ribbon.

There were three drawers at the back of the desk and he opened each carefully in turn, his eyes upon Maria to be certain she did not wake.

They were all empty. It was as if they had been recently cleared out.

Ruzsky straightened again. He listened to the sound of the clock.

He watched the rise and fall of her chest.

He leaned forward to touch her face. She did not stir.

He sat down beside her.

Ruzsky allowed himself to drift back to Petrovo and the hours when he had prayed for the dawn to be delayed. He reached forward to take her pulse.

She slept deeply.

Ruzsky watched her, lost in thought.

Eventually, he stood and moved quietly down the corridor to her bedroom. He eyed the brass double bed and turned away from it, reaching over to switch on the light.

The room was bare. There was nothing on top of the chest of drawers or beside her bed, no photographs, hair brushes, or ointments.

Ruzsky began to pull open drawers. There were a few clothes in some, but no underwear, nor dresses hanging in the wardrobe.

He caught sight of two suitcases beneath her bed. He pulled them out and heaved them onto the mattress.

Inside were clothes and possessions packed for a hasty departure, including a battered photograph album and several bundles of letters. Ruzsky looked at the album first, but he knew before he opened it what it was going to contain.

Maria's mother had looked strikingly like her. In fact, the facial and physical similarity between all three girls was remarkable. Her father was a big man, with a huge beard.

There were several pictures taken in front of a white house, smaller but not dissimilar in style to the royal palace at Livadia, a string of palm trees in the background. Maria and her sister were dressed in white, a young boy—their brother, perhaps—sandwiched between them.

Ruzsky was not aware that she had a brother. He wondered what had become of the boy.

He put the album down and untied the thickest bundle of letters. They were so dog-eared that some had almost fallen apart, and he laid each one carefully on the bed.

Most were in one hand—her mother's—and full of the kind of expressions of endearment that he could not recall having received in any communication from his own parents. Even the few from her father displayed an easy and warm affection. They had been written when her parents had been away, mostly locally—places like Odessa and Sevastopol—but once from Moscow and twice St. Petersburg.

Ruzsky folded the letters away and retied them. With a heavier heart, he sifted through the rest of the suitcase. Hidden in the bottom, he found an envelope filled with rubles and a red leather jewelry case.

The case was crammed full of everything of value she possessed. Amongst the pieces, he noticed a diamond necklace that had once belonged to his mother. Dmitri must have given it to her.

Ruzsky closed the suitcase, switched off the light, and sat on the bed in darkness.

Maria drifted in and out of consciousness. Each time she awoke, her eyes fixed upon his, but she did not speak.

Ruzsky began to smoke. He listened to the clock and watched the minutes tick past.

There was a bookcase against the far wall and Ruzsky decided to look for something to keep himself awake. The selection was not extensive, but contained most of the Russian classics. He ran his finger along the leather-bound volumes. He took out and glanced through a collection of Pushkin's poetry, before replacing it carefully.

A volume on the top shelf caught his eye and he reached up and took it down. It was a copy of *Uncle Tom's Cabin*. It was the only book in English she possessed.

It was an odd choice.

Ruzsky turned it over in his hand, then scanned the shelf once more to see if there was another work in English. There wasn't.

He thought of the claim he had made to Pavel that the marks on the ruble notes amounted to a secret message in code.

The reference book had to have been in English for the benefit of the American. Isn't that what he and Maretsky had agreed? Major works of English fiction, so that the American could get the work out of a library in Chicago, or Baltimore or Boston.

Uncle Tom's Cabin was perfect. An American novel that was popular in Russia.

The book was well thumbed and Ruzsky began to leaf through it.

He reached into his pocket, removed the roll of rubles, and returned to Maria's desk. He sat down and took out a sheet of paper. As he had done in the office, he assembled the notes in order of the numbers written inside the double-headed eagle.

He examined the figures underlined in each serial number. The sequence on the first note was 4692.

Ruzsky looked at it for a moment. It could refer to page four, line sixty-nine, and letter two. Or page four, line six, letters nine and two. Or page forty-six, line nine, letter two. Or page four, line six, word nine, letter two.

He worked through the novel. On page four, there was no line sixty-nine, so he ruled out that possibility. For the other combinations, he made neat notes on the page ahead of him.

By a process of elimination, he whittled down the possibilities until there was only one that made sense.

If the first numbers — 4692 — meant page forty-six, line nine, letter two, then what he found was "K." If he applied the same process to the numbers on the first seven notes, what he got was:

53	35	4"R"
67	13	4"E"
127	3	14"S"
71	6	10"T"
196	4	5"Y"

Kresty. If he went on in the same vein for the second seven, he got *Crossing*.

Kresty Crossing. He had never heard of it.

Ruzsky closed the book. If she had packed for a departure and this was the code book — as seemed certain — why had she not planned to take it with her?

He turned to face her. *The Kresty Crossing*. It sounded like a railway junction, or bridge.

He watched the firelight flicker across her beautiful, peaceful face, her chest rising and falling evenly.

"What have you begun?" he whispered.

———

"It's late," she said.

She was looking at him and Ruzsky realized he had nodded off.

He glanced at the clock. It was four in the morning. He sat up straight, but the expression on her face made his heart sink. "Are you all right?" he asked.

"Yes." Her voice was tired and weak, but it carried a hint of impatience.

"Do you still feel dizzy?"

"No."

"But you're in pain?"

She did not answer.

The silence dragged.

"I'd like you to leave," she said.

Ruzsky did not reply. He continued to stare into the fire.

"I thank you for what you have done, but I ask you to leave and not trouble me again."

Ruzsky did not move. He felt a tightness in his chest. "You'd like me to leave?"

She rested her head again with an almost inaudible sigh.

"Did you know the boy?" he asked.

"Not really."

"Why did—"

"Not now," she said.

"Your name is not Popova."

Maria closed her eyes.

"Your sister does not acknowledge that she has a family. Who are you?"

Maria's face was still.

"Does my brother know about your past?"

"No."

"He's an officer in the Life Guards."

"You don't understand."

"What is it that you have planned, Maria?"

"Nothing."

"Don't—"

"It is not your affair."

Ruzsky leaned forward. The stony glare in her eyes unnerved him. "All those years ago in Yalta, Vasilyev had an agent reporting on your meetings."

She did not answer.

"Three other members of your group have been murdered. The American was stabbed seventeen times. Markov's head was nearly severed . . ."

"Please go."

"Why does your sister carry a different family name?"

"What do you want of me?" she asked.

Ruzsky was stung by her hostility. "I could ask the same of you. What purpose have I served? What part of your plan was I needed for?"

Maria did not respond immediately. He listened to the sound of her breathing. "I never asked you to get involved."

"Tell me about the Kresty Crossing."

Maria slowly pushed herself upright, her face distorted by pain and fatigue. "If you're even half the man I once imagined, then you will leave now and never trouble me again."

"It's not that simple."

"Then do so for your own sake."

She lay back, exhausted. Ruzsky was on his feet. "Borodin thinks someone is closing in on you, doesn't he? Three of your number have been killed."

"I should imagine more die every second in the Tsar's army."

"You're not in the Tsar's army."

"Nor am I dead. Yet."

Ruzsky stared at her.

"What can I tell you that will make a difference, Sandro? What do you want to know? That Michael Borodin has been my lover, too? That he still is when the fancy takes him?"

She looked at Ruzsky. "Does that disgust you? Perhaps you would like to imagine the hands of the man who beat that boy to pulp tonight, all over my body. Would that convince you?"

"I don't believe a word."

"Oh, yes you do. I saw the look in your eyes when I was trying to clean him up. He's violent to me, too. Do you know what he does when we are alone together? Do you want to know what he does to me when I am naked?"

"Why are you saying this?"

"You shouldn't have been greedy. You should have taken what was offered and left it at that."

"I don't believe you. This isn't the woman I know."

"Perhaps that woman is a figment of your imagination."

"No."

She was silent again, for so long that Ruzsky thought she had drifted off to sleep. He stood and walked to the window. It was snowing, thick flakes swirling out of the darkness, into the pools of light cast by the gas lamps.

"I'd like you to leave now," she said quietly.

Ruzsky waited. "A boy was murdered tonight."

"Then come back in the morning with your constables and arrest me."

"I think you may be the next victim, and I believe that you think that too."

Maria was still staring up at the ceiling. "Please leave, Sandro. We will not be seeing each other again." She looked at him. "If you're a gentleman, you won't make me repeat myself."

41

Ruzsky let himself out into the bitter night, the hurt bewildering in its itensity. On her doorstep, he almost walked into a bulky figure huddled against the railings. He began to mumble an apology when he realized that it was Pavel.

His partner wore a thick sheepskin cap, but still looked white with cold. Ice crystals had formed in his beard and he was shuffling from one foot to the other.

"What in the—"

"I tried the hospitals. You weren't there, or at your apartment."

"Christ, man," Ruzsky said. He gripped Pavel's shoulders and began to try to warm him, then pushed the door back and forced him inside. "Why didn't you wait in here?"

"I'm all right."

Ruzsky glanced toward the hall porter's little box beneath the stairs. The man was eyeing them warily.

"Is she alive?" Pavel asked. "I saw her go under the horse."

"She's alive, yes."

Pavel took off his gloves and began to blow onto his hands.

"You need to get warm," Ruzsky said.

"No, I'm all right."

Pavel knocked the remaining snow from his boots. The hall porter shouted something incomprehensible at them.

"What happened at the factory?" Pavel asked.

Ruzsky glanced up the curved stairwell at the floors above, ignoring the question. "Are you tired?"

"Why?"

"Because I would like to go back to the factory. I'll explain on the way."

There were no trams running at this time in the morning, so they had to walk down to the Mariinskiy before they found a droshky.

The vanka was a monosyllabic Tartar who barely even bothered to haggle over the fare. He was wrapped in at least a dozen layers of clothing and as they crossed the Alexandrovsky Bridge, Ruzsky could see why. The sky was clear, a bright moon sparkling off golden spires, but it was viciously cold, a north wind sweeping across the ice and biting through their overcoats. They huddled together in the back for warmth, Ruzsky attempting to bury his leather boots beneath the straw by his feet.

He tried to explain some of what had happened in the factory to his colleague, but the howling wind made it difficult.

Pavel paid the driver outside the tall black gates and tried to persuade the man to stay for the return journey, but he shook his head, turned his sledge around, and disappeared back toward the south side of the river.

Ruzsky led the way into the courtyard. It was deserted now and bathed in moonlight. The braziers that had been burning earlier had been knocked aside.

Ruzsky marched toward the darkened entrance to the vast, redbrick building, the wind roaring in his ears.

It was quieter within, and their footsteps echoed. Pavel put a hand on his arm and drew him to a halt. His eyes questioned the wisdom of continuing. Ruzsky held up two fingers. "Two minutes," he mouthed.

He began to mount the stairs. It was dark but for fingers of moonlight feeling their way through tiny slit windows.

They reached the landing where Ruzsky had first seen Borodin, but the corridor disappeared into darkness in both directions.

Ruzsky followed the route he had taken earlier, mounting the steps and turning toward the gangway over the factory floor.

They saw light ahead and Pavel pulled him roughly back into a stairwell.

They heard voices.

The conversation grew louder for a moment and then quieter as the torchlight faded.

They waited. The factory was silent.

Ruzsky led the way down to the floor below, groping in the darkness, past giant black machines that smelled of grease and oil.

They stopped again. Above them they could see light from a series of flame torches flickering across the ceiling of the supervisor's office where Andrei had been murdered.

The voices were suddenly louder again. Two men stood in the doorway. They began to walk, their voices booming confidently across the factory floor. One of them whispered something and the other laughed.

Ruzsky edged forward, skirting one of the machines, and looked up. One of the men was Ivan Prokopiev, his closely cropped bullet head instantly recognizable, and the other was Michael Borodin.

Ruzsky stepped back, colliding with Pavel, who began to gesticulate, mouthing that they should leave immediately. Ruzsky shrugged. "How?" he mouthed back. Some of Prokopiev's men were still in the foreman's office at the end and Prokopiev and Borodin were now behind them.

Their answer presented itself when the two men returned, still in animated conversation. Ruzsky heard Prokopiev say, "Hurry up," to his officers at the far end of the walkway, and he and Pavel took this as their cue.

They moved silently up the stairs and then retraced their steps down to the courtyard. They kept moving and did not stop until they had reached the high iron fence surrounding the barracks of the Lithuanian Regiment.

"There is your answer," Pavel said, trying to recover his breath.

Ruzsky did not respond. His heart was pounding and his palms and forehead were clammy.

"It's as you suspected. Borodin and Vasilyev are allies. They must have been since Yalta. That's what lies behind our murders. Vasilyev must be eliminating everyone who is aware of that association."

"It's a neat theory," Ruzsky conceded.

"Don't tell me you're surprised?"

"Whatever one might think of Vasilyev—or his associate—I can't picture either of them following in someone's footsteps like a misguided amateur and then slashing him seventeen times for the fun of it."

"Perhaps the other one does the killing. Borodin . . ."

Ruzsky hesitated. The way in which the boy had been bludgeoned to death made some sense of this, but he still couldn't accept it. "No," he said. "I think Borodin and his allies are angered by these killings. If anything, they have disrupted their plans."

They glanced back down the street to check that they had not been followed. "What are their plans?" Pavel asked.

Ruzsky did not answer. He turned his back so that he was shielded from the wind.

"At that meeting," Pavel went on, "Vasilyev was giving Shulgin and your father the impression that these men were dangerous. Why was he doing that?"

"I don't know." Ruzsky looked at his colleague. He needed time to think. "Go home and get some sleep. We'll talk later."

"Will you be all right?"

"Of course."

"Don't do anything foolish. Remember what happened in Yalta."

Ruzsky shook his head. "I will see you in the office at one."

"What—"

"We have something we need to do."

Ruzsky tapped his colleague's shoulder affectionately and then started walking. After twenty yards, he stopped and turned back to watch Pavel melting into the night.

He and Tonya lived over in Palyustrovo, beyond the Finland Station. It was a walk almost as long as his own, but at least a warm bed awaited him.

Ruzsky turned into the wind and began the journey back to Vasilevsky Island. He didn't encounter a droshky, so had to keep walking, crossing the Birzhevoy Bridge to the Strelka alongside a peddler pushing his cart laboriously up the incline. Ruzsky helped the man for twenty yards or so—until the downhill section of the bridge—earning himself a toothless grin.

He pulled his cap down farther and narrowed his eyes against the wind as he slipped through the austere buildings that dominated this end of Vasilevsky Island. He thought of the summer days when he and Dmitri had stood with the servants close to where University and Nicholas Quays merged, listening to the whistling of the winches and the shouts of crewmen from all over the world.

The memory of such innocent pleasures troubled him. Would that world ever return? He was worried not for himself, but for Michael.

He would see his boy tomorrow, come what may.

Ruzsky was so lost in thought that he almost walked straight into them. Only the presence of a dark automobile in the region of Line Fourteen—an unusual sight—alerted him.

He stopped and ducked into the shadows. There were two officers in the car. They were Prokopiev's men, not the surveillance teams, who would have been much less conspicuous.

Ruzsky edged back into the shadows and moved silently away. Ironically, he knew there was now only one place in the city he would be safe.

At night, the servants locked and bolted the entrance to the yard at Millionnaya Street, but there was a gap above the doors that Ruzsky had slipped through many times as an adolescent.

Inside, he climbed the stone steps to the kitchen door and glanced in. A light was on. He knew that Katya awoke early. He checked his watch. It was half past five in the morning.

Ruzsky waited. Even out of the wind, it was still bitterly cold.

Katya bustled into the kitchen and he watched her for a few moments before knocking gently on the window. She looked around, startled, then frowned as she examined him more closely. Ruzsky realized that she had not initially recognized him.

She came to the back door, opening it a fraction, as if not wanting him to take his entry for granted. "Master Sandro," she said, her face flushed.

"Katya."

She did not move.

"Might I come in?"

"They're all asleep, Master Sandro."

"I want to see my boy, before they wake."

Reluctantly, and only because she felt she had no choice, Katya eased the door back and allowed him entry. In the hallway within, she examined him cautiously. Ruzsky realized, through her reaction, what a mess he must look. He hadn't seen himself in a mirror for days and he doubted it would be a pretty sight. "Thank you," he said quietly.

"Be careful, Master Sandro," she said.

Ruzsky smiled. He turned and walked up the stairs, drifting silently through the house.

He climbed the last steps to the attic.

In the darkness, Ruzsky walked forward until he stood over his son.

Michael lay on his front, his head to the side, clutching his worn-out bear. He was breathing easily. A new train track had been assembled upon the floor, reaching right to the edge of the bed.

Ruzsky studied him.

He reached down and touched his son's soft head, then leaned down and kissed his ear. "I love you, my boy."

Fatigue finally began to overwhelm him and, as he straightened, he felt unsteady on his feet. He turned and, trying not to wake Michael, slipped back across the hallway.

By the light of the moon, he saw Ilusha's abandoned animals on the shelf above his bunk and found himself moving toward them. He looked at the photograph of his brother, with the two candles on either side of it.

Ruzsky stopped. The bed was already occupied.

Dmitri sat up, his hair tousled and his face full of sleep. "Sandro? What are you doing here?"

Ruzsky did not answer. He listened to the sound of his own breathing.

Dmitri lay down again, with his back to the door. He was in the full dress uniform of a colonel of the Guards. "There is room," he said, shuffling to the side of the bunk.

Ruzsky waited for a few seconds, then walked forward. He lay down beside his brother.

The house was silent.

He looked up at the tattered toy elephant on the shelf above and the painted wooden soldier at the end of the bed. He closed his eyes.

Dmitri reached out for his hand and held it. Ruzsky gripped it tightly.

They lay still, just as they had done in the days and weeks after Ilusha's death.

Ruzsky turned over and wrapped his arm around his brother's chest.

He relaxed his grip, but did not move. After a few moments, sleep overwhelmed him.

He dreamed of her, but it was more memory than illusion. He watched the image of her crouched in front of Borodin, wiping the blood from his clothes.

The others were not there. It was just Maria and the revolutionary.

Maria ministered to him slowly, upon her knees, Borodin's dark head tilted down, his eyes upon her.

He touched her head and stilled her actions.

Ruzsky waited, his heart thumping in his chest. He closed his eyes.

He awoke, bathed in sweat—or at least, so it seemed. It took him a few moments to understand that it was his brother whose skin was clammy with perspiration. Dmitri turned and looked at him with startled eyes. "Sandro?" He stared at Ruzsky, apparently forgetting that his brother was sleeping alongside him. "Is it you?"

"It's me, Dmitri."

Dmitri slumped back down, once again turning away from him. "Thank God," he whispered.

Ruzsky placed his arm over his brother's shoulder and they lay still in the darkness.

Thoughts of her crowded in upon him. He wondered if his brother was similarly tortured and tightened his grip. Dmitri took hold of his hand. "I'm sorry, Sandro," he said.

Ruzsky did not respond.

"I don't know why I didn't stop him."

He listened to the sound of Dmitri's breathing.

"I thought you two were the chosen ones. You and Ilusha. I hated you both, did you know that? I thought Father only cared for you. Why didn't I stop Ilusha going onto the ice? Do you know, Sandro? Was I jealous? Did I want him to die?"

Dmitri was babbling, still half asleep, so Ruzsky gripped him harder, until fatigue once again overwhelmed all doubts.

42

"Master Sandro?" Katya's anxious face was close to his. "Master Sandro?" Her hand shook his shoulder.

"Yes? What is it?"

"One of the boys has drawn you a bath."

Ruzsky stared at her. The unspoken message in Katya's eyes was that she would like him to wash and then leave, before his presence was detected. "All right," he said, still full of sleep. "Where's Michael?"

"He's gone out."

"With his mother?"

"No. Mistress Ingrid has taken him to the Summer Gardens."

Ruzsky forced himself upright and swung his legs off the bunk, rubbing his face with both hands. "Thank you, Katya," he said. Then, "I'm sorry."

Her cheeks flushed. She was embarrassed by her reluctance to admit him to the house earlier. Times are hard, her expression suggested. A servant cannot afford to be without employment.

But Ruzsky saw more in her eyes than that. Katya had joined the household staff when he was nine. She had adored his brother Ilusha and treated him as her own son. It was not just his parents who had found it impossible to forget, or forgive.

Ruzsky might not have been there when his brother stepped onto the ice, but everyone thought he should have been. Hadn't his father asked him to take care of the boy? Hadn't he been told to make sure Ilusha never played on the ice?

"I'm sorry," he said again. "I will leave now."

Katya did not move. As she examined him, her face softened. "You're not cared for properly."

"I can care for myself."

"When did you last eat?"

Ruzsky felt a dull ache in his stomach. When had he? He could not recall.

"Bathe and wash yourself, then come to the kitchen."

"No." Ruzsky shook his head. "No," he repeated, in order to fortify himself. "Better not."

But he felt awake enough now to weaken at the idea of bread and cheese, or even just bread. He thought he could smell fresh coffee.

"You look thinner," she said.

"Impossible."

Katya did not move. She turned her attention to his feet. "Your boots . . ."

Ruzsky gazed at them, as if noticing the holes for the first time. His socks were still damp and his toes numb from being repeatedly frozen and thawed.

Katya turned and strode purposefully away. She returned a few moments later clutching a pair of tall, black leather boots. "He has finished with these."

"No." Ruzsky shook his head.

"Don't be so proud." Katya stared at him. It was an admonition that carried a resonance beyond the question of boots, and, knowing that she had strayed too far, she averted her gaze. "A bath has been drawn for you. Come to the kitchen when you're dressed," she said, muttering, as she returned to the door. "You need someone to look after you."

After she had gone, Ruzsky turned the boots upside down. Like all his father's footwear, they had been beautifully fashioned by Meulenhoff, a German cobbler whose tiny premises had once been squeezed between much grander shops around the back of Gostiny Dvor. The man had been interned in the first days of the war and then sent home.

Ruzsky dropped the boots, yawned, and lay back down on the bed. On the other side of the mattress, he could still see the indentation that marked his brother's presence alongside him in the night. He covered himself with the blankets and looked at the painted soldier at the end of the bed and the photograph of Ilusha on the shelf.

The house was quiet and the air still. He heard the tinkle of bells on a passing sleigh.

Ruzsky reached for Ilusha's elephant. Robbed of human affection, it smelled only of mold and dust. He held it up, looking into its one eye. "I see you, Ilusha," he said.

He hummed to himself. It was a child's lullaby.

Ruzsky pushed himself upright. He checked his pocket watch. It was eleven o'clock.

He went down to the bathroom on the floor below, where a hot bath had indeed been drawn for him in the large tin tub. Katya or one of the other servants had placed some shaving tackle and pomades on the shelf beneath the mirror.

Ruzsky turned on the tap and felt the heat of the water. It was hardly more than a dribble, but it was a luxury he had not enjoyed since he'd last stayed in this house on the eve of his marriage.

He undressed. The room was dark and cluttered, its walls covered in military prints and photographs depicting generations of Ruzsky men attending the Corps des Pages and serving in the Guards. The line drawings and photographs closest to him were of his father's younger brother, who had served in Her Majesty's Life Guard Cuirassier Regiment—the Blue Cuirassiers—at Gatchina, before retiring permanently to Paris with his Belgian mistress.

The only nonmilitary photographs were of the family's yacht, the *Sinitsa*, upon which they had once enjoyed holidays in the Gulf of Finland. Ruzsky examined it for a moment, before settling into the bath.

He felt uncomfortable enjoying the luxury that would once have been his by right.

About forty-five minutes later, freshly shaven and with a full stomach for the first time in days, Ruzsky emerged from the kitchen in the basement to find his father standing by the doorway, head bent in thought.

As the old man looked up, his expression softened. "Good morning, Sandro."

"Good morning." Ruzsky felt uncomfortably aware of the boots Katya had brought him.

"Did you sleep well?"

"Yes." Ruzsky nodded. "I'm sorry, I should have told you that—"

"Michael is out in the Summer Gardens. He's with Ingrid." The old man was staring at the rectangular pool of light stretching away from the drawing room window.

Ruzsky watched him. "Are you quite all right, Father?"

"Yes." He turned to his son. "Of course, yes."

"You look tired."

The old man attempted a smile. "Yes."

They heard the sound of horses' hooves on the cobbles and stepped into the drawing room to watch them pass. It was another detachment of the Chevalier Guard in white and red dress uniforms and blue overcoats, stiff and upright in their saddles. Their mounts were finely groomed, the men's uniforms spotless.

After they had gone, Ruzsky watched the snowflakes dancing in their wake.

A private sled passed. They heard the crack of the driver's whip.

The old man was about to turn away when he caught sight of another group of soldiers, this time on foot. They wore khaki overcoats, rather than dress uniform, but their epaulettes identified them as members of the Izmailovsky Regiment, and their demeanor as reservists.

"Dmitri says there are few regulars left in the capital," Ruzsky said.

His father did not answer. He kept his eyes upon the soldiers until they had disappeared from view.

The telephone trilled in the hall. Neither man moved, though their heads inclined toward it until the call was answered. They heard the quiet murmur of one of the servants and then a final tinkle of the bell as the receiver was replaced. The young man who had first welcomed Ruzsky to the house appeared in the doorway. He glanced at him momentarily, as if unsure as to whether he should impart information of any significance in his presence. "It was Mr. Vasilyev's office, sir," he told Ruzsky's father. "He will be here any moment. He sends his apologies for the delay."

"Thank you, Peter."

After the servant had gone, the old man checked his pocket watch. He was frowning heavily. "Mr. Vasilyev will be late for his own entry to hell."

Ruzsky was about to speak, but found he did not know how to begin. In forty years, he could not recall a conversation with his father upon matters of the world, let alone affairs of state. "I imagined you would be at the ministry," Ruzsky said.

"Not today."

"Does Mr. Vasilyev often come to see you here?"

"No." An intense weariness seemed to suck the life from the old man's face. "No," he said again.

"What does he want?"

"That is the question, Sandro. What does this man want?" He sighed. "To protect the assets of the state, he says. That is the pass he would have us believe we have come to. To protect the wealth of the Tsar from the mob." He shook his head.

"He tells you there will be trouble?"

"Yes."

"When?"

"Soon."

"On Friday?" Ruzsky asked.

His father checked his pocket watch again, then smiled. "Go and find your son."

They stared at each other. The old man's eyes sparkled momentarily with a warm affection.

"Last night, Father, I saw Vasilyev's men—"

"Go and find your boy first." The old man placed a hand upon his son's shoulder. "He is so looking forward to seeing you."

Ruzsky pulled on his overcoat and took the sheepskin hat from its pocket.

"It's a little warmer today," his father said. "You'll not need that."

Ruzsky thrust the hat back into his pocket. "I'd like to talk to you, Father. It's just about—"

"Your case. I know. After this meeting. When you come back. There is much we should have talked about."

"Yes." Ruzsky opened the door, but hesitated on the threshold.

"You'll come and stay whenever you want, won't you, Sandro?" The old man's eyes radiated warmth and sadness in equal measure.

"Yes, Father."

"It is your home."

"Yes."

"You know that, don't you? I mean, you're a grown man, you have your own life, of course, I realize that, but this will always be your home, whenever you wish it to be."

"I understand."

"Do you?"

"Yes."

"You could even . . ." He smiled, ignoring his son's unspoken question. "But I'll see you in a few minutes."

"Are you all right, Father?"

"Yes." The old man stepped back, gesturing for Ruzsky to leave with an outstretched hand. "Please go to see him. He is waiting."

Ruzsky returned his father's hesitant grin and turned away. As he walked down Millionnaya Street, he could not contain the spring in his step.

Entering the Summer Gardens a few minutes later, Ruzsky glanced at the sign attached to the heavy iron railings. *Dogs, Beggars, all Lower Ranks of the Army and Navy prohibited from entry.*

Inside the railings, another group of soldiers in long greatcoats stood around a coal brazier. They were laughing and smoking—also forbidden in public for the lower ranks—and as Ruzsky passed them, he saw that they were drunk. Like those he had seen passing through Millionnaya Street earlier, they were dressed in khaki, but this group was from the Pavlovsky Regiment, whose barracks overlooked the Field of Mars. One had a crude tin drum in his hand, filled with illegal moonshine.

Ruzsky ignored them and wandered along the line of lime trees, scanning the gardens for a tall blond woman and a small, dark-haired boy. Behind him, the soldiers began humming the national anthem, "God Save the Tsar," with heavy irony.

He wondered if they were taunting him in some way, but resisted the urge to look over his shoulder.

He stopped in the clearing, fringed by firs, known as Children's Corner. The marble statues in the gardens were all enclosed by wooden boxes in winter, but the bronze of an old man sitting in a comfortable chair here was still exposed to the elements. The statue was surrounded by high wrought iron railings and Ruzsky stared through them, thinking of the old men in high valenki who used to build snow mountains here in winter and charge the children of the rich a few copecks to sled down.

Ruzsky heard a sound and swung around. Michael stood next to Ingrid, clutching the leather lead of one of his father's dogs.

For a moment, they examined each other and then Ruzsky crossed the frozen ground as if it were the last act he would perform on earth, sweeping his boy up and clutching him with all his might. He pressed Michael's face against his shoulder.

"Hello, Father."

Ruzsky let Michael down gently and knelt before him. He touched his face, then his shoulders, as if checking that he was still in one piece. "Hello, my boy. Are you all right?"

"Yes."

Ruzsky clasped his son's face between cold palms. "Pleased to see me?"

Michael nodded. He pulled the great hunting dog closer and stroked its head. It was a gentle creature.

Ruzsky thought that his son was avoiding his eye. He glanced at Ingrid.

"You went to Yalta, didn't you?" Michael asked.

"Yes."

"Grandfather said he thought you would go to the house at Petrovo."

"Why did Grandfather say that?"

"He said you would go to the house on the way. Is Petrovo far from here?"

"Quite far, yes."

"It's where Uncle Ilusha died."

"Yes."

"Is that why you went there?"

"Part of the reason, yes."

"Can we go there together?"

"One day."

Ruzsky stood slowly. He put an arm around his son and glanced at Ingrid. Something in the way she was looking at him made him hold her eye. She rewarded him with a smile; a wry and amused gesture of undisguised pleasure.

Ruzsky studied her face. It sprung to life as her smile widened. "Mistress Ingrid," he said.

"Master Sandro."

"The winter treats you well?"

"Tolerably so."

The group of soldiers behind them began to sing more loudly, their manner boorish and designed to provoke. Ruzsky began to lead his son away. The soldiers sang still louder.

"They are always in here now," Ingrid said.

Ruzsky glanced over his shoulder. The men were smiling, pleased at the effect they had achieved.

When he turned back, Ruzsky saw the unease in Ingrid's eyes.

"The servants say there will be a revolution," Michael said.

Ruzsky did not answer. He and Ingrid exchanged glances once more.

"Why will there be a revolution?" Michael asked.

Ruzsky was about to utter something reassuring, but found he could not bring himself to lie. "The Tsar is not popular. He is blamed for the war." The soldiers' voices were dying away.

"If you are a policeman, is it your job to stop it?"

"No."

"Will the revolutionaries attack the police?"

"No." Ruzsky pulled his son closer. "Don't worry. It will be all right."

"Why will it be all right?"

"It just will."

"The servants call the police *shemishniki*."

"Well—"

"What do they mean by that?"

"Nothing of importance."

"They say it is because they get two copecks for every man they arrest."

Ruzsky looked into his son's intelligent eyes. "That's the secret police, Michael."

"You're not the secret police, are you, Father?"

"No."

"You're a detective and you investigate murders, isn't that so?"

"It's true."

"But Uncle Dmitri says the rioters hate *all* policemen."

"I'll be fine, my boy."

"I don't want them to hurt you, Papa."

"No one is going to hurt me."

They had reached the edge of the Field of Mars. Michael was still clutching his father's hand. "I'll race you," Ruzsky said, bending down, but his son shook his head. "I don't want to run, Father."

Ruzsky squeezed the boy's hand. He turned toward Ingrid and looked into her vivid blue eyes. They seemed to offer warmth and support and uncomplicated affection, but were also tinged with sadness. He saw in them an echo of his own corrosive loneliness, which made him want to offer his unqualified friendship in return. "I'm sorry," he said.

"Sorry for what, Sandro?" she asked, but he could see she knew all too well what he was referring to.

"You deserve better," he said.

"So do you." She looked at Michael. "But in one respect, you are as lucky as a man can be."

Ruzsky did not respond. Her childlessness was not a subject he felt he could broach.

In the distance, a man was running in their direction. As he came closer, Ruzsky's heart lurched. It was Peter, his father's valet.

The house was silent. The servants were gathered in the hallway, facing the study door. Inside, the old man's body lay in the middle of the rug, his head, or what remained of it, twisted to one side. He had a revolver in his hand.

There was a pool of blood on the desk, and wide smears upon the chair and across the rug where Dmitri must have dragged the body in his vain attempt to find some sign of life.

Ruzsky's brother sat in the corner, pushed up against one of the bookcases, his face and shirt front also covered in blood.

On the mantelpiece, a clock still marked the time of their father's ordered, certain world.

The old man stared up at the ceiling with lifeless gray eyes, his skin a pallid, ghostly white.

Ruzsky knelt beside him. "Father . . ."

The old man's face was almost untouched, but his brains spilled from the back of his skull.

"Oh, Father . . ."

Ruzsky bent down. He put his arm beneath his father's neck and lifted his head to his chest. He tightened his grip, his body rocking gently. Tears burned his cheeks.

The smell of blood and gunpowder caught in his throat.

"Oh Papa, Papa . . ."

Ruzsky wept.

"Papa, I'm sorry."

He had used the same words on the night of Ilusha's death. It was the last time he had called his father *Papa*.

"I'm sorry . . ."

Ruzsky half turned to see Michael standing in the doorway.

"Is Grandfather all right?"

Ruzsky did not respond.

"Is he all right?"

Ruzsky screwed his eyes tight shut and rocked harder.

"Papa, is he all right? Is Grandfather all right?"

The fear in Michael's voice dragged Ruzsky back to reality. He lowered his father's head, his face and hands covered with the old man's blood.

He knelt before his son.

"He's had an accident," Ruzsky said. He straightened and nudged Michael gently back toward Ingrid, pulling the study door closed behind him. "Grandfather has had an accident." Ruzsky wiped his nose, smearing his face with his father's blood as he tried to compose himself in front of his son. "Your uncle Dmitri and I will try to wake him; can you go with Ingrid while we do that?"

"*Is* he going to wake up, Father?"

Ruzsky tried to take the boy in his arms, but Michael recoiled, pushing past Ingrid.

"I don't know," Ruzsky said. His voice shook. "Perhaps it is time for him to go to another place."

"The same place they sent Uncle Ilusha?"

Ruzsky tried to still the fear in his son's eyes, but Michael retreated once more. Ingrid took his hand and led him away.

As he watched them go, Ruzsky realized that the servants were staring at him. He tried to wipe the blood from his face and found that his hand was shaking uncontrollably. "Go to the city police headquarters in Ofitserskaya Ulitsa," he snapped at the young man who had run to tell them the news. "Ask for Deputy Chief Investigator Pavel Miliutin and tell him to come here with Dr. Sarlov. Do not speak to anyone else."

The man was almost hopping from one foot to another.

"Is that clear?"

"Yes, sir."

Ruzsky returned to the study and closed the door. He tried to stop his body shaking, but could not. He knelt before his father, clasping both hands in front of him like a supplicant offering a prayer.

Ruzsky straightened the old man's black tie. He brushed the thick mane of white hair back from his forehead.

Outside, he could hear the murmur of conversation.

Ruzsky looked across at Dmitri. He was sitting on the floor, his head bent and face obscured. His arm rested upon the leather chair where they had once sat to discuss their reports from the Corps des Pages, or been sent by their mother to await punishment.

Ruzsky listened to the sound of the clock. It had always seemed to him that the rhythm of the pendulum altered to fit the mood of the occasion: quick, suspenseful beats back then, and slow, lingering strokes now, marking out his guilt.

Ruzsky placed the flat of his hand against his father's still-warm cheek. The skin hung from his cheekbones, leaving no sign of the soft smile he had witnessed in the hallway this morning.

Had he known he was saying goodbye?

Had he been hoping his son would stay?

He remembered his father coming up to the attic to help fix the train track. The old man had been reaching out to him, and he had given him nothing of substance in return.

Ruzsky kissed his forehead. He whispered his apology once more, overcome as he did so by a sense of profound hopelessness, of the finality of death and the futility of regret.

"Don't blame yourself," Dmitri said.

Ruzsky sat back and wiped his eyes. He did not answer, and they sat together in silence, each unwilling to intrude upon the other's grief.

Voices rose and fell outside. Once or twice they heard the noise of a sled or automobile from the street. But inside the room, only the sound of the clock marched time onward.

Dmitri came closer and they hugged each other.

When they parted, they sat together, side by side, in front of the old man. "It's the two of us now," Dmitri said. His face was puffed up, his eyes red with tears.

Ruzsky did not answer. His eyes had been drawn to a group of photographs on the wall by his father's desk. There were four of them: his mother, Ilya, Dmitri, and himself.

Ruzsky stared at his own image. In his mind's eye, this picture had been removed—stored or destroyed—a blank space on the wall where the eldest son had once gazed down upon his father.

But he was here.

They heard a knock, but neither man answered. This was the last time the three of them would be alone together, and neither of them wanted to bring it to a close.

44

Pavel slipped quietly into the room. He looked at Ruzsky only long enough to confirm that there was no need for words.

He carried out his work discreetly, without asking questions or catching his partner's eye. He examined the body, removing the revolver from the old man's grip and slipping it carefully into his overcoat. He walked around the room, checking the desk and the area beside it.

Sarlov entered and both he and Pavel came and went in silence for half an hour or more. When they had completed their tasks, they stood in front of him. Pavel crouched down with his notebook open. "He had visitors, you know that?"

Ruzsky nodded.

"Vasilyev and two of his men." Pavel looked into his eyes. "The meeting lasted about ten to fifteen minutes. Your father saw them out and returned to his study. The valet said he seemed subdued, but noticed nothing out of the ordinary. Approximately two minutes later, they heard the shot."

Ruzsky stared at Pavel. His partner was waiting for a response, but he had none to give.

"With your permission," Pavel went on, "we will . . ." He glanced at Sarlov. "If we could take your father's body down to Ofitserskaya Ulitsa . . ."

Ruzsky looked to his brother, but receiving no lead from him, turned back to his colleagues and nodded. Neither man moved. "We'll . . . arrange it," Pavel said. "Is there anything else that you would like us to do?"

Ruzsky shook his head.

"Is there anyone you wish us to notify?"

"No."

Pavel stood, but both he and Sarlov lingered. "I'm sorry, Sandro. If there is anything else . . . anything at all."

"I will see you in the office later today."

Pavel did not respond. His compassion was the more moving for remaining unspoken. He and Sarlov slipped out and pulled the door shut.

Ruzsky opened the window a fraction and looked out at the garden. He could see a snowman Michael had built earlier. He wondered if the old man had helped him. "When did you last see him?"

"Last night," Dmitri said.

Ruzsky rubbed the condensation from the window. The morning sun disappeared behind a bank of heavy cloud.

Dmitri left the room for a few moments and returned with a yellow carnation. He placed it in the buttonhole of their father's jacket.

Ever since the death of their mother, the old man had ordered fresh flowers for her bedside table every week, just as she had done when she was alive.

"Do you think they will be happy together?" Dmitri asked. "Wherever they are."

"Content, perhaps."

"Is that the best we can hope for? To be content?"

"We were born to a different age."

Ruzsky bent down and tugged the wing of his father's collar back inside his morning coat.

There was a soft knock at the door. Pavel and Sarlov slipped in and Ruzsky saw from the expression on their faces that it was time for them to take the body away. Ruzsky straightened his father's coat once more and then stepped back.

Pavel and Sarlov bent to pick up the body.

Ruzsky and his brother watched their father being carried out.

As the door was pulled shut, Dmitri moved to the old man's desk and picked up the paperweight he had always used—a rock Ruzsky had given him during a family holiday at their aunt's estate in the Crimea. He pushed it to and fro on the desktop.

Despite the sight and smell of blood, the removal of the body made the old man's death seem almost an illusion. The voices outside died away as the servants drifted back to their tasks. Pavel and Sarlov left with the ambulance.

The telephone in the hall was silent. Even the wind had faded to a whisper.

Ruzsky thought of the loneliness that must precede suicide; could he not have saved him that? Was it simply for want of another's support that his father had reached such an impasse? He'd assumed the old man would have been too proud to want to share a dilemma with his eldest son, and yet hadn't he tried?

As Ruzsky looked out of the window at the lifeless skies, he grew more certain. A liar or cheat could always dream of escape, because he did not fear his conscience, but for an honorable man, sometimes there was only one way out. The old man's responsibility was to protect the assets of the state—what mistake or threat could have demanded such a sacrifice?

"Did you know he was going to meet Vasilyev this morning?" Ruzsky asked. He was surprised by the strength in his own voice.

"No."

"Do you have any idea what they could have talked about?"

Dmitri looked at him. "No."

Ruzsky turned to face his brother.

"I sometimes think," Dmitri said, "that you believe Father talked to me in a way he never did to you, but it wasn't so. He would never have confided in me."

Ruzsky shook his head, but even as he did so he knew that Dmitri was right. "You were an officer in his regiment . . ."

"But not like he was. Not like you would have been."

Ruzsky saw the distress in his brother's eyes. As it had once before, grief diminished him and it broke his heart to see it. "Let us not quarrel," he said.

The tension on Dmitri's face eased. "Yes. Let us not quarrel."

Ruzsky found Michael playing with Ingrid in the attic. The pair sat side by side on the floor, putting together the train track. The boy looked up with a naive but brittle optimism in his eyes. "Is Grandfather awake now?"

Ruzsky sat down. He put the station at Mtsensk by the edge of the track and then assembled the house and village at Petrovo a short distance away from it. "I think Grandfather has gone to be with Uncle Ilusha." Ruzsky glanced at Ingrid.

"Does that mean we won't see him again?" Michael asked as he fitted the first locomotive onto the track and then began to hitch carriages behind it.

"Not in the way we are used to."

Michael concentrated intently on putting together his train.

"I'm sorry, my boy."

"Will you come and live here, now, Father?"

Ruzsky hesitated. "Yes."

"With Mama?"

"I will talk to her."

"I will miss Grandfather."

Ruzsky did not answer.

"Will you miss him also?"

"Very much."

"Some of the servants said you didn't like each other, but you did, didn't you?"

Ruzsky swallowed hard. "I loved him. And I think, in his way, he loved me." He pieced together two stretches of track. "He was my father, just as I am yours. It is an unbreakable bond."

Ingrid reached forward to squeeze Michael's shoulder.

There was a long silence.

"How did he have an accident?" Michael asked.

"I don't know."

"Was he sad?"

Ruzsky shook his head. "No."

"Then why did he have an accident?"

Ruzsky did not offer an answer, since he had none to give.

Michael put the last carriage on his train and pushed it around to the station at Mtsensk. He unloaded the small wooden passengers and assembled them on the platform with their luggage. One family had been modeled on Ruzsky's own: two parents with three boys and a small group of servants. There was even a troika waiting for them. "Can we speak to Grandfather?" Michael asked.

"In our dreams," Ingrid said. "In our dreams, we can talk to him."

Michael seemed encouraged. His frown eased. He loaded the passengers back onto the train, sorting each group into its regular compartment before storing their luggage.

45

In the hallway of the Okhrana's gloomy headquarters, they had clearly been expecting him. Ruzsky neither had to explain who he was nor offer any form of identification. He was led down the corridor to the elevator, almost colliding with a man bringing a box full of papers out of the printing room.

As the elevator began its ascent, Ruzsky reflected upon the bomb that had been thrown at him in Yalta. Had not the intention been to kill the pair of them then—and if so, why had the Okhrana's many trained assassins not been instructed to try again?

Were they waiting for the right moment? Had it arrived?

Vasilyev was standing by the door to his dark, wood-paneled office, and he offered his hand as Ruzsky entered. "I'm sorry, Sandro," he said, in his low, smoke-roughened voice, his eyes searching Ruzsky's own. His handshake was firm. "Please have a seat." He pointed to the table around which their last meeting had been conducted. "Please."

Vasilyev retreated behind his desk, silhouetted against the light. Ruzsky noticed for the first time an oil of the bay at Yalta above the mantelpiece. It looked like it had been painted from the window of Godorkin's office.

"You have been told of my father's death?"

"Your office informed the government and Colonel Shulgin telephoned me directly. It must have been a very great shock."

Vasilyev's insincerity brought a flush of anger to Ruzsky's cheeks. Beneath the table, he carefully clenched and unclenched one of his fists. He had promised himself he would not allow himself to be provoked.

"Some tea?" Vasilyev leaned forward to tap a service bell upon his desk.

A young boy in a starched linen jacket appeared through a side door. "Tea," Vasilyev instructed him. "Would you like something stronger?"

"No."

Vasilyev slipped his hands into his pockets, waiting for the servant to withdraw.

Ruzsky looked out of the window at the fading light that shrouded the city's rooftops. For the first time, he felt a stranger in the land of his birth.

Vasilyev smiled. It was as if he was able to read Ruzsky's mind. He picked up a silver case from his desk. "Cigarette?"

Ruzsky shook his head. Vasilyev lit one for himself.

"You came to a meeting at Millionnaya Street," Ruzsky said.

"Yes. Tragically, it appears that I was the last—"

"What was it about?"

Vasilyev gave another tight smile. Only good manners, his expression suggested, required him to continue the conversation. "I'm afraid, Sandro, that I am not at liberty to—"

"Did you arrange the meeting?"

Vasilyev did not flinch. He raised a hand and scratched his cheek with one manicured finger. "It was your father who requested that I come to the house on Millionnaya Street."

"Why?"

"He did not say."

"He must have given some indication."

"There are many meetings, in many locations."

"You had frequent contact with him?"

"He ran an important ministry."

"Would it not have been more usual for him to ask you to go there?"

Vasilyev shrugged. "His request was not unusual."

"But you knew what the meeting would be about?"

"I had some idea."

"But you are unwilling to tell me?"

"I am not at liberty to."

"The meeting was arranged to discuss the assets of the state." Ruzsky tried to recall the precise words his father had used in the drawing room that morning. The old man had spoken of Vasilyev's desire to protect the wealth of the Tsar, but to what, precisely, had he been referring? Not, surely, palaces and jewels and private wealth, which would have been neither man's concern. "You were discussing how to protect the liquid assets of the state, in the event of revolutionary threat?"

As Vasilyev stared at him, exhaling a thick plume of smoke, the picture began to come into focus. All paper money would be worthless in a time of severe unrest. But there was one asset that would be crucial to the imperial government's future financial viability.

"You were discussing what to do with the gold reserves," he said.

Vasilyev did not move, but his head seemed to sink still further onto his chest. His face hardened. "What we were discussing is no concern of yours."

"It was of concern to my father. So much so that it killed him."

"On the contrary. It would be naive to imagine a connection between a routine business meeting and the sad personal events that transpired thereafter."

"If the meeting was routine, then what prevents you enlightening me as to its details?"

"Routine or not, I draw a distinction between a high official of the Tsar and a mere chief investigator in the Petrograd City Police Department."

Ruzsky's cheeks burned. "Why was my father present at the meeting we held here yesterday?"

Vasilyev did not answer.

"What interest could he have had in two bodies found on the Neva?"

"You tell me," Vasilyev said.

"You invited him?"

Vasilyev did not respond, but Ruzsky saw that he was right. "A revolutionary group is assembled. Some personal papers are stolen from the Empress of the Russias. Something is planned for this Friday or Saturday: strikes, or more significant protests, or unrest in the capital. A meeting is convened to discuss the gold reserves, and how best to ensure their safety in the event of law and order breaking down." Ruzsky stopped. "My father had served this state for a lifetime. And yet within five minutes of that meeting, he was dead. It does not take an investigator to make a connection."

"A *connection*?" Vasilyev enunciated the words slowly and with the utmost precision. "I am not certain you understand, Sandro, as your father most certainly did, the true nature of our predicament."

"*Our* predicament?"

The young man came back, carrying a silver tray. Vasilyev poured a cup of tea and offered it to Ruzsky, who shook his head. "These are challenging times," Vasilyev went on. He moved to the window and looked out at the dull afternoon light as he sipped his tea. "When our home catches fire, we must look to see what we can save. Is that not so, Sandro?"

Ruzsky faced him, stilled by Vasilyev's change in tone.

"The bigger the fire, the greater the danger. But for each man, a different notion of what is precious: For one a painting, or some symbol of great wealth. But for another . . . a son, perhaps a grandson."

The words hung in the air. Vasilyev did not look around. "For a third, the woman he loves."

The chief of the Okhrana turned and smiled, holding the cup of tea to his lips. "Always choices to be made, Sandro. Isn't that so?"

"You think we'll disappear?"

Vasilyev took a sip of his tea, then put down the cup on the edge of his desk. "My advice to you is to save what you can before the house burns down."

"Did you make the same threat to him?"

Vasilyev shook his head. It was not a denial, but an expression of surprise at his naïveté.

"My father's opposition to you sealed his fate."

"Goodbye, Sandro."

"You told him what you would do to us if he did not agree?"

"I have a feeling we will not meet again."

Outside, Ruzsky leaned back against the stone wall and breathed in the cold winter air.

He was not ten yards from the entrance to the Okhrana's headquarters and yet all was quiet. A tram had stopped, its dull yellow light a hazy beacon against the black trees behind. A man got off and disappeared down the street, then the bell rang and it continued on its way.

Ruzsky took out and lit a cigarette. His hand shook violently.

He could see the dome of St. Isaac's in the distance and, closer, the spire of the St. Peter and St. Paul Cathedral, but this was no longer his city; it was alien and remote.

The old man's love had sealed his own fate and, if it had not done so already, old Russia was dying with him.

Then Ruzsky thought of Michael sitting alone in his room in Millionnaya Street and he began to run. "Hey!" he yelled at a droshky driver on the far side of the street. "Hey!"

46

Ruzsky burst through the front door of Millionnaya Street. Ingrid was in the hallway. "Sandro," she said, alarm on her face.

"Where is he?"

"In his room, but . . ."

Ruzsky had already reached the stairs.

"*She* is up there," Ingrid hissed.

Ruzsky stopped, looking at his brother's wife for a moment, then turned and pounded up toward the attic.

Michael sat on his bed, looking at a book. Irina was in the center of the room, packing his clothes into a leather case. Ruzsky steadied himself against the door.

Irina stopped what she was doing. Her narrow face softened for the first time in his presence for many years. "I'm so very sorry, Sandro," she said.

She did not know whether to come to him, so remained where she was, awkwardly folding one of Michael's white cotton shirts.

They were silent. Michael watched them both.

Irina was wearing an overcoat, her long, slender hands concealed in black leather gloves. A new jewel at her throat sparkled even in the dull light of the single electric lamp. Her hair was glossy and her foxlike face made up with meticulous care. It was a far cry from the radical student he had married and he saw the recognition of that fact in her eyes, also. "What are you doing?" Ruzsky asked.

She did not answer.

Ruzsky felt his son's eyes boring into him. He kissed his forehead, sat by his side, and draped an arm around his shoulder. "Where did you find this?" he asked, turning to the book's hand-drawn front cover.

"Uncle Dmitri gave it to me."

Ruzsky looked at the pictures and the neatly inscribed verse. The story recounted the preparations for the fictional wedding of Tsar Dmitri I. It had been drawn and written in the era before their father and mother had discouraged Dmitri's precocious artistic talents.

"I'm sorry I was not here," Irina said.

Ruzsky did not respond. He pulled his son closer to him.

"He was a strong man."

Strong rode high in Irina's lexicon of approval. *Strong* was everything. But her failing was that she drew no distinction between the strength of the hero and the villain. "What are you doing?" he asked again.

"Sandro . . ."

Ruzsky leaned forward, uncoupling his arm from his son's shoulder. "Where are you going?"

Irina inclined her head toward the room opposite. She wished to talk to him out of Michael's earshot.

Ruzsky hugged his son. "I'll be back in a minute," he whispered. "It will be all right."

He followed his wife through to Ilya and Dmitri's room, their footsteps echoing on the wooden floorboards. Irina shut the door and stood close to him in the half-darkness.

Ruzsky listened to the sound of her breathing.

He wondered if she would take him in her arms and what his own response would be.

"I'm sorry," she whispered, her voice hoarse. "Truly sorry."

Ruzsky did not answer.

"You know how he felt, don't you?" Irina asked him. "Whatever may have been said?"

Ruzsky wished Irina to take him in her arms now and wondered momentarily if it was too late for them. He thought of Michael sitting alone on his bunk next door.

"Irina—"

"It is not healthy for him here, Sandro, don't you see that?"

"I can't be without him."

"I cannot leave him here, Sandro."

Ruzsky looked at his wife. Even in the twilight, he could tell that she was shielding something from him. "You're going away," he whispered.

"No—"

"You were going to take Michael away from me."

"This is no place for him, Sandro, don't you see that?"

"This is his home."

"It would not be for long. Just for a few months. Until the situation here—"

"You plan to take him from Russia?" Ruzsky shook his head incredulously. "To Nice? To the Grand Duke's promenade?"

"Sandro—"

"My father's body is barely cold and you would rob me of our son?"

"Be reasonable. What is left for him here?"

"This is his home."

"But who will care for him?"

"I—"

"You're never here. You're always at work."

"Ingrid is—"

"Ingrid is not his mother," she said crisply. "I am."

They faced each other in silence.

"Think of what happened to your father," Irina whispered.

"What do you mean?"

"Do you think he was alone in feeling that way? Look about you. The tension is in every face. Look in the mirror; you will see it in your own. Old Russia—*our* Russia—is on the brink of catastrophe. The dogs in the streets know it."

Ruzsky could not think straight; she was right, but if he let her go, he was certain it would be the last he would ever see of his son. "It's out of the question."

"I'm his mother, Sandro. It's not your right to decide—"

"No. I won't countenance it."

"I'm his *mother*."

"You're an adulteress and, unless I am mistaken, society will grant you no rights whatsoever."

He had uttered harsh words more violently than he meant to. Even in the darkness, he heard her sharp intake of breath.

"Please leave this house," he said.

Irina did not move. Her silence was meant to admonish him. "It was not just your father's loss," she whispered, "that you were not your father's son."

"Please leave."

Irina hesitated a moment more, before turning and retreating rapidly down the stairs. Ruzsky walked across to the far side of the attic. He saw that Michael had heard every word of their exchange.

"Will I be staying with you now?" Michael asked.

Ruzsky hesitated. He could see on his son's face the answer he wished to hear. "Yes," he said. "Yes."

As soon as Irina had gone, Ruzsky lifted the receiver in the hall and placed a call to Maria's apartment. It rang and rang, but there was no answer.

He tried the Mariinskiy Theatre.

"I would like to speak to Maria Popova."

"Not performing tonight."

"Is she there nevertheless?"

"No."

"Would you mind going to look for her? It's important."

"She's not here."

"Could you take a message?"

"Call again in the morning. She will not be in the theater before then."

The line was cut.

Darkness crept silently through Millionnaya Street. Ruzsky worked alone in his father's study. In the central drawer of the secretary, he found a single envelope, addressed to their cousin in England but not yet consigned to the mail. He slit open the envelope and moved the letter within beneath the desk lamp. It had been written the previous evening.

My dear William,

I fear it is now almost a year since my last missive, for which please accept my most profound apologies. This war continues to take its toll upon us all.

There has been some good news. Dmitri survived frontline duty in the Brusilov Offensive with nothing worse than a relatively minor injury to his arm, and is back at the barracks in Petrograd. Sandro has, to my great relief, also now returned from Tobolsk, and taken up his former post. He is gloriously unchanged, and my grandson a constant source of joy. In other circumstances, there would be much to celebrate.

But, as I'm sure you will have read in your own newspapers, the conduct of the government, and of the war, remains scandalous. The murder of Rasputin has been greeted with universal celebration, but upon sober reflection, has been shown to have changed nothing at all. The Empress, already domineering, neurotic, and hysterical, has become quite unhinged. All men of competence in the government have been dismissed, and we have been left with men of the caliber of Sturmer and Protopopov who are universally detested and beneath contempt.

I pause, my dear cousin, in the hope that I must be exaggerating, but I fear it is not so. Such things—and much worse—are said upon every street corner. The list of those who have beseeched the Emperor to form a government led by men respected in the country at large continues to lengthen; the Dowager Empress has pleaded with him, as has his brother Michael Alexandrovich, and more grand dukes, senior members of the Duma, and foreign ambassadors than one cares to count. The Emperor listens to all of them, but says nothing, smoking incessantly and drinking tea prescribed by a quack doctor, which those around him at Mogilev believe to be a mixture of henbane and hashish, which reduces him to a state of almost complete inertia.

So, what then, dear cousin, is to become of us? I fear the worst. As each day lengthens, the few remaining officials of any honor and competence try to prevent the inevitable catastrophe. All around is panic, greed, mistrust and fear. We are increasingly in the hands of our own secret police, a group of men as unscrupulous as any enemy. A Guards officer attempted to assassinate the Empress two weeks ago, but was caught and hanged. However, it is only a matter of time before someone succeeds. There are plans to remove the Emperor and make his brother regent to his son, before the revolution on the streets begins, but I fear it is already too late. It is now only a question of when and in what form change will occur. Everyone knows it.

Forgive me, my old friend, but I find it impossible to convince myself any longer that my fears are unfounded. While I have no right to do so, I hope you will forgive me if I request that you offer those members of my family who may find their way to England all possible assistance. I will, of course, never leave my post, and the same is true, I'm sure, of Sandro. I have grave fears, however, for Dmitri's wife, Ingrid, and am attempting to persuade her to travel abroad. It may become necessary for her to take my grandson with her. I am transferring adequate funds.

It is late and I must try to sleep. Pray for us, please.

Your ever loving cousin,

Nicholas

Ruzsky folded the letter and put it back into the envelope. He sat back, staring at the ceiling.

The old man had expected disaster, but there was no sign here that he was about to give up.

Ruzsky lit a cigarette. He thought, as he smoked it, of the way his father had once revered the Emperor's father, the giant Alexander III, who had appeared to them, when they were children, as nothing short of god-like.

Then he recalled the Tsarina's strained, haunted face, upon their meeting at Tsarskoe Selo not two weeks ago.

Ruzsky leaned forward, stubbed out his cigarette, and continued with his work. He sifted through the rest of the desk drawers and made piles on the floor around him of papers that he would need to discuss with Dmitri. The biggest contained those relating to the family's financial situation. Most pressing was a letter from the manager of the Moscow Bank on the Nevsky asking for firm confirmation of the order to press ahead with the transfer of a significant part of the family's cash reserves to the bank in London. It was dated yesterday and delivered by hand. A bank statement revealed that the balance of their father's account stood at more than a million rubles. The old man had clearly been liquidating assets for a considerable period of time.

Other papers detailed the rest of the family's wealth. There were shares in three private banks and numerous companies, including several involved in arms production. But the paperwork was not assembled in order. The old man had not been intending to take his leave so suddenly.

Ruzsky worked alone in his father's study by the light of a desk lamp, looking for documents or letters relating to what the old man had told him that morning. He found nothing.

He remembered the precise words now. *To protect the wealth of the Tsar from the mob.*

Ruzsky moved his chair, knocking over a pile of letters that he and his brother had written from the Corps des Pages. He bundled them together again, then sunk to his knees and dragged his hand along the ledge beneath the desk, where his father had always kept the key to the safe.

There was no sign of it.

He stood and moved to the hall. He placed another call to Maria's apartment, but there was still no response.

Ruzsky asked the exchange to put him through to the theater again.

"Mariinskiy." He had reached the same operator, but could hear the guests gathering for the evening performance in the background.

"I would like to speak to Maria Popova, please."

"Not dancing tonight."

"Could you get a message to her, it's important."

"Call again in the morning."

As the line was again abruptly cut, Ruzsky swore violently under his breath. He stood in the silence of the dark hallway, thinking, then moved through to the drawing room.

There was a sled parked on the opposite side of the street, in a dark corner beyond the gas lamp, its driver huddled up on the front seat in swathes of blanket, as if expecting a long wait. Vasilyev's men were making little attempt to conceal that they were watching him.

Ruzsky returned to the hall. He placed a call to Tsarskoe Selo. A woman answered. "May I speak to Colonel Shulgin, please."

"Who is calling?"

"Chief Investigator Ruzsky of the city police department. If you could tell him it is urgent."

Ruzsky waited. It seemed to take an interminable amount of time before he once again heard footsteps crossing the hallway. "Colonel Shulgin is engaged. May I take a message?"

"Could you tell him to telephone me . . . Chief Investigator Ruzsky in Millionnaya Street. Petrograd 266. At once. Please tell him it is urgent."

"Call again in the morning."

"Will you tell him it is urgent?"

"I already have. He says to telephone again in the morning."

The call was terminated.

Ruzsky walked slowly back to his father's desk. He removed the silver case from his jacket pocket and lit a cigarette. For a moment, he watched the smoke curling up toward the ceiling and imagined his father sitting here alone.

Ruzsky turned over the case and looked at the family crest. It had once belonged to his great-grandfather and had been passed on to each eldest son on his eighteenth birthday.

He sat back.

There was a knock at the front door. Ruzsky stood and moved to the doorway as he heard a servant's footsteps. He reached into the pocket of his jacket and checked that he had ammunition in his revolver.

47

Ruzsky relaxed as he heard Pavel's voice.

A few seconds later, the big detective slipped into the study. Ruzsky put the revolver back into his pocket. "Expecting company?" Pavel asked.

Ruzsky pointed at the leather seat opposite his desk. Pavel took it, and the proffered cigarette. They smoked in silence. Ruzsky wondered if Pavel had noticed the Okhrana agent outside, and if so, why he had not mentioned it. Had they grown so used to being watched?

"That was where we used to sit," he said, "while Father read out our school reports."

"I'm sorry, Sandro."

"Don't tell me, you've found that all is as it appeared; Sarlov says there was no sign of a struggle, the cause of death is suicide, and the only fingerprints on the revolver belong to my father."

Pavel did not answer.

"He'd been a different person since I came back from Tobolsk," Ruzsky said. "He'd changed, and I had barely begun to appreciate it, let alone respond."

"Don't punish yourself."

"It is inevitable. If I'd taken the hand of friendship, then who knows—"

"Who knows indeed? He was a strong man. Honorable, as you have said yourself on many an occasion. He knew exactly what he was doing."

Ruzsky leaned forward. He looked at the rock on the corner of the desk. It was the most unattractive paperweight imaginable.

"Have you seen the man outside?" Pavel asked.

"Yes."

"They're not making any attempt to hide themselves."

"Whatever Vasilyev is doing, he wanted my father out of the way."

"In case you've forgotten, he wants you out of the way as well."

Pavel was silent. They both finished their cigarettes and stubbed them out in the large stone ashtray on the corner of the desk. It still had the remnants of Ruzsky's father's last cigar.

"The meeting this morning was about how to protect the wealth of the Tsar from a revolutionary mob," Ruzsky said.

"Your father told you that?"

"Not in so many words."

Pavel stared at him. His expression was wary.

"I've started going through his papers. He feared there would come a point when paper money would cease to have any value. He would not have concerned himself with the Tsar's private possessions; this must have been to do with the Tsar's gold. The imperial reserves."

Pavel shook his head slowly. "But how could that have led to his death?"

"I think Vasilyev has robbery in mind. My father stood in the way."

There was a lengthy silence. "But how would that have led to—"

Ruzsky thought of the things Vasilyev had implied that afternoon. "I think he was threatened."

"But your father was . . . He was a minister of the Imperial Court. He had many connections. Have you called Colonel Shulgin?"

"I left an urgent message. He did not come to the telephone."

Pavel stared at the light on the desk. "What do you want me to do?"

"I would ask a favor."

The big detective waited.

"There is no answer at her apartment, nor the Mariinskiy. Could you find her, try to speak to her alone?" Ruzsky ignored the look of quiet despair in his friend's eyes. "Tell her what has happened to my father. Try to convince her to leave the city. Just for a few days."

Pavel stood slowly. He contemplated his friend for a moment more. "I suppose it is too late to persuade you to reconsider?"

"Reconsider what?"

Pavel sighed. "I will do what I can, Sandro. Will I find you here tomorrow?"

"No. I will come to the office."

"Very well, then."

As Ruzsky listened to his friend's receding footsteps, he turned toward the window and looked out into the night, thinking of the things he had chosen not to share.

What was it that Borodin had planned for the Kresty Crossing?

He needed to have time alone to think.

Ruzsky sat in the kitchen. He had said good night to Michael long since, and waited until he had slipped reluctantly into sleep. The servants had withdrawn.

The house was quiet down here; it was where Ruzsky had always felt most comfortable as a child. It was where he had avoided the constrictions of his parents' world.

Though his inability to come to terms with the reality of the day's events still shielded him, that comfort was denied him now.

He heard Ingrid's soft footsteps. She had bathed and changed, her hair glossy. She wore a high-necked, rich blue dress that matched the color of her eyes. "Is he still asleep?" Ruzsky asked.

She nodded.

"He has fared well, better than I might have expected."

"Perhaps he is blessed with only partial understanding. For now, at least."

Ruzsky did not respond.

"Have you had something to eat?" she asked.

He shook his head.

"Do you mind if I join you?"

He gestured at the far side of the wooden table and she took a seat opposite him.

Ingrid shook out her hair and ran her hands through it, her head tipped forward. Then she looked at him. "If there is anything I can do, Sandro, any way in which I can help, please just tell me how."

"When did Dmitri go out?"

"Shortly before you returned." Ingrid examined the texture of the table, brushing the palm of her hand against its surface. "He often seeks comfort with her now." It was said without rancor or bitterness. "She can offer him that, at least."

Ruzsky felt his cheeks flushing and tried to conceal his own pang of jealousy. He wondered if Ingrid had any inkling that the same woman tormented them both.

"She plans to take him away," she said quietly. "By the end of this week. Do you know that?"

For a moment, Ruzsky thought she was talking about Maria and Dmitri.

"Irina," Ingrid went on. "And her Grand Duke."

"Yes. To Nice."

They were silent. Ruzsky finished his cigarette and went to find an ashtray in which to stub it out. Failing to locate one, he squashed it against the bottom of an enamel basin and threw it into a wooden bin.

As Ruzsky sat down again, Ingrid reached forward and put her hand on his. "I'm truly sorry, Sandro."

Ruzsky gazed into her deep blue eyes. He did not know whether to withdraw his hand. "He was an extraordinary man," she said.

"He was extremely fond of you."

"And he adored you," she responded.

Ruzsky withdrew his hand slowly. "We had our . . . difficulties."

"But he was always so very proud of you. Of who you are. He could not conceal it."

Despite himself, Ruzsky felt a flush of pleasure. "He concealed it for many years."

"He talked about you almost constantly over the past few months. He could not hide his excitement at the prospect of your return."

Ruzsky tried to imagine this. If Ingrid's face had not radiated such sincerity, he'd have suspected her of humoring him. "He had changed. I failed to see it." Ruzsky thought again of that last conversation in the drawing room. "I failed to respond," he said.

"Don't blame yourself. It is the last thing he would have wanted."

They were silent. The great gaping void of his suicide hung between them. How could either of them know what he would have wanted, when they had not suspected the imminence of such a catastrophe?

"Did you see any sign?" Ruzsky whispered.

Ingrid shook her head.

"Was his behavior in any way out of the ordinary, these last few days?"

"He was subdued, quite gentle. But then, that is how I shall remember him."

"Did you speak to him this morning?"

"I saw him in the hall after breakfast. I asked if he was not going to the ministry and he said, no, not today. I thought that was odd, in such times, but he did not appear to wish to converse, so I took Michael upstairs to the attic until we went to the Summer Gardens." Ingrid tried to smile. "I think Michael hoped we would wake you. One of the servants had told him you were here."

"And when you came down again?"

"The study door was ajar, and I could see a light on. I assumed he was at work. But, as you know, he did not like to be disturbed."

"Had he received any callers the previous night?"

"No."

"No telephone calls?"

"Several, but I did not answer them. Dmitri was dining at his mess; your father took his meal in the study. But he worked late. I needed a glass of water in the middle of the night—at one or two in the morning—and did not wish to trouble the servants, so I came to get it myself. When I passed his study, the light was still on."

"You did not look in?"

Ingrid shook her head.

"He never made any comment about the work of the Ministry?"

"Never. Nor about the government, except in the most general terms, and then only to discuss the progress of the war."

"And to Dmitri?"

"I . . . I do not believe so. It was Dmitri's great frustration. He said they never talked about anything in depth, merely exchanged platitudes."

Ruzsky wondered again where his brother was.

"Was there anything about the past few days that struck you as out of the ordinary? Any visitors? Any chance remark?"

Ingrid shook her head. "The city is tense, Sandro. It has affected us all. The servants . . . everyone."

"And you saw signs of tension in my father?"

"He spoke of his concern."

"What did he say?"

"He asked me at breakfast yesterday, or the day before, if I would like to consider going to Sweden, perhaps, or England, until things were calmer. Funds would be made available in London, he said, for as long a stay as I wished for."

"And what did you reply?"

"I said that I wanted to stay with my husband at this difficult time. And to help look after Michael."

"Had he suggested you go abroad before?"

"No."

"Did he give any particular indication as to why he raised the matter then?"

"No. He said we should discuss it again, perhaps tomorrow."

"Did he mention a deadline? Did he mention this weekend, for example, as a time that concerned him?"

"No."

"Did he ever talk about Vasilyev with either you or Dmitri?"

"No."

"Had you ever seen them together before that night at the ballet?"

"No."

"Did Dmitri mention it? They made . . . odd companions."

"Your father was a member of the government, Sandro. Even Dmitri understands that it requires one to deal with a wider circle than the Guards mess."

Ruzsky took out a cigarette and tapped it against the silver case before putting it into his mouth and lighting it. He offered the case to Ingrid, but she declined.

"Will there be a revolution?" she asked.

"Few seem to doubt it."

"When he is sober, Dmitri says many of the soldiers would relish killing their officers."

"Not if they're hanged for it."

Ingrid leaned forward. "A German in Millionnaya Street," she whispered. "I suppose I must fear the mob?"

"We should all fear the mob."

"It is so long since I have seen someone smile. In the street, I mean."

"They never have in the winter."

It was an evasive response, and they both knew it. Ruzsky saw the fear in her eyes now. And he realized that she had long since stopped looking to Dmitri for protection.

Ruzsky stood. He failed to find either vodka or wine in the kitchen, so opened the hatch into the cellar. It was dark, but he was able, so long as he moved cautiously, to find his way. He located a bottle on the rack and picked it up.

Back in the kitchen he saw that it was French champagne. He looked at Ingrid. "It hardly seems appropriate, but . . ."

Ingrid watched as he went to get two glasses from the cupboard and opened the bottle. "I was never an expert on vintages," he said. "Father started to explain, but gave up on me."

"I'm glad you reached some kind of understanding, Sandro."

Ruzsky sat down. He lifted his glass. "To the future."

Ingrid raised her own and looked at him warily across its brim.

They drank. The temperature in the cellar had ensured that the champagne was chilled.

"Michael asked me tonight why your father had an accident."

"And what did you say?"

"I said that I did not know, but that you would find out."

Ruzsky contemplated his champagne for a moment, before downing it. He refilled both glasses.

"Would you ever leave the city, Sandro?"

"Why do you ask?"

"It is just that your father was someone whose opinion I trusted."

"And his question frightened you?"

She looked at him, seeking reassurance. "Was that foolish?"

"No."

"Does it frighten you, too?"

Ruzsky looked out of the low kitchen window to the darkness of the garden. "It is hard to turn your back," he said.

"On a life," she answered. "Of course."

And on a love, he thought, though he did not say it.

Ingrid put her hand over his again. Ruzsky felt drunk. He realized he hadn't eaten since that morning. It already seemed a lifetime away. He turned his palm upward, so that their fingers interlocked.

"We'll be all right," Ruzsky said, looking into her eyes.

"I hope so."

Gently, Ingrid withdrew her hand. They drained their glasses slowly and in silence. Ingrid stood. "I . . . will see you tomorrow."

"Yes."

"Good night, Sandro."

"I have a favor to ask," he said. "I need a day, perhaps two. I need to know that Michael is going to be safe."

"Just tell me what you wish me to do."

"There is a man outside. I . . . I am being watched now. I cannot leave the house unless I know you have found somewhere safe."

"Where do you wish us to go?"

"The Hôtel de l'Europe, perhaps. Anywhere but here. Not tonight, but in the morning. So far as I can tell, only one of them is following me, and he will not wish to risk losing sight of his target. If you hide some spare clothes beneath your coat and do not return, it will take them some time to locate you."

"Of course, Sandro."

Ingrid looked at him with sad, compassionate eyes.

"Good night," he said.

Ruzsky did not watch her go, but he listened to her progress through the house.

He refilled his champagne glass and lit another cigarette.

Five minutes later, Ruzsky climbed the stairs from the kitchen. The desk lamp was still on in the study and he switched it off. He had intended not to linger, but that proved impossible. He sat down in his father's chair. The air was still thick with the pungent aroma of the cleaning fluid he had used to scrub the rug clean.

He sat still.

He thought of his brother in the apartment off Sadovaya Ulitsa, and the comfort that she must offer.

He wondered what his father would do in his circumstances, and realized, with trepidation, that the answer lay in that small patch of scrubbed carpet. Though he had often fought against his father's certainties, they were many times more attractive than the vacuum he was faced with now.

The house was quiet.

Ruzsky stood and moved through the shadows to the telephone in the hallway. He examined it for a moment, before picking up and dialing Maria's number. Once again, the bell at the other end rang and rang, but there was no answer.

He replaced the receiver and headed upstairs. He halted on the landing outside his parents' bedroom. On a small table beside their bed stood a vase of fresh yellow carnations.

Ruzsky walked through to his father's dressing room and opened the cupboards to the rows and rows of suits, morning suits, full-dress uniforms, frock coats, mess jackets, and tunics. At the bottom of the cabinet was a line of field boots, handmade walking shoes, dress shoes, and dancing shoes three-deep. He took out one of his father's dress uniforms and held it up to the moonlight. It had been made by Nordenshtrem, the country's most prestigious military tailor.

He replaced the jacket, shut the cupboard, and moved to the window.

The sled still stood in the shadows.

Ruzsky looked up and down the street.

He stepped back again, returned to the landing, and made his way to the top of the house. He found sheets and blankets, checked that Michael was sleeping, bent down to kiss his soft head, and then lay down on the floor beside him.

The shouts at first appeared distant, but the sound of breaking glass in the street propelled Ruzsky from his sleep. Michael was sitting up in bed.

The shouts suddenly appeared much closer.

Ruzsky rolled onto his feet and put on his trousers. "It's all right," he told his son as he picked up his revolver.

He clambered down the stairs, checking again that there was ammunition in the chamber.

He reached the first floor and his father's bedroom.

There was the sound of another window breaking.

Ruzsky looked out. "Jew lover!" one man shouted, though none of them could have seen him in the window.

There were about twenty of them in all, a ragtag collection of Black Hundred thugs. One or two carried banners emblazoned with images of the Tsar. Ruzsky could still see the Okhrana agent wrapped up in his sled, though he had moved fifty yards down the street so as not to be directly associated with the harassment. The road was darker; someone had knocked out the gas lamp.

"Jew lover!" they shouted again. Several of the group had rocks which they were throwing at the windows on the ground floor.

Ruzsky turned. He saw Michael in the doorway, his face pale. "What are they doing, Papa?" Ingrid was behind him.

"Stay here," Ruzsky instructed. He walked down the last flight of stairs to the hall. He was dressed only in trousers and a loose, white shirt, the holster slung over his shoulder. He pulled out his revolver as another missile came crashing through the drawing room window. The valet, Peter, was in the hall. "Have you got a gun?" Ruzsky demanded.

"No, sir."

"Do any of the servants?"

"I don't believe so."

Peter's face betrayed no fear. "Did my father keep any other guns in the house?"

"Only his revolver, sir, so far as I'm aware."

The shouting from the street was growing louder. Ruzsky saw his son's face poking through the banisters. "If anything happens to me—if any of them are armed—then bolt the door behind me and call Pavel Miliutin, my deputy at the police department, on Petrograd 446. Do you understand?"

"Yes, sir."

Ruzsky strode forward and pulled back the door. He charged down the steps, his sudden and violent appearance bringing a hush to the crowd.

He stopped and surveyed them. "You have ten seconds to leave the street, by official order, and I will shoot anyone who remains a moment longer."

Ruzsky looked from face to face. He saw the hunger for violence there, the desire to be bold enough to storm through to the world of wealth and privilege that lay behind him. For a few seconds, he feared that his ultimatum would not be enough, and that he would have to carry out his threat. Then one turned away, and the others slowly followed.

He saw a curtain twitching in the house opposite, but none of the neighbors—friends and colleagues of his father's for many years—had come to offer any help.

48

The following morning, Ruzsky watched Ingrid and Michael go. He had helped conceal a few spare clothes inside Ingrid's coat, and now, from the window of his father's bedroom, he kept his eye upon their receding figures until they disappeared at the end of the street.

He saw with satisfaction that the man in the sled did not follow. He barely gave them a second glance.

At the city police headquarters, Ruzsky found his colleagues gathered at the window. Beside Pavel, Maretsky looked like a dwarf. As they turned to see who had entered, the professor mumbled his condolences, then stared at the floor in embarrassment.

Ruzsky joined them at their vantage point. The man who had tailed him from Millionnaya Street had parked alongside another droshky on the far side of Ofitserskaya Ulitsa. Ruzsky could tell from Pavel's expression that the second driver was also Okhrana.

He heard chanting and craned his neck to identify its source. About a hundred or more protestors were walking in their direction, carrying a tawdry red banner bearing the slogan "Fair pay for a fair day's work."

Ruzsky watched the faces of the Okhrana men as the protest passed. "You were followed here too?" he asked Pavel.

"Yes."

"How long have you had a tail?"

"Since first thing this morning."

Ruzsky glanced at Maretsky, then tugged at Pavel's arm and moved him over to the other side of the office. "Did you manage to—"

"I could not find her. I searched half the night."

Ruzsky felt his chest tighten. "Where did you look?"

"She was not at her apartment. The neighbors had not seen her."

"Perhaps she came back later?"

"I checked for the last time at past one in the morning."

"Did you—"

"She wasn't at the Mariinskiy. They had been expecting her for a rehearsal in the afternoon, but she never showed up. When I impressed upon them the urgency of my inquiry, they gave me the name of a Guards officer . . . your brother." Pavel's tone was neutral; he offered no judgment on his partner's personal affairs. "I went over to the barracks. The officer on duty said that Major Ruzsky had been expected at dinner in the mess, but had not been present. Then I went to the Symnov factory, but could find no sign of anyone. When I got back to her apartment at one, your brother answered the door."

"You spoke to him?"

"He was in uniform—as if he had been intending to go to the dinner. He looked tired and worried, so I introduced myself and said I wished to speak to her in connection with a case. He replied that he did not know where she was."

"And you believed him? It was not possible she was inside the apartment?"

"Sandro, I could see the concern in his face. He said he had been due to meet her at seven that evening, but she had not appeared."

Ruzsky retreated to his desk. He sat and rubbed his temples. What was she doing?

"Have you ever heard of the Kresty Crossing?" he asked.

"No. Why?"

"Maretsky?"

The professor turned around, startled. "What?"

"Have you ever heard of somewhere called the Kresty Crossing?"

"Er . . . no." He shook his head. "What is it?"

"It's a place. At least, I assume it is."

"Should I be aware of it?"

"I don't know."

"Why?" Pavel asked again.

"You remember the numbers on the money we found on the American? Well, the message spells: 'The Kresty Crossing.' "

The pair of them examined him in silence. "How do you know that?" Pavel asked.

"I found the code book."

Pavel was about to open his mouth to ask where, when he saw the answer in his friend's eyes. Ruzsky offered no further clarification. He stood and moved over to the map of the city on the wall above Pavel's desk.

"Are you sure it's a place?" Pavel asked.

"It sounds to me like a railway junction."

All three were silent as they studied the map. Ruzsky traced the line of each route out of the capital, but no crossings were marked.

"What makes you think it's a railway junction?" Maretsky asked.

"Because the last thing we know the group in Yalta did was rob a train."

Pavel leaned back against the edge of his desk. "Aren't we clutching at straws?" he said gently.

"Why?" Ruzsky struggled to persuade himself that somewhere here lay the key to Maria's disappearance.

"Well . . . I mean, Ella stole something from the Empress. That's why she was killed . . ."

"We've assumed that's why she was killed."

Pavel frowned. "You don't think the two events are connected?"

"Perhaps not in the way we thought."

Pavel shifted onto the top of his desk and swung his legs to and fro, deep in thought. "But, as you said before, Ella was a shy, quiet girl. Someone put her up to that theft. Why would they want her to steal from the Empress if their intention was to rob a train? It doesn't make any sense."

"We know that Borodin assembled his people here for a specific purpose. We know that robbery is something at which they are experienced."

"That doesn't explain any of the deaths."

Ruzsky stared at the telephone in front of him. He picked up the receiver and asked the operator to connect him to Petrograd 592.

As the call was put through, he imagined the bell ringing in Maria's empty hallway.

He waited. There was no answer.

He replaced the receiver. Pavel was watching him. Ruzsky knew he was testing the limits of his loyalty.

He sifted mechanically through the paperwork that had accumulated on his desk. There was a note from Sarlov, but as he picked it up, he saw Maretsky slipping out of the door. "Have you heard from Professor Egorov?" he asked.

The professor stopped.

"You said he was going to telephone you. You showed him the inscription on the knife."

"Of course. I'll call him."

Maretsky pulled the door shut behind him.

Ruzsky sat down. Pavel had returned to the window and was looking at their watchers on the street with the fascinated air of a small child following a military parade.

Ruzsky glanced over Sarlov's note, then picked up the telephone again. "Sarlov? It's Ruzsky."

"Sandro, yes. I'm . . . well, we're all sorry. I'm sure—well, I hope you know that."

"Thank you, yes." Ruzsky cleared his throat. "You wanted to speak to me . . ."

"Yes . . ." Sarlov seemed hesitant.

"Your note referred to the body at the Lion Bridge."

"Yes." Sarlov blew his nose heavily. "Of course. Do you recall the brand on the American's shoulder?"

"Yes."

"Well, the body at the Lion Bridge had something similar."

"On his shoulder also? In the same place?"

"I can't say for certain. I didn't see it. The Okhrana performed the autopsy, if you recall."

"You discussed it with a colleague?"

"It came to my attention, yes . . . The marks sounded alike. I thought you'd like to know."

"So, both men had the mark, but not the girl." Ruzsky was referring to Ella, but thinking of Maria. He had seen nothing like it on her shoulder either.

The pathologist did not respond.

"If there is anything else that springs to mind, would you telephone me, Sarlov?"

"Of course."

Ruzsky terminated the call. He looked at the clock on the wall beside him. He tried to work out what reason there could be for the men in the group to have the mark, and the women not.

He picked up the receiver once more. "Would you put me through to the Ministry of the Railways," he told the operator.

Pavel glanced over his shoulder, before facing the street again. The shouts outside were growing louder.

Ruzsky asked to be connected to the assistant secretary to the minister. A man in this office listened patiently to his explanation, but said that he had no idea where the Kresty Crossing was or what it might be. He suggested that Ruzsky call the Bureau for Railway Building and Maintenance on Petrograd 447.

The number 447 turned out to be for the administration department at the headquarters of the North Russia Maritime and Customs Police. Ruzsky called the operator and was eventually put through to the correct department at the bureau, but the wrong individual. The man said the office he required was on the floor below, but that he could not recall the number.

More than ten minutes later, Ruzsky finally spoke to someone in the maintenance department of the Bureau for Railway Building and Maintenance. Despite it having been impressed upon him that this was a criminal investigation, the man said he was too busy to check the detailed maps that were kept on the top floor. He conceded, when Ruzsky would not let the matter drop, that he believed it was a road crossing on the line out to Tsarskoe Selo, but he could not be certain. Everyone in the department was stretched to breaking point, he said, ensuring the lines were in working order for the war effort, and he did not have time to pursue the matter further.

When Ruzsky tried to ask again, the call was terminated.

He stared at the telephone after replacing the receiver.

A moment later they heard rapid footsteps on the stairs and along the corridor. A constable appeared in the doorway, a sheepskin cap in his hands, his hair damp with sweat.

They waited while he caught his breath.

"Another body, sir," he gasped. "A woman."

49

Ruzsky flew down the stairs, the constable alongside him. "A woman?" he demanded.

"Yes, sir."

"How old?"

"I don't know, sir."

"Young?"

"I—"

"Twenty? Thirty? Older?"

"Something like that, sir, yes."

Ruzsky ran out into the street toward the droshky waiting opposite. They had lost Pavel, but he did not wait. "Where?" he demanded of the constable as the young man got in beside him.

"Vyborg side," the man shouted at the driver. "By the Finland Station."

The driver cracked his whip and the sled began to move. "Go via the quay," Ruzsky instructed him.

The man did not look around, nor did he query the instruction. Only likhachy drivers were usually allowed to take their charges along the Palace Embankment. Ruzsky glanced back over his shoulder and saw Pavel running out of the building. The big detective hailed another sled. He had two more constables with him.

Ruzsky swung back to his companion. "She was dark?" he demanded. "Dark hair? Long, dark hair?"

"Yes, sir. I believe so."

"You're sure?"

"Yes . . . yes." He did not seem at all certain. "She had a knife, through her . . ." He pointed at his eye.

Ruzsky faced the front.

It could not be her. But his heart threatened to break out of his chest and his forehead prickled with sweat.

The sled hurtled past the Admiralty and the facade of the Winter Palace. They swung onto the Alexandrovsky Bridge.

"Whereabouts?" Ruzsky heard himself shout. "Tell me where exactly."

"I'll show you, sir," the constable responded, equally agitated. "I'll show you."

They were over the bridge now and hurtling down the broad, tree-lined avenue, toward the spire of the Finland Station.

"Here," the constable shouted at the driver, pointing toward a narrow side street between the tenements. "Here."

The man slowed the horses and then wheeled them into the alley and down toward a tall, dark building surrounded by armed men.

Ruzsky leapt from the sled before it had ground to a halt.

Ten or more Okhrana agents, armed with rifles, stood in a semicircle around the entrance. The queue outside the bakery opposite stared at the scene in awed silence.

Ruzsky strode toward the officer in charge. "Chief Investigator Ruzsky," he said, "city police."

The man's broad, bearded face was unyielding. "We've instructions to let no one through."

"A murder has been reported by my constables," Ruzsky said.

The other sled drew up and Pavel strode over. He produced his identification papers. "Deputy Chief Investigator Miliutin," he said. The man remained unmoved.

The two groups faced each other. Ruzsky slipped his hand into his jacket, grasping the handle of his revolver. The silence was broken by the screech of an engine and then a loud clank as a train shunted inside the Finland Station.

Ruzsky seized his moment.

"You . . . *stop*," the officer shouted, but Ruzsky had already broken into a run, darting through the entrance, past a mound of garbage.

"Wait," he heard Pavel shout. He half expected a shot.

Ruzsky pounded up the stairs. The stench of urine and decay brought tears to his eyes. The walls glistened with water. He tried to focus only the steps ahead of him. He turned the last corner.

There was a man ahead, bent over the body.

Ruzsky saw one slim leg twisted at an impossible angle, a long leather boot.

Prokopiev straightened and turned to face him. A knife protruded from the dead woman's cheek.

"Sandro, I—"

It was not her.

It was Olga.

Christ, it was not her.

Ruzsky leaned against the wall as he tried to recover his breath. Inside his overcoat, he was soaked in sweat, his throat dry and palms clammy. The Okhrana officer caught up with him and bellowed in his ear, but Ruzsky was oblivious.

"All right, all right," Prokopiev shouted. He waved the man away, and Pavel, who stood behind. "I'll deal with him."

Prokopiev faced Ruzsky, his hands thrust into his pockets, waiting for the others to withdraw.

Ruzsky tried to control his breathing. He wiped the sweat from his forehead.

Prokopiev examined him as a gamekeeper might a cornered animal, but, as Ruzsky came to his senses, he realized that something had changed in the man.

Ivan Prokopiev appeared tired, and in those dark, intense eyes, there was a hint, if not of humanity, then at least of irony, or weary disillusion. "Are you all right, Chief Investigator?" he asked. "You do not look well."

When the others had retreated out of earshot, Prokopiev took out a silver cigarette case and offered it to Ruzsky. "Did you think it was someone else?" Prokopiev asked as his match flared.

They smoked in silence. Prokopiev glanced at his boots. They had been newly polished. "I heard about your father," he said. "I'm sorry for that."

Ruzsky did not respond. He took a pace toward the body, but Prokopiev raised his hand. "Don't go any closer," he said, smoke bleeding through his mouth and nostrils.

Ruzsky examined the dead woman. The hilt of the knife bore a striking resemblance to the one they had discovered on the Neva.

"You know who she is?" Ruzsky asked.

Prokopiev shrugged.

"Might I take a look?"

Ruzsky inched forward and this time Prokopiev made no move to stop him.

Olga had fallen awkwardly, her body twisted. Her assailant had been waiting in the shadows of the doorway and her face, never beautiful, was savagely distorted.

Ruzsky squatted, an arm resting upon his knee. He reached forward to touch the skin of what remained of her cheek. She had been dead some time.

He examined the knife. It was an ancient, simple weapon with an iron handle, but no inscription that Ruzsky could see.

There were three stab wounds: one in the left cheek, another in the mouth, and a third directly through the center of the eye. He didn't need Sarlov to tell him that the killer had been tall. The wounds were deep. A pool of congealed blood had frozen on the stone floor around her head. Her remaining eye was fixed upon him. It appeared to be as filled with hatred for Ruzsky and his kind as it had been when she was alive.

Prokopiev leaned on the iron balcony. "So, who did you think it was, Chief Investigator?"

"There are no witnesses?" Ruzsky asked, ignoring Prokopiev's knowing look. He had seen no onlookers or curious glances through half-open doors. Such was the fear of the Okhrana.

Prokopiev did not respond.

Ruzsky reached a hand toward the pocket of Olga's overcoat.

"There's nothing in there."

Olga's clothes were ill-fitting and loose, so he started to ease her overcoat away from her right shoulder.

"What are you doing?"

Ruzsky did not respond.

"Step back, Sandro. Please."

But Ruzsky had already pulled back Olga's overcoat and was now shifting the thick shirt beneath far enough to allow him a glimpse of her shoulder.

She had the mark, a dark star branded upon white skin.

"Move back," Prokopiev said.

"You see this? This brand? The American had one; so did the man we found at the Lion Bridge."

Prokopiev bent down to take a closer look. Ruzsky could see that he knew exactly what it meant.

"The mark of the assassin," Prokopiev sighed, almost inaudibly. He straightened, his eyes boring into Ruzsky's own. "Do not mourn for them, Sandro."

"You know the woman?"

"Few will regret her passing."

"You know her from Yalta?"

"An anarchist."

"How did she come to be here?"

"No tears will be shed for her. But, for *your* girl . . ." He paused. "Now she is a very different matter."

Ruzsky stared at him, searching for some sign that this was another threat, but Prokopiev's expression was concerned—almost imploring. "Did you know her in Yalta?"

"No."

"You were on the train with us?"

"When you disappeared? Yes."

Ruzsky gestured at the bodies. "Vasilyev has been behind these killings, hasn't he? He wishes to remove all traces of the connections that date from Yalta?"

"You're smarter than that. No general kills his own soldiers before the battle begins."

"What battle?"

"Your time is short."

They heard labored footsteps on the stairs below. "Back," Prokopiev instructed. He fixed Ruzsky with an intense stare. Your time *is* short, his eyes blazed.

Vasilyev turned the corner, a dark cape around his shoulders, fastened at the throat by a gold chain. He mounted the steps with his head thrust forward, his face glacial. He ignored Ruzsky and examined the body, betraying no reaction.

"Thank you, Chief Investigator. That will be all."

As Prokopiev led him away, Ruzsky dropped the remains of his cigarette and looked back at the dark figure stooped over the body. At the bottom of the stairs, he noticed a small pool of blood and stopped to examine it.

Prokopiev lifted him up gently and propelled him onward. Ruzsky tried to turn back, but the door of the apartment building was slammed in his face.

Pavel was waiting on the far side of the road, to one side of the queue. "Who was it?" His eyes told Ruzsky he knew who it was not.

"Olga Legarina."

"She's also from Yalta?"

"She's one of the group, yes."

"Did you get a look at the body?"

"It's the same killer, with a similar knife. She had an identical mark on her right shoulder."

"The same as the American?"

"Yes. Prokopiev called it the mark of the assassin."

Pavel said, "If we don't reach her, she's going to die, isn't she?" He did so without emotion, as if considering the possibility for the first time. "We had better find her."

But Ruzsky was deep in thought. "We've been foolish," he said. "Or I have. I should have spent more time looking for the families of the victims."

"I thought they were robbers." Pavel shook his head. "Armed robbery, you said."

Ruzsky was staring at the doorway opposite. He thought of the passage in the records he had uncovered in Yalta. *Popova expressed view that Chief of Police in Odessa better target.*

He turned and walked rapidly back toward the sled. "Hurry up," he said.

50

The records division of the Petrograd City Police Department was housed in the vast cellar that ran all the way under Ofitserskaya Ulitsa. It was cold, the documents it contained damp and frayed at the edges.

The duty clerk led them to the far wall and pointed at a section of buff-colored files which stretched for thirty yards or more. No one had ever counted exactly how many servants of the regime had been murdered in the past twenty years, but it clearly ran into the thousands. For each assassination, the local police office telegraphed notification and a request for information to every major city department in the country. Every crime against the regime was recorded here.

The only desk in the cellar belonged to the clerk, so Pavel and Ruzsky sat on the floor. Pavel began on the shelf for 1910, Ruzsky for the year before. Each folder contained the telegraph traffic for one week.

"What are we looking for, precisely?" Pavel began to turn over the tattered sheets of the first file. "An assassination in the Crimea?"

"And the surrounding area, unless something else leaps out at you."

Ruzsky looked up at the narrow slit in the far wall. The ceiling shook as an automobile passed on the street above. He thought again of the brief description of the group's activities in the records in Yalta and its reference to both the chief of police and governor of Odessa. "I think they concentrated on the peninsula, and possibly Odessa."

Pavel did not look convinced.

Ruzsky began to sift through the telegraphs in his hand. They provided a window on an empire in which it was all too easy for criminals to evade capture.

After half an hour, Ruzsky found a string of correspondence relating to the murder of an imperial official—the principal private secretary to the governor—in Kazan. No group was mentioned and the two suspects were "believed to have traveled to Moscow."

He replaced the file and began to work through the next, but he was finding it hard to concentrate. "It's age that divides them," he said.

"Divides who?" Pavel asked, without looking up.

"The victims. Olga, the American, and Markov from the Lion Bridge are all considerably older than Ella. And it is they who have the mark."

"So?"

"The mark of the assassin predates . . ." Ruzsky stopped.

"What?"

"Hold on a second." Ruzsky shut the folder on his lap, stood, and replaced it. He moved down the line of shelves, examining the dates. "I'm going to start earlier."

Pavel didn't answer. Ruzsky continued until he found the section for 1905. He was recalling not Ella's history, but Maria's.

Ruzsky took down the file for the first week of that year. It contained a seamless record of similar, mostly anonymous crimes, from across the Empire. They merged into each other, but he flicked through the pages methodically, before replacing the file and taking the next.

The telegraph traffic for the year was exhaustive, as the revolution which began in St. Petersburg slowly consumed the whole of Russia. It was particularly heavy from Odessa during the summer, as revolutionary fervor spread to the Black Sea Fleet, sparking a mutiny in the battleship *Potemkin*. Members of the local police department had recorded the string of ordinary crimes that occurred during the period of anarchy, even as the entire fabric of their world teetered on the brink of extinction. Ruzsky gave a wry smile.

He looked up at his partner, who sat with his head bent, absorbed in his task.

He returned to his own file and began to leaf through the pages once more.

"What are we looking for, Sandro?"

"You know what we're looking for."

Pavel had not raised his head. "If you say so."

———

They worked without a break. Stanislav appeared as the light began to fade.

Ruzsky looked at him, but remained silent.

"I'm surprised you are here," Stanislav said. "I heard—" The look on Ruzsky's face persuaded him not to continue. "I'm sorry, anyhow."

The journalist shrugged. He glanced at Pavel and began fiddling nervously with his mustache. "There's an alert for Friday and the weekend."

"What do you mean?"

"The entire Petrograd garrison. I heard Shulgin and Count Fredericks want the reserve battalions brought in from Peterhof and Gatchina, but the Tsar won't hear of it."

"I thought the Tsar was at the front."

Stanislav shook his head. "Apparently not. There are delegations on their way. Italians, French . . ."

"Why is there an alert?" Ruzsky asked, though he thought he knew the answer.

"I don't know, but the city is being divided up by military district and they are to patrol the streets before dawn. The Finland Regiment on Vasilevsky, the Preobrazhenskys on South Quay and along Horseguards, the Volynsky from the Nevsky down to Nicholas Station . . ."

Ruzsky put his folder down and stood.

"What are you doing down here?" Stanislav asked, looking about him.

"Why is there an alert?" Ruzsky asked again.

Stanislav shrugged.

"You must have heard speculation."

Stanislav said, "I heard you found another body."

Ruzsky did not respond.

"The newspapers are going to love that."

"Well, you'd better ask Vasilyev before you get them to print it."

Stanislav tugged harder at the ends of his mustache. "What are you doing down here?" He glanced at Pavel, who still had not moved.

"Some research," Ruzsky answered.

"Into what?"

"Never mind."

"It is still your case?"

Ruzsky took a pace forward. "I'd like you to do something. I want to know what all the murder victims were doing back in Petersburg, especially the American. He was staying at the Astoria, so go down there; talk to the bellboys and the chambermaids. See what you can find out. What did the American do with his time here? What visitors did he receive? Where did he go when he went out? Did the girl, Ella, ever come there?"

"The Astoria?"

"Yes."

"He was staying at the Astoria?"

"Yes."

Stanislav raised an eyebrow. "What else?"

"Just find that out, and get back to me. I want to know exactly what the American's movements were from the moment he arrived until the moment someone stuck a knife in his chest, out on the ice."

A few minutes later, Ruzsky tramped up the stairs to the deserted offices of the Criminal Investigation Division. The secretaries had tidied their desks, and all the doors around the central room were shut.

He picked up the telephone on his desk and asked the operator to put him through once again to Colonel Shulgin at Tsarskoe Selo.

It took a long time to make the connection and when it was achieved, a woman answered, her voice distant. "Yes?" she demanded.

"Might I speak to Colonel Shulgin?"

"Who is it that wishes him?"

"Chief Investigator Ruzsky, Petrograd City Police Criminal Investigation Division."

"Oh, yes."

He heard her footsteps receding.

Ruzsky drummed his fingers as he waited.

"Yes?" another voice answered. "Shulgin here."

"It's Ruzsky, sir."

"Oh . . . yes, Ruzsky." There was a long pause. "I was sorry to hear about your father."

"I called you last night, sir."

"Yes, you said it was urgent. My apologies."

Ruzsky could tell someone else was listening, or standing close. He hesitated again.

"I'd be grateful if I could speak to you in person at the earliest opportunity."

"Yes." Shulgin's tone was noncommittal.

"Preferably tonight."

"That is not going to be possible, Chief Investigator."

"My father's death was no accident, sir."

Shulgin was silent.

"It occurred within minutes of an unscheduled meeting with Mr. Vasilyev. I'm sure you will agree that it was quite out of character."

"The meeting was not unscheduled. And Mr. Vasilyev is privy, I'm afraid, to a great deal of information that disturbs the minds of the sanest of men."

"That is hard to accept," Ruzsky said quietly.

"So are many things, at this time."

"You were close to my father."

"We were colleagues."

"Close colleagues."

"I was aware of your father's concerns."

"Would you share them with me?"

Shulgin sighed. "No, Sandro. I'm sorry. I cannot."

"Am I not to be permitted to know why my father took his own life?"

There was a longer pause. "Nicholas Nikolaevich was a senior government official. Our hands are thus bound in ways we might not wish."

"So he placed a revolver in his mouth and pulled the trigger purely as a result of the situation in which Russia finds herself at this time?"

Shulgin did not answer, but his silence suggested he also did not believe this was an adequate explanation.

"In the meeting we attended, you made reference to events you expected to take place on Friday or Saturday. You spoke with Mr. Vasilyev about intelligence you had received."

"Yes."

"We have been informed that the Petrograd garrison has received specific orders relating to this weekend."

"Yes."

"Would you mind telling me why?"

"You know the answer perfectly well."

"You fear unrest?"

"Yes."

"It is more than a routine matter?"

"We would not issue an alert without specific intelligence. But what bearing does this have on your investigation?"

"I thought it might shed light on the victims. It is possible that they have been murdered as a result of activities they planned to conduct in the capital."

Shulgin was silent again.

"There has been another body, sir. A fourth victim. A woman."

"I see."

He could tell Shulgin already knew. Ruzsky pictured the colonel standing alone in the hallway of the Alexander Palace, the Tsar and his wife secluded in the rooms behind him, their children asleep. It seemed not just incongruous, but suddenly quite mad that the government of an empire should rest upon such foundations.

"I appreciate the burdens of office," Ruzsky said. "Especially at this time. But it is not just blind faith that prevents me believing in my father's suicide."

"I understand that."

Ruzsky waited for Shulgin to continue.

"Do you know who she was?" Shulgin asked. "This new victim."

"She was another of the revolutionaries from Yalta. Olga Legarina was her name."

"Have you spoken to Mr. Vasilyev about this?"

"Briefly."

"I see. If you . . . hear of anything, you will let me know, won't you, Sandro?"

The sudden intimacy surprised Ruzsky, and touched him. "Yes. Of course."

As he replaced the receiver, he had a strong mental image of Colonel Shulgin walking slowly away across the hallway of the Alexander Palace.

Ruzsky put his elbows upon his desk and his face in his hands.

He thought of his father. He wanted to be able to pick up the receiver and place a call to the study at Millionnaya Street and have the old man answer.

Ruzsky was about to push himself to his feet when the telephone rang. He picked it up.

"Chief Investigator?"

"Yes."

"Colonel Shulgin."

"Yes."

"We . . ." There was a long pause. "We would like you to present yourself here at first light."

"Yes, sir."

"Come alone."

"Yes, sir."

After a few minutes, Ruzsky walked back down the corridor and returned to the cellar.

51

The clerk had gone home, and Ruzsky persuaded Pavel that he must do likewise.

He sat in the basement, alone in his task. The work was laborious, but it was how he most liked it.

He flicked through the files covering the period from 1905 to 1908, but with the exception of the era of quasi-revolution in the first of those years, there was little serious crime reported from the Crimean peninsula and its immediate surroundings.

There were assassinations in other parts of the country, but not in Yalta, Sevastopol, or Odessa.

Pavel had checked through the records for the latter half of 1908 and the two following years, which left Ruzsky with nowhere to go but backward.

He began on the files for 1904.

He reached July before he found what he was looking for. His eyes had begun to droop, but the sight of the name on the telegraph snapped him awake.

Governor Bulyatin murdered. Bomb thrown in carriage. Wife and son also fatalities. Two daughters unharmed. Further information soonest. Yalta.

Ruzsky stared at the telegraph, then began to turn the pages. A period of intense traffic had followed, culminating in the identification of a suspect.

Suspect in Bulyatin case identified as Michael Borodin. Await further information.

But if the office in Yalta had uncovered further information, none came. The Bulyatin case was referred to with diminishing vigor for the remainder of the year, the suspect Borodin not at all.

Ruzsky took the original telegraph from the file, folded it up, and slipped it into his pocket.

The wind had strengthened again, and it had begun to snow heavily, drifts gathering against the houses and around the bases of the gas lamps. The streets were deserted.

Ruzsky crossed the canal and turned off Sadovaya Ulitsa. The light was on in her window and there was no sign of a cab or sled outside. A dark shape emerged from the shadows, hurrying toward him, a woman— old or young he could not tell—cloaked in the robes of mourning, her face covered in a veil.

Outside Maria's building, Ruzsky looked up through the swirling snow. He saw her at her window, silhouetted against the light.

He pushed the door open and climbed the stairs.

At the top, he leaned back against the wall. He thought of the document he had in his pocket, and the reason for her exile. Did she think of the white house she had told him of in Yalta, with its high ceilings, airy rooms, and views of the bay, as she stared out of the window at a dark Petersburg night?

He imagined a young girl leaning out of the window to listen to her mother sing on a warm summer's evening, her sister beside her.

Ruzsky knocked. He heard footsteps and then nothing.

He thought of her beyond the door, in the darkness.

A minute passed, perhaps more. A key was turned and the door slowly opened. She wore a long red dress, a black velvet bow in her hair. She was painfully beautiful; her lips were slightly parted and her eyes shone with a potent blend of love, loneliness, and loss.

She had been waiting for him. She had known he would be searching for her.

She took him into her arms and he breathed in the scent of her. "I'm sorry," she said. "Sandro, I'm so sorry."

Ruzsky closed his eyes, transported for a moment to the place he most wished to be.

"I wanted to come to you," she whispered.

Maria let him go, but only so that she could look into his eyes, her long fingers resting coolly upon his jaw. Her expression was intense; she wanted to offer reassurance and support in the dark hours she knew all too well. "I met your father once," she said, "before you came back, after a performance. Despite everything, he was charming and kind. He reminded me of you." She came closer, her face almost touching his. "I'm sorry, Sandro, if I'd known . . . I would have told you. You understand that, don't you?" The look in her eyes was that of a little girl desperate to be believed.

"He was as good as murdered."

Maria did not answer. Ruzsky slid down the wall, and she slid with him.

"Your group was gathered here by Vasilyev," Ruzsky said. "For a robbery. He plans to steal some of the Tsar's gold. Vasilyev duped my father."

Maria looked down at her hands.

In the riot of emotions that crossed her face, Ruzsky found the final pieces of his jigsaw. "It's going to be moved," he said suddenly. "Vasilyev would have needed someone to sign the papers, so he must have convinced my father and Shulgin that the gold needed to be moved out of the city to Tsarskoe Selo."

Ruzsky took hold of Maria's chin and forced her to meet his eye. "Talk to me," he said. "Please."

But Maria looked down, her long, dark hair shadowing her tortured face.

Ruzsky reached into his pocket, took out the piece of paper, and handed it to her.

He watched her expression as she read it.

"Have you come to arrest me?"

"I've come because I fear I'm going lose you."

Maria leaned back against the wall with an almost inaudible sigh. She raised her knees and placed her head against them. The desire to reach out and touch her was almost more than he could resist.

"Less than a second," she said, "to destroy so much. How can it be possible?"

Maria lifted her head and tipped it back against the wall, staring up at the ceiling.

Ruzsky waited.

"Sometimes, even now," she said, "when I am asleep, I can see the clear sky and the sea. I can hear the sound of the cicadas and feel the sun on my face. I was smiling. I was my father's assistant's favorite, and he was making me laugh. Father and mother, my sister and brother, were all in the carriage in front of us. I could hear Papa's laughter. He had a big, loud, booming laugh."

Maria put her hands against her cheeks. Ruzsky could not tell if she was crying.

There was a long silence.

"We had been to Livadia. It was the summer, and they had had a function in the gardens for local officials and their families. My sister and brother and I had hidden beneath the tables and gorged ourselves on cake. We had played with the older girls, the Tsar's daughters, and everything was just perfect. All the adults drank champagne and talked in small groups.

"On the way home, Father laughed and Mother started to sing and he joined in. I think they were drunk."

She smiled, her face the image of her sister's.

"We were rounding the corner. It was very hot. I could see my mother's parasol. Kitty was looking around and waving at me and so was Peter, my brother.

"A man stepped out. He wore a black suit and a fedora—a dark shadow on a bright day. I saw the bomb leave his hand and then there was complete silence. I knew something terrible was about to happen. We had heard of assassinations, of course, but never here, never in Yalta.

"The taste of my father's flesh and the sight of it on the front of my white dress; the smell; these things have stayed with me every moment of my life.

"Nobody screamed. It was still such a perfect day. Our driver stopped and his assistant, Kemtsov, stood up. He had blood on his face, too, and pieces of flesh clung to his dark suit and hat. I saw the shock on his face. He climbed down from the carriage. He walked slowly and I think he called out. But there was no answer.

"The man in the fedora was no longer there. The cicadas screeched. The sun shone. It seemed to take an age for Kemtsov to reach my parents' carriage.

"I did not want to call to him.

"I stood up and squinted at the sun. I stepped down onto the dusty road and stumbled; I could not feel my legs. When my balance returned, I walked slowly to where Kemtsov stood."

Maria's face was as still as a statue.

"Kitty was alive. My father's great body had shielded her. She didn't have a scratch on her, but I knew from the expression on her face that we had lost her. She held my brother's hand. She, too, had been dressed in white.

"There was a tiny breeze. I remember a strand of hair blowing across her face.

"Kemtsov fainted, but we did not help him. I held Kitty's hand and we stared into each other's eyes. It was as if the world around us had ceased to exist." Maria tipped her head to one side. "And it was strange, because, *then*, I could not hear anything."

Maria stared at the wall. Her face was wet with tears. Ruzsky enfolded her in his arms.

She gripped him tightly.

"It's all right," he whispered.

Her fingers dug deep into his back. "No," she whispered. "It's not all right. It will never be all right."

Ruzsky held her until the convulsions ceased and her breathing slowed. He released her and she tried to compose herself, wiping the tears from her cheeks and removing the hair from her eyes.

"Michael Borodin. *Michael Borodin*. Such an ordinary name," she said, as if in a trance. "I was at the piano when my uncle first mentioned his name. It was in the big hall of his house. The window was open and the evening was cool. The police have no doubts, he said, but the man has fled. They would put out an All Russias bulletin, but I knew even then that it would be up to me to find him."

They were silent. Ruzsky could hear her breathing.

"And you did?"

"It has not been easy."

"You infiltrated the group."

Maria did not answer.

"You infiltrated the group alone, or at Vasilyev's urging?"

"Alone."

"You have never been his agent?"

"The suggestion is obscene."

"But you did not kill them." It was a statement, shielding a question. He hoped merely that she would confirm it.

She slowly shook her head. "For many years, I had lived for their deaths," she said wearily. "But no, I could not kill them . . ."

"Does Dmitri know about this?"

"No!" She shook her head. "He knows nothing."

Ruzsky looked out at the glow of the gas lamps in the street. He thought of Ella's pretty face on the ice, then of the knife in Olga's eye, then of Maria risking her life to push him away from the Cossack's thundering hooves. And he knew that whatever she had done, his love for her was as fundamental and unyielding as his love for his son. He was bound to her.

"What shall we do?" he asked.

Maria stared at the floor. His heart ached for her.

"If I have found out the truth, then so will they. And when they do, they will kill you."

"Yes."

"Borodin still lives. Why have you not already—"

"We have tried, but he is unpredictable and suspicious. There was a meeting last night, and he was supposed to arrive with Olga, but he never came."

"But you are certain he will be at the Kresty Crossing?"

Ruzsky saw the flicker of recognition in her eyes.

"I will help you," he said.

"No."

"I will do anything you ask of me."

"You are your father's son. You are the chief investigator, and you believe in the old certainties, the old Russia. You could never be an accomplice to murder."

Ruzsky felt a knot in his stomach. He was desperate to deflect her. "They must suspect you."

"How could they? I was no more than a girl at the time of my parents' death. Soon after, I fled the unhappiness of my uncle's house and took another name. For all that anyone knows the young Maria Bulyatina might as well have been blown apart in that carriage."

"Borodin will kill you. He must suspect—"

"But he does not. You have seen how he is with me."

"And you will risk everything for this final act of revenge?"

"What is it that I risk, Sandro? What is it that I have?"

He smarted at her rebuke. "I would do—"

"It is too, too late. It was too late a long time ago."

"So you came to Petrovo to say goodbye?"

Maria did not answer.

"If I had not been married. If I had not turned away . . ."

"It was already too late for me, even then."

Ruzsky pulled her gently toward him until her head rested upon his shoulder, her legs entwined with his. He lifted her face and held it as the tears rolled down her cheeks. "What can I do?" he asked.

Maria did not answer. He cradled her head upon his shoulder and rocked her as she cried. "It will be all right," he whispered, but he knew that she did not believe him, and he wasn't sure he believed himself.

He was tortured by the image of Borodin covered in the young man's blood on that night at the factory, and of Maria bending before him to clean it from his clothes.

Could she really defeat this man?

"This will consume you," he whispered.

"Sandro . . . This is my fate. It has chosen me, but it is also the one I have chosen."

"This man has dragged you into his world. He will extinguish all the light your family once created. Is this what your father would have wished for you?"

"Do not speak of my father."

"To abandon your sister . . ."

"Do not speak of them, Sandro."

"Don't leave Kitty to her fate."

"Sandro, I beg you."

"No, Maria. I beg *you*." But he knew he had lost her. Maria's sacrifice was not wild and hasty, but gentle and considered. This was her fate. The passion they had shared at Petrovo was fueled by the urgency of the condemned. "Please," he whispered, his voice hoarse.

"You must let it run its course."

"I cannot."

"Nothing can change this, Sandro . . ."

She reached for him, her legs wrapped around his waist, her cheeks pressed to his. They touched each other with urgent desperation. Ruzsky kissed her cheeks and forehead and nose and eyes.

"Sandro," she whispered. "My Sandro. I'm so sorry."

Ruzsky crushed her to him.

"I'm so sorry," she said again. "I would do anything for you, anything except this."

Later, they stood and stared at each other in the darkness of the hallway.

Ruzsky knew he must leave, but could not. "I will try to stop you," he said.

"Then we may both pay a terrible price."

"For my father's sake, for the sake of all that he stood for, I cannot allow their plans to continue uninterrupted."

Ruzsky could not take his eyes off her. He was hardly able to breathe.

"Goodbye, Sandro."

Ruzsky walked out into the stairwell.

He faced her. He could not bring himself to say goodbye.

Slowly, and without taking her eyes from his, Maria Bulyatina shut the door.

52

Ruzsky slept fully clothed in Michael's bed, and was awake long before dawn.

He pulled back the tiny curtain. It was still snowing heavily, the gas lamps dull orbs in a sea of swirling darkness. But Ruzsky could see the sled. Its occupant was still there, wrapped in blankets.

Ruzsky checked his watch. It was almost six. The day was Friday, but he could not be certain of the date.

He walked across the hall. Dmitri had not returned. He searched the bedrooms on the lower floors for good measure, and then took a few minutes to shave.

When he had finished, Ruzsky climbed back to the top floor and walked slowly through the rooms. He wished to take leave carefully of his childhood home today. He looked at his own room, then Ilya and Dmitri's.

He went to his father's bedroom on the first floor.

Ruzsky stared at the carnations, which had begun to wilt, and surveyed his father's silver hairbrushes, neatly set out on top of the dresser. He felt like a ghost, drifting silently through a former life.

Ruzsky picked up the telephone in the hall and asked the operator to connect him to the Hôtel de l'Europe. "Madam Ruzsky," he said.

"What room number, sir?"

"I'm not certain."

After a momentary delay, he was connected and a sleepy voice answered.

"Ingrid?"

"Sandro."

"I'm sorry to wake you."

"What is it, Sandro?"

"I just . . . wanted to check you were all right."

"We're fine. Michael is still asleep."

"Will you stay in the hotel today? I know it is hard, but if it is possible . . ."

"I'll do my best."

"Just stay inside if you can."

"Have you seen Dmitri?"

"No." Ruzsky tried to sound untroubled. "But I'm going to look for him now. There's something I need to talk to him about. He's probably staying in the barracks, or perhaps he's taken a room at the yacht club."

"Of course."

"Go back to sleep."

"Goodbye, Sandro."

Ruzsky went to find one of his father's thick woolen overcoats from the cloakroom and took a new sheepskin hat from the shelf. As he put them on, he glanced once more around the darkened hallway, his gaze resting upon the scabbard on the wall just inside the drawing room door.

He hesitated only a moment more and then walked forward and out into the street, the front door slamming shut behind him.

It was snowing harder than ever. An Arctic wind chafed his ears as it whistled down from Palace Square. Ruzsky pulled down the flaps of his hat and began to walk, his eyes half closed against the driving snow. At this time and in this weather, the city was deserted; his only company was his pursuer.

Ruzsky deliberately walked through the Summer Gardens, forcing the Okhrana man to leave the sled and follow him on foot.

At the iron gates to the main Preobrazhensky barracks opposite the Tavrichesky Garden, a sergeant in the guard box eyed him suspiciously before wiping away the condensation that had gathered upon his window and pulling it back. "Yes."

"I'm looking for Major Ruzsky."

"At this time in the morning?" He was one of the old school. On his top lip, he sported a long and elegant mustache with fine, waxed curls at its tips. He consulted his list. "No. Not present."

"Has he been at all, during the night?"

"Do I look like his mother?"

"You haven't seen him?"

"Who is asking?"

"His brother, Alexander Ruzsky."

The man shook his head.

"Thank you, Sergeant."

Ruzsky retraced his steps past the Summer Gardens, through Millionnaya Street, and across the lonely expanse of Palace Square to St. Isaac's, the Astoria, and finally the yacht club. It was the same story here. The doorman knew Dmitri well—they all did. But he had not seen him for several days.

Ruzsky checked his watch once more before continuing on his cold and lonely walk down Morskaya, past the gilded window of the jeweler Fabergé, and the dusty premises of Watkins, the old English bookseller.

As he turned toward the Tsarskoe Selo Station, Ruzsky had almost forgotten that the man from the Okhrana was behind him, but when he looked around, he was only about twenty yards away. He had abandoned all pretense of concealment.

Waiting by the ornate gates of the Alexander Palace at Tsarskoe Selo little more than an hour later, Ruzsky pulled his coat tight around him. He was cold now, through to his core.

The palace grounds were deserted. The sentry had retreated to his box. In the building overlooking the gate, an officer of the palace police watched him.

Ruzsky tried to light a cigarette, but soon gave up. He had lost all feeling in his feet, and bashed his boots hard to try and restore it. His welcoming committee was taking a damned long time.

At length, the guard instructed him to proceed. He pointed at the near corner of the palace. "They are waiting," he said.

Ruzsky began to walk, his head tipped forward against the wind.

Another uniformed guard was standing outside the large wooden doors to the family's private wing, and he ushered Ruzsky up the steps and into the hall. He took off his hat, coat, and gloves and tried unsuccessfully to prevent the snow from falling on the polished wooden floor. A footman removed them from his arm.

Colonel Shulgin strode down the corridor toward him. His face was like granite, but his eyes communicated a different message, perhaps, Ruzsky thought, comradeship or compassion. "Come this way, please," he said.

Ruzsky followed.

Shulgin led him to the antechamber and they sat in a pair of upholstered chairs beneath the portrait of Marie Antoinette. Ruzsky glanced up at it. He had once been told that it hung over the Empress's desk.

They waited. Shulgin examined his hands. "I'm sorry about your father," he said beneath his breath. He stared dead ahead. "I had not imagined . . ."

"I must speak with you."

They heard footsteps from the direction of the Empress's private apartments. She swept into the room, wearing a dark dress with a cream brooch at the neck. Shulgin and Ruzsky both stood and bowed low.

The Empress waved them back to their seats and took one opposite. She was about to start speaking when they heard a child's cry in the distance. She began to get up, then chose to ignore it and sat down, smoothing the front of her dress.

There was another scream, a boy's, high-pitched and heartfelt. This time the Empress stood, turned, and departed without a word.

Ruzsky listened to her rapid footsteps. "Colonel Shulgin. I very much need to—"

"Later, Chief Investigator. Please bear in mind where you are."

At length, the Empress returned. She offered no explanation, nor apology, and after they had repeated their bows and seated themselves once more, she stared at the floor. Ruzsky wondered if she was having difficulty remembering why he was here, or even who he was. A phrase from his father's letter echoed in his mind: *She has become quite unhinged . . .*

What struck him most was how tired she looked; in fact more than tired. He himself was exhausted, and so, by the look of it, was Shulgin, but the fatigue in the Tsarina's eyes was of a wholly different nature. Her face and mouth were pinched, her eyes hollow. She gave the impression of having to exert a gigantic effort of will simply to articulate a question.

"You have not recovered . . ." She sighed and placed her head in her hand for a moment, as if once again having to steel herself to think straight. "You have not recovered the girl's possessions?"

Ruzsky did not answer. He could not imagine what he was supposed to say.

"The chief investigator is primarily conducting a murder investigation," Shulgin said. Ruzsky noticed the tension in his voice and face. He wondered whether any of them had had any sleep.

The Empress did not appear to understand. She frowned heavily at Shulgin.

"This is the chief investigator, ma'am. Chief Investigator Ruzsky. He was assigned to investigate Ella's murder. Since then, there have been three more victims."

"But you have still not recovered her . . . possessions?"

Ruzsky stared at the Empress. He wondered if she was on some kind of sedative. "No, Your Majesty."

"Then why have you come here?"

There was silence.

"You instructed me to summon him, ma'am," Shulgin said. The strain in his voice was barely hidden now.

"He has not got to the bottom of it."

"No, ma'am. He has not."

They heard a soft patter of feet. Ruzsky caught his breath. For a moment, he thought he'd seen a ghost. A girl with a shaven head, dressed completely in white, hovered in the doorway.

Anastasia. It was the Grand Duchess Anastasia.

Ruzsky could not take his eyes off her. She looked pale and unwell. There were deep shadows under her eyes. It had been two weeks ago that he'd seen her playing in front of the Alexander Palace with her brother and sisters, her long, dark hair framing a face of exceptional beauty.

"Mama?"

Anastasia came to her mother and whispered something in her ear.

The Empress hugged her, and Ruzsky noticed the way in which her mother's fingers dug into her back as she held her.

The Tsarina released her daughter reluctantly. Anastasia smiled shyly at Ruzsky and Shulgin and then withdrew, glancing once more over her shoulder as she reached the doorway.

The Empress stood and followed.

"Measles?" Ruzsky whispered, pointing at his hair.

Shulgin nodded.

Ruzsky waited. The minutes ticked by, but Shulgin did not meet his eye. "Why am I here?" he asked.

"Because the Empress summoned you."

"But why—"

"No reason is required, Chief Investigator."

"May I be assured that you will speak to me when this audience is at an end?"

Shulgin sighed. "Your father's death will be discussed at the Imperial Council tomorrow morning. In the meantime, I am empowered to offer my most profound condolences."

They heard the Empress's footsteps. As she reentered the room, she appeared to be in some pain.

She sat awkwardly, and looked at him. "You have not found the girl's possessions?"

"I was not aware, Your Majesty, that we were looking—"

"So, you have not found them?"

Shulgin's eyes flashed a warning.

"No, Your Majesty," Ruzsky said.

"You have found nothing, then?"

They endured another lengthy silence.

"Have you spoken to Mr. Vasilyev?"

"On a number of occasions, Your Majesty."

"You are working together on the case?"

"Together . . . yes."

Shulgin leaned forward. "The chief investigator's father was the assistant minister of finance, ma'am, if you recall . . ."

"Yes," she said.

Ruzsky waited for condolences to be offered, but the Empress continued to look straight through him.

"Very reliable family," Shulgin added.

"Is that reliable in the general sense, or the specific?" she asked. "As reliable as most of our reliable families?" The Empress glared at Shulgin before turning her attention back to Ruzsky. She seemed more alert now. "Your father met with an accident?"

Ruzsky hesitated. "Yes."

"I'm sorry for it."

"That's kind of you, Your Majesty."

"Does this mean you will give up on the case?"

"Of course not."

Her expression became opaque once more. "But you have not yet recovered any of the girl's possessions," she said again.

"No, Your Majesty. We were not aware any were missing."

"Has he spoken to that filthy newspaper?" she snapped at Shulgin.

"No, ma'am. Vasilyev has taken care of that."

"But they will not be publishing what the American took to them? We have a guarantee of that?"

"Yes."

They heard another cry. It was fainter now, but Ruzsky could see the son's pain mirrored in the mother. "Yes," she said, distracted. "Well . . ."

For a moment, Ruzsky saw the despair in Shulgin's eyes, before the colonel lowered his head and stared at the floor. The Empress stood. "I wish to be informed immediately when you have recovered the girl's possessions. I wish this matter to be given the most urgent priority. I don't want to have to go through this again."

Anastasia and one of her elder sisters had returned to the doorway. They stared silently, round-eyed, at the two men who had been occupying their mother's attention. As the Empress reached them, she bent and placed her arms around their shoulders, ushering them gently from the room.

Ruzsky watched Shulgin staring into the empty doorway.

The court official forced himself back to the present, sighed deeply, and stood. He muttered something under his breath, before leading

Ruzsky back down the corridor. All the doors were shut, but Ruzsky could still hear the young boy's whimpering.

In the hallway, Ruzsky accepted his coat.

"I'm sorry," Shulgin said.

"The American took the material Ella stole to a newspaper?"

Shulgin glanced around him to be sure they were alone. "The *Bourse Gazette*." He hesitated. "I'm sorry I brought you here, but she insisted."

"I had the impression that you and my father were old friends."

Shulgin stared at him with hollow eyes. "Your father knew too much, Sandro. And so do I."

"As the minister responsible for the State Bank, he had to sign papers authorizing any movement of the gold reserves from the central vault?"

"If he told you that, then he should not have."

"He was reluctant to sign the papers?"

"I simply cannot discuss this." Shulgin sighed. "He had his reservations."

"Vasilyev persuaded you all that this was necessary?"

"Mr. Vasilyev is in possession of much intimidating and unpleasant information." A muscle in Shulgin's cheek had begun to twitch. "I needed little persuading of the seriousness of our predicament." Shulgin looked over his shoulder again, aware that he had raised his voice.

"So my father signed the papers?"

Shulgin avoided Ruzsky's eye, but he did not deny it.

"But he wanted to countermand his order? That's why he called the meeting with Vasilyev?"

"He did not telephone me before the meeting."

"You must know that Vasilyev's intention was—and is—robbery. He had assembled the group, of which Ella was a part, for precisely that purpose."

"The group you refer to has dedicated itself to creating great difficulties for the government and its servants, and in that, I may say, it has been very successful, thanks largely to the activities of that silly, misguided girl."

"Vasilyev knew all of these people in Yalta. Borodin may appear to be their leader, but Vasilyev—"

"He has infiltrated the group most successfully, for which we should all be grateful."

"He controls them."

"He is able to provide substantial reports on their activities, which the Emperor, in particular, appreciates."

"They're Vasilyev's creatures. I have seen the evidence with my own eyes."

"Well, then, *present* it. I am not at liberty to mistrust a government colleague upon whose advice so much now rests."

"He has convinced you that today or tomorrow will bring revolutionary activity on such a scale that the regime's wealth must be put beyond the reach of the mob?"

"That is a matter upon which I cannot and must not comment." There was a stubborn determination to Shulgin now.

"My father didn't trust him," Ruzsky said.

"That's not a matter for me."

"And neither do you."

"I have no *choice*," Shulgin hissed, his face moving closer to Ruzsky's, his eyes blazing. "The publication of the material stolen from the Empress's private quarters would have the most damaging possible consequences."

"What was stolen?"

"I cannot say. And do not press me. As the Empress has indicated, the details are not a matter for the city police department."

"She brought me here *only* to ask about her stolen possessions."

"She is naturally concerned and, at times, confused, about to whom she has spoken, and to whom she has not."

Ruzsky looked at Shulgin. He could see the futility of his task. "Whatever Ella stole could be the final nail in the Romanov coffin," he said. "Or so Vasilyev has claimed. But my father realized what he really had in mind."

"Good day, Chief Investigator."

Ruzsky turned away, but as he did so, he caught a glimpse of Shulgin's unguarded expression. He had the look of a man who has felt someone walking across his grave.

53

The offices of the *Bourse Gazette* were close to Sennaya Ploschad, in a nondescript gray building in a narrow side street. As the droshky driver dropped Ruzsky and Pavel off at the entrance, a black automobile drew to a halt twenty yards away, on the opposite side of the road.

Their surveillance had been stepped up.

A porter ushered them through the ground floor, past a series of giant black printing presses, to a steel staircase that led up to the editor's office. As they passed through the newsroom, the noise and bustle fell away, and they were greeted by looks of hostility.

Ruzsky was glad of Pavel's robust company.

The editor was much younger than he'd expected, in his twenties or early thirties, with dark hair that hung to his shoulders and a long, narrow nose. He had bony hands, which he kept clasped together in front of his face and did not move as the porter introduced them.

"How can we help you gentlemen?"

There was another man behind him, standing in front of a series of framed pages of the newspaper and a photograph of a man whom Ruzsky took to be their proprietor. Both wore the expression of carefully cultivated disdain he had come to expect from the Petrograd intelligentsia. Another slipped into the room behind them, a notebook and pen in his hand. He was even younger, and slouched in the corner, his manner was deliberately disrespectful. "I don't think we'll need the office boy," Ruzsky said.

"I demand that you do not threaten us." The editor got to his feet.

"You *demand*?" Ruzsky said.

Pavel stepped forward, his manner conciliatory. "We are conducting a criminal investigation."

"And we are a newspaper," the editor countered.

For a moment, nobody moved, then Pavel took one pace toward the young man, picked him up and threw him out of the room, then slammed the door shut. An overcoat hanging on the back of it fell to the floor.

"How dare—"

"Sit down," Pavel ordered. The man did as he was told and glowered at them in silence.

"I apologize for our ill humor," Ruzsky said.

The men glanced at each other, without speaking.

Ruzsky seated himself, trying to shake off his fatigue. He scratched his cheek. "I am Chief Investigator Ruzsky," he said. "This is my deputy, Pavel Miliutin."

The men stared at them.

"We are investigating a series of murders. You may recall that two bodies were found on the Neva on January first."

"A series of murders?" the editor asked, his curiosity aroused.

"Yes."

"The two bodies on the Neva?"

"And two more since."

The men frowned.

"A man at the Lion Bridge with his head almost severed about ten days ago, and a woman close to the Finland Station yesterday."

He could see he had their attention now. "An American came to see you," Ruzsky went on. "Just before the first murders. His name was Robert White, though he may have used an alias."

"Anyone who visits this office with information does so on a guarantee of anonymity."

"He's dead."

Pavel took the photographs from a folder he had tucked under his arm and spread them out on the desk.

"This is the man who came to see you?" Ruzsky pointed at the American's corpse.

Neither man answered. They were staring at the photographs, which appeared to be having the desired effect.

"Whitewater," the editor said quietly. "That was the name he gave."

"What did he want?" Pavel asked.

"He said he had some material that would be of interest to us."

"What kind of material?"

"He didn't say."

Ruzsky stared at them. " 'Explosive' is what I imagine he told you."

"We have done nothing wrong," the editor said.

"No one has suggested that you have."

The man looked at the photographs again. He pulled over the picture of the bodies on the Neva. "Who is the girl?" the editor asked.

"You don't know her?"

The man shook his head. He glanced at the photograph of the body at the Lion Bridge. "Who was he?"

"His name was Markov. He was from Yalta."

"From Yalta?"

"Yes. Both men, and the woman at the Finland Station, were stabbed repeatedly. It's possible the murders had something to do with the material you were being offered."

Neither man met his eye.

"What was it?" Ruzsky asked.

Ruzsky could see that White had told them exactly what he had in his possession. "It was revealing," he went on. "That's what they told you. Something revealing that related to the personal lives of the imperial family . . ."

The editor put the photographs back in a pile and moved them to the other side of the desk, as if trying to distance himself from them.

"He said it was evidence we would wish to print."

"Evidence?"

"Yes."

"Of what?"

The editor shrugged. "Of the corruption of the Romanovs."

"What kind of evidence?"

"He was . . . vague about the detail."

"Where did he say he had got this material?" Ruzsky asked.

"He didn't."

"An American walks in alone, off the street, and promises you material such as this and you believe him?"

"He did not come in off the street. Nor was he alone."

"He was with the girl?" Ruzsky pointed at the top photograph. "With Ella."

"Not with her."

"Who then?"

"I do not feel inclined to tell you."

"Someone you knew?"

"Someone whose sympathies we know of." The editor smiled. He had recovered his confidence. "We wished to examine the material," he said, smugly. "That was all."

"What proof did they offer that it was genuine?"

"We did not get that far."

"You were told that the material had been stolen?"

"It was intimated. But, as you will understand, we did not wish to investigate that too closely until we had at least had sight of it."

"You were told you could meet the woman who had acquired it?" Ruzsky asked. He leaned forward and pointed at the picture of Ella's bloodied body on the ice. "They told you this girl worked out at Tsarskoe Selo from where the material you were promised was stolen?"

"Naturally, we would have handed any stolen property over to the police."

"Naturally. You planned a private printing?"

Neither man answered.

"Why did they offer you this material?" Pavel said.

"They did not say." The editor held his gaze.

"The American came with a man?"

"No."

"A woman. Did she give you her name?"

"I cannot give you the woman's identity," he said calmly.

"The material was never delivered?" Ruzsky asked.

The editor shook his head.

"But you were expecting it?"

"The agreement was that it would be delivered this morning before eight." The editor looked at the clock on the wall beside him. It had just gone three. "And, upon verification, we'd have printed for tomorrow morning. I imagine your presence means it is unlikely we will ever receive it."

"It was supposed to be delivered today?"

"That is correct."

"You set a deadline?"

"No. The American was quite specific; he wanted the material on the streets late this evening or early tomorrow morning. Not before, not after."

"Why?"

"No reason was given."

Pavel and Ruzsky looked at each other. "They must have given you some indication?"

The editor shook his head.

"But you accepted their demand?"

"We accepted nothing." The man leaned forward. "We promised what we needed to in order to be able to gain access to the material. Naturally, once it was in our hands, the question of its distribution was for us alone."

Ruzsky got to his feet. "Thank you for your time," he said.

They stopped in the lobby to light cigarettes. "Vasilyev has been behind this from the start," Ruzsky said. "He put Ella up to the theft. Then he must have claimed that his intelligence was that a group of revolutionaries wished to publish it . . ."

Ruzsky began walking again. "Let's go back to the office," Ruzsky said.

54

Another crowd of protesters was streaming past the entrance to the city police headquarters. The demonstrations seemed to Ruzsky to be getting bigger, but quieter. This one was led by a group of Tartar waiters carrying a banner demanding "fair tips" and he would have laughed, but there was nothing amusing about the hunger he saw in every face.

Ruzsky glanced over his shoulder at the automobile that had pulled up behind them. Vasilyev's men were also momentarily distracted by the protest.

The last stragglers passed by and Ruzsky and Pavel crossed the road. A constable stood between two men in handcuffs in front of the incident desk.

Ruzsky climbed the stairs fast, pulling away from Pavel. In the central area of the Criminal Investigation Division, he passed Maretsky, who stood at his own window, watching the march.

Another pile of papers had accumulated upon Ruzsky's desk, on top of which was a note from Veresov, headed *Bodies on the Neva*.

Veresov had found no match for the fingerprints on the dagger in their files, so, whoever the killer was, he did not have a criminal record. Perhaps it was his imagination, but it seemed to Ruzsky that the present uncertainty was seeping into every corner of the city. No one was concentrating.

He poked his head around Maretsky's door, ignoring the sporadic shouts from below. "What about the knife?"

The little man turned around, his porcine eyes examining Ruzsky as though he were a complete stranger. "I'm sorry?"

"The knife. The murder weapon."

"Oh. Professor Egorov will be back soon," he said.

"I thought you said he was due to return several days ago?"

"He has been delayed."

Maretsky faced the street again and Ruzsky returned to his office, closing the door quietly behind him. He picked up the telephone. "Could you put me through to the university?" he asked.

There was a long wait.

"Porter's lodge," a voice answered.

"Might I speak to or leave a message for Professor Egorov."

"Professor Egorov?"

"Yes."

"We have no Professor Egorov."

Ruzsky stared at Pavel, who stopped riffling through his own paperwork.

"Are you there?" the voice asked.

"Yes. You're sure?"

"Of course."

"Thank you," Ruzsky said.

The professor was sitting behind his desk, staring at his hands. He looked up as Ruzsky returned, and closed his eyes.

Ruzsky took a seat opposite and waited for an explanation.

"I admire you, Ruzsky," Maretsky said quietly, opening his eyes. "You're honest. And you don't judge people."

"That's not true."

"You don't judge me."

Ruzsky looked at Maretsky with compassion. "Who am I to judge anyone?"

"Anton is a good man."

Ruzsky did not see what the professor was getting at.

"He has tried to protect us. But they know everything that we do, so it is hard for him."

"I don't see—"

"We have to be careful what information we bring into the building, don't you see that?"

Ruzsky inclined his head.

"I gave the knife to a colleague. His name is not Egorov. I will take you to see him." Maretsky stood and put on his coat.

They crossed the bridge from Palace Embankment to Vasilevsky Island, where the cab turned left and slithered down toward the Twelve Colleges building at the far end of the street. Ruzsky made a point of not looking around to check whether they were still being followed, but Maretsky could not restrain himself. "It's all right, old man," Pavel told him jovially, but Ruzsky could sense the tension in his voice, too.

There were two black automobiles on their tail now.

They were not far from Ruzsky's dilapidated rooms here, but their surroundings could not have been more different. Built to house the government of Peter the Great at the foundation of St. Petersburg, the beautiful red and white buildings of the Twelve Colleges had long ago been taken over by the university. Like so much of the landscape of the city, they had been designed to project the power and majesty of the Russian Empire.

As the three of them climbed down from the droshky, the Okhrana's vehicles pulled up on the other side of the street. The still-falling snow blurred the day's journey into night.

Maretsky led them through the stone archway and up to a long, cavernous corridor. They passed a handful of students wrapped up against the cold.

Maretsky stopped, knocked once on a door to their right, and, upon receiving a reply, opened it to usher them in.

Professor Egorov's alter ego was a tub of a man, with a drooping white mustache and steady, pale blue eyes. His dusty rooms gave the impression of someone rarely troubled by a world beyond its four walls, and for a moment, Ruzsky envied him the tranquillity of his environment.

The professor knew immediately who he was. He emerged from behind his desk and produced the murder weapon from a drawer. He handed it to Ruzsky. "It's Persian. The date suggests it was inscribed during the period of conflict over northern Azerbaijan, which lasted through 1812 and 1813."

"What does it say?" Ruzsky asked.

"It bears the name of a Russian general."

"Which one?"

The professor did not relish the question. "Nicholas Nikolaevich Ruzsky. Your great-grandfather, I assume. Or a generation before?" He shook his head. "It belongs to your father?"

"Sandro," Pavel called as Ruzsky marched down the outer corridor. But Ruzsky was no longer listening. He moved rapidly away, eager for the cold night air to clear his head.

"Sandro, wait," Pavel called again, his voice echoing in the hallway. Ruzsky did not stop.

55

Snow swirled around the entrance to the house in Millionnaya Street. The light above its door cast thin slivers of light into the night. Ruzsky had to knock three times before there was an answer.

As Peter opened the door, Ruzsky was swept into the hall by a gust of air that scattered snow halfway up the stairs.

"It's a terrible night," Peter told him.

"Is my brother here?"

"I believe so, yes sir."

Ruzsky removed his sheepskin hat and overcoat, dusted off the snow, and handed them to the young servant. He began to climb the stairs.

The upper part of the house was in darkness.

Ruzsky moved slowly through the shadows. He tried the room on the first floor where Ingrid and his brother were officially quartered, but it was empty.

He checked all the other bedrooms on the same level, including his father's, but there was no sign of anyone.

He returned to the center of the landing. "Dmitri?" He walked up the stairs to the second floor. "Dmitri?"

He moved to the wooden steps that led to the attic, and began to climb them.

"Dmitri?"

He checked his own room—now Michael's—but it was empty, as was the one opposite. Ruzsky glanced at the soldier at the end of Ilusha's bed and the elephant on the shelf above it.

As he emerged, he sensed movement and spun around. Peter was at the bottom of the stairs. "Your brother has just gone out, sir. He said you would know where to find him. 'Where this began,' he said." The servant held up a small key. "He asked me to give you this."

Downstairs, Ruzsky walked to the far wall of his father's study, took down the painting, and slipped the key into the lock of the safe.

Alongside his mother's jewelry, he found large bundles of banknotes, some in rubles, some sterling, some United States dollars. At the back of the safe was an envelope marked with the imperial seal and his father's name and the instruction *By hand*.

Ruzsky returned to the desk and opened the envelope. He pulled out a thin sheaf of papers. Wrapped around them was a note with the imperial eagle at its head.

Nikolasha, I enclose just some of what they have to offer. Vasilyev says he has been unable to recover the rest and may not be able to do so before the weekend. The possibility of their publication then is still, therefore, significant. I feel that we must do as he suggests; perhaps not all of the gold reserves, but a significant proportion should be moved to the vault out here. He will need you to sign the order. We are considering all other options, but His Majesty will not consider recalling any further battalions.

Vasilyev says the movement of the gold should begin before this information is broadcast in the city. The atmosphere here alternates between panic and denial, so I suggest, my old friend, that we act upon our own initiative —S.

Inside was a series of neat, handwritten notes that each began with the same instruction in the left-hand corner: *For immediate transfer.*

December 2, 1916. Povroskoe from Tsarskoe Selo for Novy. You have not written anything. I have missed you terribly. Come soon. Pray for Nicholas. Kisses —Darling.

Ruzsky put the first down on the desk. Povroskoe was a remote village in the Russian interior. It had been home to the peasant priest Grigory Rasputin, who also went by the name Novy. Tsarskoe Selo meant the Alexander Palace and, by implication, the Empress.

They were messages for transcription by the telegraph office from the Empress of the Russias to a peasant priest.

April 9, 1916. Povroskoe from Tsarskoe Selo for Novy. I am with you with all my heart, all my thoughts. Pray for me and Nicholas on the bright day. Love and kisses —Darling.

Ruzsky stared at the neat, careful hand.

He turned to the last note. This was an actual telegram, complete with the stamp of the Povroskoe office.

December 7, 1914. From Petrograd for Novy. Today, I shall be back in eight days. I sacrifice my husband and my heart to you. Pray and bless. Love and kisses —Darling.

Ruzsky sat back in his father's chair.

He understood all too well the tension he had seen in Shulgin's face. The rule of the Romanovs could not possibly survive the publication of such material.

He put the documents back into the safe, locked it, and put the key in his pocket.

Lights from the upper floors of the Winter Palace blazed defiantly into the gloom as Ruzsky stared out at the frozen Neva.

He saw a dark figure in the center of the ice.

He hesitated for only a moment, before stepping out and walking purposefully toward his brother, blocking his old fear from his mind. The marine police had placed no warning flags here, or none that he could see.

Dmitri wore a long, dark blue regimental overcoat and a sheepskin hat. His hands were thrust deep into his pockets.

They stared at each other through the falling snow.

"Don't try to stop me, Sandro."

Ruzsky did not respond.

"Father is dead. You are absolved of your responsibilities."

"It's not about responsibility. It's about love."

The word hung between them. Dmitri's expression softened. He took off his hat. "Did you open the safe?"

"Yes."

"You understand, then?"

"I do now." Ruzsky wiped the snow from his eyes and face.

Dmitri lowered his head. He stared at his hat, flakes gathering upon his hair. Ruzsky thought he looked handsome in the darkness, and young—something like the boy he remembered.

"I could have warned him," Dmitri said, a terrible guilt etched into his face just as it had been in Maria's last night. "I knew they planned to steal the gold. I knew they had to trick Father to do it."

"How could you know what threats they would make?" Ruzsky answered. "Or how far Vasilyev would go?"

Ruzsky could not take his eyes from his brother. He felt not anger, but an overpowering compassion. What he saw in Dmitri's eyes now was a more confused and tortured version of what he had seen in Maria's the previous night; it was a swirling mixture of love, loss, and regret. But it was guilt, above all, that swam to the surface. He had put his love of Maria and his desire to become the man he thought she wanted him to be above everything. Dmitri had watched his father walking into a trap and done nothing to prevent it closing around him, and it was tearing him apart.

Ruzsky thought of his brother's fear on the evening of Ilusha's death as they awaited the summons to their father's study. He thought of the way they had held each other for comfort and strength. "Dmitri," he said quietly, "let us go home."

"I know how they must have threatened him," Dmitri answered. "I know what happened at that meeting. Father wanted to countermand the order and cancel the movement of the gold and I know how Vasilyev threatened him. You saw the way Father looked at Michael. You know what was in his mind every time he even glanced in his direction."

"Michael is not Ilya."

"But which one of us can look at him without—"

"That's not his fault."

"It's no one's fault, Sandro! It never was." Dmitri stared at the ice by his feet. "But Father would have moved every mountain in Russia before he'd have let anyone hurt a hair on the boy's head. He wasn't going to lose him twice." His voice quivered with emotion. "I didn't know what they would do. How could I have guessed?"

Ruzsky did not answer.

"Do you understand why, Sandro?"

"Do I understand?"

"Do you understand why?" Dmitri was pleading with him. "She makes me feel as if I have come home at last. But the past hangs heavily upon her, and, in that one way, I can soothe her pain."

"I understand."

"I'm not a coward."

"You don't have to prove anything to me," Ruzsky said sympathetically.

"She needs me. In this, at least, she needs me."

"Did she ask you to kill them?"

"Once I knew what had happened, she did not need to."

"She told you what happened to her father?"

"What I am doing is only just, Sandro."

"She has told you each name? She has informed you on each occasion where they can be found?"

"She is entitled to justice. She will not find it in any other way."

"The couple on the ice were expecting you. The American and the girl, Ella. You had met them before?"

"Maria hated the American almost as much as Borodin. She was sure the pair planned the murder of her father together. She convinced him the girl Ella was an informer for the city police and the army and that their plan here was in danger of being discovered. He led the girl out onto the ice. He was expecting her to be dispatched by an assassin on the far side, in the shadows of the fortress—that's what he'd been told. Maria begged me not to harm the girl, but I could hardly have left a living witness."

"But you left your footsteps. Those last three paces onto the embankment were designed to taunt me."

Dmitri stared at him. "Not a taunt, Sandro. I knew you would find me."

"That's why you didn't go to the Strelka," Ruzsky said, almost to himself. "You left the ice to go home." He looked at his brother. "If he was here, Father would beg you to stop."

"But he's not. He's dead and that house is an empty shell, full of ghosts at every turn. I've had enough of ghosts. If I survive, we will leave Russia, begin again . . ."

"He would still beg you—"

"He would do no such thing. I was never you, Sandro. I was never Ilusha. I was the son he didn't understand, I was the one for whom he could never conceal his disdain."

"Dmitri—"

"Though you will deny it, it is true. But he can't reach me now. I have found a purpose that I have long searched for."

"Then it is I who must beg you," Ruzsky said. "And I plead with you on my knees."

Dmitri looked at him, his anger melting into sorrow and regret. "I'm sorry, Sandro. This is all I have to give her."

"I cannot lose you." Ruzsky's voice quivered with emotion. "Don't you see that?" He took a pace toward his brother.

"I understand." Dmitri shook his head, as if to rid himself of his dilemma. "I understand, Sandro, but I must go."

"Dmitri, I beg you . . ."

"Don't try to stop me."

"In God's name . . ." Ruzsky's cry was taken by the wind.

"Stay there, Sandro!" He turned away and began to run. For several moments Ruzsky watched him go, his tall figure receding into the darkness.

"Dmitri!"

Ruzsky lunged forward, lost his footing, and crashed straight through the ice into the darkness below. The cold was savage, expelling the air from his lungs.

He bobbed up against a solid wall. He gasped, but sucked in only water and began to choke.

Ruzsky kicked down, searching for some sign of light, blood roaring in his ears.

For a moment, these strange and brutal surroundings were familiar. He recognized this place. He remembered once before welcoming its oblivion.

But in his mind's eye, Ruzsky could see his brother walking across the ice to his fate. He could not let him die alone. He began to kick, his lungs stretched, the cold numbing every fiber of his being.

He saw ripples on the surface of the water.

Lungs exploding, he pushed upward until he burst through the hole.

A hand grasped for his.

A man stooped over him and it took Ruzsky a few moments to recognize who it was. "Pavel?" he asked.

"Be quiet," the voice hissed. "Save your energy."

56

When Ruzsky opened his eyes again, Pavel was bending over him, and he could see Katya and Peter looking anxiously over his shoulder. He was in dry clothes, but he was chilled to the marrow. He was lying on the floor of the drawing room in Millionnaya Street, next to a roaring fire, the side lamps lit.

Ruzsky heard Katya whisper something to Peter and then they withdrew, leaving him alone with his deputy. Pavel moved back to the long white sofa.

Ruzsky looked up at the ornate cornices of the ceiling and the low chandelier. His gaze strayed across to the oil of the mountains of the Hindu Kush and the curved saber that hung alongside it. He grasped for the familiar in a world that was growing ever more remote.

"You've been following me," he whispered quietly. "You've been watching me from the start."

Ruzsky stared at the ceiling. He did not want to look at Pavel; he didn't want to see the guilt and regret he would find there. He had experienced too much of both. "They must have threatened Tonya, or your boy."

They were silent. Ruzsky listened to the crackle of the fire.

"They didn't have to," Pavel said. "It's been clear how the land lies for a long time. Only you refused to see it."

Ruzsky closed his eyes again. Pavel's face merged with Dmitri's in his mind. He thought of his brother's solitary progress across the ice, and of the guilt that haunted his every waking moment.

He thought of his father's body sprawled across the floor of the study.

They could have anyone. They could destroy everything. "I understand, Pavel."

He shook his head. "No, you would never understand."

There was a long silence.

"You work for Vasilyev alone? Not Borodin and his group?" Ruzsky asked.

"We all work for Vasilyev."

"In Yalta, they tried to kill us both."

"It was a warning. You were to be allowed to pursue the murder case—after all, Vasilyev more than anyone wished to know who was killing his men—but you were not to uncover the link between him and the revolutionaries. And in Yalta, you did. The bomb was an attempt to warn you off, but the young fool was incompetent and that's why he nearly killed us."

Pavel stared at him with mournful eyes.

"In your own way, you were trying to protect me," Ruzsky said. "You thought that if you watched me and reported back all that we were doing, they'd have no need to dispose of me. Isn't that the case?"

"Even if it was, it would not exonerate me."

Ruzsky looked at his friend. "For Christ's sake, you do not have to seek *my* forgiveness. What have *I* done that is of any benefit to anyone?"

"You have caused Vasilyev true discomfort." Pavel examined his hands. "He wanted to find out who was killing his creatures, but he did not want you to know what they were doing." He looked up. "He could not decide what to do with you."

Ruzsky heard the hesitation and regret in Pavel's voice and, when he looked up, saw it in his eyes. His heart sank.

Their friendship was destroyed and they both knew it. The consequences of this betrayal outran even a complete understanding of its motives. "I'm sorry," Ruzsky said.

"I deserve no pity."

"And should feel no shame. There is no one left to serve."

Pavel did not answer.

"Each of us must find his own way through. I didn't understand that before. I do now." Ruzsky pulled back the blankets and forced himself upright. His head exploded with pain.

"If you try to interfere, they will kill you."

"I have no choice."

"It is too late. The gold is already being loaded at the Tsarskoe Selo Station. There is nothing you can do."

"I cannot leave him. He is my brother."

"If that is his destination, then all you will achieve is to die together."

"But I cannot abandon him to his fate alone." Ruzsky looked at his partner. "Do they know he is coming?"

Pavel shook his head.

"Will Maretsky tell them about the knife?"

"He would not help them."

"I ask only for a chance, Pavel."

The big detective straightened, his eyes never leaving Ruzsky's own. "Of course, my friend. I will ask them to prepare a sled."

A few minutes later, Ruzsky opened the door and stepped out into the night. A plain sled had been prepared, without the family's livery. A servant was wrapped up in the driving seat and the horses shifted quietly in the wind. Pavel was waiting for him in the darkness.

Ruzsky climbed into the back, and looked into the face of his deputy.

"You are too late to reach the crossing," he said. "Try to get onto the train."

Ruzsky offered him his hand. Pavel took it cautiously. "Good luck, my friend," he whispered. "There will be many of them."

The sled pulled away.

As Ruzsky looked back, he saw that Pavel was still watching him, his big body framed by the light of the doorway.

57

Okhrana men in long black overcoats had sealed off the Tsarskoe Selo Station, standing in a ring around its entrance in the darkness. It was still snowing heavily and Ruzsky ducked his head and walked past them toward Sadovaya Ulitsa.

He had left the sled some distance away and told the servant to return home.

Fifty yards on, Ruzsky stopped and looked back to check that he was out of sight.

He reached up for the wooden fence next to the road.

It took all his strength to lever himself over it and into a drift three or four feet deep that had gathered on the far side. For a moment, he was lost in the powder, small crystals of ice in his eyes and mouth and ears.

He stood and fought his way through, until he stumbled and fell onto an icy pathway.

He picked himself up and brushed the snow weakly from his clothes. There were no lights on in the two sheds ahead, but he could see sparks from a brazier spitting into the night sky.

The coal fire stood in a small clearing. Ruzsky hesitated for a moment, then moved forward to warm himself, standing so close that sparks gathered on his clothes.

He heard voices and slipped into the nearest shed. It was dark and smelled of oil and grease. Bits of machinery—winches, old signal posts, hammers, and wrenches—hung from the ceiling alongside rows of conductors' flags. Ruzsky shut the door and waited until the men had passed. They were talking quietly to themselves, and he smelled the pungent aroma of their tobacco.

He took the Sauvage revolver from inside his jacket and checked that there was ammunition in its chambers. He wasn't certain if it would still fire after being bathed in the frozen waters of the Neva, but he replaced it and stepped outside.

He walked to the far end of the shed and looked down toward the station.

The snout of an armored train, of the kind used to transport heavy fighting equipment to the front, poked out beyond the shelter of the glass and iron roof above the concourse. Across the track, through the snowstorm, Ruzsky could see a group of men standing guard.

Above the engine, the Tsar's personal flag flapped in the wind.

To Ruzsky's left, there was a large mound of discarded equipment covered in snow and he waded through another thick drift to reach it. He felt his body temperature plunging once more, his hands icy as he touched a discarded piece of track and clawed his way up it so that he had a view into the station concourse. He was close to the platform where he and Pavel had boarded the commuter train to Tsarskoe Selo.

Behind the huge black engine were four or five transport wagons with their doors open. Through a cloud of steam, Ruzsky could make out a series of figures on the platform. Four men wheeled a trolley down toward one of the transport wagons and unloaded its contents. The gold bars shimmered in the light of the gas lamps.

Ruzsky could make out Prokopiev, who stood several inches above the group of agents around him. The Okhrana deputy threw his cigarette out into the night and then he and two colleagues strolled toward the engine and climbed in.

Ruzsky watched the last of the gold being loaded up. One of the men got into the carriage and another slammed its door shut. The other two wheeled the trolley back toward the station entrance.

The engine wheezed and hissed. A cloud of steam curled around the corner of the roof and was lost in the swirling snow.

Ruzsky stood and caught sight of two guards, right in front of him, not ten yards away. He cursed silently and dropped back down, his heart pounding.

He raised his head slowly. The men had not seen him. They were also watching what was happening on the platform, smoking and talking to each other. They began to walk around to his right, blocking his departure.

There were a series of shouts. The engine let off a loud hiss of steam and then turned its wheels once, shunting the carriages forward.

More men appeared on the platform.

Prokopiev stuck his head out of the side of the engine and looked back at the carriages. "All right!" he called. "It's ready!"

The train shunted forward once more, but still did not pull away.

The two guards stood between Ruzsky and the train.

The engine blew off another head of steam. Again it shunted forward and this time kept moving, its great iron wheels grinding their way along the track.

The guards watched its departure for a moment, then moved away.

Ruzsky edged forward. No one was visible at the rear of the train. The Okhrana men inside were behind closed doors and those in the armored engine had ducked down to avoid the blizzard.

The train began to gather speed. As the last transport carriage drew level, Ruzsky began to run. He slipped once, then picked himself up and waded through to the path. Out on the track, the snow drove hard into his face and mouth.

He heard shouts behind him and what sounded like a shot, but the train was moving at the pace of a run now and his eyes were on the great iron bar at the rear of the last car.

He reached it and took hold of its lip, but was almost pulled from his feet.

Ruzsky grunted to himself and jumped. He was half up on the ledge, one leg banging along the ground.

He heaved himself forward. Another shot rang out and he looked up to see the two guards, both down on one knee, their rifles pointing toward him, but the train roared onward, and their bullets were lost in the darkness.

When he could no longer see the station, Ruzsky pulled himself upright and climbed the ladder to the iron roof of the carriage.

The snow whipped into his face, and the night groaned and howled around him. Flat on his stomach, almost unable to see, he clawed his way forward slowly. He reached the end of the carriage and slipped down into the gap before climbing up to the next. He repeated the exercise until he was only a few yards short of the engine.

They were out of the city now, the landscape a brilliant white, the plow sending great chunks of snow flying across him. Occasionally, Ruzsky looked ahead, but all he could see was the Tsar's yellow and black flag snapping in the wind.

58

Finally, the train slowed.

Ruzsky pushed himself onto his knees. The snow had stopped and the moon cut through thinning clouds to leave slivers of light dancing upon an indifferent landscape.

They were coming down a slight incline, and ahead, Ruzsky could see a road that ran through the middle of the wood and up to the edge of the track. It had been recently cleared. A large military truck was parked across the line.

The train jolted as the brakes were applied, almost sending Ruzsky tumbling over the lip of the carriage. It came slowly to a halt less than ten yards from the obstacle. Ruzsky kept low, but the only sound was the wheezing of the engine.

Up ahead, he saw two Okhrana men walking toward the truck. He heard a shouted command, but there was no response. The men looked about them.

The engine appeared to grow quieter, the forest around it still.

One of the men moved up to the rear of the truck, a revolver in his hand. He wore a black fedora and it spun high into the air as his body slumped to the ground, the powder lifting around him as the snow cushioned his fall.

For a second, there was no reaction, even from his companion. And then the second man turned, his own hat falling in his haste.

He got no more than a yard as the air was filled with the crack and whistle of rifle shots. Dark figures emerged from the woods, charging toward the carriages. There were shouts, doors banging, more shouts, screams, and then the dull pop of shots muffled by the wood.

Vasilyev was sacrificing his own men in the interests of staging an authentic robbery.

And then all was quiet once more.

Ruzsky heard the roar of a truck being started, and he watched as from down the lane a line of headlights begin to swing through the wood.

The convoy wound its way down to the crossing.

Ahead of them, on the far side of the track, the road ran straight up a hill. Halfway up it, in the moonlight, Ruzsky could make out Borodin and Maria. She did not wear a hat; her long hair was swept back from her face, as if she wanted to be recognized. Despite her height and slender grace, she seemed a frail figure alongside him.

There was a hiss of steam, then an eerie silence.

Ruzsky listened to the clank and whimper of the engine.

There was a shout. "I have him!"

All of the men in the clearing moved at once. Figures swarmed from the shadows. There was a shot, then another.

Borodin turned in the direction of the confrontation, but Maria continued to stare straight ahead.

Ruzsky heard a distant cry.

He waited, his heart pounding.

Had they been waiting for him?

He saw Dmitri being led over the brow of the hill.

Ruzsky pushed himself up, fumbling for his revolver, and as he did so, he felt the cold metal of a gun barrel on the back of his neck. "Good evening, Chief Investigator," Prokopiev said. "Time to join us."

Ruzsky looked up. He put his revolver down. "Don't hurt him."

"We'll see."

"Don't hurt him."

He saw the tension in Prokopiev's face. "*Get down.*"

Ruzsky swung around and jumped into the drift beside the crossing. He walked forward, Maria's gaze fixed upon his.

Dmitri turned around, his face white. He was ringed by men in long overcoats, their rifles and revolvers pointed unerringly at him. There was fear in his eyes, such as Ruzsky had only ever seen in those of condemned prisoners before they were led to execution. He took his brother's hand, his grip icy cold. "It's all right," he said.

Dmitri fell into his arms and Ruzsky held him tight. For a moment, they were thousands of miles away, far from the harsh-faced men who surrounded them, clutching each other on the top floor of the house at Petrovo. "It's all right," he whispered.

He looked up to see Michael Borodin striding toward them. He saw no shred of humanity in his eyes.

Borodin pulled them apart. He kicked Ruzsky and forced him to his knees. "Mr. Khabarin," he said.

Ruzsky stared at Maria.

"Your Russia is dead, Prince Ruzsky," Borodin said. He cocked his revolver. "And your kind will soon be finished. You understand that, don't you?"

Ruzsky listened to the last gasps of the steam engine. Maria's eyes bored into his. Her expression was one of infinite sadness, as if she was reaching out to him but could never touch him again.

Ruzsky felt the cold metal of Borodin's revolver at the back of his skull, but did not flinch. He mumbled a prayer. He thought of his father's smile in the hallway of the house on Millionnaya Street and Michael pounding through the snow and into his arms.

The world around him was distorted and out of focus.

All he could hear was his own breathing.

He kept his eyes upon Maria.

Dmitri began to move, a blur on the periphery of Ruzsky's vision. He got only a yard toward Borodin before the revolutionary fired a single shot through his forehead. His body crumpled and fell.

The clearing was still. Maria had taken a pace toward them, but had now frozen where she stood.

Ruzsky crossed himself.

He waited. He closed his eyes.

"There was no need for him to die," Borodin whispered, his mouth close to Ruzsky's ear. "She wanted you both to live. That was the trade."

Ruzsky looked up at Maria.

Her sadness was not for him, but for herself. She had come to say goodbye.

He heard the snort of a horse and the bells on a sleigh.

"Start walking, get in and go away," Borodin said. "Turn around and you'll regret it."

Ruzsky did not move.

"She has paid for your freedom. Better take it before I change my mind."

Ruzsky stared, transfixed, at Michael's tiny figure beyond the crossing. Ingrid sat next to him, two Okhrana agents either side of them, their guns pointed toward him. He looked down at the body of his brother sprawled in the snow.

"Don't you want to know what she thinks you are worth?"

Ruzsky kept his eyes upon his son.

"She has offered what only a woman can give."

Ruzsky still did not move.

"She sent your brother to kill me, but when she understood that she could not stop you trying to save him, she traded her own freedom in order to keep *you* alive. It is quite heroic."

Ruzsky could not think.

"I would start walking, Prince Ruzsky." Borodin leaned closer, his breath warm against Ruzsky's ear. "Or perhaps you think she can escape?"

"We had a telegram from the local police in Yalta. They found out that a very clever chief investigator went to see a girl in a sanatorium. So I think I will have them both."

Ruzsky's head pounded. His mind screamed at him to turn around.

"Start walking, Mr. Khabarin, and don't look at her again or none of you will leave this clearing."

Ruzsky looked at the guards towering over his son. He began to walk, concentrating on the sound of his boots in the snow.

The Okhrana men watched him approach.

He walked through the quiet of the Russian forest.

He could feel her eyes upon his back. Ahead, he saw that Michael was crying, and his son's tears triggered his own.

"It's all right, my boy," he said.

As he crossed the tracks, Ruzsky whispered, "I'm sorry."

He climbed into the sled and took his son into his arms. The driver cracked his whip and the sled jerked forward.

As it climbed the hill, Ruzsky could resist no longer. He turned and saw her standing alone on the clearing, watching him.

She did not move. Her eyes were fixed upon him until they disappeared from view.

AUTHOR'S NOTE

The February Revolution in Russia broke out little more than a month after the end of this novel. It began with protests over food shortages and escalated rapidly as it became clear that the regime could no longer rely upon the loyalty of large sections of the armed forces. The fictional Dmitri had many real-life counterparts who were well aware of the dangers of having the capital's barracks entirely full of reservists. Had the Tsar kept some of his more experienced soldiers in Petrograd, revolution might have been averted.

After the revolution, the Tsar was forced to abdicate. He tried to do so in favor of his young son, but soon realized this would mean that they would inevitably be separated—for all his many faults, there is little doubt Nicholas II genuinely adored his family—and handed the throne instead to his brother, Michael. However, Michael was soon forced to concede that there was no place in the new Russia for a Romanov tsar.

Lenin and many other revolutionaries returned from exile immediately after Nicholas's abdication, but it seemed for a while as if a liberal, democratic Russia might emerge. However, a second revolution in October—a coup, in fact—left the Bolsheviks in charge, with drastic consequences. As many contemporaries predicted, the removal of Nicholas II led to a period of great suffering for all Russians. A stubborn man who had resisted all reform ended up pushing his people into a great catastrophe.

This novel is not history. I have striven hard to re-create the atmosphere of the time and to be accurate in all possible details, but it is a novel first and foremost. The telegrams quoted toward the end of the book are genuine, though it is most unlikely that the Tsarina did have a physical affair with Grigory Rasputin. Lonely, desperate, and half mad, Alexandra clung to the peasant priest spiritually, but the idea that the two could have become lovers still seems preposterous, even if it was believed by many contemporaries.

Anyone wishing to explore this extraordinary story further should read Edvard Radzinsky's brilliant *The Rasputin File* or *Alexandra: The Last Tsarina* by Carolly Erickson. The best contemporaneous account of the old regime is *Once a Grand Duke* by Grand Duke Alexander, and the most complete and scholarly study of the revolution, *A People's Tragedy* by Orlando Figes. I would also recommend *Michael and Natasha* by Rosemary and Donald Crawford, the story of the doomed love affair between Grand Duke Michael, brother of Nicholas II, and a divorcée.

Those wishing to take their research a stage further should go to a library and try to get hold of a copy of the memoirs of the French ambassador to Petrograd, Maurice Paléologue, which provide a fascinating, day-by-day account of the onset of revolution.

The imperial family and many other members of Russia's former elite were, of course, executed by the Bolsheviks. The St. Petersburg of today is still brimming with reminders of a world that disappeared with them.